Praise for *Mistletoe from Purple Sage*

"A pleasing holiday page-turner."　　　—*Booklist*

"Smith's prose is very readable, and she produces the perfect mix of mystery, character study, and suspense."

—*Mystery News*

"An effective side story with a surprise ending..."
—*Fort Lauderdale Sun-Sentinel*

"Smith's characters are appealing, and her complex plotting is entirely believable."

—*Brazosport Facts*

"...A pleasing diversion when the holidays get too hectic."

—*Orlando Sentinel*

"It's an excellent story, well-written..."
—*The Chattanooga Times*

'TIS THE SEASON FOR MURDER

Christmas Crimes

BARBARA BURNETT SMITH
FRED HUNTER
WALTER SATTERTHWAIT

WORLDWIDE.

TORONTO • NEW YORK • LONDON
AMSTERDAM • PARIS • SYDNEY • HAMBURG
STOCKHOLM • ATHENS • TOKYO • MILAN
MADRID • WARSAW • BUDAPEST • AUCKLAND

'TIS THE SEASON FOR MURDER: CHRISTMAS CRIMES

A Worldwide Mystery/November 1998

Mistletoe from Purple Sage and *Ransom for a Holiday* were first published by St. Martin's Press, Incorporated.

ISBN 0-373-26290-6

ACKNOWLEDGMENTS

I'd like to offer special thanks to Tyler Smith and Mitchell May, because some of Christopher's best lines were really theirs.

I'd also like to thank Mickie Bellah, of Mickie Bellah Advertising, and Danny and Kate Reed, of Danny Reed Advertising. In the past they kept me from starving, and showed me enough of agency life so that I could create Rose Sterling Advertising. Oh, and their agencies do far better work, and much more timely, than Rose Sterling!

Two of the great sayings in this book I snitched from friends Dee Willis and Sharon Watkins. Additionally I received invaluable information from Delphine Chavez, the "sabom-nim" of the Fighting Dragon's dojo. My thanks to all three.

I'm also grateful to my friends and readers who always improve my manuscripts: Debbie Meyer, Chuck Meyer, Susan Rogers Cooper, Susan Wade, Caroline Young Petrequin, and my adorable husband, Gary.

MISTLETOE FROM PURPLE SAGE
Barbara Burnett Smith

To my wonderful sister, Carol,
who is really my "forever friend."
With much love.

ONE

ON THE DAY before Thanksgiving I decided that what I wanted for Christmas was a little holiday chaos. Now that my son, Jeremy, was sixteen, Christmas would be a quiet event with the three of us, Jeremy, Matt, and me, sipping eggnog by the fire while Christmas carols played softly in the background. Very civilized.

When Jeremy was little, and I was a single parent, we'd celebrated with my sister or brother's family in a house too small for rambunctious kids, barking dogs, and frenzied parents. At the time it was frazzling, but now I missed those days.

Oh, I still had my annual holiday insanity of shopping and wrapping, mailing and baking, but that all ended a few days before Christmas. Then there was nothing but peace and gentle serenity, which I was dreading.

As I turned in to the ranch, and headed toward our two-story house, I remembered my mother's age-old admonition: Be careful what you wish for because you just might get it. But what could be so bad about a chaotic Christmas?

I parked in front of the house, honking the horn twice. No one appeared. My adorable new husband, Matt, had told me that morning he was spending the day in town with the CPA going over year-end tax-planning and investment strategies, something I'm delighted I don't have to think about. Apparently he hadn't made it back yet, and Jeremy had gone to a friend's house in Purple Sage to work on some project. That meant the house was all but silent as I unloaded the groceries and Christmas wrapping paper and such.

It took four trips, but eventually everything was deposited on the breakfast table except for one roll of green yarn that had found a comfortable home on the floor. I left it there, deciding I needed something to perk me up before I tackled the job of putting everything away. Heavy drugs were my first choice, but I didn't think the two Midol in my purse were going to be sufficient. Some ice tea was next on my list, and as I crossed the kitchen to get it, I noticed the light blinking on the answering machine. It was probably Jeremy saying he was ready to leave and would I come get him. I punched the button to find out.

While the message tape rewound, I pulled open the refrigerator. The tape began to play and I heard a female voice with a slight New York accent. I hadn't heard that voice often in my life, but I knew exactly who it was. The refrigerated air swirled around me as I listened, hardly breathing.

"Jolie, hi, this is Fran Espinoza at Guidry-Long Literary," she began. As if I didn't know my own agent. "Listen, kid, we got an offer on your book. I have to tell you right off it's not a very good offer, but with first books they rarely are. It's a good house, though, and a good editor. It'll get your foot in the door. So it's what time?" The voice paused. "Oh, hell, who knew it was that late? Listen, I'll be out of the office until Monday, but I'll call you then with details. Have a nice Thanksgiving." A click and a beep, and she was gone.

I closed the refrigerator door.

"I'm an author," I whispered to my kitchen. I was almost afraid to say the words out loud. "An author! Me." The blood slammed through my heart so fast I could feel it leaving stretch marks.

I grabbed up the phone and started to call Matt, but remembered that he wasn't reachable.

My hand shook as I replaced the receiver. I could hardly believe it. I had sold a book! I was an author. This was a big occasion. A momentous moment. An ecstatic event!

I let out an exuberant warhoop that echoed through the empty house.

TWO

THAT PHONE CALL went to my head like frothy champagne. Weeks later I would be in the grocery store, trying to decide between 2 percent and nonfat milk, when an uncontrollable grin would sneak onto my face. My mind would fill with visions of myself autographing books for an ever-increasing line of fans. I would begin to consider what dress I would wear for the Edgars or the Agathas, and end up drifting off on a cloud of fantasy.

Unfortunately, later at home I would come out of my altered state to discover that I had purchased both kinds of milk, as well as cream and half-and-half, but had forgotten the rest of the things on my grocery list. It was playing hell with my budget, and our eating habits. Besides, people were starting to talk.

That phone call did more than affect my daydreams, though. It also did something to my self-image. I had always seen myself as a writer simply because I wrote. In the past I had written advertising copy, news stories, and books. Even if I never got published, I could legitimately claim to be a writer. However, now that I had made a sale, I belonged in the much more elusive category known as author. I had leapt up the food chain; gone from gopher to gazelle; tripped the light fantastic into a fantasy world where I was special, invincible, and solidly okay. Even without my makeup on.

That's a heady experience, and probably the reason I said I would "love" to attend the twenty-fifth anniversary party for Rose Sterling Advertising. It was being held in conjunction with Chester Sterling's sixty-eighth birthday.

Rose Sterling was the Austin advertising agency where I worked before I married Matt. Chester Sterling and his wife, Rose, had founded it, although Rose had passed away a few years later. It was Chester who hired me away from another agency and kept me gainfully employed for almost nine years. I think he's a wonderful man, but for me to even consider attending that party was another sign of my temporary madness.

Unfortunately, before I recognized the idiocy of accepting, I had told Matt about the event. He immediately set up a trip to Austin around the party. He scheduled meetings with several companies he was involved with, and arranged for us to stay with his sister, Prissy, and her husband, where we would celebrate Christmas.

And it all would have been fine if it hadn't been for the Rose Sterling party, because that's where I would have to face the man I'd had an affair with some five years before. He had been, and still was, a married man, and although he'd been separated from his wife at the time, I still feel guilty.

In this day and age most people wouldn't think twice about what I'd done, but there is something for me that escalates the sin. Michael and I had begun our affair right there in the office, and as I later learned, despite our discretion, Audry had known what was going on the whole time. On those days when I came in looking like hell from staying up all night with Michael, no matter what excuse I made, she knew where I'd really been, and worse, where he had been. When we said we were going out to visit a client, she knew the truth of why we were leaving the office. And when she discovered us alone in the coffee room, supposedly discussing business, she knew that wasn't all that was being said. It must have hurt terribly, and if Saint Peter turns me away from the pearly gates, I'm sure he will mention Michael Sherabian's name.

There is another problem, as well: I've always worried about Matt learning the whole truth about my now all-too-close past. Matt and I began dating just two months after Michael went back to his wife. Ours wasn't a rebound romance; I've always believed I just happened to meet the right man at an awkward time. Because of that I never told Matt about Michael and me. At first it was too close and too intimate a detail to share. As my relationship with Matt progressed, it became a flaw I kept hidden for fear it would alter his opinion of me. Eventually it was too late to talk about it.

Of course, there was a part of me that was looking forward to the party. All of us at Rose Sterling had spent nine hours a day together; we'd labored to hit deadlines, suffered through personal crises, and generally functioned as an extended family for one another. I'd hardly talked to them in the four years since I'd moved to Purple Sage, and I missed them.

And so I found myself drinking tea at Matt's sister's house on the Sunday a week before Christmas.

With the party a mere eight hours away, even the smell of her Christmas tree and the sounds of Bing Crosby crooning "White Christmas" weren't bringing my mood to anywhere near the festive level.

"Your party tonight sounds like such fun," Prissy was saying. "You know, I've met Chester Sterling. Back when I was working for the Literacy Council. Such a nice man. He must have been wonderful to work for."

"Yes, Chester was, is, very nice," I said, hoping my smile looked normal.

"And he had a wonderful way of making everyone feel welcome. He reminded me of a big, ginger-colored bear. Always hugging people and thanking them, even though he was doing the advertising as a contribution. So charming." She smiled at me and I could see the family resemblance between her and Matt. Both have dark eyes and lashes, although Prissy swears that Matt's eyelashes are twice as thick and curly as hers. The eyes are striking in contrast to their lighter hair. Matt's is soft brown until he spends time in the sun, while Prissy's is artfully streaked to a much paler shade.

"Oh," Prissy added with an impish grin, "and Chester's son-in-law is to die for. Did you know him, Jolie?"

"Me? Uh. Yes. I did." I focused on Matt and smiled.

"Michael Sherabian is even better-looking than you, Matthew!"

Matt laughed. "So now I know why you give so much time to charity. Has nothing to do with the worthy cause."

"Some days it does, some days it doesn't," she said, cocking her head and flashing a mischievous smile.

"Maybe you and Ross could go with us to the party tonight," I said, thinking I had found a buffer between me and my fears. "I'd be happy to call—"

"No, no," she said. "It was at least a year ago. Probably neither of them would even remember me."

"You certainly remembered them," Matt said with a younger-brother grin. "Actually you remembered, what was his name? Michael?"

"I can't help it, Matt," Prissy said. "He was incredibly good-looking and charming. I'm serious, this man walked into the room and four women had hot flashes. Two others hyperventilated." Prissy turned to me. "Jolie, if I'd been you, with Michael around, I don't know that I'd have bothered with Matt. Or was Michael married back then?"

I reached for a cookie and said, "He was married to Chester's daughter. Audry. That's how he got started at the agency. And actually, he spent a lot of time at our Atlanta office."

"I hope Audry wasn't so foolish as to let him go off by himself."

"Oh, uh, part of the time, I think so. Then they both moved there." That was almost immediately after they got back together. Four days after the last time I spoke privately with Michael, which meant there had been no closure on our relationship. It still seemed as if there were things that needed to be said.

The kettle on the stove began to whistle and Prissy stood up. "How about a warm-up on your tea, Jolie?"

"Yes, please." I held out my delicate china cup, which she put back down on my saucer.

"I'll bring the pot," she said as she moved toward the kitchen. "Oh, and help yourself to some more cookies," she called from the other room.

In the center of the table was a Waterford platter piled with exquisitely decorated Christmas cookies that Prissy had made. "They're almost too pretty to eat," I said, then looked down and realized I had unconsciously broken all the edges off the one sitting in front of me. Like pulling petals off a flower.

Luckily Matt's attention was elsewhere. "I'd take another cup of coffee," he said, rising and following Prissy.

That left me alone and I took a long shaky breath. I had survived one conversation about Michael, but the party was still to come. I hate having things hanging over my head, especially something like this that needs some communication.

In anticipation of the party I actually had tried to bring it up with Matt a couple of times. On each occasion we were interrupted—Jeremy, the phone, Bart, the foreman of our ranch. After several tries, I decided we could discuss it on the drive down, but then we'd ended up coming on different days, so we each brought our own car. I had begun to think that I shouldn't say anything; that this was one of those old secrets better left buried. Didn't Dear Abby advocate that? It was certainly easier to deal with, at least in some ways.

"By the way, Jolie," Pris called from the kitchen, "how do you like the remodeling we did? The architect calls that the great room."

"And it wasn't just wishful thinking," I said, looking around the room that was off the breakfast nook where I was sitting. "It really is great." In both dimension and decoration—the floors were pale hardwood, and the ceiling tall and arched. To my right was a rounded fireplace, and at the front of the room a bay window that looked out onto their elegant yard.

In the curve of the window was a Christmas tree that stood at least fifteen feet high. It was lightly dusted with artificial snow and decorated with twenty-five years of Christmas memories, collected since the time when she and Ross had married. She had shown me a tiny bear ornament that their daughter, Stephanie, had made in first grade. It was faded after all these years, but held an honored spot on the tree.

"We got the last of the furniture in and the tree up this past weekend. I think it turned out rather well," Prissy said as she returned with a china teapot covered in roses, and poured tea into my cup. "Careful, it's hot."

"Thanks."

As she sat down she glanced toward the front door; her gaze lingered and grew more intense.

"Something about the foyer isn't right?" I asked. While I couldn't see the whole area, which was as large as some bedrooms, I thought it was as impeccable as the rest of the house. There were stemlike flutes of glass that formed a chandelier, and two carved niches in the white adobe that held tall baroque candleholders from some exotic spot. Artsy things, as Jeremy called them.

"Oh, no, the foyer's fine," Prissy said. "I was just remembering—never mind." She shook her head. "Christmas surprises, you know. We have several."

"Really?"

For a moment she looked undecided, then she forced a smile. "Yes. We have one for you, too, and it's arriving later."

"A surprise for me?"

"I can't say another word. I promised." She looked up at Matt, who was returning from the kitchen bearing a brilliantly glazed blue pottery mug.

"I'll give you a hint—" Matt began.

"Enough, Matthew!" Prissy cut him off quickly and firmly. "Santa Claus is coming and that's all we're saying. Is that understood?"

"A little stressed, are we, Prissy?" he asked, half teasing, but I heard some concern in his voice, too. "I was only going to give Jolie a hint."

"Yes, I'm stressed. It's Christmas, for God's sake, and with guests—" She stopped. "Damn, now see what you did, Matt? I didn't mean you two. I love having you here."

"But company always brings a little stress," I said. Except that in the past, Prissy had thrived on entertaining. Two years before she'd had eight guests staying with her, had given a Christmas party for two hundred, and had her house on the Holiday Parade of Homes for a charity that required her to serve tea every afternoon. She'd handled it all without a flutter of nerves, so what was different now?

Matt touched my hand. "Maybe I'll just run on and leave you to deal with my sister." He turned to her. "I'm assuming I can get downtown in half an hour. Is that still realistic?"

"You can get there, and probably get parked," Prissy said, "if you don't hit any traffic. You have a meeting this afternoon?"

"I'm meeting Trey at the Hyatt. We're going over the financials of Austin Edge."

Trey Atwood was the mayor pro tem of Purple Sage, as well as Matt's best friend. Both men spend a portion of their time out of town, keeping tabs on the companies they have investments in. Austin is the perfect spot for high-tech business, and Matt loves delving into a company's inner workings to decide if it will eventually be a success.

"Isn't that one of the new incubator computer companies?" Prissy asked. "Are they involved in software or hardware?"

"Software," Matt said. "I can't believe you know the difference. Aren't you the one who told me computers were a passing fancy?"

She waved away his words. "That was before I saw what all they can do. Besides, computer software companies are a very good investment right now. Ross thinks it's like the new frontier." Ross being her husband, Ross Linden, the management consultant who can steer companies toward success. "He says there's a lot of money to be made because everyone is into computing. Even *I'm* on the Internet."

Matt looked suitably impressed. "My sister the techie."

"That's exactly right. We have three computers in this house, four phone lines, and enough cord to rewire Louisiana and half of Alabama. I now speak computer. It's better than my French."

"Want to be my technical advisor?"

"You can't afford me," Prissy said before turning to me.

"Now, Jolie, what do you want to do this afternoon? Anything special?"

I wanted to adopt a new identity and live in an anonymous post office box, but it didn't seem feasible.

"I'd like to get a birthday present for Chester," I said. Chester had always protested when people spent money on him, but in truth, he loved little gifts that showed the giver knew him well. I had scoured the stores in Purple Sage and had come away with a Purple Sage mug. Chester collects mugs and this one was hand-thrown, so it wasn't a bad start. I had also picked some mistletoe to add to the decoration on his package. He would like both, but I wanted something to go with them.

"Didn't you say you had a mug already?" Prissy asked. "Does he drink coffee or tea?"

"Tea."

"We could go to my favorite little tea shop and create a blend just for him," she said, sipping from her own cup. "Most tea drinkers would love something like that." Her eyes closed appreciatively while she sniffed the steam rising from the fragrant brew.

Earlier she'd told me all about her tea blending, and how we were drinking a special combination of mango and peach, with just a hint of lime.

"This is nice," I said.

She opened her eyes. "We'll do something exotic, or whatever you think he'd like. And I can help you package it. Did I tell you I took a calligraphy class? I can add a label with the ingredients."

Martha Stewart could take lessons from Prissy Linden. Probably had. "Sounds perfect."

"My favorite thing for stress—retail therapy!" she said, jumping up. "That's 'shopping' to the layman. We don't want to get caught in the Christmas shopping traffic; it seems to be worse than rush hour." She glanced at her watch. "And, Matt, you should be going, too. What time is the party tonight?"

"Seven," I said.

"You probably won't want to arrive until seven-thirty; still, you'll have to leave by seven. And if you figure an hour to get ready, and an hour to eat dinner—oh, or are they having dinner?"

"A buffet, I think."

"Well, I'll just serve soup and bread here at the house. That shouldn't fill you up. I froze some homemade soup last week; I think you'll like it." She was clearing off the table, sweeping my crumbs into her hand. "What that means, Matt, is that you'll need to be back here by five. Can you do that?"

He nodded as he picked up our cups. "I certainly can, Julie. You are Julie the social director, aren't you?"

She swatted him on the arm. "I was just trying to be helpful. I am not the social director and I have no idea if this is the *Love Boat.*"

I only hoped it wasn't the *Titanic.*

THREE

PRISSY'S EXCELLENT French onion soup rolled on my stomach like a flimsy dinghy on a stormy sea as Matt and I stepped into the wide hallway that led to Rose Sterling Advertising.

The agency occupied a seventh-floor suite of offices in the modern downtown high-rise. To our right were two doors, both with burnished wood plaques; one said Petry & Thomas, Certified Public Accountants, and the other Rose Sterling Advertising. Matt steered me in that direction, but there was a short line in front of us.

He leaned down and whispered in my ear. "Do you recognize these people?"

I looked around at the glitter of silk, satin, diamonds, and jewels, then shook my head. I kept my voice low as I said, "I don't know a single person. I think I'm out of my element, or my league, and I don't mean as in 'Junior.'"

"Don't you believe it," he said. "You're the most beautiful woman here."

I was wearing a very expensive beaded dress that I had bought in Dallas a few years before. Matt was in a dark suit; his white shirt had French cuffs held together by carved jade cuff links, and he wore a tie that had just a hint of the same color in it. He looked far more attractive than I did, but he didn't seem to know it. I whispered back, "You're prejudiced."

"I certainly am," he said, his arms resting lightly on my shoulders. I allowed myself to press closer to him for comfort.

The elevator doors opened behind us and a swell of people poured into the area on a wave of chill air, expensive perfume, and laughter.

I closed my eyes and listened to the conversations floating toward me.

"We're glad you could be with us, Bill. Come in and make yourself at home." I could separate that voice out of the others. It came from inside the doorway, and it was Chester's. Apparently there was a receiving line, which accounted for the holdup.

The crowd moved forward. Another voice I recognized from those four years past became audible. "Willa, hello; it's so nice that you could come. This must be your handsome husband." It was Audry Sterling-Sherabian. I wondered if she still hyphenated the two names or if she used just Sherabian now. The office joke many years before had been that her monogram was appropriate, as in Audry SS.

I remember clearly the day that a videotape broke while she was playing a TV commercial for a client. Audry had been full of apologetic charm until the client was gone, then she'd marched into the creative director's office, slapped the tape on his desk, and said, "This tape broke in front of a very important client. I won't have that kind of incompetence around me, so don't let it happen again." With that she had stomped out.

In her defense, Audry had been young. She'd arrived from graduate school with a lot of theory but very little practical experience. Her idea of business chic had been to pull her ginger-colored hair back into a severe chignon and wear mannish suits with scarves tied into bows at the neck.

Interesting that, as I was about to face my own sins, I was spending time recounting hers.

Matt gestured toward a tall woman in mink in front of me. After I'd acknowledged seeing her, he whispered in my ear. "I thought furs were politically incorrect," he said. I turned around and saw the smile he was trying to hold back.

He leaned over so I could speak to him without being overheard. "Obviously a very brave woman," I said.

Matt just smiled and shook his head.

By the time I turned back around we were almost in the doorway, and another voice caught at me. A voice I knew all too well. And I knew the nuances it could contain, too. A shivery chill touched my skin.

"Richard, Pat, so glad you could come. Pat, you have to save me a dance later. Audry, you know Pat and Richard."

Michael at his most public and most gracious.

We drew closer and I could see the large Christmas tree behind where the front desk would be, had there been one. Then we were in the door and I was face-to-face with Audry. She was beautiful, no longer the awkward young woman I'd worked with. Her hair was short, sophisticated, and her makeup subtle, the perfect complement to her elegant features. It made her eyes appear large and brilliant.

When she looked at me there was only the barest hint of hesitation before she smiled and held out her hand. "Jolie, how nice that you could come. And this is your husband, Matt. Right?"

"Yes, of course, Audry. How wonderful to see you." The niceties slipped off our tongues as if they were truths. "Matt, do you remember Audry Sherabian? She managed the Atlanta office." Matt had taken me to lunch when we were dating, and he'd come into the agency, which is where they'd met briefly.

"Nice to see you again," Matt said, shaking her hand.

I thought I detected the tiniest narrowing of Audry's eyes as she gazed first at Matt, then back to me. Just the littlest acknowledgment of something that neither of us would admit to.

"I'd forgotten how handsome your husband is, Jolie," she said. "And you remember Michael." No question.

I got an impression of his suit, double-breasted, expertly cut, elegant on his tall, slim body. There was the scent of his musky aftershave that brought with it unwanted memories. I didn't quite look into his face. "Michael, hello," I said, shaking his hand quickly, then slipping my arm through Matt's. "This is my husband, Matt Wyatt."

"How do you do?"

I had to look. As I raised my face I saw those incredible eyes that could be playful, daring, sometimes compassionate. They stared into mine just a little too long before he flashed a smile. When E. M. Hull wrote The Sheik, he must have had Michael Sherabian in mind.

I nodded, tried to smile, then looked quickly at Audry, who said, "We'll talk later." She turned to greet the next couple.

With Matt at my side, I moved on—straight into arms that enveloped me in a bear hug. "Jolene Berenski, we've missed you around here. It never has been quite the same since you left." Chester was beaming.

I hugged him back. "I've missed you, too."

Chester Sterling had always been a big man, over six feet, with reddish brown hair like his daughter's and a round, slightly jowly face that reminded me of a happy sheepdog. He had lost weight since I'd last seen him, hastening nature's downward course, so that his face drooped into his neck. He now looked like a different breed of dog, more like a shar-pei. "And you remember Matt," I said.

Chester kept hold of me even as he stepped back to favor Matt with a welcoming smile. "Of course, Matt. What a lucky man you are to get our Jolie."

"I certainly think so."

"How have you been doing, Chester?" I asked.

"Fine, fine. Couldn't be better. And, Jolie, I want to hear everything you've been up to as soon as we get everyone welcomed. In the meantime, you just make yourself at home. Get something to eat, and something to drink; there are bars in every corner. Can't miss them."

He released me and we moved again. Someone took my coat, giving me a numbered ticket to reclaim it.

Inside the suite music from a live band played a bit too loudly. It was almost dizzying combined with the glitter, the lights, and the people. Luckily Chester favored wide-open spaces, so there were few real offices and only one massive conference room. All were being utilized tonight, and most of the desks and more prosaic pieces of office equipment had been whisked away to some other place, as had the temporary cubicles.

Flowers blossomed everywhere. On the tables were trays of fascinating edibles and everyone seemed so sophisticated, an elegant garden of exotic humans.

"Would you like something to drink?" Matt asked me.

Bourbon straight up and make it a double. "Maybe a small glass of white wine."

"Well, I'll be damned," said a broadly accented female voice. "If it isn't Jolene Berenski and that good-looking husband she just snatched up and took off with her! How in the world are you, girlfriend?"

I turned to find myself facing a red strapless dress on a very tall woman. From the cut and the detailing I guessed the dress was expensive, but it was far too revealing for a woman who no longer had the creamy skin of youth. "Donna Katherine," I said as I smiled up into her face. "I'm fine. How are you?"

"Honey, I haven't been doing near as well as you from what I can see, but I'm gettin' along. You going to introduce me, or do I just have to sit here and drool anonymously?"

Matt was laughing as he held out his hand. "Matt Wyatt. Nice to meet you."

"I'm Donna Katherine Phennicie and I know that's a mouthful, but, honey, some women just are."

With a perfectly straight face he said, "You two used to work together?"

"For our sins," Donna Katherine said. "But I'm just a book-keeper. I balance the checkbook and see that the bills get paid. Nothing exciting."

"And she's always done it exceedingly well," I added, trying hard not to glance toward the doorway to see where the Sherabians were now. "Donna Katherine, do you know what I can do with this?" I held up the package for Chester. Prissy had placed the mug and the tea on a bed of shimmery white grass in a white basket, then covered it with pale gold cellophane. A huge gold bow adorned the outside, and she had put some of the mistletoe inside, with another sprig on the bow.

Donna Katherine peered at it in the dim lighting. "Isn't that the prettiest thing! And look at the goodies inside. Girl, you always did have class. Here, give it to me; I know what we'll do." She took the basket from me and flagged over a waiter. "Here, darling," she said, handing it to him. "Put this on that side table in the conference room. It's one of the birthday presents for Mr. Sterling."

"Yes, ma'am." He nodded and took off.

"Quite efficient," Matt said. "We should have asked him for drinks."

"Don't you believe it. It would take an hour to get them. We've only got two waiters for this whole crowd."

"Then I'll go," he said.

Donna Katherine pointed the way, in fact offered to go with him, but he refused. "You stay here and visit with Jolie. Can I get you something?"

"Oh, darling, can you!" She stopped then and feigned disappointment. "Oh, you mean a drink. Well, I'll take a Scotch and water. The oldest they have."

Once, many years before, Donna Katherine had been a beauty, or so the story goes. I heard she had been Miss San Angelo, but that had been twenty-five years before. The intervening years had weighed heavily on both her face and body, leaving her with little of what had once been except the flaming red hair and not quite milky skin.

"Well, isn't he something?" Donna Katherine said, watching Matt walk away. "Girl, you did yourself proud. Now, what I want to know is, are there any more of him at home?"

"Sorry, just a sister."

"Damn. They should have made more of that model. It'd been a best-seller." She gestured at the offices. I glanced around, keeping my eyes away from the entrance, although I could tell by the movement of people that there was still a line at the door. It meant that Michael and Audry were still at the door, too. "How do you think the place looks?" Donna Katherine pushed. "Pretty good for an old ad agency."

This time I really looked at my surroundings. Chester likes color. Lots of color and lots of glass. There were hunter green accent walls next to navy blue ones, all surrounded by the glass exterior of the building.

Outside the lights of Austin shimmered seven stories below us. "I'd forgotten how beautiful it is. No wonder we never complained about working late."

Donna Katherine raised one eyebrow. "Honey, I don't think that's the reason, but I didn't say so."

I choked back a response. She knew. At least I thought she knew, but I wasn't sure. Luckily, just then we were joined by a few more of the old crowd.

I hugged Nola Wells. "Aren't you as gorgeous as always," I said, standing back to take a better look at her. Nola was about my height, maybe fifteen pounds heavier, with glowing ebony skin that looks like it's been brushed with peach.

Her black eyes sparkled. "I might say the same to you. And I love that dress."

"This old thing?"

"And speaking of old things," Nola said with a laugh, "you remember my husband, James?"

"Of course."

He had probably gained forty pounds since his college football days, but his smile still lit up the room. "How you doin', Jolie?"

"Fine, James. It's good to see you again." His big hand wrapped around mine in a firm but gentle handshake. James was in sales for an insurance company and he exuded trust, tempered with a little devilment that never went much beyond some sweet-natured teasing. "And how is Tisha?" I asked. "And James the Younger?"

He laughed. "Tisha is now seven going on seventeen, and James, Jr., well, it's hard to say."

"Problems?" I asked. "He's what, eight, nine?"

"Eleven," James said. "And that boy is something—"

"I'll say," Nola added. "He's either going to get himself elected as the first black president of the United States, or get a life sentence in Huntsville."

"I vote for president," I said.

"You and me both." Nola looked around. "Doesn't the old place look pretty? Although I expected more people."

Again I scanned the party. There were only fifty or sixty people, and I, too, had thought there would be more. At the front door a few stragglers were arriving, but they weren't being greeted. Chester was at one of the bars chatting earnestly with an older couple.

"I believe Miss Audry cut back on the guest list," Donna Katherine said with a wicked smile.

Nola looked far less amused. "Now, why doesn't that surprise me?"

Ralph Richardson joined us. "Jolie, hey, hi there." A smile peeked out from under his big gray mustache as he leaned over to kiss my cheek. The mustache had been brown last time I'd seen him.

I hugged him back. "Ralph, how are you?"

When I was up for the position of creative director, Ralph was the person who was brought in for the job. I should have disliked him. I'd certainly intended to; however, Ralph is a genuinely nice person. The kind who likes it best when everyone is working as a team, sharing both ideas and credit equally.

"I'm doing fine," he said. "Hey, I heard a rumor that you'd gone New York on us." He smiled. "Published a book and all."

"Sold one."

"That's great! I'm happy for you. Do you know Amber?" Amber was a young blonde who was hanging back just slightly. I smiled in her direction, but before I could respond, Matt was at my side, holding drinks for Donna Katherine and me.

Donna Katherine took hers and raised the glass. "Happy holidays," she said by way of a toast.

"Happy holidays," we all repeated dutifully.

"Enough of this holiday cheer," Nola said. "Ralph, did you say a book deal? Jolie, I thought you had a radio show."

This was my big moment, and I caught myself glancing around, wondering where Audry and Michael were. I wanted them to hear this, not as vindication, but as proof to them that no matter what I'd done in the past, I was beyond it now. It was some ridiculous need for both confession and absolution.

I saw neither of the Sherabians.

"Well, I did sell a book," I said. "My agent just mailed me the contracts, and we have a pub date of next September." I dropped the jargon as if it were part of my everyday vocabulary. Nola grinned at me.

"What kind of book?" Donna Katherine asked.

"A mystery. *Murder for Fun and Profit*," I said.

"A mystery? Really?" It was Ralph. "Do you kill off one of us?" he asked.

"No. It's not about—"

"Maybe you should hire the agency to get you some publicity." Amber, the only one of the group I didn't know, made the suggestion. She was wearing a burgundy crushed-velvet dress on a body that was fashionably pale and thin, like her hair. Her burgundy lipstick exactly matched her dress and the ribbon around her neck.

"I hadn't considered that." I didn't tell them that a first book advance wouldn't cover the minimum that Rose Sterling required of new clients.

"Can you send us some free copies, since you used to work here?" Amber asked.

"Actually—"

"Listen to this greedy little thing," Nola said. Nola's title was account executive and she was wearing a bracelet that probably cost more than my car.

"Well, I mean, I'd like to read it," said Amber, fingering the ribbon at her neck. "We could put a copy in the conference room and pass it around."

"Too many perks in this business," Nola said, with a quick shake of her head.

Donna Katherine hiked up the top of her dress where it had been riding dangerously low on her breasts, then put her hands on her hips as she stared at the group. "We are not going to set up our own lending library. You people can't even keep track of time sheets. Especially Ralph." She swatted him on the arm. "If I had a nickel for every billable hour you forgot to write down—"

"What a toughy," he said.

She waggled her hips at him. "And you love it..." She turned to me. "So, you'll have an author signing here in Austin, and you just let us know where and when. Y'all, this is a sales opportunity."

Sales opportunities were well understood by everyone at Rose Sterling, thanks to Chester's belief that every person in the agency was a selling representative of the firm.

"I'll make sure that you get invitations." All my senses were on hyperalert; things were going too smoothly to continue like this.

"I'll send out autographed copies of your mystery as Christmas presents," Nola said.

"And," Donna Katherine added, "I'll get the rest of these deadbeats to cough up the price of a book." She turned toward a makeshift dais at the other end of the room. "Oh, look. I believe the festivities are about to begin."

FOUR

DONNA KATHERINE left us to take charge of the informal portion of the activities. At that point the Sherabians reappeared; they slipped in beside Chester, smiling graciously. There was the singing of "Happy Birthday," and at Donna Katherine's insistence, the opening of the few presents. Chester loved the mug and the tea, and beamed a smile at me from across the room along with his thank-you.

Next came speeches. About Chester. About the agency. About people present, and long gone. About triumphs and disasters. The drink I'd been sipping was still jittering around in my stomach. I was tensed for whatever was coming, a careless word from someone who'd known about me and Michael, or for the moment when Audry and Michael joined us, because I knew they would.

A thirtyish woman with sleek black hair, and an even sleeker black dress on her small, athletic body, stepped up to the microphone.

I leaned over to Ralph. "Who's that?"

"Desi Baker. Used to be Donna Katherine's assistant, but she's doing copywriting now. I'll tell you about her later."

Desi began to speak, her lovely voice shaky with nerves. "In my experience in business, Chester Sterling is absolutely unique. He is the kind of man who believes in people." She glanced at Chester and smiled. The smile turned into a grimace, and her right hand briefly touched her flat stomach.

Her face flushed lightly as she raised her chin and went on. "Last week I checked the employment records of Rose Sterling and discovered that the majority of people in the agency have been promoted at least three times. Top positions are almost never filled by outsiders. To me that's proof that Chester Sterling is a man of unique vision. He believes in giving people the chance to move up, to try new things, to learn from their mistakes and to grow into the best they can be." She looked into the crowd, taking several quick breaths in succession. She smiled to overcome her stage fright, and again I saw how pretty she was. "I hope that all of us have learned this lesson as well. To give everyone a chance." She turned back to Chester. "And now I speak for every one of your employees, Chester, when I say 'thank you' to one of America's truly great leaders."

The applause was generous as she quickly hugged Chester, then stepped off the dais.

Nola's purse began to beep. She opened it and pulled out a cell phone. "Hello?" she whispered, already moving toward the front door to carry on her conversation less obtrusively. James gave us a wave and followed her.

Someone else moved to the microphone and spoke. Then someone else. It became a parade of speakers, all wanting to leave their mark on the occasion. Matt clapped politely after each; he does this sort of thing well. I began to feel sorry for him, knowing he must have felt like a stranger at a funeral. Even for me much of it seemed remote. Watching Michael and Audry on the dais was like watching a play. One I'd seen before; one I'd had a part in.

Then someone dimmed the lights, a screen came down from the ceiling, and a reel of the agency's award-winning television commercials began.

"Would you like another drink?" Matt whispered.

"I'd love one. Cyanide."

He winked and smiled as he moved away.

I turned back to watch the three shadowy figures sitting on the dais. I could see Audry, smiling as if she were responsible for all the award winners we were seeing. Michael was sitting beside his wife, but he was looking around the room, searching the crowd for something. Or someone.

His eyes caught mine and he smiled.

My stomach tensed. Once again I was reminded that if I go to hell, I will know why. Not that it was Michael's fault. I take full credit, with all due regret.

The truth is that I had never intended to have a relationship with Michael. It had started innocently. Accidentally. It was during that horrible time in my life when my father was dying of cancer, and my mother was in a state of denial that I'm sure was intended to be cheering. Unfortunately, there's no room for real emotions or real comfort when everyone is pretending that nothing is wrong. The problem was that I couldn't pretend, and it had left me bereft.

Once a week my parents would call from Dallas. Once a month Jeremy and I would drive up there to see them, but through all the conversations no one ever really talked. At first I asked for information, but I never got any. The few times I had the courage to say I was worried, or worse, scared, my mother would dismiss my feelings.

"Oh, pooh," Mom would say, "your dad will be fine. Fine. Don't mention the 'c' word to him; it would only upset him." I wasn't living close to my sister or brother, and Jeremy was only nine, far too young to bear the kind of grief that I was holding inside.

Then one day at work it all began to erupt, the hurt at being shut out by my mother, the anger at her denial, and worst of all, the fear that my father was dying. I'd run to the supply closet, the only place I could think of where I'd have some privacy. And there I'd finally begun to cry. Not a gentle rain of tears; no, this was an outpouring of gut-wrenching pain. Somewhere in the midst of it the door had opened and Michael had walked in. I'd tried to hide my face, but he hadn't let me.

"It's okay, Jolie." And with that he'd put both arms around me tightly. That physical contact, the closeness I'd been hungering for, broke down the last of my resolve to be strong, and the sobs became even deeper until there was a physical pain to match the emotional one.

He had just held on to me, saying nothing, letting me cry, letting me draw from his warmth and his strength. When I finally began to calm down, my makeup was all over his shirt, my nose was running, and I didn't have a shred of dignity left. Michael had calmly reached for the Kleenex stored there, and held on to me while I blew my nose and wiped my face.

Little tears were still leaking out, and when I tried to bumble excuses, Michael tilted up my head and kissed first my cheeks, then my lips. I was as needy for the kisses as I'd been for the comfort.

And that was how it all started. Over my father's illness. Over my need. Over my own lousy weakness. Michael had just separated from Audry at the time, and might have gone right back if I hadn't been there. Seeing them together now brought it home powerfully.

The lights came up, startling me into the moment. Everyone was applauding again. Chester stood, and said into the microphone, "Thank you. This is a very special evening for me. I hope you all are enjoying it as much as I am." With that he helped Audry off the dais and they began to dance. The party went back into full swing. Michael looked out around the room. I ducked my head and moved a little closer to the windows, staring out, as if I could make myself invisible.

When I felt a tap on my shoulder I jumped. It was Matt. He handed me a tall cool glass of diet Coke. "How is this?"

"Perfect." We sipped in silence, then put our drinks down and joined the dancers. I ducked my head into Matt's shoulder like an ostrich. Through two songs I stayed focused on Matt, and then a realization hit me; I stopped in midsong.

"What?" Matt asked.

"I'm not having a good time," I said. "Are you?"

"I always have a good time when I'm with you."

"Liar."

He smiled. "Most of the time."

"We don't have to stay here. We can leave and no one will notice. Even if they did, they wouldn't care."

"Are you sure you want to go?"

"I'm positive. Let me just run to the rest room first and then we can disappear into the night." I gestured toward the glittering sky outside.

"I'll get your coat and meet you at the door."

"Great idea."

I gave him my claim ticket and headed straight out, hurrying between people, nodding at acquaintances without stopping to chat. Now that I had given myself permission to leave, I felt lighter, but I wasn't willing to slow down. If I did, I was afraid my past would catch up to me.

In the outside hall I sucked in the cold fresh air without stopping; I dashed down the hall and discovered a long line of women, all waiting to get into the ladies' rest room.

Luckily in a high-rise every floor has bathrooms. I went to the elevator and pressed the button. When it appeared, and the doors opened, there was a security guard inside.

"Is there something wrong?" I asked, stepping in.

"Oh, no, ma'am," he said, running his fingers over his brown crew cut. "We're just here to help the guests." His badge said his name was Ted Polovy. "Do you want the lobby or the parking garage?"

"Neither actually, I want to go to the next floor down and use the rest room."

He put his heavy thumb on the "door open" button. "I'm sorry, ma'am, but I can't let you do that. The guests aren't allowed on any other floors. Security. You understand."

"Actually, I don't...." I said, but the look on his face told me very clearly that there was no point in challenging him. I could go to either the lobby or the parking garage, and neither had rest rooms.

"Thank you," I said automatically as I stepped off the elevator and turned toward Rose Sterling. I lurked at the door of the agency, and while I didn't see Matt, I did bump into Donna Katherine.

"Where you going, girl?" she asked.

"I was going to the rest room...but it's packed and the security guy won't let me on any other floors. I'm not happy."

"Then take the stairs down to six."

"Oh." Of course. The stairs. There wouldn't be anyone guarding the stairwell. "Thanks."

I turned back the way I'd come, pausing only briefly when I faced the door to the stairs. What if an alarm sounded? The doors hadn't been secured when I worked at the agency; I'd run up and down them fairly often because it was the only exercise I had time for. Michael and I had rendezvoused on the stairwell a couple of times, too.

With a quick shake of my head I popped open the fire door. Nothing happened and the metal staircase beyond was well lit, just as I remembered. I headed down quickly and dashed to the bathroom.

The lights inside were on, and I stopped in the doorway, assailed by an odor of perfume, urine, and vomit. It was enough to make me turn around and go back. Almost. Perhaps this was the reason they were keeping guests on the seventh floor—some kind of plumbing problem.

It was too late to worry about that, so I took a breath and entered. Inside the air felt chilly, perhaps because of the black and white ceramic tiles on the floor. I picked out the nearest stall, slid shut the bolt, and went to the bathroom.

When I came out I stopped long enough to wash my hands.

As I turned off the water, I heard a sound at the door. I expected the door to open, but whoever was outside changed her mind. It gave me an odd feeling. That was silly, because if I knew enough to sneak down one floor, there would be others. Donna Katherine was probably sending tours. I peeked around the tile wall so I could see the door and a movement on the floor caught my attention. At first I thought it was a bug crawling under the door, but with a second glance I saw it was a piece of paper. A note.

I walked over and picked it up.

The writing was as familiar to me as if I'd seen it yesterday. *Meet me in the lounge. I still love you. M.*

Michael Sherabian was sending me notes like this was high school.

I would never deny that Michael had stood by me when I needed him, but some part of me, the portion that didn't want all the responsibility, always believed he should have reminded me that he was married, even if he and Audry were living separately. If I had been beyond rational thought, he shouldn't have been, and some portion of my being clung to that, maybe as vindication for what I'd done.

Knowing he might be outside the door made me feel trapped. I could not, would not, leave if there was a chance of running into Michael in the hall. I let out a breath. Damn it, anyway!

Now I had to wait, in a cold bathroom, with a disgusting smell. One more thing to blame on Michael Sherabian. In two minutes, I promised myself, I would go back upstairs, get my purse, get Matt, and get the hell out of the building.

I started pacing toward the large handicapped stall that took up the entire back wall. The tiles felt cool and slippery under the thin soles of my high heels as I marched to the far wall, whirled around, and walked back toward the exit door again. I stopped midway and faced myself in the mirror.

My party face was slipping; I no longer had the devil-may-care look I'd worked so hard to achieve for the evening. In its place was stress as evidenced by my unnaturally pale skin. Or maybe it was the lighting.

I wondered what Michael had seen when he looked at me.

While he had instigated our affair, I had been as much the seducer as the seduced, and I had loved having him in my life. Our relationship had gone on for five months of incredible highs when it felt as if I were flying on pure exhilaration, balanced with soul-wrenching lows when I admitted that it couldn't last forever. During all that time I knew that Audry wanted her husband and her marriage back.

I believe in love and marriage. I believe in families and loyalty, and all the old-fashioned virtues that were instilled in me during the more conventional era of my childhood. Maybe those values, combined with all the years of single motherhood, are why I cherish Matt so.

This time when I held up the note and read it, the memories touched me; the scent of Michael's musky cologne, the way he would begin a conversation by gently touching my hand, the chocolate Kisses he often brought me—

I crumpled the note and shoved it down into the shiny metal waste container on the wall beside me. If I could rid myself of the note, maybe I could rid myself of the feelings as well.

I whipped back around and began to pace again, back to the far stall. When I reached it I slammed my fist against the wall; my feet slipped on the tile and went out from under me. My shoulder banged open the handicapped stall door as I went down.

That's when I realized I wasn't alone in the ladies' room.

FIVE

I GASPED AND JUMPED UP, stammering apologies. "I'm so sorry—"

There was vomit on the commode seat and inside it. Desi Baker was curled in a fetal position around the porcelain, her black dress twisted on her body. There was spit on one corner of her lips and her eyes were open, staring ahead. I realized she wasn't seeing anything.

The chill air seemed to permeate my being. I clung to the slick metal, afraid to breathe, too sick to move. I closed my eyes, willing her to be gone; when I opened them she was still there. My stomach lurched and for a moment I thought I was going to be sick.

Again I closed my eyes, only this time I twisted my head to breathe some cleaner air. When I turned back I saw again the once beautiful Desi Baker, still on the cold tile floor. With great care I bent toward her. Gently I felt the smooth white skin of her inner wrist. It was warm, but there was no movement of blood that created a pulse.

I straightened, stumbling backward across the tile. As soon as I reached the outside door I flung it open and sucked in air as I began to run. First to the stairs, then up toward Rose Sterling Advertising. All the way I prayed that someone would appear to help me. Someone who could work a miracle and bring Desi Baker back to life.

IT WAS THE SECURITY GUARD, Ted Polovy, who called both EMS and the police. Next he secured the area and me as well, insisting that I stand just outside the rest room door while he guarded the elevator. I was too stunned to care, and too relieved that someone else was taking charge. I'm sure the emergency medical people were there in minutes, but it seemed like hours of waiting, shivering, and hoping for something that I knew wasn't going to happen.

When the EMS team did finally arrive they looked like kids, too young for the job. They moved past me quickly and efficiently, straight through the bathroom door that closed behind them with a heavy whoosh. Then the police arrived. First a patrol officer in uniform, then later two plainclothes officers accompanied by Polovy. They went by me without any acknowledgment.

I felt a million miles away from the party, and from Matt, as if I were in a cold, distant existence without a pathway back to the real world. When a plainclothes detective came out of the bathroom I stopped him.

"Excuse me," I said, my voice swallowed up by the emptiness in the hallway. "I need to go back upstairs. Could you tell me how she is?"

He looked me over curiously. "Who are you?"

"I'm the woman who found her. They, the security guard, asked me to stay."

He nodded, rubbing a finger on his chin. I realized that I could have left at any time and no one would have known or cared.

The officer looked me over again, assessing me. "Was she a friend of yours?"

"No. I never met her. She worked for the agency and I think her name was Desi Baker."

"But you didn't work with her?"

I shook my head. "No. I left the agency several years ago. They invited me back for the anniversary party, and Chester's birthday. Is she...? Did she...?"

His face was stolid, implacable. "I'm sorry, ma'am, but I don't believe she regained consciousness."

At first I could only stare at him while the confirmation of what I knew slowly filtered through my mind, numbing it. I suddenly needed Matt, and remembered that he was waiting for me one floor up. "I have to get back. My husband is at the party. I have to let him know I'm okay."

"Certainly. I'll need some information first," he said, as he pulled out a small lined notebook and flipped pages impatiently. He was a heavy man, heavy and big, somewhere in his mid-forties, with dark brown hair that came down to the middle of his ears. He had on metal-framed glasses that had worn a ridge in his temples.

His beefy fingers fumbled with the small notebook. When he finally found a clean page he asked, "Your name?"

"Jolene Wyatt. Jolie Wyatt."

"Your address and phone?"

"Route 3, Box 213, Purple Sage, Texas."

"Is that your permanent address?"

"It's where I live."

"Where are you staying here in Austin?"

"At my sister-in-law's." I gave him Prissy's name, address, and phone number, then said, "Look, I'll be right back. It'll just take five minutes. Or you can come with me—"

"No problem, ma'am, I'll come with you."

I was ready to head for the stairs, but he turned in the other direction. I had to trot to stay up with him.

"I didn't get your name," I said when we stopped at the elevator.

"Senior Sergeant Ray Bohles."

The elevator door opened and we faced another security guard. He nodded at Bohles and we rode up one floor to the agency. Music was still playing, but it was muted, as were the voices coming from the suite. A crowd of people was just inside the door. Donna Katherine was one of them. Her eyes widened as she saw me. "Jesus, girl, where have you been? Your husband's been looking for you." She glanced at the man beside me.

Sergeant Bohles wasn't touching me, certainly not constricting my movement in any way, but it was obvious that he was with me. At least it seemed obvious to me.

"Where's Matt?" I asked.

"He's in the conference room." She leaned over and said confidentially, "They said someone was hurt. Shit, I was terrified it was you. But then Matt talked to someone, and it just got so confusing. What in the world is going on?"

I shook my head as I moved past her. "I'll tell you later." I had to get to Matt and assure him I was all right.

He was in the conference room, along with at least a dozen other people. My coat and my purse were on the table in front of him; he forgot both when I entered.

"Jolie," he said, his arms going around me. "Are you okay?"

I mumbled yes and held on to him, feeling the texture of his jacket against my face, and the strength in his arms.

It was Senior Sergeant Bohles who spoke, over my head, directly to Matt. "Mrs. Wyatt was helping us with an incident downstairs."

Matt's arms relaxed their hard grip and I stepped back. A woman's life and death had become nothing more than an incident.

"Exactly what incident was that?" Matt asked.

The officer hesitated, looked around the room at the others gathered in it. "We need to find a place where I can speak with Mrs. Wyatt privately. If you'll come with us..."

"That's fine," Matt said, picking up my things along with his own overcoat.

We passed through the remaining partygoers, who watched our progress with curiosity. Some asked me what was going on, but I could only shake my head and keep on walking. Fortunately, Donna Katherine had abandoned her post at the door or I doubt that we'd have made it out. We headed for the elevator, and once inside, Senior Sergeant Bohles said to Matt, "A young woman died in the rest room downstairs. Mrs. Wyatt found her."

Matt's glance went from Bohles to me. "Are you okay?" he asked, again.

I nodded, but I didn't trust myself to speak just then. Matt must have sensed my feelings because he slid an arm around me. "You're cold."

Again I nodded.

Within a few minutes we were in a small windowless room on the ground floor that was apparently the office of the security guards. "I just need to ask you a few basic questions," Bohles said, holding out a chair for me in front of a dirty gray metal desk. "Mrs. Wyatt, are you okay with that?"

"I think so."

Matt gave me a quick glance. My face felt frozen, but whatever expression showed must have been enough. He nodded at Bohles, then his eyes came back to me as the policeman took out a notebook.

After that, time went quickly. I was asked some very simple questions about how I got to the ladies' room in the first place, how many other people I had seen, and exactly what I had done after finding Desi Baker. It didn't take long; that surprised me.

"That's it?" I asked.

He nodded, helping me on with my coat. "Yes, ma'am, that's all. If there's anything more I need to know, I can reach you at the numbers you gave me, is that right?"

"Yes."

"Then I hope the rest of your evening is more pleasant." He handed me over to Matt and opened the door for us.

Matt and I started toward the parking garage in silence.

A young woman was dead, I had found her, and now I was going home. It made no sense to me. I had agreed to attend the party to have some moment of glory; to recoup my losses from years past. In truth, there had been no losses. Very few people had known about my relationship with Michael, so there had been no disgrace. Now it was over. Sadly, horribly.

It was then I remembered the note that had been slipped under the bathroom door. The one that I had crumpled and shoved into the waste container.

"Jolie, what's wrong?" Matt asked.

"What?"

"You jerked away from me; are you okay?"

I looked down at my hands. "I think I left something upstairs." I turned toward the elevators. "I have to go back up."

"Jolie? What did you leave? You're wearing your coat, and your purse is over your shoulder. That's all you brought." He was watching me as if I might explode.

"It was, uh, the present. I left it."

"You gave it to Chester for his birthday, remember?"

I stared at Matt dumbly.

I couldn't tell him that I needed to find a note from Michael Sherabian; one that held his scent. I couldn't say that the police might be digging it out of the trash at that very moment. I couldn't say that I had picked it up, and crumpled it, getting my fingerprints all over it.

I could only say, "Of course. We should go home." We started walking.

Again he put an arm around me. "Some of Prissy's herb tea will help. And some sleep. Tomorrow this will all be behind you."

Even through the haze of my shock one thing was very clear to me—Desi Baker's death wasn't going to go away that quickly or that easily.

PRISSY SET A SMALL BOWL of fruit on my place mat. There were three different kinds of melon, along with grapes and strawberries. If anything could have tempted me to eat, that would have been it, but I didn't want food. I had barely sipped the tea she'd put in front of me earlier.

"Did you sleep at all?" Prissy asked, sitting across from me at the table in her breakfast nook. It was already midmorning, although the gray sky outside gave the world an eerie feel as if there were no time.

Matt had left hours before to attend a board of directors' meeting at a company he was heavily invested in. His parting remarks to me had been filled with concern, but I had assured him that I would be fine. After that I had gone back to sleep, finally achiev-

ing the heavy dreamless state that had eluded me during the night.
Now I felt drugged and slow.

"I slept a little," I said.

"Matt said you tossed and turned all night."

"Matt's a blabbermouth."

"It had to be hard, though, finding that woman dead and all.
How are you feeling now?"

"Fine."

Prissy turned her gaze to the patio outside the French doors.
"Matt said she was young."

I nodded, remembering her body in its short black dress, curled
around the toilet. I tried to hide the shudder that grabbed me.
"Late twenties or early thirties." I took a sip of my herb tea and
the warm liquid slid easily down my throat as if it really might
do some good.

I sipped some more, enjoying the companionable silence. I
even tried a little of the fruit. My brain began to unclog and my
thoughts converged. After I drained my cup I set it down, and
Prissy went to the kitchen for the teapot. "You know what bothers me?" I said. "The police didn't do anything. That one detective asked me ten questions and then sent me away."

"What did you want him to do?" Prissy asked, returning to
refill my cup. She looked directly at me.

"Find out how she died. I mean, what caused her to die? She'd
been sick, vomiting...." I didn't want to go into the details. "She
was young and beautiful, and she'd just gotten the promotion she
wanted. Writing copy. So why did she die? The police should
have talked to everyone at the party. They should have sent for
a lab crew—"

"Jolie, the Austin police force is made up of trained profes-
sionals; surely they followed the proper procedure. Besides, Matt
said you left right after that detective questioned you. Maybe the
police did do all the things you think they should have. Perhaps
they did them after you left." She poured the tea, then went back
to the kitchen.

I let out a long breath while her words settled into my brain.

"You're right; I'm sure you are. Maybe *I* just need to know how she died. And somehow I think *I* should have done more. Something." I shook my head. "I don't know."

"I understand," Prissy said, as she sat down and touched my arm lightly. "But it's really not your fault. You didn't even know the woman, except for her name."

"Desi Baker."

It was an interesting name, and she'd looked like an interesting person. Young and smart, both in a fashion sense and intellectually. I wondered what Desi was a nickname for. Desdemona?

"Matt said he heard some gossip about her during the party," Prissy said, dropping her voice even though we were alone in the house.

"Really?" I felt a tickle of fear. Who was gossiping and what all had they been saying? "That surprises me."

"Well, actually he said some woman was telling him. He couldn't get away from her. Real thick accent?"

"It must have been Donna Katherine; I shouldn't have left him alone."

"He's a big boy, he can take care of himself. What he heard was rather personal."

I picked up my cup and inhaled the aroma, trying to appear casual. "What did she say?" I asked. I made myself take a sip of the tea.

"That this young woman, Desi, was having an affair with Michael Sherabian."

"What?" The word came out unexpectedly along with a shower of tea. I began to choke.

Prissy patted me on the back while I coughed and sputtered. She dabbed at my face with a flowered cloth napkin. "Oh, dear. Here, raise your arm, Jolie," she said, lifting my arm straight up into the air. "There, now take a breath."

I wheezed, and she pumped my arm until finally I could talk. "Sorry." I coughed again. "The tea went down the wrong pipe."

Voices and footsteps were coming from the patio at the back of the house. Prissy jumped up and ran for the outside door.

I swallowed twice before I could say, "Who's here?"

Prissy grinned. "Remember we said there was a special surprise coming for you? Well, actually, a treat for both of us."

As I started for the French doors I could hear a little voice saying, "Surprise! Open the door. Grandma Prissy, Aunt Dolie, surprise!"

Before anyone could knock, Prissy threw open the door to the chill grayness. "Hello! Christopher, come in and give me a hug." She scooped up her three-year-old grandson and smothered his face with kisses as she pulled him inside to the warmth.

"Not so much kissing, Grandma Prissy!"

They were followed by his mother, Stephanie, carrying a small bag and a huge purse, which she dumped on the floor before reaching around Christopher to give her mother a hug. "Hi, Mom." She turned and I also got a big hug. "Jolie, hi. Merry Christmas!"

"What a great surprise! It's so wonderful to see you two," I said, putting an arm around Stephanie. "How are you?"

Stephanie has heavy, glossy brown hair and her father's long lean body; over the years she has developed some of Prissy's impish quality, as well.

She gave me a slightly weary smile. "We're fine. Mr. You-know-who had way too much energy on the flight." She poked at Christopher through his heavy coat. "But he finally settled down. It's wonderful to be here; we've missed you," she said, giving me another hug. "Haven't we, little bug?"

"Yes, we have," he said firmly.

Just then the phone rang. Prissy muttered something about turning all the phones off before saying, "I'll be right back." She held Christopher in our direction.

Naturally I took him. "You're getting so big."

He squeezed my neck with both arms. "Aunt Dolie, I missed you too much."

"Aunt Jolie," Stephanie corrected.

He grinned. "Aunt Dolie, Aunt Dolie!"

I had been the first person, after the nurse, to hold Christopher at his birth. He had been wrapped lightly in a thin blanket, still covered in blood and fluids, but I'd felt a bonding that I'd only experienced once before with my own son. Matt, who'd been standing beside me, had worn an expression of amazement and joy as he had stroked Christopher's tiny fist.

Perhaps it was so special for us because we were the only family with Stephanie during the birth. She didn't have a husband, and Prissy and Ross weren't there. I don't think they intended to miss Christopher's arrival; I've always thought their family argument simply got out of hand and no one quite knew how to put an end to it. It started when Ross and Prissy first found out that Stephanie was pregnant, and unwilling to get married. Unwilling even to tell anyone who the father of the baby was. That didn't sit well with Prissy's fundamentalist background, and since Stephanie can be as hardheaded as her mother, things escalated until Prissy and Ross left for a vacation in Europe. Christopher came almost a month early, a full week before they got back.

When Stephanie had gone into labor she'd called us and we raced in from Purple Sage. I remember walking into the birthing room and seeing Stephanie, all alone, her face mottled with tears and pain. Matt and I had both put our arms around her, and that awkward group hug had been the start of a long night, one filled with sweat and those primal emotions that pull us out of the nice civilized world where we usually live. I wouldn't trade anything for the memory.

When Stephanie reconciled with her parents a few weeks later, unreasonable as it was, I actually felt pangs of jealousy. Not that we were left out. Stephanie and Christopher visited us on the ranch as often as they could. It was Stephanie's hideaway, as she called it, and I got to take care of Christopher.

Then last summer, on the Fourth of July, Stephanie had announced she was moving to Phoenix. This was the first time I'd seen them in almost six months.

A clatter from the stairway announced Jeremy's arrival. "Hey, Christopher. Hey, Steph." He smiled.

"Hey, yourself, Jeremy," Stephanie said, giving him a quick

hug. "My, how you've grown, and you're getting more handsome all the time." She grinned as an older sibling might. "I'll bet all the girls in Purple Sage are after you."

Jeremy actually blushed. "How come you're so mean to me?"

"Because I like you."

Jeremy shook his head and looked at Christopher. "Your mommy is silly. How are you doing?"

Christopher thought about it. "I'm fine, 'cept everybody's squeezin' me too hard."

"Oh, really?" I said, swinging him into the living room and plopping him on the sofa. "Then maybe I'll just tickle you instead!"

As I tickled he squirmed with giggles. "No more, Aunt Dolie!"

"Yes, more! Lots more." I pulled up his shirt and began to blow air on his tummy.

"Otay. More, more!"

"Actually," Stephanie said, the voice of reason towering over us, "we have to get the luggage in; the taxi driver piled it on the patio. After that we have to get Christopher fed because neither of us ate this morning on the plane. Did we?"

I stood up. "This is the nicest surprise—oh, but wait—I sent your Christmas presents to Phoenix."

"That's okay, because I brought them back," Stephanie said.

"Santa Claus is coming," Christopher explained, jumping up. "He's bringing baby Jesus."

"You're going to have to tell me that story," I said. "And I can tell you some Christmas stories, too. And then we'll drive around and see the lights, and we'll visit the tree in Zilker Park, and sing Christmas carols at the capitol building...." I lifted Christopher up and swung him around. "Lord, you're getting heavy. If you keep on growing, I won't be able to pick you up."

"Is that bad?" he asked.

"No, sweetie, that's not bad. You're always good."

"How come you never said that to me?" Jeremy asked.

I heard the phone ringing again, or perhaps it was a second phone line.

"It's a generational thing," I said. "But I promise I'll say it to your children. And I'll spoil them rotten. Really rotten. You'll see; paybacks are hell. Uh, heck," I corrected, remembering that we weren't supposed to swear around Christopher.

"Lucky me." He headed for the back door. "Think I'll go get the luggage."

I turned to Stephanie, who was pulling off Christopher's coat. "I was beginning to think this was going to be a terrible Christmas, but you two have changed all that."

"Why would you think it was going to be terrible?" Stephanie asked, setting the coat on a chair.

"Well, something happened. Nothing to do with the family; I'll tell you later—"

"I have to go potty!" Christopher said loudly.

She grabbed his hand. "Come on, then. Hurry. Up the stairs." Over her shoulder she said, "It's always an emergency."

"'Bye, Aunt Dolie!" Christopher put his hand to his mouth and blew me a kiss before he started up the stairs.

"Let me guess," Jeremy said, as he dragged in two suitcases. "If you ever have more kids, that's the one you'll have." He pulled in another bag.

After closing the door, I slid an arm around my son's waist, which is now higher than mine since he's a good six inches taller. "No, thanks. I adore Christopher, but I'm happy with the child I have."

Prissy returned holding out the cordless phone. "It's for you," she said to me. "Can you talk? It's Chester Sterling."

"Sure." I took the phone and said, "Hello?"

"Jolie, thank goodness I tracked you down. I had to call the radio station in Purple Sage to get this number," Chester said. "I hate to bother you, but I need some help."

Jeremy was watching me curiously, as was Prissy. "What kind of help?" I asked. I couldn't imagine what I could ever do for Chester Sterling.

"Jolie, you know one of our staff passed away last night; I was told you found her." He sounded like a man who was drowning, but still trying to be logical.

"Yes, I did."

"I'm sorry about that, and even sorrier that I have to disturb your vacation," he said, then swallowed. "Everyone is in a tizzy here, and I've got commercials that have to get written and produced before we can close up shop for the holidays. Jolie, would you consider coming in and working part-time for a couple of days? I'll pay you a freelance rate and a bonus, if you'll help."

I couldn't. I didn't want to. Stephanie and Christopher were here; it was Christmas, time for fun and family. Besides, I never wanted to go back to Rose Sterling. Not after four years ago, not after last night. "Chester, we have things planned...."

"Just a few hours a day. Whatever you can spare."

"Prissy, my sister-in-law, needs my help with the cooking, and my son needs me to take him places—"

Jeremy shook his head no. He whispered, "I'm fine, go ahead."

But then, he didn't know what Chester was asking.

"Chester, I—"

"Jolie, please? I'm desperate right now, or I wouldn't be calling. Would you do it as a favor to an old friend?"

That stopped me. Back in my days at Rose Sterling, when I had needed an advance to cover new tires for my car, or to pay for a window that Jeremy had broken, Chester had never hesitated. When I needed time off for my dad's illness, Chester had simply said, "Go." Never a question, never a complaint.

In thinking it through, I realized that I had to be there for him, too. No questions, no complaints.

"No problem," I said. "I'll be happy to come in."

I could hear his huge sigh of relief. "Thank you. I really appreciate this."

"What time do you want me?"

"Right after lunch would be good. Say twelve-thirty? One o'clock?"

"I'll see you this afternoon." I pushed the button to hang up the phone and handed it back to Prissy. "I have to go to Rose Sterling and write copy. Chester needs me."

She smiled sympathetically. "Christopher naps most of the afternoon, so we won't be doing anything special anyway. You won't miss a thing."

"Sure, Mom," Jeremy agreed. "Not a thing."

SIX

Ross and Prissy's house and outbuildings are a cream-colored stucco that passes for adobe, with roofs of red brick. The patio is Saltillo tile. In the center there's a fountain and at the back an atrium covered with wisteria and bougainvillea. Come spring both are a riot of greenery; additionally, the wisteria has fragrant clusters of lavender blooms that hang like impressionistic grapes. In the summer the bougainvillea flaunts scarlet petals that dazzle the eye.

But in winter the branches were like dried and twisted sticks of gray that clung to the trellis and snaked up the wall of the house that formed one side of the patio. At the top of the red tile stairs is the garage apartment where Matt and I always stay. The inside is beautifully laid out and decorated in a combination of styles that hint of French country and Victorian, with a splash of Southwestern for panache. Everything blends exquisitely despite Prissy's claim that most of the furniture is castoffs. It always makes me think her garage sales must be the events of the season.

"Aunt Dolie! Aunt Dolie! I need you."

I was in the bedroom of the apartment staring at the clothes I'd brought, trying to decide what in the world I was going to wear and wondering why in the hell it should matter.

"Coming, Christopher." I opened the front door and there he was, alone on the concrete steps, not wearing a jacket in the cold weather. I glanced at the patio and toward the house, but there was no one following him.

"What are you doing here, little bug?" I asked, pulling him inside and closing the door against the frigid weather. "And where's your coat?"

"In Grandma Prissy's house." He pointed in the vague direction. "I'm freezin'!"

"I'll bet you are. Come here and I'll bundle you up." With that I whisked him into the bedroom where I wrapped him in a quilt and set him up against the pillows on the bed like a big doll. I sat down close to him and hugged him once just for pleasure. "There you go; now you can get warm. Don't you know it's winter out there?"

"We don't have winter in Phoenix. But we have cold days."

"I've heard. So where's your mommy? You're not supposed to climb those stairs all by yourself, are you?"

Christopher's eyes were big and serious. "They're fightin'." He burrowed deeper into the quilt, like a little creature seeking protection.

"Who's fighting?"

He put a little finger against his lips. "Shh. No talking."

"Why can't we talk?"

"No talking about fightin'."

"Oh, right!" I said, laughing. "I'll talk about anything. Now, who's fighting? Is your mommy fighting?"

"Aunt Dolie!" His voice held an annoyance more typical of a forty-year-old than a child of just three. "I told you...no talking."

He was dead serious. It was a message he'd learned from someone, and whoever had taught him had done a good job. Christopher was watching me, but didn't volunteer another syllable.

"It's okay," I said. "If you can't tell me, then we won't talk about it."

He nodded.

"Instead, you can stay here and help me pick out something to wear. Can you do that? I need clothes to wear."

"Like Cinderella?"

I almost smiled, but didn't. "No, sweetie. I'm going to work today and I can't decide on the right outfit."

"Where do you work, Aunt Dolie? Can I work, too?"

"No, I have to go by myself. I'm working at the advertising agency."

He threw off the quilt and crawled across the bed to a royal blue sweater that I had been considering. "I like blue." It was lying there along with several other choices, none of which I had found suitable earlier. "It's pretty," Christopher added, patting the sweater with his little hand.

It looked particularly good with my black wool slacks and my fuzzy wool jacket. The outfit was a bit dressy for a copywriter at Rose Sterling, but I was going to wear it anyway. Somewhere I even had a gold pin with just that shade of blue enamel, if I had remembered to bring it.

I slid off my jeans and reached for the slacks as I asked Christopher, "Did you eat your lunch?"

"Yes. Tonight Mr. Javitz is coming."

And who was Mr. Javitz? A new cartoon character? Another friend of Ross and Prissy's? "Interesting." I slipped off my sweatshirt and hung it up with the button-down I'd had on under it. By the time I pulled on the blue sweater, Christopher had climbed off the bed and was poking at the computer Jeremy had transferred from Prissy's house.

"I like 'puters. Aunt Dolie, may you turn it on for me?"

"*Com*puters," I instructed. "Except I can't. Jeremy is working on this one and he gets very mad if we mess something up." He'd put the computer here specifically to keep it out of Christopher's reach.

"I won't hurt it." He was standing up on his tiptoes, his fingers mashing the keys.

"I know you won't, sweetie," I said, picking him up. "But what if *I* messed it up? Then Jeremy would be mad at me."

"Where did he go?"

"To his friend's house. W.D.'s," I said, carrying Christopher into the bathroom where I set him on the counter. "You don't know W.D."

A quick look in the mirror convinced me that my clothes would pass muster, and as I rummaged through my makeup bag for a lipstick I discovered the enamel pin. I slipped it in my pocket, then took the lid off the tube of lipstick.

"I can do that!" Christopher said, trying to get the lipstick from me. "I can do it, please, Aunt Dolie."

I moved the bag to the other side. "I know you can, but we're in a hurry. I have to go to work now, so you have to go back to your grandma Prissy's. I'll bet they're looking for you." I put the lipstick on quickly, then swept all my cosmetics into a drawer and out of reach of little hands. The nice thing about visits with Christopher and Stephanie, besides simply enjoying him, was that I could always send Christopher back to his mother. It was practice for when I became a grandmother.

"Come on," I said, lifting him again. "We'll go see what your grandma Prissy is doing. Besides, I think it's time for your nap."

"No it's not time for nappin'," he said very firmly. But he put his arms around my neck and hung on tightly as I went out the door and down the stairs. I almost lost my balance near the bottom of the steps and had to stop to regain my footing. "Well, that was scary," I said. Then I moved across the patio and heard the voices coming from Prissy's great room.

"Absolutely not!" It was Stephanie. "I won't. I mean it. This just infuriates me!"

Prissy's voice was battle-weary. "Stephanie, all I'm asking is that you—"

"You still aren't listening!" Stephanie snapped. "Every time I try telling you what happened, you blow me off like I'm some hysterical child. It's because you don't believe me, isn't it? I'm your daughter, doesn't that mean anything to you?"

"Of course it does. I just think—"

"Damn it, there you go again!"

"Stephanie, there is no need to yell. I'm sure the neighbors aren't interested in hearing about this." She lowered her own voice as I backed away from the French doors.

I couldn't help but wonder if this was what I had to look forward to with Jeremy, or if this only happened with daughters. And what kind of thing was this?

Christopher's arms were like a hangman's noose around my neck. "See? I told you they're fightin'," he said.

I rubbed his back. "It's just an argument. People do that sometimes."

"I don't like fightin'."

Before I could respond, Stephanie's voice came again, more sarcastic than before. "Oh, wait, I get it. You think because it's Christmas we can all kiss and make up—"

I turned around and panted back up the stone steps. "We'll call your grandma Prissy on the phone and tell her we're coming down."

Christopher had goose bumps from the cold and he didn't need to be listening to the argument. I didn't need to be either.

Back upstairs I dumped Christopher on the bed and wrapped him in the quilt a second time. "There you go," I said. "Now you can be my little papoose while I call the big house."

Before I could move, Christopher said, "Aunt Dolie, I love you."

I stared into his big brown eyes, then leaned over and kissed his forehead. "I love you, too."

Christopher continued to watch me. I said, "Look, about this fighting—" I stopped. Whatever I said, Christopher would no doubt repeat to Prissy and Stephanie, and it was apparent that there were already firm rules in place when it came to fighting. My own philosophies, however right I might think they were, wouldn't necessarily fit the family mold. I smiled; what the hell. "Your mommy and Grandma Prissy still love each other, but sometimes people just forget that they can talk things out. That's when they start yelling. It doesn't make them bad. It just means that they disagree about something, okay?"

He nodded as if he'd understood every word of my little speech, and for all I knew, he might have.

"So, now I'm going to call," I said. I used the phone in the living room, which was on a separate line from the main house.

It took four rings, but eventually Prissy answered. "Yes?"

"Prissy, hi, it's me, Jolie. I have Christopher over here and I need to leave for the agency. Should I bring him back?"

"Oh, dear, I didn't even notice he was missing. I'll meet you on the patio." She hung up.

I hurried into the bedroom, grabbing my jacket from the closet and my purse from the chair. "It's all right, Christopher," I said, turning to face him. "They're all done arguing, and they're waiting for you. Are you ready?"

He considered the question with that serious, pensive expression, then said, "Okay. But may you hold my hand?" He climbed down off the bed and put his hand in mine before we headed for the stairs a second time.

INITIALLY my title at Rose Sterling Advertising had been junior copywriter, meaning that I wrote television and radio commercials, newspaper and magazine ads, as well as press releases and industrial films. As time progressed I had moved up to senior copywriter, and then producer, a title that reflected new job duties including the casting and producing of commercials.

I should have been promoted to creative director. That's the top spot in the creative department, but Audry had seen to it that I didn't make the cut, all because of Michael. I could hardly blame her, and I had been as angry with myself as with her, because I had worked hard to get that job and knew that it was forever out of my reach.

After I had moved to Purple Sage I let go of any hard feelings, hoping that Audry would do the same. As I crossed the hallway from the underground parking garage I wondered if she had. The night before hadn't been much of a test.

On the drive downtown I had developed a strategy on how I was going to handle working at Rose Sterling. I planned to get copy notes and see what else was needed; then if I was uncomfortable at the agency, I'd work at Prissy's house and just fax things to Ralph, the creative director. All I had to do was get through this afternoon.

In the lobby I almost bumped into Ted Polovy, the security guard who'd called both police and EMS the night before.

"Good afternoon," I said.

He looked at me for a moment before he recognized me, then said, "How you doin' today?"

"Better thanks, and you?"

He fell into step beside me as I walked toward the elevators. "Can't complain." We stopped and he touched the button to get an elevator car. "That was a bad thing last night. Real bad. Sorry you had to get involved."

"Yeah, well..."

"Maybe you should've gone to the parking garage like it was suggested."

I stared at him for a moment before I realized he was at least partly kidding. "When you gotta go, you gotta go."

He smiled. "You must be one of the writers at Rose Sterling."

The elevator arrived and we both stepped in. I pressed the button for seven, while he touched the button for the third floor. The doors closed and we began our ascent.

"Actually, I used to be with Rose Sterling," I said. "Now I live in Purple Sage. I'm just filling in for a few days."

"Purple Sage? I've been there." The elevator stopped and the doors opened. As Ted stepped out he gave me a quick salute. "Stay out of trouble."

Then he was gone, and I caught myself hugging my fuzzy wool jacket around me while the elevator made another upward run. When the doors opened on seven I stepped out into the wide hallway that would take me back to Rose Sterling. My stomach tightened and my breathing quickened. As Yogi Berra said, "It's déjà vu all over again."

SEVEN

A LARGE CHRISTMAS TREE glimmered with lights, and blue and silver ribbons and balls just behind the front desk. Sitting at the desk was Amber Hadley, the young woman from the party last night.

"Hi. I'm Jolie Wyatt. I think Chester is expecting me," I told her.

She blinked as if moving out of a fog into clear air. "I'm sorry, what did you say?"

She'd verged on beautiful the night before, but today her festive look was gone along with the burgundy crushed-velvet dress. In its place she wore jeans and a red sweater that only heightened her paleness. Her eye makeup was smeared and her nose red, both, I assumed, the result of crying.

"Jolie," I repeated. "Jolie Wyatt. Chester called me to come in—"

"Oh, of course, I'm sorry. We met last night. You're the writer. Right before he left, Mr. Sterling told me to expect you. He wanted you to meet with Ralph Richardson." She stopped and rubbed her hand across her forehead, brushing her eyes and smearing more makeup in the process.

Three workmen walked toward us on their way out of the agency. One was pushing a dolly stacked with blue quilting material; he stopped. "That was the last load," he told us as the other two men went out the door.

"What?" the receptionist said, her face still cloudy. "Oh, thanks."

He addressed the rest of his remarks to me. "All the furniture's back in place, and everything's hooked up. I left the invoice with your bookkeeper." He grinned and shook his head. "That's some lady."

"Yes, she is."

"Man, she went over that invoice with a fine-tooth comb. I thought she was going to get a magnifying glass!"

"That's Donna Katherine for you."

"And then she went through some desk drawers and some file cabinets." He shook his head. "I told her we're bonded, and besides, who would want papers? Diamonds I could see checking on, but papers?" He grinned again. "You know what she said to ol' Ernie, my buddy that just left? 'Honey, with you around, a girl better check everything she's got.'" He started laughing. "Well, you have a merry Christmas."

"Thanks, you, too." I held the heavy door for him as he whistled his way out.

Amber shook her head. "Donna Katherine will flirt with anyone. At least the furniture's back. When I walked in this morning I didn't even have a desk. It's been so crazy. It would have been bad enough with all the things we had to do to the office, but then with—" She stopped and bit her lip as a huge tear rolled down her cheek. She looked young and very unsophisticated. "I'm sorry, just give me a minute." She reached into her desk drawer and pulled out a tissue; the polish on her fingernails was half chewed off.

"It's okay," I said. "I'm in no hurry."

"You must think I'm nuts, but Desi was a friend of mine, and I just, I don't know."

"I'm sorry."

She nodded, causing more tears to fall. "We started working here at the same time, a year and a half ago. Then we started rooming together; she just moved out a couple of months ago. She was wonderful to me, like a big sister, only better." Amber blew her nose, threw the tissue away, and got a fresh one. "Wait, aren't you the one who found her? Did she—? Was she—? Oh, God, I don't know what I want to know. Maybe nothing." Amber blew her nose again. "I just can't seem to stop crying. I was okay until I had lunch, and then I went down to the deli and the guy asked me where my friend was. He meant Desi, only—I just couldn't—'' The words were choked out by her sobs. She put her head down on the desk and let the tears flow.

She seemed so young and vulnerable I couldn't stand to leave her. "I'm so sorry," I said, moving around the desk to put an arm around her heaving shoulders. Her pain was so intense I could almost feel it. She sobbed even harder and I mumbled soothing phrases, hoping she could find some comfort in knowing that she wasn't alone.

After a few minutes I took tissues out of a box on her desk and put them against her clenched fist. She raised her head slightly. "This is so awful."

"I know it hurts."

She cried some more, and eventually rose up and blew her nose. "I meant for you. I'm sorry. I hardly even know you and you've been so nice."

"It's okay," I said, patting her shoulder one last time before I straightened up. "Can't you go home?"

She shook her head, then wiped her nose. "Mr. Sterling wanted me to, but I thought it would be better if I was busy. You know. Some people are already gone, because of Christmas and all, so they need me. And besides, I feel closer to Desi around here."

"I understand."

"I don't even know what she died of. Someone said a heart attack, but that's just crazy; she was only thirty. I mean, she did have something wrong with her heart. She had some disease as a kid, but still, you just don't expect people to die." She blew her nose. "God, a heart attack."

"Is that what the police said?"

She shook her head and let out a long shaky breath. "No, it was just a stupid rumor. Donna Katherine's trying to find out."

I moved back to the front of the desk, and Amber straightened her body as if in response to our new positions.

"What about Desi's family?" I asked. "Surely the police will tell them."

"Her dad is dead, and her mom is in a home someplace in Kansas."

"She's sick?"

"Senile dementia. She needs someone to take care of her twenty-four hours a day, and, well, you know." She sighed again. "It really bummed Desi out."

"It must have been hard on her. And you, too. Did Desi have any brothers or sisters?"

"I don't think so. The only other person Desi talked about much was her ex-husband. He lives in Europe and he's a pilot with some airline. KLM, I think."

"The police will find out."

"Yeah. They took her employment file last night. That big cop."

"Senior Sergeant Bohles," I supplied, as I remembered again that he might also find my fingerprints on the note from Michael.

I was trying to push the thought away when the phone in front of Amber buzzed and she answered it with, "Yes?" Obviously an internal call. Then she said, "She's right here, Ralph. I'm sorry, it's my fault. I'll send her back." She turned to me. "Ralph's waiting for you. Down at the end of the hallway. On the right; it's the next to the last cubby." She pointed her index finger with its dark, chipped nail polish.

"Thanks. I'll see you later." I moved around the modular wall of navy blue that had closed off my view of the rest of the offices. I was keenly aware of my surroundings, and my muscles were tensed in the old fight or flight response. I wouldn't be fighting, but I would have loved to flee.

At first I saw no one, and there was a somber stillness to the office, with only a few floral arrangements serving as reminders of last night's party. This was a working office again, with the modular walls back in place, forming small, functional cubicles. Chester had never grasped the concept that floor space in an office was highly prized by his employees. Nor did he understand that privacy and real walls were much-sought-after commodities. We had accepted his idea of an office, but it may have been one of the reasons that employees were so motivated toward promotion. Some video equipment was being loaded by a young man in jeans, and I nodded as I passed by him on my way to find Ralph. Ralph's cubicle was on the outside of the building, so one entire wall was glass. Beyond were the executive offices. First was Chester's in the corner, then Michael's, and finally Audry's. With a peripheral glance all I could see was Chester's empty office. I couldn't see into Michael's.

"Ralph?"

His body was hunched over his computer keyboard, and he was frowning. When I spoke he swung his chair around as if I'd surprised him. "Oh, Jolie! Come in."

There were plastic cartoon characters dancing on the top of his computer, four-color magazine ads pasted above his desk, and a large cork storyboard on the right-hand wall. It made the office seem young, hip, and busy, not the image projected by Ralph himself. In person Ralph's main characteristic was nice, but I'd never hurt him by saying so.

"Chester said you needed some help."

He grimaced as he stood up and hurried out of his office, returning with a second chair for me. "Here have a seat. I'm really glad you came. I'm in the middle of a twenty-page newsletter for Bank of Balcones that has to be mailed right after Christmas, plus some year-end stockholder reports, so nothing else is getting done. There's a little backlog."

"Little backlog?" In advertising when you have a backlog you have real trouble. A client never hires you to do a campaign when you get around to it. They want it for their high season, their low season, a trade show, or whatever. But their request is usually that you have it done yesterday. It's an impossibility considering the limited availability of commercial advertising space with the major media, at least here in Austin, but we always did our best. *Backlog* wasn't a word I'd ever heard within the offices of Rose Sterling before. "So what exactly does that mean?" I asked.

He sighed and slumped in his chair. "We're in deep shit. My assistant quit a month ago and they haven't hired anyone to replace her. Audry thought she could save money, only with the party and the holidays and everything, we're so far behind it's not funny. We're short an artist and a layup person, and now our usual freelancers are gone for the holidays. With Desi dead..." The Ralph I remembered, a man who was easygoing, in charge, and always solid, had been replaced by someone who reminded me of Willy Loman. Tired, harassed, and frustrated.

"Can I see the hot list?" I asked.

He swung his chair around, and when he turned back he was holding two full pages.

"Are you serious?" I asked.

"At least we got all the Christmas campaigns finished in time; of course, I haven't seen my kids in a week, and my wife is so angry she refused to come to the party last night." He ran his hand over his head, rumpling his hair.

"So tell me what to do."

It didn't take him long to show me what had to be done immediately and what was only needed for tomorrow. We went through several client folders so I could see the most recent campaigns for each one. Then I stood up. I felt like a soldier thrust unexpectedly into battle. "Point me to a computer." There was no time to drive back to Prissy's.

He grabbed a pile of folders. "This way."

He trotted me to a tiny cubbyhole built with temporary walls of a rich red burlaplike material. There were no windows, and the secretarial chair was wobbly. "This was Desi's," he said. "You can work here."

I scanned the tiny space. The desk was clean, the same as the credenza since all of this had been stored elsewhere for the party. The only things in sight were those affixed to the modular walls: three snapshots stuck in the edge of one, a couple of Christmas cards, and some cheap plastic Mardi Gras beads held on with pushpins. There was also a small sign that read, "The First Draft of Everything is Shit." Ernest Hemingway.

That is one of my favorite quotes, and it brought home to me that Desi Baker had been a living human being, and she and I had a lot in common.

Just Friday, two days before, she had worked here. She had

typed on that keyboard, had looked at that quote. It was obvious she had not been ranked high on the agency's totem pole, but she was in the right space to move ahead. If Audry didn't block her way.

Again I remembered the note that had been pushed under the bathroom door. The one from "M" that was now at the police lab with my fingerprints on it.

It was only at that moment I realized the note hadn't been for me—it had been intended for Desi.

In a way I was relieved, but something else shivered through my body, too. Desi Baker and I had more in common than I'd known. What would the police think when they discovered that fact?

Ralph placed the large stack of files on the desk, then opened desk drawers, pulling out pens and pencils. He even put a box of white Posh Puffs on the file cabinet. "There. That should be everything you need," he said. "There are more client files in here." He pulled out a file drawer. "And if there's anything you can't find, I'll be in my office. Okay?"

I looked at him, seeing his discomfort.

"Ralph, it's okay." Only I wasn't sure it was.

"Oh, I know. I'll just stay long enough to get you started."

I sat down at the computer, which, thankfully, had all its cords reattached. I turned it on, then waited until it asked me for a password. "Any idea what that is?" I asked.

"She had two—I have a master one written down in my office. I'll be right back." As he whipped out, I typed in the word *Michael*. I don't know why; there was no premeditation on my part, it just seemed right for Desi.

The computer refused to let me in. I tried her first name, then *Baker*, and then the word writer.

The computer began setting up icons.

Apparently we'd had dreams in common, too.

Before the computer had finished loading programs, the phone rang. I answered it without thinking, my mind still trying to digest all this new information. "Rose Sterling, this is Jolie."

"Jolie, it's me, Ralph. The word is *bingo*."

"Thanks."

"I'll let you get right to work. And me, too. If you need anything, I'm at extension three-twelve."

"Got it."

"And don't forget the password."

"Bingo."

WHEN I WAS LITTLE, third or fourth grade, I began making up stories. One summer in particular the neighborhood kids would gather in the evenings under a big pecan tree in our yard, and I would tell ghost stories. Not long after that my grandmother came for a visit, and one night when my parents were out and she was baby-sitting, I started telling her one of my stories. She responded with, "Jolene Berenski, if you think I have time for this nonsense, you're sadly mistaken. Any fool can make up tall tales, and if you don't believe me, you just ask your mama about your great-uncle Jack. Now, git. I'm busy."

It was a rude awakening, and I quit thinking that my stories were anything special. I still needed a creative outlet, though, so I tried out for the talent show at school where the teacher put me in a skit with some other girls. After the performance, while I was still backstage, Paul somebody-or-other's mother had looked straight at me and said, "It takes no talent whatsoever to act silly, and that's all you girls did up there." Paul played accordion.

It might not have been such a big deal except that my younger sister, Elise, played the piano and could sing. Beautifully. My older brother was an athlete, and wherever you found sweaty boys winning at any game, you'd find Win leading the way. Win was short for Winthrop, but nobody teased him about his name.

After that I made one last-ditch effort to find an arena where I could excel. I begged my mother to send me to a new art school. She finally relented. After only six classes the instructor took her aside when she came to pick me up. I'm sure I wasn't meant to hear, but I did. The instructor said it was a waste of money sending me to art classes—I had no visual artistic acuity and would be better off doing paint by numbers.

I retreated to my writing, only I didn't tell the stories out loud anymore. I wrote them on paper, and once accepted an F in English rather than turn in a story and let someone else judge it. Luckily my overall grade remained sufficient, because my test scores pulled up my average.

Writing was my joy, my solace, and even when I got over my shyness and early insecurities, which, of course, were replaced by adult insecurities, I kept my love of writing. I consider it a privilege to be able to put words on paper. Sometimes they aren't great words, or in great order, but I love the process even when it's a struggle and seems beyond my abilities.

My early training as a professional writer was in radio. When I discovered how fickle that world can be I moved into advertising, and my current job consists of writing and voicing radio news in Purple Sage. Everything is always on a deadline, and the one thing I had learned was that Jack London was right. "You can't wait for inspiration, you have to go after it with a club."

I stretched my wrists and started in. First I wrote two press releases, and admittedly they required more than one phone call to Ralph to ask questions and get a translation of someone's scrawled notes. And then I rewrote and rewrote them again. The third press release was for a client of Michael's, and his notes, written in heavy black ink, were easy to read. By that time I wasn't quite in the writing zone, but at least I knew there was one. I plunged into two radio campaigns, and realized I needed more information. I set the copy notes aside and dug into the folder for Bank of Balcones to see what they had done in the past. The first thing I found was a radio commercial written by Desi Baker.

It featured two squirrels discussing where to store their winter supply of nuts. One was partial to an old tree down on campus, while the other wanted a safety-deposit box at Bank of Balcones. According to Desi's production notes, the voices were to be sped up enough to make them sound cartoonish but still understandable. At the end, the bank president invited both squirrels and the listeners to drop by the bank, just to make sure it was secure enough.

Reading that script was like seeing into the mind of Desi. Clever and whimsical. I hadn't expected that humor, and it caused me to readjust my picture of her. She had been beautiful and funny. I sighed and plunged back into work. Using the same theme she had created, I wrote two more after-holiday commercials for the bank.

Next I turned to a magazine ad. It was complete except for the small square of body copy, so that was relatively easy. Everything I had written was still what I considered first draft, and I needed hard copies to edit. I sent all my work to the laser printer, then without thinking, pulled open a drawer looking for something to munch on. What I found was some trail mix. When I realized whose it was and where I was, I closed the drawer with a snap, almost catching my fingers.

I needed a break. My joints were stiffening; I stood and stretched. As I did I spotted the pictures on the modular wall. The first showed Desi with an older woman, presumably her mother, beside a wintry pond. Desi was younger, probably late teens, but much the same as the beautiful young woman I had seen. In the photo both mother and daughter were smiling, bundled up in winter clothes, their noses red from the cold. The second photo was of a tanned Desi, wearing short cutoffs, a tank top with a flannel shirt tied around her waist, and heavy hiking boots. Sunglasses hid her eyes but not the jubilant smile on her face. She was standing on what looked like the top of a mountain, deep blue sky behind her; her arms were raised in triumph.

The last picture was of a big yellow Labrador with his tongue hanging out and a bow perched incongruously on his head. A birthday cupcake was in front of him.

Desi Baker's life in three pictures.

A woman I'd never met was haunting me, perhaps because I was working in her office, touching all the things that she had touched, breathing into the same phone she had used just three days before.

I had to know more about Desi Baker, and if I could, I wanted to find out what caused Desi's death. There was only one person who might be able to tell me—good old Donna Katherine, our source of news and information. Better than a KSGE news bulletin.

EIGHT

GIRL, I CAN'T BELIEVE you're back here, just like you belong!"
Donna Katherine said when she saw me.

She'd been standing at a five-drawer filing cabinet in her office.
Today her look was gypsy modern, a good choice for her tall
frame and red hair. Her skirt was a wild print that reached almost
to her ankles, which were encased in soft, black leather boots.
With it she wore a deep turquoise sweater. On her ears were large
gold hoops, and on her wrist were over a dozen matching bangles.
Unfortunately her makeup was too heavy and it brought attention
to the fact that she was no longer an attractive woman. "You
thinkin' about movin' back in permanently?" she asked, a half
smile on her lips.

I shook my head. "Absolutely not. I'll be here two or three
days at the most," I said.

"That's because of that handsome husband of yours." She patted her chest. "Be still my heart."

"You are something."

She grinned, cleared her throat, and said, "Now, let's get down
to some business. Chester told me he wants to treat you like
contract labor. I have everything you need to get paid right here."
Her bracelets jingled as she pulled three sheets of paper from her
out box. "I filled them in since Chester said you were going to
be so busy and all. All you have to do is put your John Hancock
on them."

"What, you didn't sign them for me? Seems to me you used
to forge everybody else's signature—"

"I never! Jolie Wyatt, there are some things it'd be a lot
smarter to forget—if you get my drift." She gave me the evil
eye.

"I've got it."

"Smart gal. Just sign here and here," she said, pointing to sticky tabs attached to the spots, "and we're all done but the crying."

I looked the papers over quickly, found everything accurate, and signed where she'd indicated. "That was easy." I handed her back the forms, which she slipped into a folder that was prepared and waiting.

"We aim to please." She pulled out the second drawer of the cabinet and filed the folder. "Fill out a time sheet when you finish. We pay in forty-five days, fifteen longer than we used to, and I'll just mail you the check."

"Fine," I said. As she sat down, I reached for a second chair. "Mind if I visit a minute?"

Donna Katherine used to be the chief source of information at Rose Sterling. For example, when a rumor was going around that the offices were to be remodeled, she knew who was doing the work and what the time schedule was. She also knew that Michael and Chester were selecting the colors and styles. Donna Katherine explained that Audry wasn't getting involved because that was stereotypically a woman's role, and Audry had refused to play it. By the time the memo about the remodeling came out, for me it was junk mail.

"What's on your mind?" she asked.

"Desi Baker. Have you heard anything from the police?"

Donna Katherine scooted her chair closer to mine and whispered, "Let's take a little break to the ladies' room." She looked around. "Even these temporary walls have ears."

THE BATHROOM was almost identical to the one just a floor below, except that the accent tiles were black and deep rose. It was a nice change.

Donna Katherine walked along the row of stalls and peeked under each one, then rejoined me at the mirrors. "Don't sit up there," she said, gesturing toward the faux marble counter. "The faucets all leak. I reckon management doesn't get to the ladies' room on our floor, although you'd think Audry would have gotten it fixed. Woman gets everything else she wants. Maybe she's never noticed because she doesn't pee like the rest of us mortals."

I wasn't going to respond to that. "So tell me, has anyone heard from the police?"

Donna Katherine rolled her eyes. "They were here first thing this morning, and I'm tellin' you, it was not pretty. Not that I was in the room, mind you. It was a private conference with the royal family." Donna Katherine's office was next to the conference room, though. "First thing that cop said was that it wasn't a normal heart attack. He suggested that maybe Desi had committed suicide. Chester wouldn't stand for that. Not for one minute."

Chester believed in people. Suicide was something outside the world as he knew it.

"But what do you think?" I asked. "Did she kill herself?"

There was a long pause while Donna Katherine considered the possibility. Finally she said, "I don't know; but Desi could be moody sometimes." She shrugged the thought away. "Anyhow, I figure this Bohles was on a fishing expedition, as my daddy used to call it. When no one went for his suicide theory, he said it was more likely a drug overdose."

"Drugs? What kind of drugs?"

"He said he suspected cocaine."

"Cocaine?" It made no more sense than saying Santa Claus had slipped down the chimney and given her the drugs. "Cocaine?" I repeated. I had seen no signs of it in that other bathroom.

As I thought about it, there was something even more out of kilter—Desi Baker hadn't looked like a woman on cocaine. She had been poised and clear-eyed, and slender, too, but well muscled to the extreme, as if she worked out hard and was proud of the effect. Her black dress had skimmed along her body, and her arms had been taut and firm as she had stood up and delivered her speech about Chester. Drugs aren't part of that healthful regimen.

"Desi didn't look like someone who did drugs. Does it seem possible to you?" I asked.

Donna Katherine didn't even consider her answer. "Girlfriend, I know nothin' about drugs. I smoked pot once in my life and spent the rest of that night in the emergency room. I'm allergic to the stuff, and that one experience was enough to keep me real straight for a real long time. Like my whole life."

I was no more experienced than she was. I'd smoked pot with my first husband, Steve, a few times until I became pregnant. I decided that the natural high of having a healthy baby was far better than an artificial evening of silliness, so that was the end of my experimentation.

"When Chester and Audry heard that word cocaine, that's when Chester got real firm with the cop," Donna Katherine went on. "Chester told him he had friends on the city council, which he does, and friends high up in the police department, which he does, and that Sergeant Bohles better find out the truth about how Desi died pretty damn quick and stop trying to palm off these *scurrilous* rumors." She grinned. "Nice word that, scurrilous. I looked it up. 'Low indecency. Abuse.' Sure put that cop on notice."

"I guess."

"Bohles told Chester it was the medical examiner's office that had the final decision, and those folks usually take up to a week for an autopsy. Chester said something like, 'Perhaps you should try to hurry them.' Bohles was pretty nice about the whole thing when you figure the kind of pressure they were putting on him. He said he'd try to get things moving. Course, Chester called some old bud of his, anyway."

What little I knew of law enforcement and police procedure came from experiences in Purple Sage, admittedly a much smaller place than Austin. There, if the sheriff's office sent anything to the DPS lab, it could take up to a week for results. It wasn't because of lack of caring, it was simply the heavy workload. Apparently the medical examiner's office in Austin had the same problems, and this being Christmas week no doubt made things worse.

"This could take a long time," I said.

"Maybe not." She shrugged, then reached up to scratch her neck. The movement set up a soft clattering as her bracelets clashed together. "Bohles said he'd call or come by first thing tomorrow. I figure we'll see."

"How did the others take it?" I meant Audry and Michael, but I couldn't say names.

"I was real proud of Audry," Donna Katherine said with a grin. "She just told that policeman that she wasn't buyin' any of his conclusions so far, and that was that. As for Michael..." She lowered her voice. "He was all but silent when that cop was around, but I was standing near the water fountain in the hall about an hour later, and I swear the sounds comin' from the men's room made me think there was some new Wailin' Wall in there. Weepin' and gnashin' of teeth like you never heard. He hasn't been back since, so he must've left. I figure he'll just say he was seein' clients."

I was wholeheartedly glad I hadn't been at the agency that morning.

"Oh, and I was going to tell you last night," Donna Katherine said, "I think Desi Baker was special friends, if you get my meaning, with someone in the agency. But I figure you know that by now."

"Michael."

"Right."

I let out a breath. Donna Katherine hadn't known about Michael and me after all, or she wouldn't have told me about Desi. I hoped.

"So, Jolie," she went on, "you're a big mystery writer now, what do you think Desi died of?"

"Not a big mystery writer, just an aspirant." But I had been mulling over her question for some time. I always came back to the same answer, and I wished I could feel more sure of it. "I've thought of some kind of poison. You know, something that she accidentally ingested." I have read up on poisons for my writing, but it's a vast subject and almost anything can be poisonous if given to someone who has an allergic reaction. "I suppose it could have been natural causes, like a brain tumor, but in the bathroom she'd vomited.''

"Wait, how about this one," Donna Katherine said, leaning against the sink. "Maybe she was allergic to one of the hors d'oeuvres. Of course, we didn't have much but fruit, raw veggies, and cheese. And that steamship round of beef.''

"There were rolls. And alcohol. I wonder if she had too much liquor and died from that.'' I hardly had to think about it. "No, couldn't be. She was perfectly sober, or at least she looked sober, when she was on the dais. How could she be dead drunk an hour later?'' It was an unfortunate choice of words.

Of course, there was another option—someone could have purposely given Desi Baker a poison.

"Sorry, gal, but I've got to run," Donna Katherine said, looking at her watch, straightening up, and smoothing her skirt. "I'll let you know if I hear anything.''

"Thanks, I'd appreciate it.''

We left together and when we entered the agency, Donna Katherine went toward her office. The reception area was empty and I assumed Amber had finally gone home. There was a note on her desk with my name on it; I picked it up and began reading as I walked around the partition. It was from Matt, asking if I would give him a call at Prissy's.

Unfortunately with my head down, and my attention on the note, I walked straight into someone.

"Excuse me," I muttered, then detected a wave of the musky aftershave that pulled me into a distant past. I didn't need to raise my head to know that Michael Sherabian was right there, inches from me. "Oh. Michael. I'm sorry." And then I had to look up.

His normally dark skin seemed pale. He appeared stunned. Not from running into me, but I assumed from the bigger shock of Desi's death.

"How are you doing?" I asked. "Are you all right?"

He stared at me for a moment, then said in a low-pitched voice, "Yes, of course. Why wouldn't I be?" Anger, sorrow, and resignation were all crammed into those few words, although on the surface he appeared poised.

"I'm sorry." It felt inadequate. "I didn't mean—"

"This is difficult for all of us. It's hard to lose someone you've worked with, especially because Desi was a unique person. Ask anyone at the agency, anyone who knew her."

"Well, if there's anything I can do—"

He stared at me for a long time, his eyes so intense I could feel a surge of heat that coursed through my body.

"Actually, it's like a miracle that you're here," he said. "Just when I need someone, you're at the agency. Come and talk with me?"

"Of course." Michael had been the one to help me through my father's death; I was obligated to be there for him. "In your office?"

He shook his head. "There's a new little coffeehouse not far from here. Very quiet and private."

Coffee with Michael? My warning sensors prickled.

There had been so many times in the past when we had gone off to have coffee together. Just the two of us, slipping out of the agency, pretending even to ourselves that it was business.

I brushed that aside; I had changed, grown, and so had he. There was no reason not to go.

"Now?" I asked.

"Yes. That would be good; I have the time." He tilted his head to watch me, our eyes held, and it was like the fleeting moment at the top of a roller coaster with all its quivery anticipation. Next would come the incredible downhill rush that no one could stop. "And thank you," he added.

Like a cobra he had me mesmerized; even my breathing was shallow. "Of course. I'll have to get my coat." But I didn't move, couldn't move. "Are you sure?" I asked, perhaps more of myself than him.

"Of course." He held me with his eyes, but didn't touch me again, he didn't have to. I could sense him as clearly as if our skin were touching in a thousand places.

I wanted to comfort him, but just to talk.

Just to talk, I reminded myself again. But would there be that moment when, just as in the past, our hands would accidently brush? Some part of me grew shivery at the memory.

"Would you like me to get your coat for you?" he asked.

If Michael went for my coat, I would be committed to leaving.

Once he returned with it, he would slide it over my shoulders, just as he had so many times in the past. It was impossible not to think of how his hands used to slide along the collar on the pretext of straightening it, and how my body would begin to vibrate in response to his fingers gently brushing my neck.

Clearly I saw that this was how all the problems had started the first time, but surely I was beyond that now. Stronger than that. I could talk to Michael without having anything happen.

I tried to break whatever mystical hold he had on me, but my body wouldn't respond. It was an effort to force out words. "No, I'll get my coat."

He nodded, his eyes still watching mine. "Then I'll meet you in the parking garage. Second level up by the elevator."

Just the way we used to meet.

He turned to leave, and the finality of his move jerked me out of whatever spell had held me captive. I thought of Matt.

"Michael," I called. He turned, and I spoke quickly. "I'm sorry, I've changed my mind. I don't have the time."

Confusion crossed his face. "Jolie, you said you'd go." It was voiced with innocence, as if he honestly couldn't understand my reluctance.

I looked away and forced myself back a step; it may have appeared to be a retreat, but it felt like a safety precaution, like moving away from a live bomb. "I'm sorry, Michael, I don't think I'd better."

His eyes searched my face, looking for something. He seemed to find it. "You're angry."

"No, not at all." I shook my head quickly. "I don't belong here," I said. "I feel like all of this, you, everything is from some dark part of my past that should never have happened. Even a conversation—'' At the expression on his face I stopped. "Michael, I'm sorry. I know you must be in pain, but I'm not...it just...I can't do anything to help." I was stammering, and I knew it. "I have to get to work—there's just no time."

Michael stared in disbelief, then his elegant nostrils flared. "But there was time to gossip in the ladies' room with Donna Katherine?"

Before I could think of a way to escape, Michael's eyes went soft and his voice became gentle. "Jolie, I'm sorry. That was unforgivable." He reached for my hand, kissed the palm, and hurried off toward his office.

I probably stood there a solid minute, staring after him, before I realized I had to move.

As a child I had once seen a Hollywood film device for making people look like they were sinking into quicksand. The actor stood on a raised platform, and under him was a flattish box of mud, with a heavy rubber center that had two crosscuts. Initially the actor positioned his body on the center cuts, actually standing on the raised platform. Then slowly the platform would lower so that eventually the actor was "enveloped" by the muck.

I could almost feel the platform going down under me. Rose Sterling Advertising was sucking me back in. It mattered to me that the agency was behind in the work for its clients, and somehow it had become my responsibility to bail them out. And now Michael—

Coffee. Just coffee. But not with Michael.

I was having feelings for these people again. It was the last thing I'd envisioned when I'd accepted the invitation to the party.

The front door opened and the balls on the Christmas tree swung together in the whoosh of air. I stepped around the partition to cover the front desk, hoping my face didn't show all the things I'd been experiencing. It was Audry Sterling-Sherabian who'd come into the agency.

"Jolie," she said, when she saw me. "You're exactly the person I want to talk to."

NINE

I FOLLOWED HER as she knew I would. With unerring accuracy, Audry skirted the cubicle where I'd been working and went straight to the laser printer in the hallway outside. She picked up all the copies in the tray, flipped through them quickly, left behind those with someone else's initials, and said, "Is this everything you've written so far?"

"That's everything."

I had to wonder if she knew everyone's working habits so well, or just mine. And how much more did she know of the things that went on in the agency?

"Let's talk in my office." She led the way.

Audry's office was large, but then, it needed to be to accommodate her massive desk, topped with a slab of black marble veined with white. Three walls were burgundy, the accessories all sleek and black, from the floor lamp to the bookends on the shelves. There was a splash or two of dark turquoise for accent, but very few; even her computer was black.

It would have been like a dungeon, except the back wall was glass with a view of downtown Austin. I could see the river as it meandered below us; even in winter there was an unspoken invitation in the running paths and biking trails along its banks.

Without a word, Audry gestured to a black leather visitor's chair while she sat behind her desk. She began reading through the pages in her hand.

Sitting there in my low chair with her massive desk in front of me, I felt like a child who'd been called to the principal's office, a child who was guilty as charged. Audry finished the first page, started on the second, and frowned first at the paper, then briefly at me. I wondered if she hated me. She had good reason to.

I'd even understand if she did, because I had hated my first husband's girlfriend.

I'd never even suspected her existence until, late one night when Jeremy was just a month old, Steve had come home and told me he was leaving. There had been no discussion, he was in a hurry. After all, Candy was waiting downstairs in the car.

With only the dim glow of the teddy-bear night-light to relieve the blackness, I had rocked Jeremy as I listened to Steve pack in the other room. I'd been at such a disadvantage suffering with postpartum blues, my pregnancy weight gain, and no job. I'd had no weapons to fight with, and so he'd walked out the door leaving $43.27 in the checking account, the rent due, and no car. But all those things piled together weren't as bad as the hole he had left behind. Jeremy had never had a father until Matt came along just four years ago. I'd done everything I could to make up for it, but I was afraid Jeremy had suffered in ways that I didn't even know about.

As for me, I'd never been the homecoming-queen type, but when Steve left, my self-image shattered. Even now, sixteen years later, I sometimes found myself reacting out of the old insecurities Steve's defection had caused.

Looking at Audry, so cool, so self-assured, I couldn't help but wonder if underneath there was proof of the damage that I had done to her. At that moment I would have given a lot to undo the past and erase my relationship with Michael, but my remorse wouldn't make a whit of difference to the pain I had inflicted. My only saving grace was that when Audry convinced Michael to try and repair their marriage, I had stepped aside. There had been a brief phone conversation between Michael and me, but nothing more.

I'd always wanted to apologize to Audry, to let her know how truly sorry I was, but I could never find the right moment. Certainly not when Michael first went back to her because then I had been the wounded party. Later it had seemed too late, like bringing up the past for no good reason. Yet even now, I could feel myself squirming with guilt.

Audry's expression changed as she went through the next several sheets of paper. At one point she almost smiled; twice she nodded. When she was finished she picked up all the sheets and handed them across the desk to me.

"Very nice," she said. We were back in the land of polite, where façades were kept firmly in place. "One suggestion—the press release on Mangason's charity Christmas gift is too terse. It reads like a news story."

"It is a news story."

"It needs lightening up. Add some humor, a twist of some kind."

Before I could defend myself further, she went on. "You're very good, but then you always were. I like that bank spot. Nola's out today, so I'll fax it to them this afternoon for approval."

"Thank you."

"I'm the one who needs to thank you." She leaned back in her chair and seemed to relax slightly. "You didn't have to work during your vacation; I'm sure the extra money won't even be noticed at your house." Her quick glance took in my cashmere sweater and the heavy gold balance bracelet that Matt had given me for our anniversary. "Certainly not like before."

"No," I said. "But when your dad called this morning he said he needed help. He'd do the same for me. He certainly always has in the past."

I thought I heard a touch of envy as she said, "He's wonderful with people."

"Yes, he is. Is he in today?"

"He's delivering Christmas baskets. He's almost completely retired now."

"And you're running the agency?"

She nodded. "We moved back from Atlanta last year. I think the change will work well, once everyone has adjusted."

"Who's running the Atlanta office?"

With the light behind her it was hard to tell, but it appeared she stiffened before she said, "We're downsizing Atlanta. There's no need for a full staff; what with E-mail and computers, almost everything can be done from here. We'll keep one account executive and one artist.''

Downsizing, rightsizing, capsizing. Business as usual in the nineties. I was very glad that I was out of it, rather than a potential victim to the mercenary slashing that was going on.

I started to say something more, ask how business really was and how she was doing, but Audry stood up. Maybe she sensed that we were treading close to personal communication. ''Thank you, again,'' she said with a quick smile. ''Even if you're here just as a favor to my father, you're helping us all.''

''You're welcome. I'm glad I could do some good for you.''

The words only hinted at my regrets, and the protectiveness I felt toward her. There wasn't time for more, because she reached for the phone and began dialing; for all her toughness, in some ways Audry was very vulnerable.

I headed straight back to my little cubby, shifting all my attention to the offending news release as I went. It started out well enough, but as I went through it I realized Audry had been right, it was more like a terse news bulletin than an inviting story. Damn.

MANY HOURS LATER I left Rose Sterling. I was feeling pulled in a dozen directions as I drove home through the dark sea of traffic. When I arrived at Prissy's I wanted to run up to our little apartment and shower, a long shower that would wash away all the feelings and needs of Rose Sterling Advertising, but unfortunately there wasn't time.

I hadn't seen Michael again, although Chester had stopped by late in the afternoon to give me a warm hug and a key to the offices since I would be needed again the following morning. The key felt as heavy as lead, weighing down my purse, a physical reminder that I was back at Rose Sterling whether I liked it or not. It took the entire drive to Prissy's to break free of the hold the agency had on me. The cold winter air helped, as did the walk from the drive to the patio.

Once there I stopped to glance through the French doors into

Prissy's living room. A grouping of poinsettias brightened a corner of the fireplace, and pine boughs graced with glittering Christmas balls were draped across the mantel. It was like watching a play through a proscenium, a Noel Coward play, with Prissy and Matt looking elegant as they sipped coffee in the beautifully decorated house.

Prissy's husband, Ross, was sitting on the couch, his long rangy legs stretched in front of him. Beside him was another man I'd never met before. He appeared to be about the same age as Ross, possibly even a few years older, late fifties, early sixties, but of a totally different type. With his thick silver hair and tanned skin, he looked like an actor. His eyes were such an intense blue I could see the color from outside; they were set off by the pale blue sweater he was wearing.

Presumably he was the owner of the classic bathtub Porsche that was parked in the driveway, its smooth body shimmering silver in the streetlight. A rich man's car, my father used to call such automobiles. Not because the initial cost was so high, although it certainly was these days, but because the upkeep was tremendous and, according to my dad, you had to have a second car to drive while your expensive car spent most of its life in the shop.

With one last martyred sigh, I dashed across the cold patio. The house was warm inside and smelled like Christmas as I joined the gathering.

"Jolie, hi." Matt stood up, and I moved into the circle of his arms, getting a welcome-home hug that I needed. He gave me a quick kiss before saying, "How was your day?"

"Oh, fine," I said, trying to dismiss it with a shrug. "Mostly it was productive. And yours?"

"Okay."

As I slipped off my jacket Prissy began the introductions. "Jolie, this is a, uh, an old friend of ours. He just recently divorced. Peter Javitz—"

"I should have introduced you—" Matt began.

In the jumble of words, their guest, who was already up off

the couch, held out his hand to me and said, "Just call me Pete." We shook. His grip was firm and his smile dazzling. "Matt was bragging about you earlier," he said.

"I pay him to do that," I said as I sat on the love seat beside Matt.

"He said you have a book coming out. Congratulations, that's a tough field to crack from what I hear."

"Well, I think so, but I may have done everything wrong at first," I said with a smile. "Do you work with Ross?" I asked.

"We don't work together," Ross explained, gesturing with one of his long thin arms. "But Pete is the one who got me started in consulting." He seemed annoyed about it, although Pete laughed.

"You love it. Fly in, work a few miracles, fly out. And get paid very well for it—I can't think of a better life. You've even built up a clientele right here in Austin, so you don't have to travel that much, you lucky dog."

"That's easy for you to say."

Prissy explained, "Pete is taking an early retirement, and while he's in the process of the sale, any of the clients he can't accommodate, he's sending to Ross."

"It's a mixed blessing," Ross said.

There was something going on. Pete's conviviality appeared forced next to Ross's barely concealed dislike of the man. I wondered what that was all about.

"Retirement," Prissy was saying. "I can't imagine people our age retiring. My father retired. My grandfather."

"Call it a lengthy sabbatical. From which I'm never returning."

Having done what she could to smooth the conversation, Prissy offered me coffee. After I declined she said, "A glass of wine? I have a new white from Château St. Jean."

"That would be great."

"Are you starving?" She stood up, and I got the impression she was relieved to have an excuse to leave the room. "I have some hors d'oeuvres."

I followed her to the kitchen.

"I'm not really hungry." I was dying to ask what the story was on Pete Javitz. "Can I help?" I asked.

"There's really nothing to do." She seemed distracted as she scooped warm appetizers from the oven and slid them onto a red tray with bright green Christmas trees. She set them on the counter, frowned, then said, "Actually, you might get some napkins from the pantry while I pour your wine."

"Be happy to." I found some green napkins to complement the tray and placed them on the side of it. "By the way, where's Jeremy?" I asked. "And Stephanie and Christopher?"

"They should be back anytime. They wanted to let Christopher see the ice rink at Northcross Mall, and then they were going to rent a couple of movies for this evening. I think Stephanie wanted to supervise the movie selection, and Jeremy wanted to make sure they got something besides Disney films."

Now that I was at the back of the kitchen, I asked, "So who is Peter Javitz, besides an old friend?"

Prissy looked at me and I could see her weighing her answer. It seemed she was just about to talk when she tipped her head in a way more suited to a Barbie doll. "Oh, you know, just an old acquaintance." She turned to me, wineglass in one hand, tray in the other. "Ready?"

So much for that. "Sure." I followed her back into the living room with its crackling fire.

The men were talking about the company Matt had been looking at, and I sank onto the love seat, grateful that I didn't have to join in. Prissy handed me the wine, and I sipped it slowly, letting the conversation simmer around me.

After a few minutes, maybe it was longer, I wasn't paying attention, the front door opened and Christopher came toddling in.

"Hey, Christopher," Matt said. "Did you get some good movies?"

"*The Rescuers—*" Christopher stopped and looked around the

room at the assembled group. "Oh, no. Peoples!" He ducked behind the Christmas tree.

Jeremy and Stephanie hurried in. Jeremy was carrying a sack of movies, and while he stopped to shut the door, Stephanie brushed past him. "Pete! I'm sorry we're late." She went straight into his arms. Before my mind could accept their very warm hug, she planted a kiss on his lips.

His blue eyes glowed as if he'd just spotted the seventh wonder. "Hello, beautiful."

I waited for Stephanie and Peter to break apart. To tell us that they'd been joking. For them to say something, as if they'd just mimicked a movie scene, but it didn't happen. Pete sat back on the couch, pulling Stephanie down with him.

"Christopher," she said. "Did you say hello to Mr. Javitz?"

He peeked around the tree. "Hello, Mr. Javitz."

Pete kept his arm around Stephanie's waist as he leaned forward to say, "How's it going, young man?"

"Fine."

I looked at Prissy to see what she thought about all this. It was obvious from her expression; she wanted to wrench her daughter away from Peter Javitz and send him packing. Permanently. But being the perfect hostess, she took a breath and her face became placid again, as if I'd imagined the anger.

Nevertheless, I was feeling angry. Angry at Pete for taking advantage of Stephanie, and at Stephanie for behaving so uncharacteristically. And all the while the word *trophy* was screaming in my head. As in trophy wife, or trophy girlfriend.

I am always appalled when an older man divorces the woman who'd had his children and helped make him successful, and then replaces her with a trophy wife. I've seen it happen to two of my friends, and in my opinion that's two too many. Both times when the husbands walked out, they walked almost directly into the apartments of young women in their twenties.

They act as if the practical lifespan of a woman is fifty. As if after that she is no longer up to the current standards. The worst of it is that it's the young women who perpetuate the myth in their quest for the money and reflected status of the older man. If only they realized that their time is coming.

I watched Stephanie pick a piece of lint off Peter's sweater. I couldn't dismiss Stephanie as if she were some little gold-digging bimbo. She might be acting like one, but I loved her dearly. She didn't need the money, so what did she see in a man the same age as her father? A father figure?

"Hungry?" Pete was asking Stephanie.

"Of course. Aren't I always?"

He laughed and gave her a quick hug. I wanted to slap him.

"Good. I have a wonderful new restaurant for us to try. I'd like your opinion of it." He glanced toward Ross and Prissy. Ross was poker-faced; Prissy was doing her best not to glower. "We'll see all you nice folks later." He stood up and grabbed his jacket off the couch beside him, then helped Stephanie up.

She went over to Christopher, who was now poking around under the Christmas tree. "You be a good little bug, okay? Grandma Prissy's going to put you to bed, and I'll bet Aunt Jolie would read you a book, too."

"I know," he said, hardly even looking at her.

"Don't I even get a kiss good night?"

He turned. "Good night, Mommy." He kissed her quickly, then scampered back to the far side of the tree.

"And stay out of those presents."

"I'm just hidin'! In case Madame Medusa comes here."

None of the other adults said a word, which made me suspect they were thinking about other things, primarily Stephanie and Peter.

Stephanie kept the mood light. "Well, don't let her find you and don't open any presents." She stood up, waved to the rest of us, but before she left she leaned close to her mother and said quietly, "I'll be home early. Remember your promise."

"I remember," Prissy said, a touch of annoyance lacing her charm.

Stephanie watched her seriously for a moment, as if judging

her mother's truthfulness. Prissy added, "Don't worry, I'll be here the whole time."

"Thanks," Stephanie said, before she gave us all one last smile and swept out the door on Pete's arm.

"That's her boyfriend?" Jeremy asked, speaking for the first time since they'd returned.

I shot him one of those looks. Prissy glared at him, too, although her anger was more likely intended for Pete than Jeremy. "Unfortunately," she said, "it is. Temporarily."

IT WAS LATER, much later when Matt and I were in bed, that I asked him what he thought.

"I don't know. I guess I think Stephanie's making a mistake. Maybe not."

"Remember Tom and Beverly?" Friends of ours in Purple Sage.

"It's Tom and Leigh."

I refrained from making a gagging noise. "Now it is."

When the divorce between Tom and Beverly had first occurred, Matt and I had had differing thoughts on it. He believed that Beverly had changed from a bright, funny woman into a shrew, and it was amazing Tom had put up with her behavior as long as he had. The fact that it was a hormonal imbalance as a result of menopause didn't sway Matt's opinion. "Does that mean Tom should have to take that kind of treatment? No, sorry. You can't condone verbal abuse for any reason, and that's what she was doing."

When I reminded Matt that Tom had a daughter two years older than his new girlfriend, Matt had merely shaken his head. I never could get Matt to denounce Tom as an idiot, which I was perfectly willing to do, although he did finally say, "I don't know how Tom communicates with Leigh. It's the ultimate generation gap."

Now we were looking at the gap, and a similar relationship, from another point of view. "Stephanie's perpetuating the obsolete-wife myth," I said. I was ready to fight this one all night if necessary, as if by convincing Matt, I could stop my own fears that someday I would be treated as if I were archaic. "She could do so much better. Someone younger. Someone willing to share her dreams and help her reach them.''

Matt made a sound as if he were coming out of sleep. Or dropping off. ''Maybe Pete can give her what she needs. He seems devoted.''

''Lust and devotion are two different things.''

Matt, who had both arms around me, snuggled my body closer to his. ''How do you know that?''

''Because I'm very wise.''

''Hmmm, I see. Well, I'm both lustful and devoted.''

''So?''

''And you're very sexy.''

''You're just trying to distract me.''

''How am I doing?''

I didn't even have to think about it. ''Keep working at it, I think you'll have it in a minute.''

AN HOUR LATER Matt was asleep and I was awake staring at the ceiling. I had come close to dozing off after we'd made love, but there was simply too much rustling through my head. Bits of anger mixed with worry about Stephanie refused to rest. Concerns about the agency and curiosity about Desi Baker kept after me, too. The more I tried to sleep, the faster the thoughts seemed to scurry through my mind.

As carefully as possible I slipped out of bed and dressed in clothes that were lying on the chair. I would make some warm milk in the house and perhaps that would help me sleep. Still in the dark, I took Prissy's house key off the hook near the door and slid outside, quiet as a ghost. It was colder than I'd expected, so I moved quickly, silently skimming down the stairs. A night-light from Prissy's kitchen was on, and it dimly illuminated the patio so I could see the two tubs of pansies that flanked the back door, the start of the trellis against the far wall, and the dead leaves scattered along the tiles.

As I turned to make my way to the back door, I could see that a man was there before me. He was silhouetted in the weak light from the kitchen, and he was watching me.

TEN

BEFORE I COULD SPEAK, he opened the door and stepped out.

"Hello."

After the initial jolt of finding a man I didn't know, I realized that his face was vaguely familiar. Not someone I knew... someone I had seen.

"I have an advantage over you," he said, moving into the reflected kitchen light. "I know that you're Jolie, but you don't know that I'm Todd." He smiled again, held out his hand, and said, "Todd Rainey. My mom was a friend of Prissy's."

He was in his mid-twenties, and the reason he looked familiar was that he resembled his mother, Olivia Rainey, whose smiling face I had seen many times in the picture on Prissy's dresser. Olivia had been Prissy's best friend all the way back to junior high school. She had died just eight months before of breast cancer. "You're Olivia Rainey's son," I said.

His eyes were much like his mother's, and at the mention of her name they briefly dipped closed, I assumed to hide his sadness. Then he looked at me and offered a simple, "Yes."

I remembered Prissy talking about how, after marriage, the two women hadn't kept in close contact until Olivia divorced maybe fifteen or sixteen years back. She'd been living somewhere in the East. Maryland? Pennsylvania? I knew, too, that Olivia had moved home to Texas for a while and then they had done some traveling together. Most had been around the state, but they'd also cruised the Bahamas. Ross had been working; Prissy claimed it was better that way since he wouldn't want to know what kinds of things they'd gotten up to.

This was Todd's first Christmas without his mother.

"Hi, nice to meet you. Prissy didn't tell us you were coming; you're here for the holidays?" I asked.

Todd nodded. "It was kind of iffy until this morning. Work and school and all. Getting time away is tough sometimes, but you probably know how that is." He waited for my nod, then added, "I got here just after you and Matt went up to bed."

Ah. Something tickled the back of my mind.

"Where do you live?" I asked.

"Takoma Park in Maryland. I grew up there, then we moved out here for a couple of years, so I could go to UT." The University of Texas at Austin. "Only after Mom died"—again his eyes dipped closed—"I've kind of been floating; you know, here, there. We... I still have the house in Maryland, but I don't stay there much."

His pain was still alive and I didn't know how to respond to it.

"Prissy's mentioned you." I wrapped my arms around my shoulders to hold the chill at bay, and still I shivered.

Todd noticed. "You're freezing. Were you going in?" He gestured toward Prissy's kitchen.

"I was, but I really should get some sleep. I'm working in the morning." I rubbed my forehead. "I think I just needed to clear my brain. This cold certainly did that."

He laughed, and I could see his breath in soft puffs. "I was clearing my head, too. I could give you my jacket—" He started to pull it off.

"No, thanks. I need to get back up to bed. I'm sure I'll see you later."

"You will." He put the brown leather jacket back on, and zipped it as he spoke. "Prissy made it sound like the holidays are going to be great. I have friends to see, too."

"And I have to work," I said, with a quick smile. "No rest for the wicked, I guess. Well, good night."

"Good night," he called softly, as I turned to go.

Todd Rainey, son of an old friend, spending Christmas with the family. Prissy collected strays for every holiday, at least that was my impression, and Todd would certainly find himself lonely this year, even among friends. However, I had this sneaking suspicion that Prissy might be doing some matchmaking, perhaps to ease old Pete out of the picture.

Interesting speculations were drifting through my head, but they were as soft and slow as my movements as I undressed, pulled on silk pajamas, and crawled back into bed. Matt didn't even stir when I slid the covers over me, and finally went to sleep.

THE OUT BASKET on the credenza had been emptied once, and there were already three more scripts in it, ready for production. It was amazing what Ralph and I were accomplishing with me doing the writing and him producing.

Audry had come in like a whirlwind, grabbing copy, picking up phone messages, and issuing commands all at one time. Then she'd swept out with hardly a glance at me.

Michael had arrived shortly after that, and he had made a point of coming into my cubby to say good morning. His eyes had traveled around the small space, taking in the pictures on the wall and the Mardi Gras beads, but then he had focused his attention back to me.

"How are you this morning?" he'd asked.

"I'm fine. How about you?"

Michael had smiled gently, studying my face. "Still the same as ever; aren't we all?"

"Actually, I've changed a lot. I've grown up, sold a book—"

"So I heard. Congratulations. Am I in it?" He was teasing me, those playful eyes dancing with a mischievous joy most adults have forgotten.

"Guess you'll just have to buy several copies and find out, won't you?"

"Tell me the name and I will."

I gave him the name, even wrote it down for him. Michael read the slip of paper, then pulled over a second chair and sat down, resting his briefcase on his lap. "Oh, and here, I have something for you."

My heart nearly stopped beating as he popped open his brief-case. How often in the past had Michael done exactly the same thing, opening the briefcase and pulling out a Hershey's chocolate Kiss? He would place it on the desk in front of me, leaning forward to breathe softly into my ear, "For the real thing, meet me in the parking lot. Ten minutes."

I would always shake my head no, protest in some way, but Michael would touch my neck, or stroke my arm, and I would give in. He'd leave then, quickly, and I would check my makeup, my hair, and wipe off my lipstick. After a few minutes, which seemed interminable, I would scoot out of the office, saying breezily to the receptionist, "I'm running down to the deli. Be back in a few."

There was a second elevator in the far corner of the parking garage that had a small enclosed waiting area. Very few people used that means of access to the building, and so Michael and I would meet there. Our time together was always rushed, always breathy, as if we couldn't pause even to take in air. We would say those repetitive phrases that lovers always make new, then kiss and hold each other as if each moment might be our last. A few more kisses, then we would break apart.

"This isn't right," I would say. "I hate this."

"And I love you." Michael would touch my chin gently, kiss me lightly, before adding, "Maybe after work."

"No. Absolutely not." Then I would stop. "Maybe."

I was always fighting to get away, even as I was wanting to get closer.

Now I watched as Michael shuffled some things in his briefcase. He must have heard my intake of air, because he looked up and smiled. "I thought about bringing you chocolate, but—"

"But I'm happily married," I said quickly. "And so are you."

He looked sad. "Yes." Then he brought out two sheets of paper with notes for new commercials.

"And there was Desi," I added brazenly.

He paused, first puzzled, then there was another emotion I couldn't identify. "Desi and I weren't lovers. We never had been," he said. "It wasn't that kind of—"

"Don't, Michael. You don't have to tell me, and I don't want to know."

"I want you to understand, Jolie—"

"There's no need. Really." I had promised myself that for as long as I stayed at Rose Sterling, I would keep my distance from Michael Sherabian, and it should be easy to do. "It's better if I don't know." I reached out a hand and took the papers from him. "Here, I'll take them. When do you need these? Does it say?"

He stood reluctantly, an injured expression on his face. "I didn't mean to hurt you. I really—"

"Michael, it would be better if I could just write. Work. You know."

"Sure. Whatever you say." But he left with that sad look still in place.

I forced myself to focus on the writing. The notes he'd given me had everything I needed to know, and I placed them at the side of my computer while I went back to what I'd been working on. Just as I had placed Michael aside when he had gone back to Audry.

It's hell when the skeletons in your closet start to dance again.

TWO HOURS LATER Ralph departed for a recording session at one of the TV stations, leaving instructions that if I had time, I was to help with the client newsletter that was consuming him. We both knew that was wishful thinking.

At least all of the copy I'd written the day before had been approved and turned over to the art director. There was still much to finish before I could leave, but the most urgent work was getting done.

"Hey, look at this. I heard you were back here." Nola, Rose Sterling's high-level account executive, stuck her head around the corner. "How's it going?"

"Good, thanks. Come on in." I smiled as she pulled off her navy blue cashmere coat and draped it over the top of the temporary wall. "I was here yesterday, too, but I didn't see you," I said. "So where'd you go the other night? After the phone call at the party?"

"It was the baby-sitter, and Tisha was sick. Stomach flu. We zipped home and by the time we got there, James, Jr. was sick too. Not a good evening. Yesterday I made chicken soup and dry toast and kept everyone in bed. Actually, yesterday was a pretty nice day." She sat down on the filing cabinet, spreading her wool skirt to avoid wrinkles, then shook her damp, frizzy brown hair. "It's misting."

Droplets spattered me and the computer. "That's the heaviest damn mist I've ever seen."

She flicked a few more drops at me, grinning her smart-aleck smile. "Did I get you?"

"Weren't you intending to?"

"Okay, first question," she said, signaling the beginning of an old game we used to play. "Best adventure movie of the nineties."

"The nineties? That's a tough one, I don't see many movies in Purple Sage."

"No excuses; I need an answer."

"Uh, *Jurassic Park.*"

"Good choice."

"Thank you. Best political figure in Texas? In the nineties."

"Ann Richards. Here's one," she said, grinning. "Sexiest actor from the sixties."

"From the sixties? Are you serious? I can't even name an actor from the sixties." I stopped to think. "Wait—I've got it. Moondoggie!"

"From Gidget? No way! Did you see Sydney Poitier in *To Sir with Love?*"

"Yes, and I thought he was too schmaltzy."

Nola made a face. "And Moondoggie wasn't schmaltzy?"

"I liked his smile." This was the whole point of the game— to argue over the choices. It was something we'd done through lunches and breaks, on the way to visit clients, and even when we'd snuck out to smoke.

"It's nice to have you back," Nola said, the smile still in place. "Of course, you're still wrong about certain things like sexy actors, but I've missed you. It's been like a ghost town around here, and now with Desi dead—oh, crap, I didn't mean that. You know what I mean."

Open mouth, insert both feet, and then try to dance. That was Nola, but clients loved her.

"I know," I said. "The whole office seems empty. Are you short-staffed?"

She puffed out air in a gesture of disgust, then peered around the corner before continuing. "Who's here? Anybody important?"

"Besides us? Audry is out, Chester hasn't been in, and Michael is in his office. At least I think he is."

"Well, then let me fill you in on the situation." Nola lowered her voice. "Audry keeps letting people go, all the while telling us we're 'outsourcing' our work to get higher quality at a lower cost. So why does the client need us, that's what I want to know? Any of them could go direct to an artist and then to a printer without paying our commission. Chester always ran this place like a family business, and that included client service. I think it made a big difference. Well, you know; you were here."

Rose Sterling had for the most part been a big warm happy place, always busy, always buzzing with people, including clients. Sometimes tempers flared and there were loud arguments, but those had been like family flurries, too. It didn't take long for everyone to kiss and make up. When Audry had arrived the atmosphere had shifted, but the rest of us had usually banded together against her. Behind her back, of course.

Nola leaned even closer. "Audry's even been making noises about cutting my commission on new accounts, but I'm telling you right now it's not happening." She turned her head around to check behind her before continuing her whispered diatribe. "She's already done it twice, and I'm not taking another cut. I'm working on a big new client and I'll blow this pitch before I let her keep all the money."

We used to have a saying at the agency, "Everybody makes their own deal." Meaning that everybody got something a little different depending on what they asked for. It hadn't been that way with Chester, but it certainly had after Audry started. With Audry's involvement absolute, it appeared Nola needed to be making a hard deal. Fast. And one that was in writing.

The front door opened.

"Look at me in here gossiping," she said, standing up. "Like you don't have anything better to do."

I heard Chester and Audry speaking as they walked to their offices.

Nola raised her voice to a normal level. "What I really came for was to tell you how much you're appreciated, Jolie. I was afraid I'd start losing clients, but with everything finally getting done, my clients are happy little people."

"All kudos gratefully accepted," I said.

"Oh, you're welcome. Just don't let it go to your head; we don't need any more people thinking they oughta just climb over everyone else to get to the top." She clamped a beautifully manicured hand over her mouth. When she pulled it away, she said in a soft voice, "Would you just listen to me? There I go again. If I don't watch my tongue, something evil is going to come after me."

"Wait, I don't get it. Who are you talking about? Who tried to climb over you?"

"I'm not saying a word."

"Oh, come on, Nola. It's me." We were speaking barely above a whisper, not that anyone was officed close enough to hear us. "If you don't tell me, I'll blab to everyone about the first time you—"

"Shh!" She lowered her own voice even more. "It was Desi Baker."

I glanced at the three pictures pinned to the burlap wall. "Are you serious? What did she do?"

"If I tell you, and vampires come to my door, will you be there to protect me?"

"All you have to do is call." But I wasn't feeling flippant.

"Damn. Just don't repeat it. See, I asked her to write a bank commercial, and she wants to see the whole place right down to the vault. Which I arranged. Then I figure out that she really wants to meet the bank president, and next thing I know, our Miss Desi is having drinks with the man. Pitching my account! That girl had designs on my job, and when Desi wanted something, she got it. There were times I was ready to shoot her!" Nola stopped and scrunched her face in disgust, and said, "You hear what I said? I'd better go."

"See you later."

She grabbed her coat and went out, leaving me with the realization that I was sliding even further into agency life. Nola was gossiping in my office again, only there was a difference. I didn't know the object of her gossip, not like the people she'd talked about in the old days. And I didn't want to know things that were detrimental to my opinion of Desi. She was dead, and by some strange quirk of fate I felt linked to her in her passing.

I shut it all out of my mind and turned around to work, but my fingers had barely touched the keyboard when I heard a deep male voice coming from the front office. Immediately I had a vision of the large police officer from the night of the party, Senior Sergeant Bohles.

I went back to typing, but when the conversation with Bohles continued for more than a few minutes, I paused, craning to hear words in the outer office. Before I could discern what was being said, Amber was hurrying down the hall and into my cubby.

"The police want us in the conference room," she said, her pale face almost ghostly. "They didn't say why, though."

"Do they want everyone?"

"Yes." She scraped at her nail polish with her front teeth, then pulled the finger away from her mouth. "This is scary."

I stood up and put my arm around her. "Not to worry. They can kill us, but they can't eat us."

She gave me a horrified look. "What?"

"It's an old expression. Never mind. It was supposed to make you feel better,'' I said. "Why don't you get Nola? Do you want me to call Ralph?" He was still at the TV station.

"No, I already did." She started toward Nola's office. "We're going to go ahead without him."

"Fine." While she went to gather the rest of the staff, I saved the document I'd been working on. Once it was safely tucked into the bowels of the computer, I headed for the conference room. Despite my assurances to Amber, my own stomach produced a sudden gush of acid. Whatever the police had to tell us would not be good news.

And then there was the little problem of my fingerprints on that note.

Even with the lights on, the pervasive gloom of the misty day made its presence known in the conference room. The faces staring at me matched that brooding sky.

Audry was standing at the far end of the table. Her black suit accented the creases on either side of her mouth. They were far more pronounced than when I'd seen her earlier, making her appear tired and angry. Chester and Donna Katherine were sitting together, both of them staring straight forward as if waiting for a funeral to begin.

Michael was also in the room; I didn't look at him.

Then there was Fred, the art director. He was a short, reedy man with thin salt-and-pepper hair pulled back into a ponytail. A leather thong around his neck had a shark's tooth on it, and a hand-tooled belt held up his well-worn jeans. He was typical of one segment of the Austin population, none of whom appeared to have realized that the sixties were gone.

Sergeant Bohles nodded as I came in and gestured toward a chair on the far side of the table. It put me directly in front of where Michael was standing. Michael didn't seem to notice; his eyes were glazed, and he stared out the glass wall as if he were alone, contemplating the growth of the city.

When Amber and Nola came in, Bohles asked them to sit as well. If this was the entire group, it was a very small staff compared to what the agency had employed before. We were down a good ten people, even if there were some employees out for the holidays.

Bohles waited until everyone was seated, then glanced around the room, taking in each one of us, and waiting some more. Another officer arrived and took a place beside Bohles. Both had their feet apart and firmly planted on the carpet; their shoulders were stiff with their hands clasped behind their backs. They looked tough, and maybe even angry. Perhaps they were.

It was Bohles who spoke. "I'm Senior Sergeant Ray Bohles with the Austin Police Department. Beside me is my partner, Senior Sergeant Billy Dempsey. For those of you who don't know, I was called to this building two nights ago as part of a routine investigation of the death of a young woman who was employed here at Rose Sterling Advertising. Her name was Desiree Ann Baker, Desi Baker as she was better known to you. She was found in the sixth-floor women's bathroom by Mrs. Jolene Berenski Wyatt." He nodded in my direction, never taking his eyes off the rest of the group. "Miss Baker was dead upon the arrival of the EMTs. Mrs. Wyatt did not know Miss Baker, but I'm sure many of you did."

There was no sound in the room except the distant hum of the central heating, which had just clicked on. All eyes watched Bohles.

He continued. "At the time I suspected that Miss Baker had died of a drug overdose. The assumption was based on the fact that a big party was going on, and it was consistent with what we found at her death scene. That assumption was wrong. The autopsy showed that Miss Baker had not taken any street drugs. We have subsequently learned she died from ingesting a poisonous substance. We do not at this time believe that it was self-administered, therefore we will be conducting a homicide investigation and request complete cooperation of every person in this room. At this time I would like to read all of you your rights so that you will understand what they are."

Hearing the Miranda rights on television or reading them in a book is nothing like having them read to you in real life. Bohles's deep voice was almost a monotone, yet his words hit like projectiles, tearing away at the veneer of politeness we all wore. There was fear underneath our façades, and my hands were suddenly icy.

Amber was so pale she was almost blue. Nola's upper body was rocking slightly side to side as she listened, openmouthed. Deep emotions were churning in Michael's dark eyes, and though I suspected one was anger, the others were a mystery. Audry had withdrawn to some mental executive suite where nothing touched her. Chester looked ill. Donna Katherine had taken his arm, I assumed to give him comfort. Fred merely looked surprised.

"Do you all understand these rights as I have read them to you?"

We all nodded or mumbled, but that wasn't sufficient. He went around the room, asking each person individually. Everyone said yes. When he was done he nodded, satisfied. "Good. Now I need to talk to each one of you separately.

"Mr. Sterling, I'd like to begin with you. The rest of you are requested to stay here. Sergeant Dempsey will wait with you."

There was more silence as Chester, looking old and confused, left with Sergeant Bohles. There was nothing for the rest of us to say with the watchful eyes of Dempsey on us. Even my thoughts seemed to halt until twenty minutes later when Bohles reappeared. He said, "Mrs. Wyatt, come with me, please."

ELEVEN

BOHLES TOOK my fingerprints first. When he was finished he handed me a paper towel soaked in some kind of fluid, and said, "I appreciate your time, Mrs. Wyatt; I know this is difficult for you."

I said something nondescript and polite.

Sergeant Bohles was sitting on the edge of Audry's desk, while I sat in front of it. With the light behind him he was a faceless profile.

No doubt he had selected this office because it was farthest away from the conference room, assuring that our words would be private. Unfortunately, for me this was the least comfortable office in the suite. Bad vibes, as they say.

"Do you mind if I record our conversation? It will help with the transcription later."

"That's fine."

"Good." He started a tape recorder. "Now, would you tell me again about the night you found Desiree Baker's body. Please begin with the party and tell me why you were there."

"Of course." I took a breath, wondering how in the world I could explain my motives for some official report. How could I make him understand that I had wanted to brag about my book contract, and laugh with my old friends? That I needed a homecoming? Looking at the very sturdy Sergeant Bohles, I doubted that he would comprehend, even if I could get the words out.

I started slowly. "It was a combination birthday party for Chester and anniversary party for the agency. Rose Sterling has been a big part of my life, and so has Chester; I felt it was important to be here. We combined the trip with my husband's business, and time with his family. For the holidays."

"Thank you. I understand that Mr. Sterling received some gifts; did you give him one?"

I told him about the mug and the tea.

"What did the box look like?" he asked me.

"The box?"

"The outside of the package."

"Oh, I see." I concluded he had a picture of the table that held the gifts and was trying to determine which was mine. "It wasn't in a box. It was in a basket." I told him about Prissy's fancy wrapping.

"So it was a white basket with gold cellophane."

I nodded. "And of course, it had a big bow, and I had brought some mistletoe from Purple Sage that Prissy put on the outside—and some on the inside, too."

Bohles's attention intensified as I spoke. The package was important, but why? I paused to consider the possibilities, then I stopped and looked straight into Bohles's face. A shudder caught me and my shoulders contracted with the chill of it. I knew how Desi Baker had died.

"It was poisoning from mistletoe, wasn't it?" I was appalled that I'd said it out loud.

He responded with a question that was asked as if the answer didn't matter. "Why would you say that?"

"Because. Because I looked up mistletoe in a book once. I'd been thinking of using it as a murder weapon. In one of my mysteries." My mouth felt very dry. "People can become very ill from eating the leaves. Or the berries." I felt nauseous as the vision of Desi Baker, dead on the floor, came back to me.

"Take a deep breath," Bohles commanded. "You may want to put your head between your knees. Go ahead."

I did as suggested and stayed down until I felt steadier. Desi Baker had eaten mistletoe, just like what I'd brought from Purple Sage. It might even have been the same mistletoe. Someone could have taken it off the package, and—

No, that wouldn't work. There was merely a sprig on the outside, and it was still there when Chester opened his presents.

Besides, mistletoe was everywhere; there was no need to blame myself.

Cautiously I brought my head up, and when that didn't cause any adverse reactions I sat up. "I'm better." But I didn't nod my head or make any other sharp movements. "I saw the berries." They had been in the toilet.

"I'm not saying that you're correct in your assumption, but I would like you to avoid speculating out loud with the others."

Because I'd been right. "Certainly."

"So you left the party, went straight to the bathroom, and discovered Miss Baker upon entering. Is that correct? And why were you alone on that floor? I understand guests were not supposed to be there."

As a starting point for my explanation I used my encounter with the security guard in the elevator; from there I went straight through the story.

Except for the note, of course.

I faltered when I came to that part, but only for the merest second, and then went on until I reached the end. Bohles continued to watch me as if expecting more.

We stared at each other, and I was the first to look away. "That's all there is," I said.

He waited, then with the timing of an actor he slowly reached behind his back. His eyes never left my face as he brought out a clear plastic Baggie with a file label on the back. Inside was a piece of Michael's notepaper, creamy and rich, only this piece had been crumpled and smoothed as an afterthought, leaving deep wrinkles on the paper. I didn't have to see the handwriting, or read the words, to know this was the note Michael had slid underneath the bathroom door. Bohles continued to watch my face as he said, "You didn't say anything about this."

My reaction was the same as when I was a teenager and the police had caught a group of us toilet-papering a house. My blood seemed to stop in my veins and my body temperature dropped.

The note remained in the bag; Sergeant Bohles held it motionless between us like a battle flag. I couldn't deny seeing it before—my fingerprints were on it and I was sure Bohles already knew that.

"I forgot," I said. "I heard a sound at the door and when no one came in, I went to see what it was. That was on the floor."

"And you read it."

"Yes, of course. I couldn't help it. It was faceup, not folded or anything."

"Did you recognize the handwriting?"

The lie was conveniently close, but I knew I would be caught. "Yes. I've seen Michael Sherabian's writing many times. It's very distinctive."

"And what did you do with the note after you read it?"

"I, it seemed so strange. I didn't understand. So I guess at some point I must have thrown it away." The words were as new to me as they were to Bohles. "Yes, I remember that; putting it in that silver container on the wall."

"You crumpled it first."

I swallowed. "Yes, I guess I did."

"And you didn't go outside to confront Mr. Sherabian about the note."

"No." The temperature in Audry's office was as cold as her decor.

"And he wasn't outside the door after you'd found Ms. Baker's body."

"No."

"Why did you crumple the note and throw it away?"

"Why?" I frowned; it was a true reflection of what I was feeling. Why? Why? Why would anyone? I fumbled the words. "I knew that it, the note, wasn't for me, and I didn't want to leave it for just anyone to see. I guess."

Bohles waited, still watching. I waited too. Finally he nodded. "I'd like you to do two things. Please write down your movements from the time you entered the offices of Rose Sterling the night of Desi Baker's death until you left to use the rest room. Please include approximate times." He handed me a fresh yellow legal tablet and a new number-two pencil. "Then draw me a map of this suite of offices."

"Now?"

"Yes, ma'am."

The term *writer's block* was the first thing that came to mind. Beyond that were disorganized images that would never translate to paper.

With a feeling of hopelessness I ducked my head and tapped the pencil eraser against my front teeth. I stared at the blank sheet of paper.

"What time did you arrive?" he coached.

"About seven-thirty or so. We didn't get in the door for a few minutes."

"Just start with that."

I did, and the physical act of writing the words broke open my thoughts. I listed people and conversations, because those were most memorable; exact times were more difficult. I had checked my watch once during the presentation, and once when I was getting ready to leave. In between I could only guess, so on the sheet of paper I left blanks rather than provide the police with incorrect information. "Is this okay?"

He glanced at the tablet and nodded. "We know when the video started, and the speeches, so if you remember any of those events, you might want to jot them down."

I did so quickly and realized that I had been alone for almost ten minutes, staring out the window, while Matt had gone for my drink. No doubt Bohles would spot that time period and question me about it, if not today, then later. "I'm done," I said, holding the yellow tablet up toward him.

"The map, please."

I sketched it quickly on a second page. I'm not a draftsman, which became readily apparent; the proportions were off in several places. "Not perfect," I said, standing up. I was grateful to discover that my muscles held me upright.

He glanced at the map. "Close enough."

"May I go?"

He answered by leaning forward. "Do you like writing commercials?"

"What? Do I like writing commercials?" This wasn't a cocktail party, and I tried without success to figure out where his question was taking us. "Um, yes. Sort of."

"It must be satisfying, seeing your commercial on television, seeing the end product."

"Yes. It is."

His nod was slow, almost lazy. "That's why I like being a detective. I like seeing the end product, but I enjoy the investigation, too. Getting to the bottom of things. Finding the whys, and digging out the truth. I always know the truth before it's over." There was a long pause, followed by a half smile. "You can go now." I started toward the door, but he called me back. "Mrs. Wyatt?" When I was again facing him he said, "I'll need to talk with you again. Save some time for me tomorrow."

It was like the dream where you run but don't get anywhere. "Tomorrow? Certainly."

"Good. I'll look forward to it."

This time I made it out of the room, but once outside the door, I stopped. I couldn't think where to go. I felt as if I'd miraculously escaped some brutal ordeal, and I wasn't certain how or why. The one thing I did know for sure was that Sergeant Bohles was going to keep asking people questions until he knew about my affair with Michael Sherabian. I could feel it coming like an arthritic person can feel the onset of rain; his persistence was going to make my transgression public knowledge.

Had the windows around the building been the kind you can open, I might have considered jumping.

Donna Katherine appeared beside me, chatting away as if it were normal to find me paralyzed in the hallway. "I was fixin' to make a cup of herb tea for Chester. They let me out because I was nice and said, 'Pretty please.' You look like you could use a cup, too."

"Yes." The act of nodding, speaking, and moving broke the feeling of rigor mortis. "I'd like that."

She led me into the little break room. It was outside this door that the dais had been set up at the party.

"You okay?" she asked.

"Sure. Fine."

"This is very hard on Chester. He had a heart attack a few years ago; I think it aged him. You maybe noticed how thin he is."

"Yes."

"I sure hope this mess with the police doesn't cause him more problems." Donna Katherine pulled mugs out of the cupboard and rinsed each with hot water before filling them.

"Is he feeling ill?" I asked.

"Says he's not, but I don't like his color. I'm making him some chamomile tea, that ought to help." She put the two mugs on the counter. Donna Katherine had always had a very special relationship with Chester. She did everything for him; picked up his laundry, his lunch, and his prescriptions. It was a platonic relationship, but she was combination mother hen and old-time secretary, always seeing to it that his needs were taken care of.

I waited until she was finished, then ran my hands under the tap, rubbing at them as Lady MacBeth must have rubbed hers.

"At least it's over," Donna Katherine said, opening the door of the large microwave oven. We were assailed by the nostalgic odor of the hundreds of once-frozen entrées that had been cooked in there. It was mixed with a dusty scent like weeds.

It brought me back down to earth.

"Smells like someone cooked a bush," I said as Donna Katherine placed the cups in the microwave and closed the door. "With marinara sauce."

"Always does," she said, setting the timer. Once the oven was humming she turned and asked quietly, "So really, you doin' okay?"

"I'm fine. Honest." At least I was breathing, and able to form short sentences.

"So what went on? Was it rotten?"

"Oh, not so bad." Or it wouldn't have been if I'd told the whole truth. "There were no bamboo shoots, whips, or chains."

"Damn well better not be. This is a polite society. What did he want to know?"

Some part of me didn't want to discuss it, as if my refusal would alter the fact that it had taken place. However, in an agency as small as Rose Sterling, I knew that wasn't going to work for long.

"Bohles seems thorough, and I guess that's good," I said. "He asked again about the things that happened before I found Desi's body. I've been over it with him several times now; I'm sure he just wants the timing straight. He had me write things down. I guess it's a way of tracking people."

"We all had to do that after you left the other night."

"Really? Did you have to draw a map, too?"

"A map? Of what?"

"Of the offices, and the rest of the floor."

She stared at me. "No way. Now, I can see wantin' to know where folks were, because obviously someone was doin' something they weren't supposed to be. But a map? Now, why would he do that? And did he say what killed her?"

"No." I lengthened the one-word response with a shrug. "The whole thing is a big mystery, I guess. Besides, you know the police, they don't give information, they just get it."

"I *don't* know the police except for a deputy I used to date, and it was never information that he was after, if you get my drift." She reached into a cupboard and pulled down a box of chamomile tea, then turned to me. "So you're telling me you spent all that time in there and you didn't—" She stopped, swallowed, and went on smoothly, "Buy a single thing? Honey, even if you had your husband with you, you should have taken a little time. A woman is supposed to shop till she drops. Haven't you heard that? Isn't that true, Sergeant?"

Sergeant Ray Bohles was in the door behind me.

Donna Katherine fancies herself an actress, and having gone to a few community plays to see her, I'm sorry to say she is terrible.

She is of the "look, Ma, I'm acting" school of theater, so I was amazed at how smoothly she'd transitioned into the questions.

"Not my call, ma'am," the sergeant said. He reached beside the door and pulled up some yellow tape I hadn't noticed. Printed on it were the words Police Line, Do Not Cross. "Didn't you see this? I'm going to have to ask you to put everything down and come out of there, please. Without touching anything else."

Donna Katherine stared at the tape, same as I did.

"I didn't notice it," I said, bowing my body away from him as I slid past him out the door. "I'm sorry."

"What I want to know," Donna Katherine said less than graciously, not even budging, "is how I'm supposed to make a cup of tea for Mr. Sterling."

Bohles shrugged. "That I couldn't tell you. The guys from the lab will be here any minute to examine this room."

"Well, then just help yourself to whatever you want," Donna Katherine said with exaggerated graciousness. "I'll skedaddle. And when Chester has a heart attack, or hyperventilates, we'll just call you so you can put up more of your little yellow tape. That ought to be real helpful." With that she flounced out of the room.

For the first time Bohles looked like he wanted to smile. He called after her, "We'd like to speak to you next."

"Well, I'm lookin' forward to it," she said with one more flip of her hip.

He turned to me. "Oh, and, Mrs. Wyatt, I understand you're working in Desi Baker's office." When I paused to listen he added, "You'll need to relocate temporarily; the staff from the lab will be going through that area as well and they may take a few things with them. I hope it won't inconvenience you."

"Certainly," I said.

"You can wait in the conference room, if you don't mind."

"Right."

As I passed Donna Katherine's office I saw she had pulled out wrapping paper and was wrapping a Christmas present. When I paused, she scowled. ''Well, I've got to do something useful, or I'm fixin' to go downright crazy. You know what I mean?''

I knew.

TWELVE

THE MARBLED TILE of the lobby floor was damp and smeared with footprints tracked in from the sluggish rain outside and I had to step carefully to avoid slipping as I moved from the elevator to the garage stairs. Ted Polovy was at the security desk, running his hand across the top of his short bristly hair; I slowed.

"Don't you ever get time off?" I asked, pulling my coat tightly around me.

"Why? You want to take me out?"

It took me a moment to understand what he meant, then I smiled, almost laughed. The smile felt like something I'd needed to do for a long time. I moved closer to the desk. "I think my husband would object. It's just a guess, of course...."

"Yeah, well, you change your mind, and I'll consider it. I'm not saying yes, but I would think about it." He threw me an exaggerated wink. He'd changed from the grizzly he'd been the other night to a teddy bear.

"I'll remember that," I said. "You seem to be around a lot."

"Don't I know it. It's the holidays. We've got one guy out with his wife having a baby, and two others on vacation. I'm putting in some extra hours since we have to have three people on every shift."

"Really? That's a lot of security."

He cocked his head. "It's a tough world these days. There's more crime than there used to be, and with computers and stuff, one burglary could wipe out any business in the building."

"I see." After a pause, I said, "Ted, on the night of the party, could a stranger, you know, someone not invited, have gotten up to the agency and killed Desi Baker?"

His response was swift. "No way. I was in the elevator, and Lina was on the desk. You think I'm tough, you should meet her.

I guarantee you, she made sure every person got on the elevator; we only had one running, and I took it straight to the seventh floor. Nobody was slipping around on their own.''

No one could get in the building without passing this spot.

"What about when you two were on break?" I asked.

He gave me a look of disbelief. "What break? Does Superman take a break? No. And neither do we."

"Right, I'm buying that."

"Okay, so maybe once in a while. But Travis was our third that night, and this guy was on the Olympic karate team eight years ago. People don't sneak past him, either." Ted studied my face for a moment. "You're hoping whoever killed Desi Baker was an outsider."

"Is that wishful thinking on my part?"

"I'm afraid it is, kiddo. Besides, if you were going to sneak into a building during a party to kill someone, you wouldn't use poison. You'd get them to some empty spot and use a gun or a knife, and then you'd leave. Poison is for when you're hanging around and can't get away."

An interesting thought, and it made as much sense as anything I'd come up with. Unfortunately, it also limited the possible murderer to the employees and guests of Rose Sterling. Most likely to the employees. "And there were no other parties that night? No one working late?" I asked.

"Not on a Sunday night." When I sighed, he said, "Checkmate."

"It's not over till it's over." I hiked up my purse strap and waved as I turned toward the elevator. "Thanks."

"See you later," he called after me.

"Right."

Inside my car the air was that crisp cold that hasn't yet reached unpleasant, and it was tinged with the bayberry air freshener I'd put in a week earlier during my pre-trip car cleaning.

After the engine was warm, I put the transmission in gear and headed out of the garage. It was almost dark outside, with the lights of the city twinkling invitingly. Rose Sterling was located in the maze of one-way streets that run through downtown Austin, and as I turned in to it I began noticing Christmas decorations and lights on many of the stately buildings.

I rolled down my window as if to suck in the Christmas spirit. It seemed unfair that Desi Baker was missing all this.

The traffic was heavy up to the freeway, and then stop and go on Mopac, the taillights in front of me a stream of red. My thoughts were a jumble of pictures and feelings, past and present woven together to form a rope that held me tight. I couldn't shake it loose and I hardly noticed the other cars as I drove.

Michael and Desi formed one picture. Donna Katherine with Chester in the conference room, another. There was a quick flash of Nola and James ducking out of the Christmas party, which was replaced by Nola and me ducking out of the office to smoke. God, had we ever been that young?

Eventually I exited, still fighting the past. After a few more turns I drove into the driveway. A car was there ahead of me and that's when I realized I hadn't driven to Prissy's, but instead had gone to my old house as naturally as if it were four years before.

I had no idea what my subconscious was suggesting, and I wasn't willing to dwell on it long enough to figure it out, but looking out at the houses in my old neighborhood was comforting. Jeremy and I had lived much of our lives here, and we'd had many good times. They seemed as vivid as the bright star on the roof.

What the heck, no one would worry if I was a few minutes late.

I backed out of the drive carefully and cruised the car-lined street until I found an empty spot, then parked and walked back to my old house. It was small, just two bedrooms, with a big den and a kitchen with lots of cupboards but no room for a table.

The yard looked as it always had in winter, the grass a golden color, the juniper bushes a soft gray-green in the reflected porch light.

The drapes were pulled back on the front window to show off the Christmas tree, which was flocked and decorated with a mixture of ornaments, beads, lights, and bows. It looked a little more sophisticated than anything we'd ever had, but pretty just the same. By moving a foot or two down the sidewalk I could make out the corner of the fireplace and see a stocking hanging there. It appeared to be a knit sock, long and striped, and it hung dangerously low, just missing the opening of the firebox.

It made me think of the time Jeremy's stocking had gotten so hot it had started smoking. Luckily it hadn't caught fire, but it was good that we'd been there to see it.

I shook my head at the memory. There were so many memories. Like the time Jeremy had hidden in the garage, working on a birthday present for me, a specially painted and lacquered computer disk box. I had noticed his absence and gone hunting for him. He was only eight and thoroughly disgusted with me for ruining his surprise.

And then there were those wonderful evenings when Matt had been our guest at the house. At first he had picked me up at the door, saying little more than hello and "How are you doing?" to Jeremy. But then, on our sixth or seventh date, when I knew I really liked Matt and was harboring some secret hope for our relationship, things changed completely. What a night.

I had agreed to let Jeremy stay home alone since it was summer, still light outside, and we were only going to be gone an hour or two. Except as I called good-bye he appeared in the hall doorway, looking waiflike. His voice had been barely a notch above pathetic as he'd said, "Mom, what am I going to eat? I'm starving."

I had tried to smile sweetly. "You can make a sandwich, we have cheese, and there's frozen pizza, or leftover spaghetti."

Pitifully he'd shaken his head. "Oh, thanks a lot—those really sound appetizing."

It was a ploy to make me look bad so Matt would go away. My son was being territorial, the age-old battle of male dominance; after all, he was the man of the house, and Matt a potential interloper. Jeremy had pulled similar stunts when he was younger, although they'd been less subtle.

While I recognized the reasons behind his words, they had left me in a stupefied silence. I debated whether to respond or just kill him on the spot, thus solving the problem permanently.

"I have an idea," Matt had said in an easy tone of voice that I have come to know, and usually love. "Jeremy, why don't you have dinner with us? I was planning on taking your mom to Chez Zee, but we can do pizza if you prefer."

Expressions flickered across Jeremy's face with amazing speed: shock, dismay, distrust, and finally, after a good thirty seconds, delight. He'd looked at me. "Really? Can I go?"

I'm not a suspicious person, but I'd had the horrible fear he was ready to take the battle for male supremacy to a public arena. And yet, if I said no, how would that look to Matt? "I don't know if it's a good idea," I'd said, giving Jeremy the beady-eyed stare mothers are renowned for. "Do you think we could all have a good time?"

He knew exactly what I meant, and he grinned. "Oh, sure we can." He'd turned to Matt. "And Chez Zee is cool. I'll have Sharon's Angel Hair Pasta."

My son the sudden gourmet.

Matt had nodded. "That's one of my favorites too." He was an innocent about to be cannonballed by an eleven-year-old.

"Cool. Be right back." Jeremy had raced out of the living room and returned in literally seconds wearing presentable jeans and a golf shirt with a collar.

I vividly remember locking the door as we left, thinking that I had made a terrible, horrible mistake and this night would live in infamy. It would have a special name in future annals, called Jolie's Last Date with that Wonderful Matt.

Once we were seated at the restaurant, Jeremy began some macho posturing unbecoming a boy of his age. I kicked him under the table several times until he gave it a rest. Matt and I chatted for a moment, then Jeremy started a new tactic: an interrogation of Matt.

"So what do you do in this Purple Sage place, anyway?" he'd asked.

"I have a ranch," Matt had responded easily.

"What's on the ranch?"

"We run cattle and a few sheep."

That had slowed Jeremy. "No kidding?"

"No kidding."

"Do you have horses, too?"

Matt had shaken his head. "No, I don't raise them, if that's what you're asking. I only have a few for work and for guests to ride. There are eight in the stable right now."

Jeremy's eyes had widened like sunflowers. "Are you serious? You have eight horses?" It was spoken with the same amazed admiration an adult might use on someone who owned eight Rolls-Royces.

"Uh-huh. Why?" Matt had said. "Do you like horses?"

"Oh, yeah!"

"Really? Would you like to come out sometime?"

"Oh, wow!"

"You and your mom can come spend the weekend anytime. I've got a big house, and I always need someone to exercise the horses."

I had jumped in then to stave off the inevitable questions from Jeremy, which would be, "Can we, Mom? And when?" But that was the end of Jeremy's skepticism toward Matt. The rest of that evening involved a swapping of information between the two, with a lot of "wows" and "cools" coming from Jeremy. He added a few stories of his own, and while most were wild exaggerations, it was fun. Back at the house we made popcorn and played Pente until I was falling asleep on the couch. Matt kissed me good-bye softly and Jeremy let him out, but only after making Matt promise to come back for dinner the next night.

It wasn't until months later that Matt admitted he'd been searching for a way to get to know Jeremy. In the country they call it salting the calf to get the cow. He told me he'd realized he was falling in love with me, and he'd thought that by winning Jeremy over, he'd have a better chance with me. That part always amazes me. I still can't believe that Matt could worry about such a thing, but he says that what with the distance between our homes and the slow build of the relationship, he was sure someone else would come along and sweep me away before he could.

And now we were a family. We appreciated each other in a way that natural families may not, and I was happier than I'd ever been. The only blot in my life at the moment was that damn thing with Michael. And Desi Baker's death.

As I stared at the house in the cold December air, I pushed those thoughts aside and let the other memories wash over me in waves of happiness, sorrow, laughter, and some regret.

Suddenly the front door opened and a woman stuck her head out. "Can I help you?"

It surprised me to be caught and it certainly must have startled her to discover a stranger standing on the sidewalk, staring at her house.

"Oh, I'm sorry," I said, keeping my distance so as not to concern her any more. "I used to live here and I just wanted to come back and see my old house."

She stepped around the door. "Are you Jolie?"

That surprised me even more. "Yes. Jolie Wyatt. How in the world did you know that?"

"How's Jeremy?" She was smiling now as she cut across the winter gold grass toward me. "Are you still in Purple Sage?"

I went to meet her. "Yes, but, uh, I don't understand. How do you know all this?"

"The present you left for us. Don't you remember?"

Present? "I don't know you, do I? Oh, wait. Of course!" I hadn't given it a thought since the day we'd loaded the moving van for the trip to Purple Sage. "It was a candle, a housewarming gift for the new people who were moving in."

She nodded, smiling broadly. "It was the most wonderful surprise to find that huge, white candle on the mantel. It was just beautiful, and the whole house smelled like lemons. It was really nice of you."

"We'd just had so many good years in this house, we wanted to wish you the same happiness. Did it work?"

"You know," she said, after a moment's thought, "I think it did."

"Good; I'm glad."

"Me, too. And now I get to thank you. And please, thank your husband, Jeremy, too."

I laughed. "Jeremy's not my husband—he's my son. He's sixteen now."

"Oh, you're kidding! The card just had your names, and we assumed... Isn't that funny? I've thought about you so many times, and all these years I've had your relationship wrong."

"My husband's name is Matt. I'm sorry, I don't know your name."

"I'm Keri. That's my daughter, Hana Pearlson." She hugged her sweater tightly around her body, and pointed to a cherubic little girl peeking at us through the window. "Why don't you come in? Wouldn't you like to see the house again?"

"The inside?"

"Of course."

I stared at the front door, catching a glimpse of the tree and the stockings on the mantel. Inside that house were a million memories, but in fact, they weren't really in there; they resided in the house that still existed in my mind. It was decorated differently than this one, and it probably felt different, too.

I shook my head and took a step backward. "Thank you, that's really nice of you, but I need to be getting on."

"Are you sure?"

Again I glanced at the house, then back at her before I said with a firm nod, "Yes. I'm sure." I felt a compelling need to get to Matt.

"I WAS GETTING WORRIED," Matt said as he gave me a welcome-home hug on the chilly patio.

"The police," I said, hugging him back. "They were at the agency, and it took up time we didn't have to spare. Are we going in or up?" I gestured to our apartment.

"In," he said, opening the door for me, so that I could smell gingerbread and pine mingled in a heady Christmas welcome. "Everyone else is getting ready to leave for the evening. We have a few minutes."

I could almost hear the hum of activity coming from upstairs as he led me toward the living room couch. I said, "Want to make out?"

He grinned. "On the couch?"

"Or the floor."

He started to laugh, then slid his arms around me and pulled me close. "Actually, when I start kissing you, I prefer to be in a spot that's a little more private. You never know where that kind of behavior can lead."

I tipped my head up to gaze at him. "Oh, yes, I do."

"What I want to know," he said, kissing me once lightly before setting me on the couch, "is what got you into this mood. I want to remember it."

"I went by my old house."

"Ah, I see, and how was that?"

I let the memory wrap around me, brief yet warm, before I said, "It brought back a lot of old memories. And it made me homesick for you." I curled back against him before I added, "It was a nice ending to a perfectly rotten day."

Matt held me tightly. "What was rotten about it?"

"The police came to the agency; they brought some bad news." I was serious now and Matt's expression changed to match my somber tone. "Desi Baker was murdered."

He nodded. "I heard."

"You did? How? Did Nola call you?" I slipped out of my coat, leaving it on the back of the couch.

"She didn't have to. The police stopped by here."

"You're not serious?" A burning log hissed from the fireplace as if in echoed protest. "What did they want?" I asked.

Matt shifted my coat slightly. "I had to give them a written schedule of my movements during the party, and then draw them a map of the Rose Sterling offices and the rest of the floor. It was a pretty sketchy map."

Maps and mistletoe, motives and—

"Aunt Dolie! You're here. Hip hip away! Hip hip away." Christopher plunged into the room from the staircase, ran across it, and threw himself into my arms. "I missed you too much."

"I missed you too much, too, but you aren't supposed to be running on those stairs," I said, pulling him onto my lap and kissing him on the head at the same time. He felt warm and cuddly, exactly what I needed. "Where have you been hiding? And where is everyone else?"

"Parties," Christopher said fervently. "Grandma Prissy and Grandpa are going to parties and my mommy's going to a party, too. They're gettin' ready."

"That's nice."

"No. I can't go."

"You get to stay home with us," Matt said, tickling Christopher. "We'll have more fun."

Christopher was unimpressed. "I can party."

"I'll bet you can," Matt agreed.

"So where's Jeremy?" I asked.

"On the 'puter, and I can't touch it."

"Poor guy." I hugged him again and smelled the baby-shampoo scent of his hair. "Sounds like you're having a rough day."

A timer went off in the kitchen and Matt rose, moving in that direction. "Jolie, would you like some tea?"

"I'd love some. The police cordoned off the break room this afternoon, so I haven't had any all day."

Tea and break rooms. There was something important in these associations, but I couldn't put it together.

"Christopher, would you like some juice?" Matt asked from the doorway.

"Nope. Thank you."

As Matt disappeared Christopher pulled a tiny plastic bag out of his pocket. "Aunt Dolie, look what I founded. It's for treasure." He whispered the last word, a grin on his face.

The bag was only two by two, and not something I could see

Captain Kidd using. It was instead the kind individual servings of vitamins are packaged in at convenience or health-food stores. "Very tiny treasure; they must be worth a lot of money."

"Diamonds and gold," Christopher said, his eyes glowing. He hopped down off my lap. "May you go find diamonds with me?"

I smiled. "No, sweetie, I just want to sit down, relax, and drink some tea."

"I'll bring you some," Christopher said, racing up the stairs.

"Slow down on those stairs, and hold the banister," I called, watching him. Once he was safely on the second floor I pulled off my boots and wriggled my toes comfortably, then slumped deeper into the couch cushions.

Treasure and tea. Mistletoe. Again the words were pinging at me, but I was too tired to connect the dots.

Interesting that the police had come to see Matt. Had every guest been contacted, and had they all been asked to make a schedule and draw a map? I closed my eyes and let the thoughts drift away. At least we didn't have any parties to attend tonight.

I opened my eyes as I heard Matt approach. He was carrying two cups, one of which he handed to me. "Prissy would have done this better."

"Prissy does everything better," I said from my less-than-graceful position on the couch. I balanced the cup. "Matt, what did your map look like?"

"Like everyone else's, I imagine. Not very artistic, just a plain rendition of Rose Sterling's suite of offices." We were silent a moment, drinking our tea, before he added. "No, that's not true. I wasn't sure about the location of some things, so my map may not have been completely accurate."

If this was important to the police, then I wanted to understand it, too. I sat up and pulled a pen out of my purse, along with the small notebook I always carry. "Could you redraw your map? I'm wondering what you saw."

He gave me a curious look, but said, "Sure. It was nothing fancy." With smooth, flowing strokes he outlined the offices, putting things pretty much as they'd been the night of the party, including the temporary walls and dais. When he was finished I studied his work. The scale was probably more accurate than I would draw, but as he'd said, it wasn't perfect.

"Close, but no banana," I said. "See, you're missing the supply closet." I pointed to the spot where the infamous supply closet should have been. Matt had distorted the dimensions in that area, leaving that and the break room out completely. "And you forgot—"

Tea and break rooms, mistletoe and murder.

"What?" Matt asked.

It fell into place as easily as a drawbridge lowering into position. Desi Baker had died from mistletoe, probably administered in the form of a tea, made in the little break room.

"Jolie?" Matt said again. "What?"

"The police think that someone, the person who killed Desi, made her mistletoe tea in the break room." I was breathing rapidly. "Except the door to it was closed and the dais was in front of it. Most of the guests don't even know that room exists. That's how they're narrowing the list of suspects. The police. If you didn't put the room on your map, then you're safe."

Disjointed as my explanation was, I knew I was right.

"Uh, Jolie, you know, the murderer could have left the break room off his map, too. Murderers have been known to be tricky like that." Matt had an amused glint in his eye.

"But he wouldn't. He wouldn't understand the purpose of the map. Desi didn't die in the break room. I'll bet she didn't even drink the tea there." I stood up and walked to the fireplace, then turned around. "But then why wasn't Bohles more upset that Donna Katherine and I were in there?"

"You were in where?"

"Oh, wait, I know! Because it's been two days since Desi died. Most of the evidence is gone, but he's hoping not all. Of course."

Matt rose and joined me in front of the hearth. "We have two choices here," he said, his arm brushing my sleeve. "Either you can explain what you're talking about, or I can leave and let you carry on the conversation uninterrupted. You choose."

So I explained what I was thinking, and as I did I realized that the cordon around the suspects was tightening. Audry and Michael were securely within its bounds, as were a number of other people. Ralph Richardson was such a nice man, but wasn't that what they'd said about Ted Bundy? Amber seemed too young and too naive to kill, but she displayed some hero worship where Desi was concerned, and it could have skewed toward hate; that happens sometimes. Donna Katherine, loose-lipped and loose-hipped, didn't seem a likely candidate any more than Chester Sterling himself, but both had opportunity. And what about Nola?

And then I realized that I, too, had opportunity. And, in the view of the police, I could also have a motive. As soon as Bohles learned of my affair with Michael Sherabian, I was in for some very intense questioning, if not something far worse.

It felt as if a ball of black tar were growing in my stomach. Fear can do that to me.

"Matt," I said, championing my courage. "I think there's something I need to tell you about—"

"I didn't stole it!" I heard Christopher's cry as he raced across the landing at the top of the stairs. There was a bump, then another cry, and he was on the staircase, falling toward the bottom.

THIRTEEN

MATT AND I were up in a flash, running toward the stairs. We reached them just as Christopher bounced on the last step. Matt caught a leg, I grabbed a shoulder, stopping him before he hit the ceramic tile floor. We raised Christopher, turned him upright, and I wrapped my arms around him.

"Christopher! You have to be careful," I said as he began to cry. "Are you okay?" Cautiously I ran my hand along his arms, hoping I wouldn't find anything broken. "Where does it hurt?"

"I didn't stole it, Aunt Dolie, I didn't."

"I know, sweetie. Are you hurt?"

"No." But he cried even harder.

"It's okay; hey, it's okay." I rubbed his back, and my hand brushed Matt's. He was also trying to soothe Christopher.

"You scared us, Christopher," he said. "You have to be more careful on those stairs. You could have been hurt."

"But I, I, I not bad." He hiccuped twice through the faltering tears. "It was for treasure."

More footsteps clattered above us and Todd appeared at the top of the stairs. "Christopher—"

"I din't stole it!"

"It's okay," I said. "Relax, it's all right." I looked up. "Todd, what's the problem?"

He came down the stairs gracefully, his beautiful face showing a flick of anger, and something more that I couldn't define. "Is he okay?" he asked, gesturing to Christopher. "Are you okay, little guy?"

"He appears to be fine, physically." Matt said. "What's going on?"

Todd seemed reluctant, but said, "Christopher was poking around in my room, again. I told him this morning he wasn't supposed to go in there.'' I moved toward the couches to sit down and he followed along, explaining as we went. "I didn't mean to scare him, but I did tell him to stay out. Isn't that true, Christopher? Didn't I tell you that? Twice?''

Christopher rubbed a fist across his tearstained face and nodded; more huge tears fell down his cheeks. "I'm not bad.''

"Of course, not,'' I said, hugging him tightly as I looked at Todd. "I know it can be frustrating, but he's just three. Little kids forget things. As the adults, we have to take responsibility for putting things up so that Christopher can't get them.''

Todd twitched his shoulders, hesitating before he said, "I'm sorry. I overreacted.'' He was young, too; I could see that in his face. "You okay, little buddy?''

"I didn't stole!''

Matt took a relaxed posture, his voice easy as he asked, "What didn't you steal?''

"I din't stole—'' Christopher began.

"It's okay, Christopher,'' Todd said, kneeling beside the couch so he could pat Christopher on the back. "I'm sorry you fell; I know you didn't mean anything.'' Then he looked up at us. "Christopher had one of my cuff links. Gold nuggets with a little diamond in it. My mom gave them to me last year for my birthday.'' He swallowed hard and stopped as if he couldn't say anything else.

I began to understand why he seemed young and upset. Some things have value beyond price.

I rearranged Christopher so that I could look into his face. "Christopher, you mustn't ever take Todd's cuff links again, do you understand?'' I waited until he nodded. "Those are very special to Todd. Very special. You wouldn't like it if someone took something very special of yours. Like your teddy bear.''

He sniffed and nodded. "No.''

"And you can't go in my room anymore,'' Todd said. "You have to mind, don't you?''

"I know.''

"One more thing," Matt added. "You cannot run on those stairs. Got it? You were almost hurt."

Christopher nodded again. "Okay."

I wondered how much of this a three-year-old could take in. I hugged him. "I'm glad you're all right. And we'll just forget the whole thing. Deal?"

"Deal," Christopher said, solemnly.

Todd stood up. "Deal for me, too." He patted Christopher. "Well, I guess I'd better go." He looked at Matt. "It's been a while since I've been in Austin. Lots of old friends to see." He trotted toward the front door as Prissy came down.

"Todd," she said, "did I hear Christopher crying? I had the blow dryer going—"

"He's okay, Aunt Prissy," Todd said. "He almost tumbled down the stairs, but Matt and Jolie caught him."

"The stairs? Oh, my God—" She hurried over and swept Christopher into her arms. "Are you all right, little bug?"

"I'm otay. Aunt Dolie saved me."

"And here I thought I was going to be the big hero," Matt said. "I didn't even get a mention."

Prissy was still clutching Christopher. "We're all so busy running around that we haven't been watching Christopher. And I promised Stephanie that I wouldn't let him out of my sight while she was in the shower! She made me swear, and he could have been killed. Oh, my angel." She squeezed him so hard he let out a squeak. "I could put up a baby gate, but I just hate those things. You have to step over them, and then if someone else fell and hurt themselves in the process, I'd feel terrible. I thought Christopher knew better. Don't you know better?"

"I know better, Grandma Prissy," he responded.

Matt took Christopher out of her arms and put him on the floor. "You're overdoing it, Grandma," he said to Prissy. "He's fine. Don't make a big deal or you'll s-c-a-r-e him. Go get ready, we'll baby-sit."

"You're just so pragmatic, Matt!" She looked at me. "Jolie, I feel so bad. I thought this was going to be a fairly relaxed holiday season, but I opened Ross's briefcase and he had nearly a dozen party invitations that he'd forgotten to tell me about! Can you believe that? And these are all clients. We have to show up."

"It's not a problem for me," I said. "I'd just as soon kick back and relax."

"You see, Prissy," Matt said, "Jolie doesn't mind, and she said that even before I told her that *White Christmas* is on TV tonight."

"Really?" I said. "That makes my evening complete."

"Jolie has this weird belief about that movie," Matt went on, getting the *TV Guide* from the television and handing it to me.

"It's not weird," I said. "It's very simple: If you don't watch *White Christmas* or *Miracle on 34th Street,* then Santa won't come to your house. If you watch both, you get anything you want."

Christopher jumped up on my lap. "I want to watch movies!"

"And I'd better go," Todd said. He went over to Prissy. "Good night, Aunt Pris. I'll see you later."

"Oh, Todd, I feel like I've been ignoring you, too," she said, putting an arm around his waist. "The holidays are almost too much. Have you even met Jolie?"

Todd smiled in my direction. "We met on the patio last night when I was getting some air. Don't worry, we're all fine and you're a wonderful hostess." He kissed her on the cheek and she flushed happily.

"Thank you."

A phone rang, and at the same time Ross called from upstairs, "Pris, which tie do you want me to wear?"

"See you all later," Todd said as he turned and headed out the door.

It was like prom night, only I was staying home, and grateful about it. Matt went for the phone, Prissy went upstairs, and I took Christopher to the kitchen. The refrigerator held the makings for some rather terrific sandwiches, leftover soup, and even a fruit salad Prissy had somehow found the time to make.

"Are you ready to eat, little bug?"

"Just soup. I don't eat fruit," he said as I fixed him a plate.

"Of course you eat fruit. Everyone eats fruit. Uncle Matt is having some. I'm having some, and your grandma Prissy made it special for you. So you can grow up big and strong."

"Call me Bernard. He's a Rescuer."

"Okay, Bernard, here's your plate. And just a little fruit. Rescuers need fruit."

He made a face, but once he was arranged on his booster chair, he began spooning soup into his mouth.

Food is imperative to life. And poison—poison could come in many forms. Most adults knew the difference and were careful not to ingest the wrong one. But mistletoe had been swallowed by Desi Baker. She had seemed like an exceptionally bright young woman, so she must have trusted whoever fed her the parasite.

"Mom, can you fix me a sandwich before I go?"

I looked at Jeremy, who had appeared in the dining room dressed in clean, ironed clothes. "Where are you going?" I asked.

"You know Alicia Willis? Remember, she was a friend of Suzie's when we were at Lucy Reed Middle—"

"Not really."

"Well, anyway, I ran into her at the computer store today, and we got to talking, and there's this big party tonight. She said I'd know almost all the kids that will be there, so she invited me. She's even taking me, because she has a car of her own." A pitiful yet accusatory stare was directed at me, apparently intended to make me feel guilty. "She's picking me up in ten minutes, so could you, like, make me a sandwich?"

"I didn't say you could go."

"Mother! You know her aunt. She's in the Austin Writers' League. She had a signing at Mysteries and More and you took me. It was right before we left Austin. Remember she wrote a book about something? There was a cowboy hat on the cover."

I did remember the aunt, although not the hat. Unfortunately I couldn't remember the woman's name, and even if I had, she wouldn't have had any knowledge of her niece's social plans.

"I just don't know—"

"Mother, I'm sixteen. You have to start trusting my judgment; it's just a party."

"Fine. Go talk to Matt and I'll make you a sandwich," I said, and he took off.

It was my way of bowing to greater wisdom; Matt was more evenhanded, perhaps because he was Jeremy's adopted father. Or perhaps because Matt is that way in all of life. Still it let me off the hook. If Matt said no, I was safe, and if he said yes, then I was being overprotective, which I suspected was the case.

"Good fruit, Aunt Dolie," Christopher said, bobbing his head up and down as he chewed.

I finished putting together a plate for Jeremy. "I'm glad you like it."

I tried to imagine Michael in this setting, but he didn't belong.

When Matt and Jeremy returned, Matt sat down beside me, while Jeremy merely snatched his sandwich off the table, almost at a full run, as he raced outside and up the staircase to the little apartment. I assumed he was after money—money Matt had promised him for the evening.

"Softy," I said.

Matt smiled as he reached for a plate.

Next came Stephanie, hurrying through on a cloud of Giorgio. She was in a festive red dress trimmed in black piping. Something by a designer, and probably borrowed from her mother's closet. It aged her, and at the same time softened her slender figure and added color to her cheeks. A good choice for business parties.

"Give me a kiss, angel," she said, bending over Christopher. After a quick kiss she took a bite of his sandwich. "Mmmm. Good stuff."

"Aunt Dolie made it."

"And she did a great job." Stephanie looked at me. "Are you sure you don't mind staying with Christopher tonight? Matt kind of volunteered you."

"I don't mind a bit," I said. "We're going to have a fun evening. Don't worry about us."

"But I do. Where is Todd?" She glanced around as if she might have missed him.

"He left a few minutes ago to visit friends," I said, wondering if the matchmaking was working.

"Oh." She ate a piece of Christopher's fruit, then said, "Pete has so many of these obligatory Christmas parties. You know. I'm surprised you and Matt don't have a dozen, too."

"Oh, we do," Matt said, then added with a drawl, "but not so many as you, bein' from Purple Sage and all."

Stephanie snorted, blowing her bangs off her forehead. "Uncle Matt, you can't even do a Texas accent anymore! You're going to have to practice. But I do appreciate your help with Christopher. You're not going to leave or anything, are you?"

"Stephanie, of course we won't leave Christopher alone," I said. "What is with you?"

"I'm sorry—"

"I have a plan," Christopher said. "We can make popcorn, and I can party!"

The doorbell rang and Pete was there, kissing Stephanie; I didn't look until he'd moved over to the table and was shaking hands with Matt.

"Matt, good to see you again." He leaned over Christopher. "Hello, young fellow."

"Hello, Mr. Javitz. I'm eating."

"So I see. Well, we won't interrupt your dinner. I'm taking your mother to a couple of parties. I hope that's okay with you."

Christopher looked at both of them seriously, as if weighing his options. Finally he said, "Okay."

There were more kisses from Stephanie, along with some final instructions for Christopher—instructions that were also aimed at us. "Christopher, you have to take a bath tonight, and don't leave a big mess in the bathroom. Also, you have to go to bed by eight o'clock. And no milk for your midnight snack because you know what happens. And you stay right with Aunt Jolie. No wandering around upstairs by yourself, because you get into things you aren't supposed to.'' When Christopher continued to eat without looking up, she added, ''Do you hear?''

He looked at her and nodded. ''I hear, Mommy.''

''Good. 'Bye, little bug, I love you.''

Finally they were out the door. Then Jeremy whizzed back through, clutching Matt's newly purchased duster, made of khaki canvas with brown leather trim. Matt had been wanting a long coat like this for years, not that he rides horseback a lot in the rain, but when he does, he says wearing wet jeans for any length of time chafes his thighs. I applauded fixing that problem; I wasn't sure I applauded Jeremy wearing the duster on its first outing.

Jeremy slipped it on, lounging in the doorway to give us the full effect. When he moved, the split in the back revealed his jeans. Apparently Jeremy's new persona was city-kid-gone-country. I shot a glance at Matt, who was nodding.

''Looks fine on you,'' he said very seriously.

Jeremy grinned. ''Cool.''

The doorbell rang, and he raced for it. I gave Matt one of those sidelong glances and he followed Jeremy at a discreet distance.

Matt discerned the young woman's name (by way of a simple introduction), as well as the name of the hosting family, where they were going (by cautioning of some road construction and discussing alternate routes), and approximately what time they would return. The last question he had to flat out ask, although Jeremy didn't seem bothered. Maybe because he was wearing Matt's duster and, as I learned later, carrying two of Matt's twenty-dollar bills in his pocket.

I was introduced from across the room. Alicia was a bubbly brunette with a sweet smile and dimples. I said hello without getting up, just to show how cool I could be.

After they left, Matt sat back down at the table.

''Big night,'' I said. ''Are we the dorm parents?''

''Yes, we are,'' Matt said. ''Luckily it's a very small dorm.''

Next Prissy and Ross came down. Ross had misplaced his wallet and began hunting. Prissy tried to kiss Christopher and smeared her lipstick. Ross found his wallet while Prissy wrote down a list of phone numbers, ending with their cell phone. "Which I promise you Ross will keep with him all night." When they, too, had gone, I jumped up, saying to Christopher, "That's it! They're gone. We can party and trash the place!"

"Hip, hip, away!" he shouted, giving me a full view of his partially chewed bit of fruit.

"See what you started," Matt said.

So we partied, right up until eight-thirty when I fell asleep on the couch.

AT SEVEN-FIFTEEN in the morning I quietly unlocked the door and stepped into the offices of Rose Sterling Advertising; there was an eeriness in the still empty suite.

The heat came on, and a gust of not-yet-warm air touched the Christmas tree, causing the ornaments to dance and jangle gently. I swore I could hear a soft humming that floated on the air current, but the very practical portion of my mind convinced me it was a mechanical sound and nothing more. The office was unpleasantly chilly; lower temperatures had blown in with an overnight cold front that left weathercasters predicting one of Austin's very rare snowfalls. Driving down Prissy's street, I'd seen plants shrouded in blankets to protect them from the frost.

Trying not to think about the temperature, or the solitude of the offices, I moved down the hall to the cubby that once had been occupied by Desi Baker.

When humans depart a company or the earth, they leave something behind them. I always expect some residual aura, intangible yet present, but I've never gotten it. Instead it seems that most people leave a legacy that is a reflection of what they did in their lives, like a happy family, a profitable company, or just a cupboard full of prescription bottles.

Desi had left unfinished business and unwritten copy, the result of a life cut short.

She had also left relationships incomplete, like the one she'd had with Michael. Luckily, that was not my problem. My only concern was the commercial work she'd left undone; my intention was to finish it so I could leave Rose Sterling with a clean conscience and a clean slate.

The police had spent several hours in Desi's former office just the afternoon before. I hadn't been close enough to see everything they'd done, but I knew they had gone through the files and the desk, removing whatever it was they'd thought important. I did see a young woman holding the trail mix in a gloved hand—no doubt that had gone to the laboratory. Then some computer person had come in and copied off the contents of the hard drive. Audry Sherabian had signed a receipt for all of the things they'd taken, and I had been allowed back in there late in the day.

Now as I stepped around the temporary wall that formed Desi's office, I stopped in surprise. The computer was already on and humming, drawers stood wide open, and file folders were everywhere. I had the eerie thought that Desi Baker had returned. Especially since I'd left the office in perfect order the evening before.

FOURTEEN

MY HEART pounded and there was a metallic taste in my mouth as if my adrenaline had come from the superleaded pump.

Instinctively I backed away. I started to turn and rammed into something soft. There was a grunt at the same time as my own.

"Damn!" Nola was clutching the temporary wall. I had almost knocked her over.

"You scared the hell out of me!" I said.

Nola's normally dark skin had lost its glow. She took several deep breaths before she said, "It's mutual! What are you doing here at this hour?"

"I couldn't sleep, so I came in early. Did you do this?"

She glanced around at the mess. "I didn't realize it was this bad. I'm sorry; I'll clean it up." Without a word of explanation, she got down on her knees and began picking up folders, refilling drawers as she went.

"Here, I can help," I said, bending down and reaching for a stack of files.

She scooped them up first and shoved them in a drawer, saying, "No need, I've got it."

"Well, pardon me. What were you looking for?"

"What? Oh, nothing."

I stood back up. "There was obviously something."

"Just some copy I needed for a client, but it isn't here."

I glanced at my watch. It was barely seven-thirty, and to Nola that is like the middle of the night. Unless she had changed her habits drastically, this was not usual behavior. "I can't believe you did all this for a missing commercial, at least not at this hour."

"It's an important client."

"You could have asked me yesterday and I'd have helped you

look. Or you could have checked with Ralph.'' I waited, watching her efficient movements. A sick feeling began in my stomach— Nola had been searching Desi's office. It looked suspicious and my mind made the easy jump to link her with Desi's murder.

Not Nola. Anyone but Nola. I couldn't keep silent. ''Come on, Nola, this isn't your style; tell me what's really going on.''

She stood upright, her arms full of papers. ''You are so damn pushy.''

''Then talk to me—''

''Do you mind?'' She shoved the remaining folders at me. ''Go flap your lip at someone else!'' With that she whipped out. And not just out of my cubicle. I heard her slam a drawer in her own office and then head for the front door.

''Nola, wait a minute,'' I said, starting after her.

The clamor of the ornaments on the Christmas tree told me it was too late; she was gone.

I blamed myself; she wouldn't have left if I hadn't insisted on knowing what was going on. She probably had some perfectly logical reason for coming in so early. Maybe she really had lost some copy for a big client. I turned back to the office and looked around at the small cubicle. No matter how much I wanted to, I couldn't convince myself to accept that explanation. If there was a problem with a client, Nola would have said so. She would have asked for help.

Nola Wells and I had worked together for eight years, and she was probably the person I'd missed most when I left Austin. We had a history together; in fact, I had been the one who'd convinced her to go on her first date with her husband, James. She'd said no, and had been vehement about it when he first asked her out.

''He's a damn football player, and we know those guys are just raw-meat-eating animals. I don't need someone like that in my life.''

''That was in college,'' I'd protested as we rode up in the elevator after arguing about it for most of lunch. ''Nola, that was how many years ago? Give the guy credit for growing up.''

"There are plenty of other men out there—"

"Name one who is as charming and good-looking *and* as interested in you as James."

"I don't have to answer that."

"Because you can't." I'd been at the media party where she and James had met, and I had sensed a spark between the two. Beyond that, I had liked James. There was something about him that just seemed right. "Look, tell him you'll go to dinner, but tell him you want to double-date. I'll come along and I'll bring the biggest guy I know with me. If James does anything he shouldn't, my date can corral him. At least you'll get to know him a little better."

It had taken a bit more talking, but finally she had agreed. "One dinner, Jolie, but it's just to get you off my back, not because I like James."

Less than a year later they were married.

We'd had some bad times, too, but while Nola could be fiery, her brand of anger was the get-in-your-face kind. I was the one who would sputter and dash out the door. Nola would plant herself in front of whoever had displeased her and vent until she was damn well through, thank you very much. Either she had changed a great deal, or something was very wrong.

I couldn't shake the worry as I began putting away the files I held in my arms. The client names on the bulging folders were some of the agency's old guard, familiar to me from my tenure at Rose Sterling: Bank of Balcones; Chez Zee Restaurant; Petry & Thomas, CPAs; the Travis County Zoo; Ant Computing; North and South China Restaurant; and the Austin Aqua Festival. It appeared Nola hadn't found what she was looking for here, so it didn't make much sense for me to go through these folders again.

What I really wanted was to help her. I pulled open the second file drawer hoping that something might occur to me. Desi had kept folders for dozens of clients, many I'd never heard of before. There was one whole section of hanging files bearing names new to me, each holding only a few pieces of paper. There were names like The Witch Stand, Iced Treats, Card Capers, and a business called Stuff 'N Puff.

Curious as to what that might be, I opened the manila file and discovered Stuff 'N Puff was a balloon company out of Friendswood, Texas. There was a print ad showing a teddy bear sitting on a nest of curly ribbon all inside a huge balloon. The next sheet of paper was a piece of radio copy that touted a holiday shopping fair held back in November. Stuff 'N Puff was one of the participants listed. The last thing I found in the folder was an eight-page newspaper called the *Holiday Bulletin*, obviously printed just for the fair. It was beautifully laid out with lots of graphics, and on the front page was a small article about Stuff 'N Puff. The other articles and pictures featured more sponsors of the event.

While it seemed likely that Nola had been through this section of hanging files already, or hadn't been interested in it, I put the folder on top of the desk and flipped through a few others. Most folders had three or four print ads for different fairs, and three or four pieces of radio copy, although a few had less. At the back of the hanging file I found full-page newspaper ads for the November Shopping Fair, a June Bridal Affaire, and a Spring Garden of Delights. Each had a special border around the outside, with the small client ads inside it.

As I closed the drawer I heard the front door of the agency open and the Christmas tree ornaments set up their holiday clamor.

I turned and jumped up, hoping it was Nola returning with a simple explanation. Instead it was Ralph Richardson who appeared in the doorway of my cubicle. I tried not to show my disappointment.

"Ralph, good morning."

"Good morning. You beat me here."

"Oh, not by much."

"It's still pretty early for someone who's supposed to be on vacation." He shifted his body and became more serious as he said, "I don't know if anyone's told you or not, but we really appreciate all the time you're putting in. I can't think of very many people who'd pitch in like you and be so serious about getting us out of our bind."

I responded lightly. "Well, you need to know I'm also serious about leaving here early today. Two o'clock at the latest, police or no police. I have a hot date with a young man named Christopher to do some heavy Christmas shopping, and I'm not letting him down."

Ralph appeared puzzled. "I thought your son's name was Jeremy."

"It is. Jeremy is sixteen and these days he goes off on his own to do his Christmas shopping. This is my three-year-old nephew. More dependent *and* he still lets me hug him."

Ralph grinned. "We're expecting our first grandchild next month, and Mary already plans to kidnap the baby twice a week and teach it quilting and gardening."

"Sounds like a great plan to me," I said, putting away the last of the folders. "And it's a small step from there to mud pies."

"As long as I don't have to eat them. Have you had your coffee yet?" he asked. When I shook my head no, he gestured toward the break room. "Come on, I'll make you some. My treat."

"Except," I said, following him, "that I quit drinking coffee almost a year ago. Only tea now, so I'll make my own."

"We have lots of different kinds. Donna Katherine thinks we're some kind of International Tea House; you can have your pick."

"Is the break room open again? The police had it blocked off yesterday."

We arrived at the door and the yellow police tape was gone. "It was open last night when I left here," he said. "Guess that was around nine or so."

Advertising can be rough when the pressure's on, although usually our Christmas rush came earlier in the season. Then you had to deal with all the after-holiday sales, and before you knew it, it was time to advertise soft drinks and outdoor garden furniture.

Ralph flicked the light switch. In the fluorescent radiance, I could see that the break room was spotlessly clean.

"I'm impressed," I said, running my hand across a counter. It came up dust- and dirt-free. "I expected fingerprint powder and chalk marks, all kinds of things like you see in movies."

"Not a chance," Ralph said. "The janitorial service comes through around midnight, and I'll bet they cleaned it up. Not that there would be chalk marks. You're dating yourself, Jolie." By this time he had pulled open the cupboard doors. "What the hey?" he said, staring at the almost empty shelves.

"What?"

"Things are missing. The fancy tea that Donna Katherine collects for Chester is gone. All of it's gone." He opened the refrigerator; it was empty and clean. "Everything's gone. The police must've had some tea party in here yesterday."

Except it hadn't been held here. My guess was that the party took place at the lab where they looked for poison mixed in the tea tins. Most likely the search was still going on.

"Doesn't matter," I said. "I'll take whatever is available."

He handed me a brand-new, shrink-wrapped box of blackberry-flavored tea, and I proceeded to open it while he filled two cups with water and put them in the microwave.

"Did the police talk to you yesterday?" I asked.

"They tracked me down while I was in production at KVUE. I suppose it was unavoidable, but it was a bit embarrassing." His ears turned pink at the mention of it; most people would have complained loudly, maybe even rudely, but he wasn't that kind. "I thought about coming back here when Donna Katherine called," he went on, "but I felt like I had to stay. You know how it is. The station would have charged us for the studio time anyway, and you can't blame them. The biggest problem, though, was that I couldn't have rescheduled until tomorrow and then I'd only get an hour, not the whole day like I needed." He shook his head. "At least Sergeant Bohles came himself, and he wasn't in uniform."

"What do you think of him?"

"He seems competent."

"Except he didn't realize it was murder at first."

"But that's understandable. A young attractive woman dies at a big party? That scenario would indicate drugs to me, too."

I raised one eyebrow. "Oh?"

He looked embarrassed. "I was an MP in the service and I ended up doing a lot of investigative work."

"Really? I never knew that. And you gave it up when you got out of the military?"

"Sure. I never wanted to be a cop, and even worse is a private investigator. Who'd want to be one of those?"

I didn't admit it, but actually, I think I would. Or would have in my younger days. Not that thirty-nine is old, but I'm probably beyond the physical rigors of that profession.

By now I was dunking a tea bag in a cup that had an Austin Aqua Festival logo painted on it. The building was quiet, with only the creaks and groans that came with the cold winds outside. The break room was like a cozy retreat from the real world, and Ralph's presence was like the comfort of an older brother.

I took my tea and sat at the small table. "Ralph," I said, "what do you think of Desi's death?"

He spent some time formulating his answer while he pulled out a chair to join me. "It was a terrible thing," he said, when he finally sat down. "Desi Baker was a nice person."

Not the kind of in-depth response I'd been looking for. I wondered why he was being so vague. "Who do you think killed her?" I probed.

"I couldn't say." He became very busy pouring Equal and powdered creamer into his tea. Then he stirred, tasted, and poured some more.

"If you'd rather not talk to me—"

"It isn't that," he said, sniffing his tea as if it were a vintage wine. "I'd like to believe Desi's death was an accident. You know, she ate or drank something and had an allergic reaction."

"Wouldn't the police know that by now?"

"Probably."

"So you and Desi were friends?"

Ralph's eyes focused on something in the distance as he said,

"I thought very highly of Desi. She was the kind of young woman I want my daughters to grow up to be like." He looked at me. "Sorry, it's just not something I can talk about easily." He took a swallow of his drink.

"Of course, I understand." In the past year I'd lost someone I thought a great deal of, too. Actually, he'd been closer to Jeremy, but it had disrupted our world in ways I hadn't expected and gave me an empathy with Ralph and what he was going through. Still...he seemed more than just a little reticent on the subject of Desi.

"Tell me about the fairs that Rose Sterling has been handling," I said, just to keep the conversation going. "That holiday gift fair and the Spring Delights sound like fun. Were those your ideas?"

His face brightened as he said, "I had nothing to do with them, although my daughters spend a lot of money at them. Actually, it was Audry who thought of putting them on, as a way to boost revenue. They're a quick influx of cash, from what I understand. Thirty clients at a thousand dollars each is a nice chunk of change. Not that we keep it all. We have to pay for the space and cleanup, and some ad placement, but it's still fast profit."

"Audry handled those?"

"Actually, somehow Donna Katherine got involved about three years ago, and she did the last couple of years practically on her own. Oh, she'd hire an intern to help and Desi worked with her on the last two, but they were Donna Katherine's babies. She designed the flyers so they looked like hometown newspapers with articles on all of the sponsors; it was a nice concept. And she grew the events into what they are today. Our first fairs only had fifteen booths, and some of those were comps to radio stations and such. The last fairs were at least twice that. In fact, I think she squeezed thirty-five or forty booths into the show right before Christmas."

"That's a lot of work."

"You're right, but you know Donna Katherine."

Donna Katherine had always been known for her efficiency. Deposits were made and invoices went out with the precision of a military drill unit. Donna Katherine could find something as small as a penny missing from a bank statement. When I'd had a problem getting my own bank account to reconcile, Donna Katherine had sorted it out, and had straightened out the accounting people at my bank, all in less than a day; before I'd gone to her for help I'd been struggling with it for weeks. She might be loud, and she might be brash, but she had a work ethic that was enviable. Whatever it took to get the job done was what she put into it. I couldn't ever remember her taking a vacation.

I started to say something about her, but another of Ralph's comments suddenly struck me. Fast profit. And here we were, sitting alone in the coffee room, without another employee in the office because of the pared-down staff. There was more to that theme, too. At the party, Donna Katherine had said something about cutting back the guest list, as if it were a money-saving measure.

There had always been ups and downs in the agency's fortunes, and I assumed it was that way with any business. You lose clients, budgets get cut, expenses go up, and then there are those times when the workload is heavy and the bank account is flush. Obviously this past year had been off, and it appeared to be by quite a bit. Odd considering all the production we were handling now.

I wanted to ask Ralph about it, but he stood up and gestured toward the door. "Guess it's time to get after it. Are you ready?"

"Is there an option?" I asked, rising to my feet and taking my cup with me.

"You could just leave, but then I'd be writing copy while other people were opening their Christmas presents."

"Well, we can't let that happen, can we?"

I followed him back to his office, keeping one ear cocked toward the front door. In part I was hoping Nola would return—another part of me was tuned to Michael's arrival. I wasn't sure what I was going to say to him, but I felt I had to say something to clarify things.

Ralph was talking and I paid closer attention as he went over everything I'd done the day before. He was generous with his praise before he portioned out another stack of work for me to start on. I went back to Desi's cubicle and did just that.

I'd been writing for almost two hours, glazed eyes on the computer screen, the keys almost like extended appendages, when I was interrupted by a young man in the doorway. I had to blink several times before I could refocus enough to recognize him. He was one of the men who'd returned the office furniture and equipment the day before; he'd left while I talked to Amber at the front desk.

"Brought back one more," he said, holding out a cardboard file box. "Where do you want this?"

"Here, set it here," I said, sweeping things off the top of the cabinet. "Where did it come from?"

He swung the box over and put it down with a thump. "When we brought all the other furniture back, someone must of missed this one. There weren't supposed to be boxes, anyway, just furniture. It wasn't on the instructions, so don't let your redheaded friend in there think she can take more off the bill."

I don't deal with billing; never did, never will. "Well, have a Merry Christmas."

"Oh, yeah. You, too."

"One more thing," I said, and he turned around, his expression saying he had known this was coming. "Did the receptionist tell you to bring this to me?"

"No, she didn't say nothing about that. I just knew where I got it from."

I nodded. "Well, thanks again."

FIFTEEN

AFTER HE LEFT, I took the lid off the box. Four or five army green hanging files were lying flat on the bottom of it with an address book on top. More of Desi's things that were coming back to roost on my doorstep, just like her memory, adding to the subtle haunting that wouldn't release me.

I told myself how foolish I was being and turned to the more practical issue of the items in the box. Did the police need any of these?

Amber appeared in the doorway of the cubicle. "Uh, Jolie?"

I picked up the box and slid it back under the desk.

When I straightened up, I said, "Yes? What's up, Amber?"

Her eyes were wide. She said, "That policeman is here. He wants to talk to you. Again."

"Me?" And I thought of the note.

My stomach went into a tailspin. I'd almost forgotten about the note, or perhaps it would be more accurate to say I had conveniently repressed the memory of it. "Is it that big cop?"

"Uh-huh, that senior sergeant. He wants to see you."

This would be my third interview with Bohles. "Does he want to see me now?"

"Yeah, he said now."

Damn. There were too many things I didn't want to discuss with him. All those things that would lead him to my past relationship with Michael.

"Tell him I'll be right there."

"Sure, okay. No problem."

I slid on my jacket like some kind of protective armament and started after her. Bohles was waiting for me in the conference room. We finished with the niceties in a few short sentences, and when I was seated he began asking questions, covering the same ground we'd been over before. I might have been bored except for the little knot of fear that rested in the bottom of my stomach. It was coiled, waiting, just as I suspected that Bohles was waiting.

A couple more questions, and while Bohles didn't shift his large body, something about his eyes changed. They became tighter, more intense and focused, much like those of a bird of prey before an attack. He said, "Mrs. Wyatt, I've been going over your statement and I'm unclear about some things. The timing. Would you help me out?"

Only a fool would decline. "Yes, of course."

"Good. Is it correct that when you went into the ladies' room by the stairs, your first stop was a stall nearest the door?"

"Yes."

"After that you stopped to wash your hands and look in the mirror."

"Correct."

"You heard a noise near the door, went to it, and found the note from Michael Sherabian."

I was hardly breathing, so I merely nodded my agreement.

"Then you marched to the far end of the rest room, opened the handicapped door, and discovered Desi Baker."

"Yes." The word strangled in my throat.

"I see. Mrs. Wyatt, why did you walk to the handicap stall? Was there a sound? Was Ms. Baker alive? Did she do something to alert you to her presence?"

"Oh, no. I'm sure she was already dead." This was safe ground, territory I could easily tread. "I didn't do a lot to make sure, but I did feel for a pulse before I ran to get help. There was nothing, although her wrist was still warm."

"So you heard a sound near the door. You stepped around the wall, spotted a note that had been slid under the door. You picked it up and read it. You recognized Michael Sherabian's handwriting immediately, is that right?"

"Well, it took a second, but yes."

"Good. Then after reading the note, you crumpled it, pushed it down into the trash container, and then walked to the far end of the rest room, opened the handicapped door, and discovered Desi Baker. Is all of this accurate?''

"Yes. It's close."

"Where am I off? Explain it to me."

"No, I guess you have it all correct."

"Good. But none of it explains why you crumpled that note. Or why you walked to the far end of the bathroom."

I had no explanation—I merely stared at him. When that became impossible I lifted my shoulders and shook my head. "I don't know. I just did. And when I found her, I checked her pulse before I ran to get help."

He reached behind him on the desk and brought out the plastic Baggie with the note from Michael Sherabian.

He brought it up close to me so that I couldn't avoid the black pen strokes of Michael's writing. "Let me make sure I'm clear. This is the note, and you recognized the writing almost immediately?"

"Yes." I swallowed, my throat suddenly dry.

"And"—he paused—"you thought this note was for you, didn't you?"

"No, no."

"You crumpled it and threw it in the trash. Are you having an affair with Michael Sherabian?"

"No! The note was for Desi Baker. He was in love with her."

"Maybe. And maybe he was sleeping with you at the same time."

"That's crazy! I haven't been in Austin since last spring. I haven't seen Michael since I left the agency four years ago."

My voice was rising, and I was afraid it would become a hysterical wail. I stopped to breathe, to think. In my avoidance of the truth I had triggered an even worse suspicion. If I were to tell the whole truth right now, Bohles would have no reason to believe me, and he'd certainly try to verify anything I said with others at the agency. Everything would come out in the ugliest possible way. In desperation I said, "I'm very happily married."

Bohles continued to watch me, waiting for me to go on. I had no more to say.

After a time he nodded and said, "So tell me again how you found the note, and what you did after that."

As clearly as I could I told about hearing the sound near the door, finding the note, putting it in the trash, and discovering Desi Baker's body. The holes in my explanation were big enough to house a mausoleum.

"Again, please." His tone was deceptively gentle. He knew he had me.

I repeated my story. I still didn't say why I had walked to the back stall of the rest room, and I knew that was what he wanted to hear.

He asked me to tell it again. After that third telling he nodded. "Why did you throw away the note if you didn't think it was for you?"

I shook my head no.

"You won't tell me?"

"I, I don't know."

"Why did you go back to the handicap stall?"

There was nothing to do but shrug and look into those small intense eyes. He waited, stared, as if it were a game and he already knew he'd won. At last he said simply, "You can go."

I jumped up and almost fell over with the suddenness of it. "Thank you," I said, nearly running in my desire to be away from him. God, if only I had told the truth right away—but there was simply no way I could have. At the time I'd thought the note was for me, Matt had been there, and I hadn't wanted Matt to know about my past relationship with Michael Sherabian.

The phone was ringing as I hurried back into my cubby, and I grabbed it up as if it might transport me away from Bohles and Rose Sterling.

"Yes? This is Jolie."

"Aunt Dolie, come see us! We're playing."

Hearing Christopher's voice was like an invitation from another world.

"Christopher? Where are you?"

"At the Chirden's Museum. May you come and play? Here, Mommy wants to talk to you. 'Bye."

The phone banged against something before I heard Stephanie's voice. "Jolie?"

"I'm here."

"We're at the Children's Museum and we thought you might like to join us. It's just over on Fifth."

I glanced at my watch; it was after eleven-thirty. "I don't know that I'd be very good company—"

"Things pretty tense there?" she asked. Stephanie knew about the murder, but she wasn't aware of my personal link to it.

"Very," I said with more emphasis than I'd intended.

"Then this is exactly what you need, a hundred happy kids. Christopher begged me to call you. How about it? We can even have lunch later if you have the time."

I started to hedge some more and changed my mind. "I'd love to come over for a while. I doubt that I can take time for lunch, but a little break would be wonderful."

"Christopher will love it."

"I'll see you in a bit," I said as I hung up and reached for my purse.

I suspected the effect of the museum would be akin to the old veterinary cattle medicine, in that it would either "cure or kill in thirty minutes." Not that I thought I'd die from the noise and chaos, but if it didn't pull me out of my current mood, it would certainly send me screaming for the door, grateful to get back to the agency.

I hadn't taken more than five steps out of my cubicle when Bohles appeared. Stolidly he watched me, then gave me a non-committal nod, accompanied by a flat, "Mrs. Wyatt." As if he were the new hired gun in town and I was—

I wasn't sure what he thought I was, so I nodded in return. "Good-bye, Sergeant."

He stared a few moments more before he said, "I may need to talk to you again. At your convenience, of course."

"Sure. Fine. Whenever." I left the building on automatic pilot. My mind was a canyon and Bohles's words continued to echo back at me. *"I may need to talk to you again. At your convenience, of course. Why did you go back to the handicap stall? And maybe Michael Sherabian was sleeping with you...."*

Had I thought it would do any good, I would have put my hands over my ears and shut out Bohles's words and their damning implications.

The absolute worst was that I had no one to blame but myself. I was the one who had decided to come back to Rose Sterling for the party. Had it not been for my own vanity, I would be in Purple Sage, contentedly swearing about my job, or at my writing, or at the fluorescent light in my kitchen that intermittently flickers. I would be worrying about normal, everyday, sane things.

Instead I was here in Austin, worrying over things that should have been none of my business. Things that threatened my happiness in a subtle, insidious way.

I arrived at the Children's Museum in just minutes and found a parking spot in front. The entire complex is one large, flat stucco building that rambles around a series of semiopen hallways, all one level down from the parking lot. It houses not only the museum but a dance studio, the Austin Writers' League, a recording studio, and many other small offices, most of a creative or theatrical nature. I went down the outdoor steps and hurried into the open hallway, grateful for some protection from the cold wind.

Rather than the happy shrieks of children, the first thing I heard was Stephanie's voice; it was loud and angry as it reverberated through the barren halls.

"Damn it, you have to stop following me! Do you understand? Stay the hell away from us!" To my left was the door to the Children's Museum; Stephanie seemed to be down and around the corner to my right, but I couldn't be positive.

A man's voice responded to her, but I couldn't make out the words.

"Forget the justifications," Stephanie snapped back. "I've told you before, I want you to go away. I mean it. Now. Forever."

I'd determined she was somewhere to my right, and I was about to hurl around the corner to protect her from this intruder when she added, "And next time I'm telling everything. Do you understand? Every fucking thing!"

I stopped. This was someone she knew, and I wasn't sure I wanted to plunge into the midst of it; it also didn't sound like she needed me. With my coat wrapped tightly around me I edged nearer the museum door, just in case reinforcements were called for.

When the door eased open, I turned. Christopher was struggling to get out. "Aunt Dolie!"

"Christopher—" I helped him into the hallway, then bent down and gave him a hug. "How are you, little bug?"

"I'm fine. Where's my mommy?"

"I'm right here." Stephanie rounded the corner briskly, her face pinched and tight. I waited for the other person to follow her, but no one did.

"Are you okay?" I asked.

She flashed me a quick nod as she shooed us inside. "I was just in the bathroom. And, Christopher, you were supposed to stay in the museum. You can't go running off like that." She moved us both around the corner of the gift shop, and bent down to lecture him. "I mean this, and I want you to listen; it's important. A bad person could get you."

"I found Aunt Dolie—"

"Yes, you were lucky, but I want your promise that in the future you will stay just where I tell you to. Promise me."

He looked into her eyes, raised his hand, and said, "I promise."

"Thank you."

There were things going on here that I didn't understand. We do live in a world that is hazardous to children. The statistics are enough to frighten any parent: when children are abducted, they will never make it home alive unless they do something to free themselves. It makes sense to teach our kids ways to fight back, or at least protect themselves, but Stephanie's fears seemed rooted in a more immediate threat. My concern was, how immediate? And how dangerous?

I wanted to ask questions, but before I could formulate any, Stephanie stood up and said to Christopher, "So where do you want to go?"

"I know!" Christopher said, in a quick mood shift from the solemn promise he'd just made. "Let's play in the music room." He grabbed my hand and pulled me farther into the museum. "Hurry, Aunt Dolie, they have a whole bunch of stuff. You'll like it..."

"Just a minute, I think I have to pay—"

Stephanie said, "You two go ahead, I'll take care of it."

"Good plan!" Christopher said, tugging me forward.

I went with him, but I couldn't help myself from turning around, just on the off chance that I would see the person Stephanie had been arguing with. Through the glass doors I glimpsed the hallway, but, it was empty. Stephanie saw my glance, and waved us on as if nothing had happened.

SIXTEEN

CHRISTOPHER BALKED as we loaded him into his car seat. He had played hard and run us hard as well, so now we were all showing signs of wear.

"Christopher, stop wiggling!" Stephanie snapped.

He slapped at the webbing as Stephanie pulled it over his head. "It's too tight! I told you, Mommy, it hurts me."

"And I told you that it doesn't hurt, and you have to wear it. It's a law, Christopher."

"Here, I have an idea." I jumped in and pulled at the underside to release the belt some, giving him an inch of breathing space. "It's the heavy coat—they take up so much room."

Stephanie looked annoyed. "Thank you. Now, Christopher, it's fixed; time to go home and take a nap."

"I want pizza! You said pizza."

"You can have soup at Grandma Prissy's and then you have to sleep. You're tired and you're cranky. You haven't been sleeping."

"Mommy—"

Before there was a full-scale outbreak, I leaned in and kissed Christopher. "I'll bring you pizza for dinner if you take a good long nap." I noticed Stephanie's scowl. "And if your mommy says it's okay."

Here in the gray light of the parking lot Stephanie's face looked drawn. Christopher wasn't the only one who was tired.

She shrugged. "Pizza's fine. Whatever."

I touched her arm. "Steph, look, I know it's none of my business, but it's apparent something's going on. You know I'm here for you and Matt, too. If there's anything we can do to help, we'll do it."

The sun broke free of the clouds and she blinked at the sudden brightness. For just a moment she looked relieved, perhaps expectant, as if we really could make things better, then something in her face shuttered and she flashed a determined smile. "I appreciate that," she said, turning to make sure the buckle had caught on Christopher's seat belt, "but everything's fine. Really. Except—" She stopped, and waved away her irritation. "Never mind. Okay, Christopher, time to go. Give Aunt Jolie a kiss."

Which meant I had to lean in and kiss Christopher good-bye, giving Stephanie a chance to get in the driver's seat and start the car. It was an effective escape method.

"We'll see you tonight," she said over her shoulder. "Don't hurry home on our account; we'll be napping until at least five-thirty." She put the car in gear.

"Have a nice rest." I closed the door; Christopher was already nodding off, and Stephanie was anxious to be on her way. Which left me with another load of concern and unanswered questions. Maybe I would detour by the mall on the way back and ask Santa if he could bring solutions instead of presents this year.

MATT CALLED about three-thirty. My mind cleared, I had eaten a sandwich for lunch, and plunged back into work afterward. There was no need to rush back to Prissy's house with everyone else already occupied. Prissy had gone off with Todd to do some last-minute shopping; Jeremy was out cruising the city with Alicia acting as tour guide and chauffeur, while Stephanie and Christopher were sleeping. I hadn't known where Matt was until I picked up the phone.

"You were among the missing," I said.

Matt's normally easygoing voice sounded tense. "No, I'm not missing. I've been working on Austin Edge. How is your day going?"

"Does the term 'like crap' ring any familiar bells?"

Instead of laughing, he responded with a terse, "Yes. That's how mine feels, too."

Not what I had expected. "Sounds serious. Can you talk?"

"A little." I heard phone rustles as if Matt were repositioning himself. "I'm at the CPAs right now, and we've found some financial irregularities that need to be straightened out. If we can get it done by tomorrow, then Trey will come back up here and address the management team with me. If not, it's going to have to wait until after the first of the year."

"I'm sorry." Matt is wonderful at both the financial end of business and dealing with people, but this didn't sound easy regardless of his skills. "Are you saying someone was embezzling money from the company?"

"Not outright; as of yet I'm not even sure what they've done is illegal. That's part of what has to be determined, and I'm meeting with some lawyers tomorrow morning. Apparently the management staff took out loans against the capital, and then used the capital to give themselves perks and bonuses. In effect, it gutted the company financially."

"Do they know you're on to them?"

"Not yet." The words sounded as hard as an ax hitting bone. "I may bring some of this home to work on, if you don't mind."

I had intended to talk to him about Stephanie, but it wasn't the time. "Whatever's best is fine with me. I'm just sorry this is going on."

"Me, too. I'll see you tonight."

"Okay. I love you."

"You, too," he said as we hung up.

I plopped down into my chair—Desi's chair—and my feet kicked at the box I'd tucked under there. I tapped my fingers on the keyboard and stood back up. As my friend Liz Street would say, "The vibes were all wrong." There didn't seem to be any peaceful haven this holiday season—no place where I could stop, relax, and simply enjoy. Everywhere I went, every which way I turned, there seemed to be undercurrents of trouble.

The atmosphere at Prissy's was especially distressing because it involved people I loved. Stephanie could protest all she liked, but there was something wrong in her life. There had to be if she was being followed.

I rubbed my stiff shoulders and took a new position in the chair.

Maybe my mood was all from unbalanced hormones; it was an encouraging thought, but unless menopause was striking ridiculously early, it wasn't true. What I needed was to get Stephanie alone and get her to talk. Or perhaps Prissy had some idea what was going on.

I fretted for a while, tapping the keyboard until a line of *j*'s appeared on the screen. Had Matt been there, he would have told me unless there was something I could do at that moment to solve the problem, my worrying wasn't helping her or me. Matt gives great advice, and sometimes I take it to heart, changing my outlook completely. At other times it merely leaves me more frustrated and wanting to clobber him.

Desi was grinning down at me from her picture on the wall, the one taken on top of the mountain. Today her smile seemed to hold more dare than triumph. It seemed personal, as if directed at me.

I jumped out of the chair and reached toward the box under the desk. Just touching the rippled cardboard made me nervous, and rather than pull it out, I left it where it was and started through the agency to see who was where.

"Everything okay, Jolie?" Ralph asked as I passed his office.

"Fine. Just stretching." I slowed. "I thought you were going to The Production Block?"

He looked at his watch. "I don't have to leave for another few minutes."

"How's the newsletter coming?"

"Very s-l-o-w-l-y. This computer barely has enough memory, so if I get too many pages opened at once, the whole thing locks up on me and I have to shut it down and start over." He made a crashing sound in his throat and aimed a karate chop at the air just above the computer. "My kingdom, such as it is, for more RAM."

"I'm sorry I asked."

"I should have this finished by tonight. If not, I'm quitting my job and moving to the outback."

"Out back of your house?"

His grin was rueful. "That's about all I'll be able to afford."

"I won't keep you, then. See you later."

I kept moving. The place was like an abandoned ship; there were two empty cubicles before I found another human, and that was Fred, the graphic artist. He was hunched over his drawing board making tiny marks on a poster for a local bed and breakfast.

"How's it going?" I asked, lingering in the doorway.

Fred started, clutching his shirt near the region of his heart. "I was concentrating."

"I'm sorry, I didn't mean to startle you."

"That's okay, come on in."

"I'm Jolie Wyatt; I don't know if we've officially met. I'm writing copy and I used to work here."

"I know." He held out his square hand and his shirtsleeve pulled up to reveal a woven copper bracelet tarnished with patches of green; I wondered if it really did help arthritis, as I'd heard it was supposed to.

As we shook hands he said, "I used to work for Mickie Bellah Advertising when you were here. We pitched a couple of accounts against you."

"Did we win or lose?"

"A little of both."

"Well, that's good, I suppose." I stared at him a moment longer. "Oh, yes. I remember, you were, uh, uh, the artist." The word *artist* was in lieu of what had almost slipped out; I'd been about to say he'd been slimmer, and when I realized that was unacceptable I couldn't think of anything to replace it except younger, or cleaner-looking. I vetoed all three.

"Right." He laughed, as if he suspected what had been on my mind.

I moved closer to the drawing table. "I didn't see you at the party the other night."

"I was out a week for the holidays," he said, as he turned back to his work, shading in a pale green on the stalk of an iris. "Missed the whole thing."

"You must have celebrated early."

He looked up. "Hanukkah. I'm Jewish."

"Oh, damn. I mean, of course." I was beginning to bumble like Nola. "I'm sorry, I live in a small town now and it's so firmly fundamental I forget there is anything else. That's what happens when you move off to the Hill Country."

"No biggie. But don't tell my mom." He smiled and he looked both younger and happier. "I'm trying to talk her into moving to Fredericksburg."

"She'll love it. How was your vacation?"

He laid down the green pencil and picked up a lavender one, which he used to shade the tip of the flower. "I don't know if I'd call it a real vacation." He shook his head and turned to face me. "Ten full days at my mom's house in Cleveland was a lot of time; I mean, I could have gone on a cruise to Alaska with all that time."

"But I'll bet you made your mom happy."

"Yeah. I did." He grinned as he tugged at the shark's tooth around his neck. "She say's I'm a good boy."

"You see? Now, there's an endorsement."

"For what it's worth. Except I really wish I'd been here."

"May I?" I asked, gesturing to a tall stool opposite him.

"Sure."

As I sat down I said, "Why? Too much work when you got back?"

"No. Because..." His face grew long and sad. "I didn't get to say good-bye to Desi. Desi Baker. I guess you didn't know her."

How could I explain she was a specter haunting my office? "I heard her speech about Chester. It was very effective."

"Was it? I'm glad. She was nervous about that speech. She practiced it with me a couple of times before I left." He stared out the window. Then he said, "How'd she look in her black dress?"

"Gorgeous."

He nodded and smiled. "Yeah, I knew she would. She was tellin' me about that dress; she'd bought it special for the party. She was pumping weights a lot and eating special stuff so she'd look extra hot. Crazy kid. She was a knockout anyway, but she just didn't get it.'' He shook his head, for once looking straight at me. ''I miss her. She was a real different kind of person, if you know what I mean. And honest. If I asked her something she didn't want to tell me, she'd just say, 'Fred, there are some things I can't talk about.' Like about her mom. Or one time this fall she was real stressed, and she never did tell me what it was about. She just wasn't the kind to cry on anyone's shoulder. I like that in a woman.'' He shook his head as if to shake away the memory.

His next thought was brighter. ''Oh, and she did funny stuff. Like she dressed up as a pumpkin for Halloween, and went around the building giving out apples and oranges. That was really nice, you know?'' His grin faded and his face aged in the process. ''And then some asshole comes along and kills her.''

I nodded, thinking again how unfair life can be. And death. ''At least she was happy about getting to write copy. Wasn't she?''

''Oh, yeah, she was real happy. Man, she hated that accounting stuff, but it was the only job she could get in advertising. It's tough right now.''

''I've heard.''

''It wasn't until about a month ago that she got to change jobs, and she was like a little kid, she was so excited. It wasn't because she couldn't do the accounting; she could. Desi worked hard at it, you know? She was just that way. Real hardworking, straight-arrow kind of person. Like she was John Wayne inside. But female and hip. Didn't smoke, was a vegetarian, worked out all the time. A real straight arrow.''

My brain was busy digesting all this new information on Desi Baker. ''I guess I'd better get back to work....'' I said, sliding off the stool and moving toward the doorway.

''Yeah, me, too. But hey, thanks for listening to me.'' He appeared sheepish. ''I didn't mean to dump on you like that, but Desi, she affected people. I guess she got to me, too.''

''That's okay. And I do understand, because I've been affected by her, too.'' I waved and started down the hall toward the front office, trying to fit these new facets of Desi's character into the picture I already had. I'd made some assumptions about her and now I had to question them.

"Whoops, excuse me." Ralph whizzed past me carrying a battered briefcase and a folder of copy. "See you tomorrow. Half day—your last day, I promise."

Before I could say good-bye the tree ornaments clattered and he was gone.

Who did that leave in the building? The Sherabians? Donna Katherine? Nola?

When I reached the front office Amber had the receiver to her ear taking a message, and Donna Katherine was standing in front of the desk, tapping her foot, like a mother waiting for her teenager to get off the phone.

"Leaving early?" I asked. Donna Katherine was wrapped in a full-length coat and carrying her big black leather purse.

"Christmas shopping. I swear, I haven't had a day off in years, so I'm heading out now. I'll be back in the morning." She jerked a thumb in Amber's direction. "Tell her when she gets off the phone, will ya?"

"Sure. Have fun."

"Fun? Darlin', this is going to be like rounding up livestock at the rodeo. A timed event. I don't have even seconds to spare if I'm going to get everything done before Christmas!" Then she whipped out.

Amber thanked the caller and hung up. "I don't know why Donna Katherine thinks I'm deaf if I'm on the phone. I heard every word she said. They probably heard her in Louisiana!"

"Then you know she's out."

"Right."

"So where's everybody else?" I asked. "This place is like a—a library."

Amber counted off the staff on her fingers. "Chester went to a thing at the Headliners Club, Nola is working out of her house because now James has the flu, and the Sherabians are looking at new office space." She scrunched up her face and then smiled weakly. "I didn't say that, okay?"

"Didn't say what?"

"Thanks."

New office space. Smaller offices? Probably, and most likely in a less expensive building.

I hated that things were so rough, not so much for Audry or Michael, but for Chester. He and his wife, Rose Sterling, had built this agency from a little mom-and-pop shop that consisted of a typewriter and a copier on their kitchen table, to a viable and respected agency. They'd weathered the economic storms of the eighties, which made it especially unfair that they were facing trouble in Austin's affluent nineties.

While Amber took another call I thought about that. Beyond unfair, it seemed odd. The agency should have been prospering, especially with their experienced staff. There were ways an advertising agency could get in trouble, but they seemed unlikely with Chester at the helm. Underbidding jobs or undercharging for work could cause problems, but you caught those mistakes and corrected them; you didn't continue them until the business faltered. Bad debts could also hurt, but Rose Sterling had a pretty solid client base, at least from what I'd seen. Most of the businesses had been around a long time and were fiscally responsible. They paid their bills, something that's considered a nice quality in a client.

I thought about what Matt had said, management borrowing against capital and using the money on themselves. There were only two people in the agency in a position to do that—Audry and Michael. I found it hard to believe they would do that to Chester. Sort of.

"Are you leaving or what?" Amber asked, punching a phone button with finality and putting down the receiver.

"No, just taking a breather. I was beginning to feel permanently hunched over the computer, like a mannequin in a store window."

"I saw a movie like that once."

"Sounds like science fiction—I only write mysteries."

Amber made a sad little face and said, "Like Desi's murder. That's a mystery." Her eyes reddened as if she might start crying again.

"There are a lot of mysteries around here," I said, intending to distract her, then realized how suspicious it sounded.

"Oh, yeah? Like what?"

I had to think up an answer. "Why the copier is always out of paper just when I need to use it." That got a weak smile out of her. "Why it never rains until it's time to go home."

"Yeah, I know about those. Like, why I always get a zit just before a big date." The phone buzzed and Amber reached for it. "Rose Sterling Advertising." After a short pause, "Oh, hi, Mom. What's up?"

I turned away to give her privacy.

Outside the tinted windows the winter sky looked ominously dark, while inside, the agency was almost empty, the kind of quiet that creates intimacy. I looked back at Amber, who was saying into the receiver, "Of course, I'm fine. A little depressed, but I told you all that last night. No, I don't think I'll get there in time for dinner. Probably not until seven or so."

Today Amber was dressed in black with burgundy lipstick and fresh nail polish. Her straight hair was clean and shiny as if she'd made the effort to pull herself together.

I wondered if she was strong enough to talk about Desi. Something was bothering me, and Amber was probably one of the few people in the agency who could explain it to me.

"Okay. Okay. Sure; I'll see you Christmas Eve. 'Bye. Okay, Mom. 'Bye." She put the receiver back.

"Amber," I said, wondering if I was doing the right thing, "there's something about Desi I don't quite understand. Would it be hard for you to talk a little about her? Just to help me on this?"

She looked puzzled and bit her lip. "Yeah, I guess I can. What is it?"

I paused to phrase my question delicately so as not to distress her. "I've heard some people say that Desi was very straight. Honest—"

"She was. That's exactly the way Desi was. I mean, she would tell you the truth no matter what." She gestured with her hands as if trying to make the picture of Desi clear enough for me to visualize. "Like this one time, she saw this kid, and he was like a big kid, you know, maybe fifteen or sixteen. She saw him steal some stuff from a store, and she grabbed him and said that either he could put it back, or she was calling the police and the store manager." Amber rested her hands on the desk, shaking her head in amazement. "He could have pulled a knife or something, but Desi said it was important that he knew he'd been caught. And I said she could have called the police, but she wanted the kid to have a chance to make restitution. That was important to her."

Straight arrow and moral. Although that was with a stranger.

I asked, "How was she with people she knew?"

Amber answered instantly. "The same. Honest. Last year I was going out with this guy, and he was real scum, but I didn't know it. Well, Desi saw him out with another girl. Even though she didn't want to hurt my feelings, she told me because she thought I needed to know." Amber lifted her shoulders in a gesture of resolution. "She was just that way. She said I should date people of a higher caliber."

Which brought me right where I wanted to be. I reached for the stapler and picked it up, opening and closing it casually, as if to make my words less important. "So tell me, who was Desi dating recently?"

SEVENTEEN

"DESI USED TO BE MARRIED. Did I tell you that before?"

"I think you mentioned it."

Amber nodded solemnly, her fingers tugging on a lock of hair that swung forward. "He was a pilot for some airline. They divorced about three years ago. Bastard." She leaned forward to add, "He was one. A bastard. She never came right out and said it, but I think he used to hit her. He'd be like gone on a trip, and then he'd come home and accuse her of fooling around."

The heat in the building suddenly came on. "I'm sorry for Desi. He must have been a jealous man."

"A horrible man," she corrected. "I mean Desi wouldn't do something like that, so he couldn't have known her very well, and he was gone a lot, anyway. But from what she said he was older, you know? And here he had this young beautiful wife—well." She shrugged.

Trophy wife, like Stephanie. I wondered if Desi would have been considered a trophy for Michael. While he was older, it wasn't by that many years, and he was simply incredibly handsome, which seemed to alter the circumstances.

"Some women like older men," I said. "Apparently Desi was one of them."

"Not after that," Amber said. "She didn't like older men at all anymore. Except for friends, like Fred, who's kind of strange, but really a nice guy." She jerked her thumb to indicate his not-too-distant cubicle. "But she wouldn't go out with those kinds of men. She said you should only date younger guys, because then you could train them right." This time Amber laughed. "Only I was dating an eighteen-year-old, and Desi said maybe I had gone too far. Then I was going out with—"

"Wait." I held up my hand to stop her, and my own confused

thoughts. "I'm sorry, I was getting lost. You said that Desi only liked younger men, but she wasn't actually dating any, was she?"

Amber pulled on the blond lock again and thought about the question. "Sure. Well, no. Not now. Last summer she was dating two guys; one was some kind of engineer at some computer company. Real cute guy; I can't remember his name, but I think he was about my age. I'm twenty-three. And then there was Rudy. He was older, well, older of the younger ones, maybe twenty-eight, only Desi couldn't get serious about him. I'm pretty sure he moved to L.A. around Halloween."

The thought of the cardboard box under my desk tickled my brain. That was now a more potent pull. So I hurried the conversation.

"Amber, was Desi dating anyone recently?"

She didn't have to think about that. "No. She had some guys who asked her out, but Desi could afford to be picky, because she was really beautiful, and she had that great bod. In fact, she was taking something new to pump up her muscles; it was kind of like"—she rolled her eyes—"far out, and she was going to tell me about it—"

"I heard she was going out with an older man."

"You did?" Amber stopped and cocked her head to the side. "How old?"

"Thirty-eight."

"Ooh, that's just icky!"

"I heard he worked here at the agency, too."

For a moment she looked like an angry child, and I half expected her to jump up and stomp her foot. "I sure would like to know who's badmouthing Desi that way! I heard that rumor, too, that she was going out with Michael Sherabian, but beside the fact that he's too old for her, he's married. Desi wouldn't do that!"

"I'm sure you're right."

But who can say what any of us would really do? Matt would probably swear that I wouldn't date a married man, either. Even one who was separated from his wife.

I looked at Amber, knowing that these were lessons she would learn somewhere along the way, just like the rest of us. It wouldn't help to tell her, she wouldn't listen. I did give her a hint. "Sometimes life isn't the way we think it ought to be."

"Yeah," she said, then added, "Death isn't much of a picnic either."

I was torn between laughing and patting her hand in sympathy. Neither felt appropriate, so I glanced at my watch. "Guess I'd better get back to work."

Amber was staring intently out the front door as I left; I couldn't begin to guess what she was thinking. I, on the other hand, had a very focused thought and it was finally time to act on it.

Back in the office I shared with Desi's memory, I pulled out the cardboard box and put it on top of the desk. Once the lid was off, I peered inside. It appeared to me that Desi had packed the bottom of the box carefully, then at the last minute, shoved in those things that might get lost somewhere else. There was the small brown teddy bear that probably sat on her computer. I put it aside. As my skin made contact with the fuzzy body I thought for the first time about fingerprints. They weren't going to appear on the bear, but they would show up on any of the paper I touched.

While it felt silly, I got my leather gloves from my coat pocket. They were tight-fitting, and in other circumstances, not too clumsy. I just hoped no one would see me digging in the box with them on.

After one more peek into the empty hallway, I went back to my exploration. I removed a small bag of red jelly beans that Desi had tucked away, no doubt to avoid temptation. A wrapped present with a tag that said it was for Amber was next; I would let the police deal with that. There were two bottles of nail polish, a bottle of glue, a wrist brace like those used to avoid carpel tunnel, some blank postcards from various cities in Colorado, a stapler, a porcelain pitcher with eight or nine pens and pencils, and a basket containing potpourri. None of it seemed important. This was simply the stuff she'd had on top of her desk or file cabinet, and had ended up throwing it all in a box for safe storage.

Even surmising that, I handled everything as gingerly as possible, touching as little of each surface as I could.

Next came the hanging folders, and while not as interesting to look at, they were more intriguing to me. After all, words are my life, and they were Desi's, too.

Touching only the edges, I went through the papers, careful to keep them in order. The first file was overstuffed with a hodge-podge of old commercial copy. Some of the radio scripts covered end-of-summer sales, and there was one for a spring closeout. By rifling through I discovered that most were over six months old. I suspected what I had just found was Desi's filing. That had been my job when I'd first started as a copywriter, and as I remembered, they'd saddled me with almost six months worth of stuff that no one else had bothered to put away. I set the whole stack back in the folder. I wasn't going to file it either.

The next folder was labeled Planned Purchases. There were maybe eight pieces of paper inside. On top was an order form from an herb company. There was a page torn out of a magazine that showed a model wearing a short, lime green skirt with a skinny white T-shirt. There was a catalog from one of those specialty houses; one page was dog-eared and on it were various types of decorative fire logs and fireplace accessories. Desi's new apartment must have a fireplace.

There was also an ad for an Exercycle and a catalog with personalized stationery. My mind went nuts making up all kinds of stories about that. Was Desi planning on getting married? Was she looking for new thank-you notes with her married name? As I flipped through the catalog I found a circle around some return-address labels. New apartment, new address, new labels.

The third folder was simply marked Fun Stuff. There were cartoon clippings from half a dozen strips ranging from Garfield to Cathy. There were E-mails with jokes. There were Crash Jet advertising slogans: *First with nonstop flights into the Grand*

Canyon. I found lawyer jokes: *"As medical examiner, how many autopsies would you say you have performed on dead people?" "I would say I have performed all my autopsies on dead people."* Even a sheet labeled Philosophical Sayings: *Eat a toad first thing in the morning and nothing worse will happen to you all day.* The eclectic bits of trivia that every office collects. At least mine always does.

By this time I was wondering if I could make some copies so I could share the humorous items with my friends back in Purple Sage. I was beyond hope of finding anything that might point to Desi's murderer, but not quite ready to put everything away. As I picked up the next page, it slipped between my gloved hands and floated toward the floor. The print on it was slightly fuzzed and curved as if it had been photocopied from a book. I picked it up and was about to flip it aside when a word in the heading caught at me. *Mistletoe.*

My brain went on red alert.

It was a portion of a chapter about how mistletoe as a food could be a foundation for any bodybuilding routine. *"...The study showed that mistletoe when taken in large quantities acted as a natural hormone...helped build muscle rapidly...burned fat... turned into essential proteins to rebuild cells damaged from environmental factors and poor eating habits."*

I couldn't believe anyone had written such a thing! It was wrong, flat wrong. Mistletoe was a poison. Everyone knew that; certainly anyone who grew up in this part of the country. I grabbed the dictionary from the side drawer and flipped to *M*. I was sure I was right.

The dictionary said mistletoe was a parasitic evergreen with waxy berries. There were also two mentions of its uses in certain customs, one being for kissing at Christmastime, while the other was in Druid ceremonies. There was nothing about its poisonous qualities. It didn't prove a thing.

Still outraged, I set the paper aside; I was going to do some further research on the subject as soon as I finished with the box. The next piece of paper was a copy of an article on mistletoe torn from a newspaper. On the photocopy the ragged edges showed up like the dark outlines of a map. It said that scientists at Sloan Kettering in New York had discovered that this common parasitic plant, "once thought to be poisonous," actually did a number of beneficial things for the human body. "Mistletoe increases the metabolism, burning unwanted calories even while the body is at rest." Additionally the story said it was a muscle builder. There were several paragraphs more, including research statistics and some very impressive reasons to eat mistletoe if you wanted to strengthen and build muscles quickly, with less workout time and less concern about caloric intake.

My brain continued to fight against accepting these purported facts. Mistletoe grew like the parasite it was on half the trees on our property, and while it looked festive, it was nonetheless poisonous. I had researched mistletoe for a manuscript, and according to every source I had checked, including the Poison Control Center, mistletoe could be lethal.

So where had these articles come from? And why were they here?

The answer began to filter slowly through my anger. These articles might induce anyone, even Desi Baker, to drink mistletoe tea. What a perfect way to commit murder, and how insidious.

I picked up all three sheets of paper and held them close to my chest as I whipped through the hall to the copy room. The police needed to see these, but I wanted my own copies first.

As I placed the sheets in the automatic feeder, I realized that if I were caught, I was going to have a hell of a time explaining just what I was doing. Especially with gloves on.

The machine whirred and a light told me to wait while it warmed up.

I waited. I breathed. I worried.

The light went off and I pressed the button for one copy. With the slickness of modern technology, the machine clamped down all three pieces of paper, and whisked one off the bottom to send it into the entrails of the machine where magic would take place and a copy would be made. The moving light spilled out from the flat tray on top, and then a paper ejected from the side of the machine. It was my copy and I grabbed it up and flipped it over, putting the original facedown beside it.

By this time my heart was pounding as if I had been eating mistletoe with the results predicted from the articles.

While I waited the machine stopped its work and a new light flashed. *Original jammed.*

My gloves caught on the metal as I pulled open the front of the machine and stared into its bowels. Damn thing—where was that paper? With great haste I pulled out a metal rack, looked behind it, and shoved it back in. I shut the door with a snap. Work now, damn it.

But the machine refused to operate and the light flashed again. *Original jammed.*

Original, original. Not the copy!

I lifted the lid of the feeder and saw my original stuck in a white belt.

"Son of a—"

I pulled it out, placed it facedown on the glass, closed the lid, and hit the start button again. The familiar whir started up, and the light began to move.

The heat came on, blowing from an air duct above me. It was totally unnecessary since I was already sweating. There was also a tear in my good gloves. That would teach me to dig in copy machines, except I knew it wouldn't.

My second copy ejected and then the third; I practically fought the machine for the paper as I ripped it out of the feeder. I counted the copies and the originals twice. Three of each. Then I ran back to Desi's office.

Once there, I couldn't even stop to breathe. What I had found could be important to the police investigation. These could be the very leads that would take them to her murderer. There were two more files in the bottom of the box; one was labeled AbScan. I flipped it open and found a fact sheet for writing copy. Something about a computer company here in Austin. The next folder contained a couple of invoices. The top one was a November bill for

Stuff 'N Puff in the amount of two thousand dollars. I was beyond reading anything more.

I began putting things away in the box, just exactly as I remembered they had been. The fun-stuff file went in on top of AbScan and the invoices, with the mistletoe stories last in the file. On top of them went the jokes, and finally the cartoons. I closed the file, sucked in air, and stacked the planned-purchases folder and the old commercials on top.

My hands were actually shaking, something that rarely happened to me, as I hastily deposited everything else in the box and replaced the lid.

I was trying to get the gloves off my sweaty hands, my teeth clenched on the tips of the right-hand fingers, when Amber walked in.

"Did you hear someone running in the hall?" she asked.

"Uh..." I took my teeth off the glove. "Yes. That was me. I was leaving, but then I remembered something."

"Oh, yeah? What?"

Like everyone ran through the hall with their gloves on. My hands were feeling claustrophobic, and I grabbed the fingers again and ripped it off.

"Damn, it's hot in here," I said, pulling the second glove off.

"It's always that way. Or cold. I think some gremlin in the basement controls the temperature."

Actually there was a thermostat in Audry's office, but I didn't have the patience to explain heating and cooling.

"Listen," I said, trying to gesture casually to the box that now sat innocently on the desk. "Some guy brought this back this morning. He said it was Desi's."

She nodded in agreement. "Oh, yeah, I remember."

"Well, I think we need to call the police and have them pick it up. They took some of her other things. They will probably want this, too."

"You really think so? What's in it?" She pulled the lid off before I could stop her.

"No! Don't touch anything." I grabbed the lid out of her hand

and replaced it. "I'm sorry; I didn't mean to yell. It's just that there could be fingerprints, and you don't want to mess them up. Or add yours."

She brought her hand up to her mouth as if it had been burned. "Oh, wow, I didn't even think about that. You better call that Sergeant Bohles. I'll buzz you with his number."

"Why don't you make the call?"

She pointed to her watch. "It's five o'clock. I leave at five."

EIGHTEEN

"SO THE BOX WAS DELIVERED by some man, and you don't know his name or the name of the company he works for."

It's the details of life that will trip you up every time. I had thought Bohles would find me a hero, but instead he was asking questions I couldn't answer. I began to wonder if he suspected me of filling the box myself, just to move his suspicions elsewhere.

"Sorry. I'm sure if Amber had stayed, she could tell us. Or Donna Katherine. I could have them call you in the morning."

He shook his head as he eyed the box carefully, then removed the lid. "You think this was some extra stuff that was in Desi Baker's office?"

"Right." I had expected him to heave the box up on one large shoulder and walk out with it first thing. Instead he dawdled. He asked how things were going and if Desi had left behind a lot of work. He wanted to know if she had been any good at her job. Interesting questions that I would have preferred to answer at another time.

Without seeming to touch things, he rearranged the contents of the box so that he could flip open the folders with a pencil. "These are commercials, right?"

I peered in as if I hadn't seen them before. "Yes. We call that copy."

He went through a dozen or more sheets of paper, lifting them so I could see what was printed on each one, and what was underneath. "Why do you think she put them here?" he asked.

"Well," I said, "I think that copy should have been filed and she didn't get around to it."

"Like hiding the laundry?"

"Something like that."

He opened the next file, and we looked through the planned purchases, both of us peering into the box. When he got to the lime green skirt he made a sound, something soft and unhappy. I looked up to find that he was shaking his head sadly. Without my asking he said, "She had a skirt just like that in her closet. Still had the tags on it."

"Oh." Before his comment, Desi Baker had become like a new pen pal to me—someone I was just getting to know and whose messages I enjoyed very much. Now I remembered the reality of the situation.

Bohles opened the next file. I tensed in anticipation of what we were to find; it was like knowing the scary part of a movie was coming, but pretending you hadn't seen the film before.

"That's great." He was grinning openly at one of the cartoons and he looked up to share the laughter with me. I tried my best to laugh, at least to grin, but the skin on my face felt too tight to let the muscles move naturally. I grimaced instead, hoping he'd buy that.

Next were the jokes and finally the articles on mistletoe. His eyes moved quickly to capture my response. I felt my stomach quiver. "Mistletoe." I breathed the word; my voice sounded sick.

It must have struck him as a natural reaction, because he went back to scanning the article, frowning as he did. "You ever read anything like this on mistletoe?" he asked.

"Never." I shook my head, vehemently. "I think I read it was supposed to prevent abortions, or maybe cause them. But I've always heard it's poisonous, especially in large doses." I stepped back away from the box, as if disavowing any association with what it held. "What about you?" I pointed but kept my distance. "Have you heard anything like that?"

He shrugged a big shoulder. "I leave all that to the experts." He slipped over the next two articles and went directly to the last green hanging folder. "What's AbScan? Do you know?"

I peeked into the box, then back up at Bohles. "It's a computer company here in Austin, isn't it?"

"Sounds right; that's probably where I've heard of them. Are they a client?"

I shook my head. "Not that I know of. Of course, I don't know all their clients anymore. And it could have been a pitch they made that they lost. It happens." With three or four agencies going up for every account, it happens on a regular basis. You get used to losing, although it's never enjoyable. I started to add something more, but Bohles was again poking in the box.

"Why would she have invoices?" he asked.

"I don't know." The telephone rang, the sound echoing from several phones around the agency. I hit the speaker option and said, "Rose Sterling Advertising."

"Hi, Aunt Dolie!"

"Well, Christopher, how are you?"

"I'm very hungry. May you bring my pizza?"

"Oh, no!" I looked at my watch; five-twenty. "I'm sorry, sweetie, I'm running a little late. Let me talk to your mommy, okay? I'll have it delivered right to your door. You could eat some fruit while you're waiting."

"I don't eat fruit. Here's Mommy."

"Sorry," Bohles said to me, as if he were responsible for my neglect of Christopher. He began putting everything back in its place. "I didn't mean to keep you."

Stephanie's voice sounded less strained than earlier. "Forgot us, huh? Christopher never forgets."

"I got tied up. How about if I order pizza, or you do that, and I'll be home in time to pay for it. Would that work?"

"Actually, I already ordered it. Take your time." She was definitely her mother's daughter; well organized and still silly enough to call and give me a hard time just for the fun of it. Actually, that reminded me more of her grandfather, Matt's dad.

"Good, then traffic notwithstanding, I'll be there in twenty minutes."

Bohles waited patiently until I hung up. He handed me a sheet of paper. "That's a receipt for the box and the contents, just to keep this on the up and up. I'll walk you out."

"Sure," I said, slipping on my coat. I left the gloves in the pocket. My luck, Bohles would notice the rip and then find matching leather DNA on the paper. Assuming there was such a thing.

We walked together toward the front desk. Fred was still there, still hunched over the drawing board, and I called a quick good night as we passed his cubicle. We stopped twice on our way to the door, once so I could turn off the copy machine, and once to check that the coffeepot was turned off.

"Just like home," Bohles said as I dropped the receipt on Amber's desk and we exited the offices. "Do you need to lock up?"

I shook my head. "No. Fred will do that."

"But you do have a key."

"Chester gave me one on my first day back. Does it matter?"

"Nope." We were at the elevator, and after I pushed the button he said, "Not near as much as why you walked back to that handicapped stall the night of the party. Or why you crumpled that note from Michael Sherabian and threw it in the trash." He smiled. "You ever going to tell me that?"

It was like a joke shared with a friend, but something inside me stiffened. This man was not a friend. He was like a crocodile, circling playfully, and I knew that the unwary who played back could be in trouble.

Instead of smiling, I shook my head seriously, pensively. I lifted my shoulders in a shrug. "It's the oddest thing, I guess we'll never know. What does Michael say about that note?"

He watched me carefully, the wide eyes shrinking. "He says he never wrote it." He blinked as we entered the already-packed elevator. "I have my own theory. Maybe I'll tell you about it the next time I see you."

The thought of telling the truth about the note, and my reaction to it, wasn't so frightening now that I knew Bohles a little better. If I were honest about it, and honest about why I'd been circumspect initially, my gut feeling was that he would use the information to help with the investigation, but would also protect the confidentiality of it.

I glanced over at him. I was pretty sure my secret would be safe. By the time we arrived at the lobby level and were propelled out of the elevator by the crush of people, I was actually on the verge of asking him to come back upstairs so I could tell him the whole story but we were stopped by Audry Sterling-Sherabian, who planted herself directly in front of us.

Amber had told me the Sherabians were out looking at property; the angry set of Audry's face, coupled with the fact that Michael was no longer with her, made me suspect things had not gone well. Audry took in me, Sergeant Bohles, and the box in his arms in one agitated sweep.

"You're taking more from the agency?" she demanded.

"Yes," Bohles said casually, moving out of the way of the stream of people hurrying through the lobby. "A box of Desi Baker's things was returned by the storage company. Apparently it was overlooked earlier."

"And how did you find out about it?" she asked him, throwing a sharp glance at me.

"Mrs. Wyatt called me. There's a receipt upstairs, and if you're concerned about the contents, Mrs. Wyatt went through the box with me."

"Oh, really?" She paused and in that instant she transformed back to the old Audry I had known too well. "As if you didn't know, Sergeant Bohles, Mrs. Wyatt is not an employee, nor a representative of Rose Sterling Advertising. She is merely contract labor who happens to be working out of our offices, using our equipment. Furthermore, Mrs. Wyatt does not have the authority, or the power, to turn our records over to the police. Nor does she have permission to act on my behalf."

I had wondered if Audry held a grudge against me, and now I had my answer. She did indeed, and this was my punishment for what I'd done to her. It may have been well-deserved, but as I stood there in the lobby with people scurrying around us and Christmas carols playing in the background, something shifted inside of me. I had been punished enough. Even if Audry had never said a word to me, I had browbeaten and bludgeoned myself for years over my affair with Michael. It was time to get over it and move on.

Time for both of us to move on.

I looked squarely at Audry and said, "I'm sorry. I'm very sorry."

Her eyes told me she knew exactly what I was talking about. She watched me to be sure, then her mouth moved as if she had much more to say, but this was not the time or the place. After one last angry look at me she spoke directly to Bohles. "I think we should go upstairs and you can go through that box again. With me."

Bohles had been observing the two of us with an expression of smug fascination. When Audry rounded on him he lifted an eyebrow in surprise. "We can do that," he said.

"*If* I don't think the contents are crucial to the business of the agency, then you may take it with you." She tilted her head like a queen who'd just chewed up and spat out a peasant. "Of course, if you have a warrant, I suppose you can take it regardless."

"No, ma'am, I don't. I didn't think that was necessary since you were so anxious to help clear up Miss Baker's death."

It was time for me to make my exit. "It appears that my presence is superfluous," I said. "If you will excuse me, I have a dinner engagement. Good night." I added as gracious a smile as I could muster and headed for the garage. On the way I passed Ted Polovy at the security desk. He winked.

WHEN I ARRIVED at Prissy's my intention was to tell Matt the whole story and get it over with once and for all. I'd already thrown out my original agenda for the evening, which had been to go by the central library and research the articles on mistletoe. My curiosity wasn't as strong as my desire to spend time with my family.

The whole plan went out the window, though, because Matt wasn't there. He was still working with lawyers and CPAs, according to Prissy, who'd spoken to him on the phone not ten minutes before I arrived. She said he'd gotten three other large shareholders involved in the irregularities at Austin Edge, and while that meant shared responsibilities, it also meant more opinions to be heard and researched, with more suggestions to be weighed.

Jeremy was also out, ice-skating with Alicia. Todd had spent the afternoon with friends and wouldn't be returning until late, while Ross was attending a cocktail party on the way home, then picking up Prissy before they proceeded to two other client affairs.

Lucky for me I still had Christopher.

"Aunt Dolie, eat your pizza," he said, gesturing to my plate. "Todd will eat it all."

"Todd isn't here," Stephanie said. She looked around the table. The bowl filled with greenery, red balls, and two tall slender candles had been pushed to the side along with the lace tablecloth. In its place were two pizza boxes, both half-full. We were drinking our diet drinks out of plastic glasses and using paper plates, while paper napkins from the pizza parlor littered the table along with the crumbs.

"Civilization has finally left my mother's house," Stephanie said. "Or do I mean it's finally found my mother's house?"

Prissy frowned. "I wish you wouldn't talk like that. You make it sound like I'm living some slick plastic life, and it's just not so."

"Slick crystal life," Stephanie corrected. "Do you know this is only the third time I've ever seen a pizza box on this table?"

"Get used to it," Prissy said as she got up, taking her paper plate and a couple of crumpled napkins with her. "I'm getting old, and I'm getting tired, and frankly, my dear, I don't give a damn."

"Whooh!" Stephanie made a face and grinned at me. "For my mom that's heavy swearing."

I was tempted to say it was because she'd been goaded into it, one of the things that happens during the forced togetherness of the holidays when there are too many people jammed together in the allotted square footage. And perhaps it wasn't the closeness so much as it was the niceness. I certainly didn't feel free to swear or yell, or just be my normal self. I'm sure the others were experiencing the same constraints, including Prissy. It was like living on a sitcom.

"Looks like it's just us women tonight," Stephanie said, closing a pizza box. "Except for you." She stood up and popped Christopher with her finger.

"Ouch. You hurted me."

"Oh, Christopher, don't be a baby." She made a swipe at the table with her napkin. "Jolie, do you want any more?"

"No, thanks, I've had my fill."

"I'm filled, too." Christopher said.

He started to climb down from the table, but Stephanie grabbed his arm. "You're not going anywhere until you wash those hands. I don't need red sauce all over Grandma Prissy's house."

I picked him up. "Come on, I'll wash you."

As I carried Christopher into the guest bath to clean him up, the phone rang and Stephanie jumped for it. I was hoping that after we got Christopher to bed there would be time to go through Prissy's library to see if she had anything on mistletoe. I seemed to recall that she'd been very involved in the herb society when I'd first met her. She might even recognize the articles I'd brought home.

"All clean," Christopher said, holding up soapy hands.

I rinsed them off, handed him a towel, and when he was dry, herded him back into the great room. Prissy was straightening the kitchen and Steph was still on the phone.

"I'd love to go, Peter," she was saying, "I really would, I just can't leave Christopher again. Of course, you're more than welcome to come over here."

Christopher walked over and tapped his mother's knees. "Aunt Dolie can baby-sit me."

Stephanie put a hand over the mouthpiece of the phone. "No, little bug, we can't ask Aunt Jolie to stay home with you again."

"Aunt Dolie loves me," he said firmly. "We party."

Stephanie threw a questioning look at me. Damn. I didn't mind taking care of Christopher, my hesitation came because I appeared to be encouraging Stephanie to go out with a man her father's age. I wasn't, but what were the alternatives?

"I'd love to take care of Christopher," I said.

"Are you sure?"

"Of course." It was that nice quotient again.

"Peter? I can go."

I had thought, or perhaps just hoped, that the relationship between Peter and Stephanie was one-sided, but there was too much excitement in her voice for that. "What time will you be here?" she asked.

When she was off the phone, Prissy said, "Why don't you bathe Christopher before you go, so Jolie can relax for at least a few minutes?"

Stephanie saluted. "Consider it done. Come on, bug, we have things to do."

They went up the stairs, and I found myself on the couch being served hot tea by Prissy. "Thought you could use this," she said.

"Oh, thanks."

"How was your day?" she asked.

I raised an eyebrow and we both started to laugh. "Sorry," she said. "I'm so used to saying that to Ross after dinner, I guess I'll ask anyone who sits on the couch." She sat on the love seat and actually let herself loosen up a little. "But seriously, how are things at the agency?"

"Fine, I guess."

"You guess?"

"Oh, it's that murder...." I remembered the copies I had folded in my purse. "Something came up today that has really piqued my curiosity." I couldn't resist reaching for my purse and pulling them out. "Prissy, you used to be involved with the herb society, weren't you?"

"Second vice president, but I dropped out before they could move me any higher. Why?"

"Would you look at these and tell me what you think?"

She took the papers from me and moved over to a spot on the couch under a good light where she began to read.

NINETEEN

PRISSY TURNED the page over, probably knowing full well that it was a copy and there was nothing on the back. Then she peered at me over her glasses. "The byline says this is an AP story, but what newspaper is it from?"

I could only shrug. "I don't have any idea. You have everything I know about the copies right there."

"Very odd." She pushed her glasses back up on her dainty nose and, after a puzzled glance at the first page, went on to the second.

I was close enough to see that she was reading the magazine article. Her frown grew even deeper. "*The Herbal Medical Journal?* I've never heard of such a magazine; is it new?"

"I can't answer that; I've never heard of it either."

She went on to the book excerpt. Then she took off her glasses and brushed her bangs off her forehead, prior to giving me a very perplexed stare. I could certainly identify with her reactions.

"Well?" I said.

She dropped the copies into her lap. "Jolie, where did you get these? While Arundales is an authority on herbs, I've never heard anything about mistletoe being a muscle builder, or a fat burner, or any of these things. If it really works, I want some."

"Don't we all. So do you think the information is accurate?"

"I wouldn't have questioned it if you'd just given me this," she said, holding up the book excerpt. "but there's something about these other articles that bothers me. For one thing, they're written in a style that smacks of sensationalism, like one of the supermarket tabloids." I didn't ask her how she knew that. "I'd like to do some research, but what's this all about?"

I had expected that, and I was prepared. "Just one of those

interesting little turns that life takes," I said, then gave her a quick and dirty version of where I'd gotten the copies.

"The police could arrest you!" she exclaimed once she heard the story.

"If they do, I think it will be for something more than just making copies."

That gave her pause. "Like what could they arrest you for? I thought you didn't even know the woman."

"I'm kidding," I said.

Prissy and I have never spent much time together, nor have we been through anything emotional that would help draw us closer. Thanksgiving dinner with its obligatory football games has not been a bonding experience for Prissy and me. I didn't think telling her about an old affair was the place to start.

"Does knowing where these came from change your opinion?" I asked.

She picked up the copies and again read them over. "Wait a minute!" She jumped up. "I think I have an herb book upstairs. Come on."

I followed her up the stairs and down the hall into the library. That sounds more grand than it was, but there were a lot of books. Two walls were completely covered with books, plus there was a small book stand next to Prissy's desk, which had been overrun with electrical equipment. On it was a computer with a twenty-one-inch monitor. There was also a laser printer, a scanner, and two telephones. A second desk, which was a new addition since my last visit, was shoved up under the window and it held more computer attachments.

"And you know what else?" Prissy said. "We could also look it up on the Internet. I'm a whiz at that." She began scanning the bookshelves. I would have helped, but I suspected she knew exactly what she was looking for and where to find it.

Instead I gawked at the computer equipment. "How many modems do you have?"

"What? Oh, two, I think. I keep trading up, but they keep getting faster. And then I had an entire hard disk crash a couple of months ago, but everything off it was retrieved, including files I'd erased months ago. Isn't that amazing? Now, where is that thing?'' She pulled a thick, pea green book from the shelves and held it up to show me. ''Voilà! Let's see the copyright date.'' I peered over her shoulder as she flipped to the title page. ''Great,'' she said, the irony apparent. ''It's already two years old.''

''We could at least see what it says.''

She thumbed through the pages until she found mistletoe. We read it silently together, and neither of us was surprised to discover that mistletoe was listed as a poisonous parasite.

Prissy closed Arundales. ''But this is two years old, and new information is always coming out.'' As she returned the book to the shelf she said, ''Amazing when you consider how old plants are, and how long they've been used by one culture or another. You'd think we'd know all there is to know by now.''

''We have to keep relearning. Rediscovering. Like teenagers.''

''Isn't that the truth. We certainly can't take anyone else's word for anything. And neither can our children. What we ought to do is access the word *mistletoe* on the Internet and just see what comes up.'' Prissy glanced at her watch. ''Darn. Ross is going to be here any minute, so we'll have to do the computer work later. Actually, if you want, you can use this computer while Ross and I are gone. Or I can do it tomorrow.''

The front door opened and after a moment Ross called up the stairs, ''Anybody home?''

''We're up here,'' Prissy responded.

''Hi, there,'' I called out.

''Prissy, are you ready to go?'' he asked.

We were already on the landing. ''Let me grab my coat. I'll meet you downstairs.''

I waited while Prissy went to her room. Across the hall from the master bedroom was a full guest suite with a tiny sitting room. It was easy to tell by the scattering of toys, children's books, and kids' paraphernalia that this was where Stephanie and Christopher were sleeping. Next to them was the office, then the smallest of the rooms, which was being used by Jeremy. Across the hall and on the other side of the landing was a room with its door closed. I assumed that was Todd's.

Prissy emerged already pulling on a beautiful long black coat.

Ross was at the bottom of the stairs. "Your chariot awaits, my lady."

I followed her down.

IT MAY HAVE BEEN all the activity, or the sugar in the hot chocolate that I had given him, but whatever it was, Christopher became rowdy when I tried to put him to bed. I couldn't even call for reinforcements because everyone else was gone.

"It's very late," I said, firmly.

"Aunt Dolie, I'm not tired." He was squirming and fighting as I tried to get him dressed for bed. He kicked away the pajama bottoms.

"Christopher, don't do this. You have to put these on." I grabbed his leg and thrust it in the bottoms. He was wriggling so hard I was afraid he was going to fall off the bed. "Stop it!"

"I'm not tired." It was the whine of an exhausted three-year-old. There can be no more aggravating sound to an adult, simply because the cure for it, sleep, is what the child is fighting.

I lifted him physically into the air. "I'll read you a story, but I can't until you have these on. Stop wriggling."

He kicked harder until I put him down on the bed, then he thrashed his arms, too. "No, no! I'm not nappin'! I'm not."

"Christopher!" The loud commanding voice from the doorway scared us both. It was Todd, his face both older and fiercer-looking than usual as he strode into the room. "You settle down now."

Christopher stopped moving immediately, and I took advantage of it to yank up the bottoms and then sit him upright.

"You worked some magic," I said to Todd as I pulled the pajama top over Christopher's head. When his sullen face popped out of the neck I kissed him, then put an arm into the sleeve. "You see how easy it is if you'll just hold still?"

"I didn't mean to scare you," Todd said, moving to a rocker

where he sat down. "My dad always said a man's voice is more commanding."

Christopher started to cry. "Aunt Dolie, I'm tired."

"I know you are, sweetie." I got the last arm in place and picked him up, hugging his stiff little body against mine. "Now you can get some sleep, and when you wake up it's only two more days until Christmas."

"A story. You promised a story."

"Christopher," Todd snapped, "you are pushing the limits again."

I held up my hand. "No, he's right, Todd, I did promise him a story." I smiled at him. "It's important to teach by example, and promises have to be kept."

Todd looked straight at Christopher. "You have too many women spoiling you, do you know that?"

"No," Christopher said, still hugging me. "Aunt Dolie, read me *The Cat in the Hat,* please."

Round one to Christopher, not that I wanted him fighting me, but I didn't like Todd walking in and being bossy, either. "Okay, little bug, you find the book, and I'll read." I set him down and he grabbed my hand, pulling me into the sitting area.

I seemed to remember that this had been Stephanie's room before she left home. There were still some signs of that, a pair of pom-poms with their handles tucked behind the mirror, a shelf of stuffed animals on one wall. Now several suitcases were stacked in the open closet, and a tennis bag of toys spilled over on the floor.

In the corner was a large wicker basket filled with children's books and tapes. Christopher headed straight for it. "See, Aunt Dolie, it's here. We can pick it out. Or we can pick two books. I like books."

Todd had followed us, and now he gestured down the hallway. "I'll be in my room if you need me."

"Sure, and thanks again," I said as he turned and left.

Now that Christopher had settled down, tucking him under the covers, reading him a story, and then saying a bedtime prayer with him became a treat. It was like having Jeremy a baby all over again, only better, because I wasn't responsible for his every move, and I wasn't nearly so worried about how he would turn out.

"Good night, Christopher," I said, giving one final tug to his covers and kissing his forehead.

Todd's radio came on, and after a short blast he turned it down to a white noise in the background.

"May you stay here with me, Aunt Dolie?" Christopher said. "We can make a pallet on the floor by my bed."

It actually sounded inviting, but I said, "No, thank you. I have to go, so you can sleep."

"I'm scareded of the dark."

"No one can hurt you while I'm here. I'll tell you what I'll do, I'll leave the door cracked so you can see the light. Will that help?"

"Where you goin', Aunt Dolie? Are you driving away?"

"No, of course not! I'll be right across the hall in your grandma Prissy's office. You'll hear me working on the computer; if you need me, all you have to do is call and I'll run across the hall so fast I'll be here before you finish saying my name. What do you think about that?"

"Real fast?"

"Real fast. And if the door is closed, I'll run so fast I'll knock it down and put a great big hole in the wall!"

He giggled. "Can you run so fast I can't see you?"

"Yes, I can. And I'll come in and check on you, too. So now do you feel better?"

He nodded. "Otay."

I kissed his forehead again, tiptoed out, partially closed the door, then popped it open. "Hello! I'm checking on you!"

"Aunt Dolie, you're silly."

"That's right, I am. And I'll be right across the hall. So good night again. I love you."

"I love you, too."

AUSTIN IS a computer mecca. Admittedly there are others around the country, but that doesn't dim the reality that Dell Computer began in Austin, that IBM has a major presence here, that Samsung, Apple, Power PC, Motorola, and Austin Computer employ thousands of citizens. The University of Texas plays a part by having what they call the Incubator, a program for start-up computer companies. The saying is that even if you're at the back of the pack in Austin, computerally speaking, you're still ahead of most of the world.

I am not at the back of the Austin pack. Unfortunately, I'm behind even in Purple Sage, so you can judge where that put me with all of Prissy's equipment. I could, and did, turn her computer on. Since I use a computer every day with my writing, I just assumed I could take a little extra time and walk my way through getting on the Internet. That was delusional thinking.

I pointed at icons with the mouse and ended up in bizarre locations within Prissy's computer, rather than where I intended to go. I couldn't even get the machine to hook up with the Internet; instead it gave me error messages.

Finally I stepped back mentally and started over. When all else fails, you check hardware. Are the plugs in correctly? Was there even a modem attached to the machine? I studied all the wires leading into the computer and determined, at least to my satisfaction, that they were properly, or at least firmly, attached. Next I got on the floor and started following wires to see where they went. It didn't take long to discover they went everywhere.

Above the music coming from Todd's room I heard a door open somewhere in the house. I waited, listening to see who it was, then Matt's voice called, "Hello?"

"Up here," I yelled, momentarily forgetting that Christopher was trying to sleep.

I found what I was sure was a modem and followed the phone plug to a multiple jack in the wall. Four lines, just as Prissy had told me earlier in the week. I touched all of them, pulled a little on the plugs, and decided everything was secure. I followed a second wire out of the wall socket and discovered it was attached to a small black box that was tucked unobtrusively behind the leg of the desk. At first I thought it was another modem, or some kind of surge protector, but on closer inspection I recognized the little machine, and would have even without the label: Tele-Recorder. It was a microcassette recorder, which seemed a very odd thing to have attached to a computer. Not only that, a few feet away, an identical black box was hidden behind another leg.

"Well, now, that's what I've always wanted," Matt said from the doorway. "A beautiful woman on her knees to me."

I raised my head and smacked it on the underside of the desk. "Ouch."

"Are you okay?"

"Fine. Confused. Lost." I turned around and sat on the floor. "How are you? You look tired."

Matt let out a sigh and rubbed his face. "Let's just say this hasn't been my favorite day. So what are you doing?"

"Well, I was trying to do some research on the Internet, but I couldn't get the computer to sign on. Come here and I'll show you what I found."

I crawled out from under the desk and knelt down at the far side of it where Matt joined me. I pointed to the small recorder that couldn't have been over six inches long and two inches wide.

"What do you think of that?" I asked.

TWENTY

MATT CROUCHED DOWN. "Let me get in there a second." I scooted out of the way and he proceeded around me until he could touch the box. Gingerly he pulled it toward him. "Amazing. Did you see what this is? A tape recorder, and it says that it's voice-activated."

The tapes themselves are only a little over an inch wide, and not quite two inches long, and the recorders are two by five. I carry a similar one in my car to talk out story ideas when I'm traveling. It's a great idea in theory, but the batteries are always dead on mine.

"It's attached to the phone jack in the wall." I said, pointing. "So where does it go? It can't be plugged into the computer. Wait, I'll check the other one."

I got around to the far side, and without touching the recorder, followed the thin wire up to the phone that was on top of Prissy's desk. "I don't like this," I said.

Matt was tucking the small black box back where it had been. "I can't say that I'm crazy about it, either. Did you notice? These are new. There's no dust on them like there is on the modem."

"I hadn't gotten that far." Great detective that I was. "What is yours attached to?"

"Apparently it's recording the other phone line. The one that goes to our apartment."

I shivered. "That's nice. And they're new devices." I stood up and dusted my hands off, as if something ugly had gotten on them. Todd's music was a steady background noise, assuring that he couldn't hear our words. "What do you think this is all about?" I asked. Who in this house was tapping the phone lines, and why? I could hardly believe it, let alone understand it.

"I'm not sure, but it's not the kind of thing you expect to find in the house of a loving family." He stood with his hands on his hips, his focus on the black recorders. "At least I wouldn't think so."

I turned off the computer; I wasn't in the mood for research anymore. "Let's go downstairs, Christopher is supposed to be sleeping."

"Just let me wash my hands."

While Matt did that, I went to check on Christopher. I found him with his eyes wide open; he watched me come into the room. "You're supposed to be asleep," I said, sitting beside him on the edge of the bed.

"Aunt Dolie, I had a dream and now I was thinkin' about something."

"What are you thinking about?"

"Well, what if a bad person comes here, and takes you away, and I can't hear you?" The question was phrased very seriously.

I put my hand on his arm. "First of all, no bad person can get us. I have all the doors locked, and your grandma Prissy has an alarm system, so nobody could get in without a key."

"Some of the times bad people get you because they aren't scareded of alarms."

"Well, this alarm rings at the police station, so the police would come right away. Not only that, Todd and your uncle Matt are here, and they won't let anyone get you, either."

I heard Matt come out of the bathroom and make his way through the little sitting room, only tripping once over the things that were scattered on the floor. He didn't even swear. "See, here's your uncle Matt," I said.

"Hello, Uncle Matt."

"I thought you were asleep."

"I think Christopher had a bad dream," I said, making room for Matt to sit beside me.

He held out his arms and Christopher climbed into them, saying, "I missed you today. Were you working harder?"

"That's exactly what I was doing. I didn't get to have fun, like you."

"We went to the Chirden's Museum, and I worked on the computer, and I bought groceries."

In the dim light I could see Matt smile. "Sounds like what your aunt Jolie does, only she doesn't think it's that much fun." With his free arm he pulled back the covers on the bed to make room for Christopher to lie down. "I'm sorry that you had a bad dream. Are you better now?"

"I'm better."

"Good, then I think you need to sleep so you can play some more tomorrow. How does that sound?"

"I could go with you. I'm not tired anymore."

"Yes, well, that may be true, but I think you should rest anyway. You want to get lots of sleep so that when Christmas comes you have the energy to play with your new toys."

"What new toys?"

"Oh, the ones I think Santa is going to bring you."

"I like toys!"

"So I've heard." Matt put Christopher down on the bed and gently pulled the blankets up around his chest. "Now, how about going to sleep?"

Christopher reached out a hand and caught hold of Matt's arm; I could see the tiny fingers tighten on the tanned skin and blond hair. "Uncle Matt, if you and Aunt Dolie go away, will you come and take me, too? Please."

Matt placed his hand gently over Christopher's. "We aren't going anyplace tonight. And if something should happen so we change our minds, I promise we'll come and wake you up and take you with us. But you have to go to sleep now. Is that a deal?"

"Deal." Christopher nodded his head, then looked at me. "Aunt Dolie, when I grow up, I want to be Bianca in the Rescuers."

"Honey, Bianca's a girl."

"No, Aunt Dolie, Bianca's a mouse."

I exchanged a smile with Matt, then said, "When you grow up, Christopher, you're going to be a man, like your uncle Matt."

He thought about it. "Oh. Well, otay."

"That's good to hear," Matt said. "We'll be right downstairs; can you sleep now?"

"Yes, please."

Matt and I both kissed Christopher on the forehead, and then the two of us headed out of the room. In the doorway I stopped to look back. Christopher had his eyes open, still watching us. On impulse I said, "Would you like to come and sleep in our apartment?"

Christopher sat straight up. "Yes, please."

"Then come on."

Matt didn't question the suggestion; when I grabbed an extra blanket and started to hand it to him he said, "You get those, and I'll carry Christopher."

"I'll get his coat, too."

I turned on the light, then went around the room collecting a teddy bear, a pair of Christopher's tennis shoes, an extra pillow, and his heavy coat. I don't know why, it wasn't rational, but I felt an urgency to get Christopher, in fact to get all of us, out of the house. When I had everything, I headed for the door and turned off the light. Matt was waiting for me on the landing, Christopher in his arms. "Go," I said.

"I like this, Aunt Dolie."

"I know you do, but you have to go right to sleep when we get there."

A door opened down the hall and Todd came out. "Hi, what's going on?" he asked. When he saw Christopher he looked concerned. "Is everything okay?"

"Fine," I said. "We're going over to the apartment and I thought we'd take Christopher with us."

"Oh, that's cool. I was just going out," he said, and I realized the music was turned off. He leaned over and touched Christopher on the cheek. "You get some sleep, little guy; it's way past your bedtime."

"I know."

We went down the stairs together, Matt in the lead. At the

bottom I bundled a quilt around Christopher, grabbed my purse and keys off the couch, and we all went out the back door at the same time.

"See you in the morning," Todd called as he went around the corner of the house.

"Good night." We started up the stairs.

Matt put Christopher in our bed, firmly tucking him in with instructions to go to sleep. Christopher nodded, his little body seeming more relaxed now. "Otay."

"We'll be right on the other side," I said, as Matt pulled shut the white folding doors and we moved into the living room.

I felt better to be in the apartment, too. Normally when we spent a weekend at Prissy's we had a wonderful time, but this wasn't a normal trip and it was longer than a weekend.

"Does it feel like there are undercurrents around here?" I asked Matt, who was pulling off his boots.

"Yes, not that I've been here much to notice. But those recorders bother me." He placed the boots neatly beside the couch, leaned back, and put his feet up on the coffee table. "This feels good."

"It's like the whole trip is off kilter." I stretched out the length of the couch and put my head on Matt's lap. "And you know when I said Christopher had a nightmare? Matt, I don't think he'd gone to sleep. He was lying there with his eyes open, watching the door. He was scared about something else."

Matt stroked my hair and said, "Do you think it could be the movies he's been seeing?"

"I don't know." I took a breath. "There was a whole conversation that you missed earlier, about bad people taking me away. And he said something about being left alone, too, just like he did to you." I could feel my frown, a reflection of the concern that was building inside me. "That's a terrible thing for a child to even think about; why would he worry about that?"

Matt took a moment before he responded. "That might have something to do with Stephanie being out with Peter Javitz all the time. I don't know what we can do about that; parents do have to go away."

"You're right, and that's better than anything I've come up with. But still, I don't like it." I thought of something else. "And then there are those damn tape recorders."

"That doesn't work for me. I'm going to talk to Prissy about those tomorrow."

"You think she hooked them up to check on Stephanie?"

"I don't know what to think. It, it, I..." He stopped. I had rarely heard Matt at a loss for words before. "I hate to think that my sister would stoop to something like that. Stephanie is a grown woman, and monitoring her conversations that way is wrong. The other part of this is that Prissy's violated our privacy, because she has our conversations on tape, too."

"I know." I was getting a headache and I rubbed my forehead. "You realize that it might not have been Prissy who put the recorders there. It could have been Ross, or even Stephanie. I can't think of why either one of them would do that, maybe checking on Prissy. You said the recorders are new, at least not dusty, so there's the possibility that Stephanie brought them with her."

Matt shook his head. "I don't like that any better."

"Matt, I keep wondering how long Stephanie has been dating Peter Javitz. I mean, if she lives in Phoenix, and he lives here...and how did that get started?" I didn't say, "And how can we stop it?" although the thought crossed my mind.

"Apparently Stephanie had some problems after she moved out to Phoenix; I don't know what they were, Pris didn't say, but she mentioned them in a phone call a couple of months ago. Maybe it was financial, or maybe Stephanie was homesick. I didn't get the impression that it was anything serious; if I had, I'd have called her. At any rate, Peter has several clients in Phoenix, so when he went out there Prissy asked him to check on Stephanie. Of course, the result was not what Prissy had in mind. Now he sees Stephanie as often as he can, which is much too often, according to Prissy."

"How long ago was it that they started dating?" I held back a yawn.

"You mean, is there hope it will burn out soon?"

I grinned. "Okay, that, too."

"I think only about a month or so." His head nodded. "She hasn't been gone all that long."

"Since August," I said, letting out the yawn. "So tell me what's happening with Austin Edge. Anything good on that front?"

"I'm not sure that good is even a possibility, regardless of what we do." He started explaining, and I closed my eyes and dozed off.

IT WAS THE POUNDING on the door that woke me. Matt jumped and I almost landed on the floor.

"What in the world—" I said, trying to figure out where I was and what was happening.

Luckily Matt was quicker. He pulled open the door while I was still getting to my feet.

"Uncle Matt," Stephanie said breathlessly. "Where's Christopher? He's not in his bed and—" She stopped when she spotted me.

"What?" I said.

"Christopher is gone!"

"He's asleep in there." I pointed to our bedroom.

"Oh, God." She ripped back the folding doors and saw Christopher. "Oh, my baby." With that she moved to the side of the bed and knelt down to take hold of Christopher's hand.

Matt and I tiptoed in beside her in time to see Christopher mumble in his sleep, then shudder slightly and open his eyes. When he saw all of us, he said, "Hi, Mommy."

"Hello, sweetheart. Are you okay?"

"I'm restin'." He closed his eyes and fell back into sleep. Poor little guy was exhausted.

Stephanie paused a moment longer, touching his hand and

watching his rhythmic breathing. When she stood up, we all moved into the living room.

"I'm sorry," I said softly. "I should have left you a note. I didn't think—" I shook my head to clear away the fuzz. "I guess I didn't think at all."

Matt closed the sliding door behind us.

"I thought—I was sure—" She was breathing hard, her skin flushed. "I guess I just panicked when he was gone and I couldn't find you."

I put an arm around her. "You're shaking. Come and sit down."

"It's just the cold." She tried to laugh it off as we moved toward the sofa. "I overreacted. Mom says I do that; I'm sorry, I didn't mean to be that way."

"How about if we make you something hot to drink?" I asked.

"Oh, no, thanks. It's late."

Matt sat down on the chair. "Are your mom and dad home yet?"

She shook her head. "No, not yet. Just Jeremy's there, and he's sound asleep."

"Then you don't need to get back right way; I will make coffee," I said, standing up. The only lucid thought I had was to keep Stephanie as long as possible, although I wasn't sure why that was important. Maybe I wanted her to feel protected with us around, the same way Christopher seemed to feel safe. Or on some level I may have wanted her to talk so we could discover what was really going on.

Matt is one of the best listeners I know, and if Steph wouldn't talk to him, she wouldn't open up to anyone.

I started to reach for the coffeepot, but Stephanie stood up. "Don't make any for me. I'm exhausted, and I'm sure you are, too." She started toward the bedroom. "I'll just get Christopher—"

"I'll carry him for you," Matt said, rising.

"Steph, why don't you leave him?" I asked. I gave Matt a quick look. "He's sound asleep, and we don't mind."

"But he's in your bed."

"It doesn't matter; there's plenty of room." Again I shot a glance at Matt, and this time he got the message.

"It's fine with us," he said. "Maybe Christopher will sleep better without all the activity you've got over there."

Stephanie hesitated. She glanced toward the bedroom and bit her lip while seeming to consider. Finally she nodded her head, speaking slowly. "Okay. I think maybe you're right. If you're sure."

"We're sure," I said with finality.

"Just let me kiss him good night."

Matt slid back the door enough for her to get through, while I found an extra blanket to wrap around her shoulders.

When she came back out she said to me, "I really am sorry, Jolie, for barging in here like I did."

"It was my fault." I held out the blanket. "You'll want this."

"No, thanks, I'll just run." She went to the front door. "Call me if he wakes up and needs me. Good night," she said over her shoulder as she hurried out, closing the door behind her. She was gone and only a chill from outside remained.

I looked at Matt. His expression told me he was as worried as I was. "Tomorrow," he said, "I'm talking to Prissy. And then I'll see what I can do with Steph. I don't like this." He slid his arms around my shoulders, pulling me toward him. "I feel like I've gotten you involved in something, and it worries me."

"It's not your fault; I'm the one who wanted to come to Austin for the party. That is why we're here."

"Oh, that's right, the Christmas party."

"And now you have all the problems at Austin Edge."

Matt rested his head on my shoulder and groaned before he looked up. "I will be so glad when this week is over and we can go home."

"And we'll live happily ever after?"

"At the very least."

TWENTY-ONE

HANDS TOUCHING MY FACE woke me.

I opened my eyes to find Christopher patting my cheek as if I were a family pet.

"What are you doing, little bug?"

His voice came back a whisper. "Checkin' on you, Aunt Dolie. Are you sleepin'?"

"I was." The room was dark, so while I couldn't see Matt clearly, I could detect his unmoving form. "Come here. You don't want to wake your uncle Matt; he's very tired." Christopher curled up close to me and I said softly, "You're supposed to be sleeping, too."

"I am."

Christopher wriggled in my arms and I kissed his ear. The feel of his baby-fine hair and the soft skin brought back the days when Jeremy was that little. There is what I like to think of as a universal motherhood reaction to young, whether they are babies, puppies, kittens, or most any other warm-blooded creatures; at that moment I was overwhelmed with it, and with the feeling that Christopher needed protection.

"Get some rest, little bug. I love you."

He closed his eyes and let out a satisfied sigh. "Night, Aunt Dolie."

I held him like that for a long time, while my mind worried over all the little oddities that had me concerned about Christopher and his mother. When I finally realized that worry wasn't going to help, I crept out of the bed and began getting ready for the day. I had a plan.

IT IS NOT physically possible to close a car door without making noise, but I did my level best in the dark of that cold morning.

In my hand I had two microcassette tapes that I'd taken from my own recorder. One was blank while the other had ramblings on a mystery I was plotting, and both were being sacrificed for the cause.

Skirting the dead leaves, I crossed the patio, punched in the alarm code, then used the key to let myself into Prissy's house. Once in the warmth of the kitchen, I slid off my coat and waited to see if I could hear any noises from above. There was nothing except the soothing hum of the central heat.

With great care to avoid bumping into the furniture, I headed for the stairs. A night-light on the upstairs landing helped me see the way as I tiptoed carefully up each step. I silently blessed Prissy's contractor for making the flooring so solid there wasn't even the tiniest creak or groan. On the landing I left my shoes and moved in my stockings toward the office. At the door I paused again, but still there were no noises.

Not waiting for my luck to change, I went straight to the desk and ducked underneath it, removing the tapes from inside the recorders and replacing them with my own. It hardly took a minute. Then I was up and out the door, but this time I did hear sounds and they seemed to be coming from Stephanie's room. I moved closer to her door and pressed my ear to the wood; there weren't specific noises that I could identify, just a rustling as if someone might be walking the carpet inside the sitting room.

I started to go in, actually had my hand on the knob, but I discovered that the door was locked from the inside. The soft rattle I'd made with the knob silenced all sounds from the room.

"Steph?" I whispered. "Are you okay?"

The door opened and in the dimness, with her long hair flowing over her white flannel nightgown, she looked like Lady Macbeth.

Her face appeared pale. "Is Christopher—"

"He's fine. Sound asleep," I assured her quietly. "I just came in to get something and I heard you moving around. Are you okay?"

She nodded. "Of course. Just restless." She took in my clothes. "Where are you going so early?"

"The agency. I want to be home by noon. Two at the latest. I'm tired of missing all the fun."

Her voice sounded rueful. "Has there been a lot of that? I seem to have more fun away from the house."

"I'd love to come in and talk."

More than anything I wanted to make things better for her and for Christopher, whatever that took, but until she chose to tell me what was going on, there was nothing I could do.

"It's too early, and besides, things are fine." The determination in the rigid set of her mouth made it obvious she wasn't going to let me close enough to help just yet.

I forced myself to smile. "Then when I get home we'll start having fun." I added a wink. She looked dreadful. "Get some rest; I'll see you in a couple of hours."

She nodded, and as I turned to go I heard her close and lock the door.

THE TINY TAPES were like hot coals in my coat pocket, and my fingers hovered, never quite touching them. As I crossed the empty lobby the beautifully blended voices of a chorale were singing "Silent Night," and Ted Polovy was unlocking the second elevator.

When he turned and saw me, he saluted and said, "Getting a jump on the day, huh?"

"Something like that." I veered around him, head down, plowing forward like a bull. I was on a mission.

"You ever worry about going up there?" he asked, moving just enough to block my path. "To Rose Sterling?"

I stopped. "No, why would I?"

"One copywriter died up there. Someone killed her, and the cops don't know who did it yet."

A feather of cold whispered across my shoulders and down the neck of my coat. "That's an ugly thought. And I wish you hadn't brought it up."

"Spooked you, huh?"

"Maybe. Would you like to go up there with me and check the place out, just in case?"

He grinned and rubbed his fingers across his short hair, scratching just above his ear. "I figure you'll be okay."

"Thanks."

He continued to touch his bristle of hair as his face grew serious. "You know, I still feel bad about Desi dying. Kind of responsible. Damn, feels bad, you know? Like I should've done something—"

"They say if someone wants to kill you, they will. Even the president is vulnerable, and you weren't here to protect Desi."

"I'm here to protect everyone."

"That's a pretty big job. Seems impossible to me."

"That's what the boss keeps sayin', but for me, I just don't like it. And I mostly don't like that it was Desi." He seemed almost wistful. "So many lousy people in this world and it had to happen to her. It doesn't seem fair; should'a happened to someone else—not someone of her kind."

"I guess it happens to any kind."

He brought his hand down and looked at me, sad-eyed. "But it shouldn't." He shrugged. "Maybe I'm just being fanatical, and what do I know? I'm just the security guy."

"A nice security guy," I said. "And you see a lot."

"Just doing my job."

I smiled, and finally said, "And I think it's time for me to start doing mine."

"You have a nice day, now, hear?"

I nodded and waved as I moved away.

By this time Brenda Lee was Rocking Around the Christmas Tree, but when the elevator doors closed, they shut out all sounds except the whir of the machinery. I pulled my coat tighter around me and jammed my hands into my coat pockets; my fingers touched the two tapes nestled in the bottom. There didn't seem to be much holiday cheer anywhere this season.

When the elevator doors opened I found myself enveloped in

the silence of the seventh floor. I felt nervous about entering the empty offices, and that was Ted Polovy's fault.

Inside the door the scent of the Christmas tree calmed me. What is more inviting than the smell of pine and the jangle of holiday ornaments?

Almost in passing I stopped in my cubicle to toss my coat and purse on my chair before hurrying on to Nola's office; I seemed to remember that Nola carried a microcassette recorder to client conferences.

Hers was perhaps the prettiest office in the suite, with a beautiful wooden desk with Queen Anne legs. On top of the desk was a green Acer computer—that was Nola's style. Near the door two client chairs flanked a small wooden table that held one of the holiday floral arrangements left over from the party. Brass accessories glowed in the gray dawn light, adding a warmth and richness conspicuously absent elsewhere.

I glanced around but didn't see a recorder out in the open, so I tiptoed to the desk and slid open the top drawers. I felt like a party guest poking through the host's medicine cabinet. When I didn't find what I was looking for, I closed the drawers and started out of her office. On the way out I happened to spot a large leather sample case tucked back behind a tufted chair. It seemed the natural place to keep a small recorder, and I justified looking inside by telling myself that if Nola had been there, she wouldn't have minded.

When I lifted the flaps I found several bright blue folders leaning enough so that I couldn't see the bottom of the case. I lifted two out. The labels read Precis Computing and Mind Games Unlimited.

If they were clients, I'd never heard of them. In retrospect it seems rude, but there was no premeditation involved when I opened the top file and discovered a marketing proposal for Precis Computing. The budget was almost a million dollars. The odd thing about the proposal was the letterhead. Rose Sterling used a dusty rose paper with silver gray script at the top. Proposal covers were gray with raised silver lettering. They were striking enough to be recognizable even at a distance. The paper I was looking at was a textured gray-blue with a sweeping logo in navy. Millennium Advertising. The address at the bottom on Far West Boulevard seemed vaguely familiar, but I couldn't place it.

I flipped two more pages and discovered some advertising copy for Precis, again on Millennium letterhead. Desi Baker's initials were at the top as the copywriter.

The proposal brought up a number of interesting questions, such as: Who was Millennium Advertising? Were they a competitor and had Nola just happened to get a copy of the proposal? Why had Desi been writing for them? Had she been moonlighting and Nola discovered the transgression? Or were Desi and Nola both involved with Millennium? Perhaps jumping ship to join them?

If Nola was in a better mood today, I decided I'd ask her.

With real purpose I looked under the files, didn't find a recorder, checked in the side pockets of the case and again came up empty, then put everything back and slid the case to its original position.

I decided on a quick visual search of the other offices. I stressed the *visual* to myself, meaning that I was only going to look without touching a thing. I did just that in Ralph's office, slowing only to take in the weird arrangement of the plastic cartoon characters on top of his computer. They were in a V formation, all facing down one character—a beleaguered Dilbert.

I looked around the desktop, credenza, and file cabinets. No recorder.

If I waited until the staff arrived to ask for a recorder, it would be too late to listen to the tapes, so I did a quick search of Fred, the art director's, office. I came up empty and checked Amber's desk, where I found a drawer practically filled with nail polish. The space not used for cosmetics contained a vast assortment of promotional pens from what looked like every radio station, printing company, and specialty firm in the area. It didn't yield a cassette recorder.

The offices of the royal family, as Donna Katherine called

them, were almost as intimidating to me now as they'd been when I worked full-time at Rose Sterling. I merely glanced around Audry's office from the doorway, and did the same at Chester's.

In Michael's I caught myself drifting forward, pulled in by the scent of his aftershave. I had come into this office too many times in the past, supposedly to drop off something I had written, but sometimes, tucked between the pages of a proposal, I would have a card for Michael. Or a note. It had been dangerous, leaving written proof, but in retrospect the danger was part of the attraction.

One time in particular I remembered I slid the papers across his desk, and Michael had looked up, smiled, and while we casually discussed a client campaign, he had been stroking my hand with his fingertips. It gave me a shivery feeling just to think about it.

Then I remembered that Audry had come swooping down into the office. I had heard the step outside the door just in time to pull my hand away and fall back into the client chair. As if I had been sitting there the entire time, as my mother would say, keeping my hands to myself.

Looking at Michael's desk, his space, I felt remorse, along with the recognition of thrill at the danger I had faced.

Maybe all of us have that little bit of excitement junkie within us, just enough so that when we have no exhilarating highs in our own lives we read books or go to movies to experience it vicariously. The daring have always captured us, from Amelia Earhart to Buzz Aldrin. And sometimes we are the daring—for good or for evil.

I stepped into the hallway, then turned to look toward the offices one more time. From that spot I saw not only Michael's office, but Chester's as well. The similarities caught me. Neither Michael nor Chester had a computer, a file cabinet, or any stacks of files sitting around cluttering the tidy surfaces of their office furniture. They did have some newspapers and magazines, mostly the same ones, such as *Austin Business Journal, Advertising Age, Broadcast Weekly, Newsweek,* and the *Wall Street Journal.* They also had lovely seating arrangements for their clients, and large executive chairs for themselves.

In looking around something else struck me—except for the tree by the front door, Christmas was absent from the suite of offices. In years past there had been decorations everywhere. The agency decorated the open areas, and the rest of us had added special touches to our own offices. A garland of plastic ivy hung with real candy canes had circled my cubicle, and I'd put red bows and silver tree balls in a pothos that was my permanent companion at Rose Sterling. That was another thing that was missing—plants.

I could understand how the party had created some problems; after all, most of the furniture had been shifted elsewhere, so decorations would have been just that much more to move—but plants?

As I stood there wondering, the lights in the building across the street came on, reminding me that the rest of the staff would be arriving soon. I shifted my brain to business mode and scanned Chester's office, then Michael's one last time. Neither had a microcassette recorder sitting around.

Next I poked my head into Donna Katherine's office, and literally stopped short to take in the transformation. It was as if she had gotten everyone's Christmas spirit and tried to cram it in too small a space. A two-foot-tall angel with a creamy satin gown and glittery gold wings was hung so that it hovered in midair in the center of the office. A wreath of hard candies, complete with a small pair of red scissors for snipping off the little goodies, graced the cloth of her temporary wall. A flocked artificial tree was attached to the top of her computer. It was surrounded by a red felt skirt that had small packages affixed. Three poinsettias were grouped near the door with a small train and village circling them.

On the temporary wall above her computer was a sign that said, I Only Have Two Speeds And If You Don't Like This One, The Other One Will Really Drive You Crazy. She had tacked some fake holly and a puffy red Santa to it.

I didn't think she'd have a recorder, I couldn't come up with any reason why she would have, but I looked around anyway. Her files were locked, as was her desk, which I suppose made sense for a financial person, and there wasn't anything in sight that wasn't for decorative purposes.

Without much real hope I moved down the hall and popped into the conference room. It was amazing—there, right on top of the credenza, along with a metal insulated coffeepot and some nondairy creamer, sat not one, but two recorders. As the old saying goes, whatever you are hunting, you'll find it in the last place you look.

I snatched up the recorder closest to hand and hurried back to my own office to listen to the tapes.

TWENTY-TWO

PRISSY'S WAS the first voice I heard, convincing a woman to serve on the Friends of the Library board. The woman was apparently new to the community and Prissy made her feel welcome, as if the post were a special privilege; for all I knew, it was. I stayed with the conversation until the end, expecting something major to be said. There was nothing.

Next I heard Stephanie calling the Children's Museum checking on their hours. I ran the tape forward, listening to the high-pitched garble of voices, and after a short tone I slowed the machine and heard a male voice say, "Hello?"

"Hi. It's Ed."

"Hey, Ed, how're you doing?"

"Fine. I wanted to find out what you thought of the office space you found. The one over on Spicewood."

"Right, the one I viewed on Saturday. I thought it was great. Good location, nice view, and the management group seems anxious to get it leased. They want too much for it, of course, but that's Austin for you."

I finally realized it was Ross who had taken the call. He is somewhat of a specter to me; while I've been around him, I never really talk to him, or more important, listen to him talk. He always seems the peripheral person—the floater loosely attached to Prissy.

He has always seemed nice enough, but his energy had always appeared to be expended outside the house. As if his career was more important than his family, or maybe he worked long hours to support the lifestyle they had chosen.

I'd never noticed any particular bond between Ross and Stephanie, and now it left their relationship open to questions. At some point I had even wondered if Ross was the source of Stephanie's problems.

"If you want to take a look at it," Ross was saying. "I'm going back there at noon today...."

It didn't tell me anything new about the man.

Next Ross spoke with a woman I presumed was his secretary. They went over airline and rental-car information for a trip in early January.

I kept trying to figure out when these calls had taken place, but there was nothing to pinpoint the dates. At least a few days earlier.

Another short tone and I heard a male voice say, "Hello?"

Stephanie cut in quickly, "Peter, thank God! I'm about to lose my mind! I tried talking to her, just like you suggested, but it didn't do any good. My mother is living in some dreamworld—"

"Whoa! Slow down, take a deep breath." I recognized the mellifluous tones of Peter Javitz.

"I can't slow down; I can't even think." But she did take a loud breath.

"Good," Peter said. "Now, you tried to talk to your mother, and what happened?"

"I told you, nothing. She won't even listen to me. She's like a Stepford wife! She just keeps saying that I have to stop acting like a little girl—like it's my fault."

"You know that's not true. Nothing that happened was your fault. You do know that, don't you?"

A pause before she said, "Sometimes I blame myself."

"That's crazy, Stephanie. All that expensive therapy and you're going to start beating yourself up again?"

"I know, I'm just so confused. And I know it could have been a whole lot worse. Maybe that's what scares me."

I realized I had clenched my fists as I listened to Stephanie continue her outpouring of half sentences. I was imagining some very ugly scenarios.

"And since she won't listen, she doesn't know the whole truth. She doesn't want to know. Oh, God, Peter, you can't imagine how I'm feeling. And my own mother, but then in a way, I guess

I can't blame her. I mean, she's such a loyal person, but she doesn't have any idea what could happen."

"*Nothing* is going to happen. He's not drinking or taking drugs, and didn't the therapist say that was the cause?" Cause of what? I wanted to know. "If you see him even touch a glass of wine, or if you see any sign that he's using cocaine again, you run straight over here and stay with me until he's safely in jail."

"I can't do that. The whole story would come out and I can't handle having everyone know. Especially not Jolie and Uncle Matt." A shuddery sigh. "I hate feeling vulnerable like this."

When I had met Stephanie, shortly after her eighteenth birthday, I had marveled at how pragmatic she was and how smoothly she handled problems. Two years later, even after she'd had Christopher, I still believed Stephanie was far more competent at that age than I'd been. Since then I'd been certain Christopher hadn't suffered because of her single status; now I wasn't sure.

Peter began using a lighter tone. "We're always vulnerable, though, aren't we? Lesson in life number four twenty-two." As if he were trying to tease her out of her fears. I was beginning to dislike the man more than before.

"I know, I know. It's just, you know me, I hate pretending nothing happened. I hate being nice."

"My little firebrand." What an ass he was. "You did act; you got the situation handled, and now you live with the aftermath, just like we all do."

It didn't sound like he was taking her fears much more seriously than Prissy, but I was. I had seen Stephanie last night on the verge of hysteria when she couldn't find Christopher. Whatever had happened in the past, real or imagined, it had scared the hell out of her.

A scenario was edging into my consciousness, one that repulsed me and heightened my worry. I rubbed my forehead as Peter's voice went on.

"Let's talk about it at dinner tonight. I'll see if I can help you forget your troubles."

"I can't go, Peter, I just can't. I can't leave Christopher. Why don't you come here and I'll fix us dinner?"

"That won't work. After dinner I have to attend a party at the university; they're honoring a friend of mine and I'm making a speech about him." He dropped his voice and said softly, "I want you at my side. I want your strength and your beauty with me, just like I always do. What do you say?" When she remained silent he added, "Let your aunt and uncle baby-sit, then you won't have to worry about Christopher. Nothing is going to happen, and getting away will help you put things in perspective."

Stephanie took her time responding. Finally she said, "Okay, I guess. What time?"

"I'll pick you up at seven-thirty."

Which effectively cut off my chances of hearing what I wanted to. Damn. If anyone asked me for an opinion of Peter Javitz, they would certainly get a biased one.

Another short tone came from the tape and Jeremy was on the phone talking to Matt. Something about a Christmas present. I hit the fast-forward button quickly just in case it was my present they were talking about. After that Prissy had a hurried conversation about a New Year's Eve party that she and Ross were going to drop by. While she was getting directions I moved on, and when I stopped the tape a female I couldn't identify was speaking.

"There just isn't anything available on that day. If you'd like, I can put you on a wait list for standby."

"No, not during the holidays." I recognized Todd's voice. "Look, while I'd rather leave on Thursday, if you can't get us anything, I'll take Friday. We can fly into Dulles, National, or BWI, it doesn't really matter."

Todd just now booking his return trip? That would mean he was staying in Austin several days after Christmas, and if he was the reason for Stephanie's fears, this wouldn't be good news.

But what if he wasn't the source? What if someone else in the house was causing her fear? There was only one other man, and I shivered at the ugliness of the thought.

"Would you hold a moment?" the woman, apparently a travel agent, asked. "I'd like to check something."

The soothing effect of the instrumental Christmas carol that followed was disrupted by Todd's muttering. "Sometimes, Todd-boy, you act like you aren't bright. You knew better than to put off making these reservations. I mean, right in the middle of the holidays and you just blew it off. I hate it that Dad was right, but sometimes you don't—"

The music and the muttering both stopped as the woman came back on the line. "I think I have something. It's not a direct flight, and you're going to have a three-hour layover in Atlanta, but it's at five-fifty in the evening on Friday."

Friday, one week from today; that seemed awfully far off.

"Layovers aren't important," Todd responded. "Just book it."

"One more thing, because of the holidays and the late date, the cost is going to be substantially higher, but I can get both of you on and seated together."

"Great. That's good."

A flight for two? Was that why Todd was always chasing out of the house in such a hurry? A new girlfriend in Austin? An old girlfriend? I wondered what Prissy thought of that. Not that I was *sure* Prissy had been attempting to get Stephanie and Todd together, but I suspected it despite the apparent mismatch. Stephanie preferred her men more mature, and seemed to need someone solid to lean on, although had anyone asked me, Peter Javitz wasn't that person.

The agent was rattling off flight numbers and times, so I hit the fast forward, and when I heard a new timbre of voice I slowed the tape again.

"How about if you meet me at the Hyatt? I always seem to get lost up in Round Rock." I recognized our friend Trey Atwood's voice immediately, but then I hear it all the time when I call his wife, Diane.

It was Matt who responded. "I don't mind, but I'll have to beat you at tennis tomorrow."

''In this weather, have you lost your mind? They say it might snow. Just get me a map for Christmas—''

I had been in the room during that conversation, so I skimmed on, still listening carefully, despite the fact that I had little hope left that I could identify the person who had attached the recorders. Prissy was the obvious choice, since it was her house and she was a whiz at computers and such. Ross was number two on my list, but I couldn't quite work out why he'd do it. Prissy might be checking up on Stephanie, especially because of her involvement with Peter. But Ross?

Stephanie might also be responsible, although she wasn't into electronics and didn't seem to have any reason to be spying on her family. Or did she? Was the victim fighting back? Damn. And who was the aggressor?

The tape ended, and after muttering at least one or two words that didn't reflect the true spirit of the season, I put the second microcassette in the recorder.

The first voice I heard was Jeremy talking to a young woman I assumed to be Alicia. There are some things a mother shouldn't hear, and I felt strongly that this was one of them. I moved past it to the next call, which was merely a series of computer-generated sounds. I suspected it was a modem connecting to the Internet. I heard that same sound five more times before a human voice was discernible. It was Matt speaking crisply and using succinct language that let me know he was talking serious bidness as it's known in the South.

''...assume the majority of the stockholders are unavailable during the holidays, and I feel that leaves us in a precarious position. We can't in good conscience get a stay, while the board could...''

It was not something I wanted or needed to know. The finger that was on the fast-forward button was getting sore, but I pushed it again, only to be rewarded with more computer sounds and then the end of the tape.

I scowled at the tape, willing it to speak. And not only did I want it talking, I wanted it saying what I needed to hear.

When the agency phone rang, I almost jumped.

"Rose Sterling."

"Good morning," Matt said, in his sexy just-awake voice.

A wave of guilt swept through me; while he'd been innocently sleeping, I'd been listening in on his phone conversations. It seemed to me that if I was to have any scruples at all, I was going to have to get a cat and name it that.

"Good morning," I said. "Did you just get up?"

"About twenty minutes ago. Are you all right?" he asked.

"Of course. Why wouldn't I be?"

I could hear the smile. "You sound like you've been up to something. Eh, 'Lucy'?"

"Not me."

"You got up awfully early." The smile was gone when he added, "Did you have trouble sleeping?"

It brought home to me how lucky I am to have Matt. He is a wonderful man, kind, intelligent, and even handsome, but his best attribute is that he loves me steadfastly, regardless of my mood, or his, and despite any untoward circumstances. Standing in the middle of Rose Sterling, where my past tugged at me like a demanding child, it was good to remember that.

"Thanks for asking," I said. "Actually, Christopher woke me up, and then I couldn't seem to drift off again. Where is he?"

"Believe it or not, he's still asleep." I could hear the concern. "I wish I knew what's going on. Before I leave I'm going to talk to Prissy; maybe there's a simple explanation for all of this, but I can't think of what it could be."

"Me neither. And I guess I should tell you that I took matters into my own hands. I did something...." I paused. Taking the tapes had seemed righteous and moral, practically heroic, at the time I'd done it, but now I wasn't sure.

"So what did you do?" he asked.

"Well, I took the tapes out of those voice-activated recorders and brought them to the office."

"Oh, good. Instead of having some anonymous person tapping our phone lines, it's my wife who's doing it."

"I just thought I could figure out who put the recorders there, except now that I've listened to the tapes, it seems everyone in the house has been on the phone. Or one of the phones and they didn't say a damn thing important."

"You calling us boring?"

"Neil Simon didn't write our dialogue," I said. I added seriously, "And no one seemed to be cautious of what they were saying, either."

"Why should they be?" Matt asked. "Whoever hooked up the recorders didn't plan on anyone else listening to the tapes."

I knew that, or I would have if I'd thought it through. "Well, hell. So I learned nothing, and wasted time listening to boring conversations. Although there was a call of Stephanie's with Peter Javitz that concerns me. Not their relationship, either, but Stephanie sounded really scared. Something bad happened to her, Matt, and during the call she told Peter that Prissy wouldn't listen to her. She was really upset."

Matt paused before he spoke. "I'm not much for jumping into the middle of someone else's business—"

"I know, but I think she needs help. Moral support if nothing else. It sounded—" I fought down my suspicions. I had no proof of what I was thinking, and no reason to malign anyone, yet. "It sounded serious."

"Okay, I'll try to find out what's going on. If there's some way we can help, I'm for it, but..." I could almost hear his frown. "But if Stephanie and Prissy shut me out, we'll have to accept that as their decision."

I let out a relieved breath. If Matt was going to get involved, I was sure everything would be all right.

"But don't forget the recorded phone calls," I said. "Those are our business since someone tapped our conversations."

"Which my wife listened to."

"In my favor, you should know that I fast-forwarded through a call of Jeremy's and several others."

"The boring ones or the personal ones?"

"Cute, Matt. So here's the deal. I replaced these tapes with some others, so the machines aren't empty. Unfortunately, anyone who listens to them is going to know the tapes have been switched.''

"As long as they don't know that it was you who switched them." I was silent for so long that he added, "Obviously they will know. How is that?"

"One of the tapes has my voice—I was plotting a short story. Of course, anyone could have taken it out of my car."

"I may have an extra tape in my briefcase, and if I do, I'll replace that one."

"Thank you." I let out a sigh. Then I remembered. "Oh, shit!"

"What?"

"We're being taped! And I can't tell you which recorder it is."

"Great. Look, I'll go in and pull both tapes. Damn." Matt swears only under extreme circumstances.

"I'm really sorry—"

"It's not that," he said. "It's just everything. This was supposed to be a vacation, and you're working every day, and I'm involved in Austin Edge. We were supposed to have some time together."

"I know." I hadn't intended to sound quite so wistful.

"Next month," he said. "I don't care where we go as long as it's just the two of us. Together."

There was a delicious flutter in my stomach region; from Matt's voice it was apparent that was going to be some wonderful vacation. "I'm ready," I said, my voice a croak.

"Good. Maybe we'll try a beach in Mexico? Someplace warm."

"Sultry," I purred.

"I'll tell the travel agent you said so."

I let out a long sigh. Too little of life was like this. "Okay. And I'll dream about it while I look out the window at the cold."

"Ah, yes. The cold." Damn. I'd pulled us back to reality. "And now," he went on, "I'll go get those tapes. And talk to Prissy."

"And handle the problems at Austin Edge."

He swore softly again. "I may be late tonight, but it won't be by choice."

"I know. Just hold the thought of that vacation."

"I will. I love you."

"I love you, too."

I sighed, knowing there was a sappy smile on my face. I wanted to bask in the glow of that, but before I could even get the receiver back on its hook, the other line rang.

TWENTY-THREE

"JOLIE, HI; it's me, Prissy."

"Prissy," I said. "How are you?"

"Fine. Listen, I've been in my office—"

My stomach tightened. I simply wasn't cut out to be a spy among family. "Prissy, I'm really sorry...."

"For what? I don't mind looking up these articles. It's actually been fun." In my fear, I hadn't noticed the excitement that underscored her words. "But, Jolie, you won't believe what I've found out."

"Articles?"

"The ones you gave me last night on mistletoe. Someone doctored them. The copies you have are not the same as the original articles that were published!"

My brain was making slow manual shifts. "Are you sure?"

"Absolutely! Most were originally a warning to parents to keep it away from their children and pets. And listen to this. 'Both children and adults have died from eating the berries, although it is rare.' The toxicity level is low for a poison."

"Interesting. I would assume that meant she had to ingest a lot of it."

"That's what I think. But wait, there's something else I have to tell you. When I compared the articles, you know, the copies you gave me to the originals, the look was almost identical. Font, type size, column width, and all, copied almost perfectly."

I had to think about it. "So how did that happen? I don't get it—oh." I got it.

"Someone," Prissy was saying, "rewrote the articles and laid them out on a computer. It wouldn't be hard to do. I could do it in three different software programs I have. Then you print it out, and make a copy so the difference in paper doesn't show. Voilà!

A magazine article, a newspaper article, and an excerpt from a book all look genuine.''

And it would certainly be easy to do at an advertising agency. We had two graphic design programs that would make it a snap. We also had dozens of different fonts, so the letters would match either magazine or newspaper type. And once those were photo-copied, they could be given to Desi as reason to eat or drink mistletoe. A plant that would kill her.

The skin between my shoulder blades prickled into goose bumps. "Pris, could you fax the articles you found over to me?"

"Sure. What's your number?"

I gave it to her, and after she had written it down and repeated it, she asked, "Do you want me to talk to the police?"

It was tempting. "No, that's okay. Just fax the things to me, and I'll handle it. Oh, and, Prissy, thank you."

"Actually, it was fun. Let me know if there's anything else I can do to help. I'm going by the library later, if you need more research."

I promised I would and hung up. Rather than stand hunched over the fax machine, waiting, I first found Sergeant Bohles's card in my purse and carried it with me while I made myself a cup of tea.

A number of people at the agency were capable of dummying the articles on mistletoe, but another question I hadn't spent much time thinking about was, who had the motive to kill Desi?

Who indeed?

My first thought was Audry, if it was true that Desi and Michael were lovers. The jilted wife had reason for anger, especially if she thought that Michael was going to leave her again. I wondered if Audry would kill to keep her husband. It didn't seem likely; it supposed a level of passion that I'd never seen in Audry except toward her work.

There were also a lot of ifs. If Michael and Desi really had been lovers. If Audry had known about it.

Something else occurred to me; the note shoved under the bathroom door had said, *I still love you,* as if the affair between Michael and Desi had ended, but Michael wanted it to continue. That brought up another scenario. Suppose Desi had walked away from Michael for whatever reason, and Michael decided that if he couldn't have her, then no one could. It was all too common a motive for murder.

I shook my head. I could imagine Michael loving Desi; I could even see him loving her passionately, but I couldn't accept him trying to possess her. Michael simply wasn't a possessive man.

The microwave dinged and I took out my cup and put the tea bag in it. The word *possessive* was reverberating around in my mind. Donna Katherine adored Chester, might even be considered a little possessive of him. What if she felt that Desi was replacing her in Chester's affections? After all, it was Desi who had given the speech about Chester during the party.

I thought about that one for a while, then discarded it as unlikely.

So what about Fred or Ralph? Or even Amber?

Would they? Could they? Did they?

It set up a chant in my head, like a riddle with no ending and one I couldn't solve. Time to get moving.

I went into the copy room. Three sheets of paper plus a fax transmittal page were on top of a pile of recently received faxes. Prissy had done great work; she'd found the original book page, the newspaper and magazine articles. All said more or less the same. Mistletoe was a poison, and all parts of the plant were toxic, although the berries were the most dangerous. It caused symptoms such as vomiting, diarrhea, and slowed pulse. The book mentioned digitalislike symptoms, and listed drugs that could cause the same types of problems when taken in large doses. Crystodigin, Lanoxin, Digitoxin, and last, Purodigin, which could only be administered through an IV.

I handwrote my own cover sheet to Bohles explaining what he was getting and faxed everything over to the police station. He could call me if he had questions, or he could fax or E-mail me. Ah, the wonders of modern technology.

SOMEHOW I put my brain into work gear and plowed head. I had done what I could for Desi Baker; now I would finish her job.

When the rest of the staff began arriving I didn't even look up. I did, however, stop when Chester came in and began to rub my shoulders and tell me what a wonderful person, and writer, I was.

"Thank you," I said.

"Oh, and look, your tea is cold. I'll get Donna Katherine to make you a fresh cup."

"No, no," I said. While Donna Katherine may pamper Chester, she wouldn't appreciate serving me. Besides, I didn't want to break the flow of work. "I'll get some when I finish this ad."

He patted my shoulders. "I won't disturb you then," he said as he tiptoed toward the door.

I was nose-down in my keyboard sometime later when Sergeant Bohles called. "You sent all these articles?"

"Yes. Those are the originals. My sister-in-law pulled them off the Internet somehow."

"What do they tell you?"

I tried not to sound as if he was disrupting me, but frankly, he was. "That mistletoe is a poison, just like I knew before." I stopped. "Is that what you wanted me to say?"

"So how did the articles get changed?"

I saved the piece of copy I was working on and turned my attention to the conversation. "Graphic design and layout," I said. I went on to tell him what could be done with a computer and a little skill.

"So a graphic artist could have done it."

"Well, yes." Funny, until then I'd pretty much ignored Fred, but the man was obviously a whiz at graphic design. So was Ralph Richardson. For that matter, so was Prissy, and my son, Jeremy. There was no telling how many people had the means and method to re-create the articles. Motive was another matter. "Actually, a lot of people—"

"Mrs. Wyatt, can I get back to you? I have another call I have to take."

"No need. Unless you have something else you want to ask me."

"Not a thing. Unless you want to tell me why you walked back to that handicap stall." He paused and I could almost hear his smirk. When I didn't respond he said, "Didn't think so. Thanks for your help."

Desi Baker smiled out at me from her photo on the wall. Maybe she was thanking me for doing what little I could to see that her work was finished and her killer caught. Or maybe she was in a place where it no longer mattered who had murdered her.

"Jolie?"

It was Michael, standing inside the doorway, close enough to let me know he wasn't just saying hello in passing.

"Good morning," I said.

Michael was in his casual Friday attire. Khaki slacks that fit beautifully on his long legs, loafers with print socks in colors that matched his collarless print shirt. Michael always looked like a male model, perhaps because his dark eyes held enough intensity to remove him from the everyday, and his smile was the earthly equivalent of a solar flare.

"How are you this morning?" he asked.

"I'm fine."

He glanced at the stack of files on the edge of my desk, and at the computer screen, which held an ad for a car dealer.

"You have turned out an incredible amount of work this week. I'm not sure what we would have done if you hadn't been willing to help. The one thing most of us aren't able to do is write copy."

He was right about that. Chester, Audry, Michael, and even Nola seemed incapable of that task. Chester had once said that even classified ads were beyond him, much less anything that required creativity. It was an amazing statement considering that they were all in advertising.

"Oh, you'd have figured out something," I said. "You always do."

"Perhaps, but you've still been wonderful." Michael glanced

again at the desk, saw my empty teacup, and said, "Can I have Amber bring you some fresh tea?"

The simple question caught me off guard. "What? I'm sorry, what did you say?"

"Would you like some fresh tea? I could have Amber make it for you."

I stared at him. The tilt of his head, the inflection of his voice along with the offer itself, were echoes of an earlier conversation.

That's when I saw the truth of it all. Michael was a younger, more handsome version of Chester Sterling. Chester had lost the good looks of his youth by the time I'd met him, while Michael could have replaced David, if Michelangelo had known him. It was those differences that had kept me from seeing that underneath their physical attributes both men were the same.

Both were kind, charming, and easygoing, but neither one was very productive. It had been Rose Sterling, Audry's mother, who had built the agency from its inception. I now realized that after her death, Chester had let the business function as best it could until Audry came along. She was the one who took the reins, because someone had to, and she was the one who got it growing again.

Audry Sterling-Sherabian had married her father.

"You've done so much," Michael was saying. "Worked so hard..."

"I've enjoyed it." I assessed Michael Sherabian in a way I should have done years ago.

He twitched his shoulders. "I understand you're almost finished with your work here."

"Another hour or so and I'll be done."

His dark eyes melted with sadness. "And then you'll be leaving again."

"Yes."

It should have mattered that my absence would affect Michael, but now that I could clearly see him, I also realized some truths about my feelings for him. Our relationship hadn't been about Michael, it had been about my need. My father had been dying,

Jeremy had been growing up and pulling away as little boys do, and there had been a horrible hole in my life. I had needed someone to love, and someone to love me in return, so I had created a Prince Charming. He was my own perfect man, but he was a mirage that I had clothed in Michael Sherabian's body.

As I looked at Michael I felt an incredible sadness mottled with guilt. I had never loved him. Not really. Probably because I had never really known him. I had never gotten beyond the exterior to find out what was inside. I had to wonder if anybody ever had.

I stood up because it was time for closure. "Michael, I owe you an apology. I'm sorry that I hurt your marriage—" I fumbled. Knowing the truth and offering it to him were two different things. I swallowed and said with painful honesty, "I'm sorry for everything."

He nodded slowly, looking terribly vulnerable and alone. I think he understood, and it had to hurt like hell. "It's been wonderful seeing you again, Jolie, whatever the circumstances. Your husband is a lucky man."

"Thank you. Audry's pretty lucky, too."

His shrug said it all. He knew that Audry didn't think that, and he suspected she was right.

In that moment I came closer to truly caring about him than I ever had, but it was love mixed with pity, not a combination that Michael would welcome.

"Well," he said, stepping back awkwardly. "I guess I'd better let you finish. Did you want that tea?"

I started to say no, but it occurred to me that Michael would like to feel useful. "I'd love some. Some mint tea would be nice." I handed him my empty cup.

He took it with a brief smile. "I'll send Amber right back with it."

Useful in his own way. "Thanks."

I sat down at the computer, feeling lighter than I had in months. I still wasn't proud of what I'd done, and I'd always regret the hurt I'd caused, but at least all those feelings didn't have to cloud my future.

For a moment I was tempted to call Matt and tell him what I'd discovered, but besides the fact that I didn't know where to reach him, I didn't think this was something he needed to hear. He could just benefit from my discovery.

In the picture on the wall, Desi's smile seemed to reflect my own. She looked so fresh and young, so unburdened, which was much the way I felt now. It made me think she hadn't been having an affair with Michael. Instead, I hoped she'd been a friend to him; that would explain Michael's grief.

And somehow I had the feeling she'd seen the real man more quickly than the rest of us. Certainly more quickly than I had.

Another thought struck me—I wondered if that had been the cause of her death.

"I'm sorry," I said softly to her beaming photo. Sorry she had died, sorry that my feeble efforts hadn't helped find her murderer, and sorry I hadn't known her.

I brought my eyes down to the computer screen and rested my fingers on the keyboard. My presence at Rose Sterling Advertising had become a mass of sorrys, and it was time to get to work so I could put them behind me.

"GIRL, you take good care, you hear me, now?" Donna Katherine said as she gave me a hug.

"I hear, and I will." We were standing in her office, her Christmas wonderland glittering around us. It even smelled like the holidays. "It was great seeing you."

"It was, and if you get tired of that good-lookin' husband of yours, you just send him out this way. I'll put him to good use."

I didn't like that thought, but then Matt wouldn't much like it either. "Got it. You take it easy, too."

She twitched her hips and flipped a shoulder before she said meaningfully, "I always do."

This time I laughed. "Seriously, it was good seeing you again."

"You, too, and I'll be putting your paycheck in the mail before you hit retirement age. Oh, yeah, and, Jolie, you be sure and send us a card when your book comes out. I want to read it."

"I'll arrange a signing in Austin and see that you're all invited."

"Good, girl. Now, did you get a chance to say good-bye to Chester?"

"He's gone and Amber didn't know when he'd be back. Everyone's gone." I wasn't sure if I was sad about that or relieved. Chester's party, which now seemed aeons ago, was supposed to have been my triumphant return, a glorious tribute to my brilliance for writing and publishing a book. Amazing how life twists in its own way. Instead I had found Desi Baker dead, and ended up a copywriter, just what I'd been before I'd left.

As my dad used to say, the more things change the more they stay the same.

Donna Katherine's phone rang and she made a face. "Well, guess that's the bell calling me back to the salt mines. 'Bye again, Jolie."

Before she picked up the phone I waved and started for the front door. When I heard the swish of the ornaments on the Christmas tree I stopped. I didn't want any more drawn-out good-byes. I didn't want to see Audry and feel the guilt again, or the pity for Michael. I didn't want to wonder if Ralph or Fred were murderers, which was a thought that continued to haunt me. It would even have been hard to face Chester, now that I understood him better.

I couldn't remain motionless in the hallway forever, though. With a forced smile on my face, I sucked in a breath and stepped around the corner, moving quickly, as if the momentum would push me out the door without any conversation. Nola was at the front desk, glancing through her messages.

"Hey," she said.

I slowed. "Hey, yourself." Those were the first words we'd exchanged since she'd stormed out. I nudged her elbow, causing the strap of her purse to slip off her shoulder. When she pulled it back up again I smiled. "Got ya."

She returned the smile. "You just now leaving for lunch?"

"No. Just leaving."

"You're not getting much of a send-off. How about if we have some hot chocolate first?"

Outside the window the sky was a dismal gray and tiny ice crystals had formed intricate patterns along the metal strips. The streets below were so hazy the sodden pedestrians had become shadows against the slick sidewalks.

"It looks pretty bad out there.... You think it will get any better if I wait?"

She shook her head. "Not a chance. But I'll tell you a shortcut to get where you're going."

Another of those old jokes we shared. Nola had come from radio sales, outside sales she'd always called it, where time was money and you had to know the fastest route to anyplace in the city. She'd also bragged she knew where all the best public rest rooms were, and where to find the quietest and cleanest pay phones.

Not that she needed pay phones anymore. The antenna of a cellular stuck out of her purse.

When I brought my eyes up to Nola's face she was watching me. Something was up; it mattered to her that we talked.

There was nothing to rush back to Prissy's for. Matt was no doubt at Austin Edge, fighting the good fight for the investors. Jeremy was wrapping Christmas presents at Alicia's. Christopher would be taking a nap.

Nola was waiting, still watching me.

"Sure," I said. "I'd love some hot chocolate, but you're buying. And flying."

"We're flying," she said, taking my elbow and ushering me out the door. "I don't want to stay here, and neither do you. There's a new little coffee bar we can get to by cutting through the parking garage."

"How come nobody told me about that sooner?"

"You don't ask, you don't get." She sounded grim as she added, "Especially around here."

TWENTY-FOUR

As NOLA AND I hurried across the lobby, Ted Polovy jerked his head toward the outside. "Be careful out there, it's getting slick."

"We're just going to the coffee bar, Mom," Nola replied with a grin.

Then we wrapped our coats tighter around us and hurried through the parking garage. Its half-empty state was a testament to the fact that people were leaving early, either because of the bad weather or for the holiday.

At the coffee bar Nola selected a small table that looked out on Sixth Street. I had expected charm and warmth, but the place was almost pure white with cheap plastic chairs and flimsy white metal tables. The most inviting element was the aroma. I imagined it as a mixture of every submarine sandwich that had passed through there with garlic, vinegar, and Italian sausage vying for the most attention. I sniffed a couple of times, trying to talk myself into something to eat, although I knew better. Too many meals mean too many pounds.

"There must be a million calories in this thing," I said, warming my hands around the cardboard cup of hot chocolate topped with a small mountain of whipped cream.

"Consider it an emergency measure," Nola said. "Without it we could freeze to death."

Outside the window I was grateful to see that there was none of the real ice the weatherman had threatened, but the frigid snap to the air suggested it was coming.

"So what's up?" I asked, huddling close to the table.

Nola made a quick face. "No pleasantries? 'Nice hair'? 'I like your coat'? 'How are the kids?' None of those things?"

"Your kids are fine or we wouldn't be here; I love the coat, probably because it's almost identical to mine, and your hair looks a bit windblown. As, I'll bet, mine is.''

"You're a hard woman, Jolene Berenski."

"Wyatt," I corrected. "Jolene Wyatt. Matt says it has a nice ring to it."

Nola sat back in the chair. "When you start bragging on your husband, it's time to get down to facts."

"I wasn't bragging—"

She ignored that. "You know the other morning when I was in your office?"

"And trashed the place?"

"And cleaned it up," she added. Then she stopped, her expression going from playful to serious. "Damn, Jolie, this is really hard for me. It's all hard."

I blew on my hot chocolate, my eyes still on her. For the first time she seemed like an older woman to me, as if the sedentary culture of middle age gripped her so hard she couldn't do any of her customary quick movements. She didn't raise an eyebrow, fidget with her ring, or twitch her shoulders. She merely sat.

"Nola, what is it? You look so, so unhappy."

Another sigh, and a slow nod. "I am." Her eyes narrowed as she focused on mine. "Would you say I am a loyal person?"

"Of course."

"A good person?"

"Yes. You're one of the best people I know. You're kind, you're generous, you care about other people's feelings—"

"You're prejudiced."

"I probably am," I responded. "But for good reason. So what's going on? What was going on the other morning when you were looking for something in my office?"

The sigh she let out this time was almost a shudder. "I needed some copy. Remember I told you I was pitching a big new account?"

"Right. And you said that Audry was talking about cutting your commissions again."

"Yeah, she is, and when she told me that, it was the last straw.

You can't believe what it's been like around there. I can't make a long-distance call without writing it down and justifying it. Hell, I was going home to phone my out-of-town clients because it was just easier to pay for it than put up with the nonsense, but James put his foot down. He said no matter what kind of trouble Rose Sterling was in, it wasn't our place to subsidize them. Especially because he just started his own insurance agency last year, and we're still not seeing a profit. I'm supporting the family and his business.''

Which could certainly put a strain on anyone, especially a woman who took her responsibilities as seriously as Nola.

"I'm sorry," I said.

"Not your fault."

"No, but I'm sorry it's happening to you. It's got to be difficult."

She nodded. "Not that anyone at Rose Sterling seems to care. Hell, Jolie, I don't think they've even noticed. Certainly not the Ice Queen."

"But what about Chester? Have you tried to talk to him?"

She took her time formulating a response, and when she spoke the words came out slowly. "I know you think a lot of Chester, and I agree with you he's a very fine man, but, Jolie, I don't know if he's much of a force at the agency right now. Used to be that he'd do something if you asked; he really cared about us, but he's just a figurehead now. Audry has the say-so. Only Audry."

Her words saddened rather than surprised me; they merely confirmed my own conclusions. "I can appreciate that," I said, nodding. I sipped some chocolate before I asked, "So what are you doing about it?" I already suspected the answer to my question, and even had some proof at the office, but she needed to talk.

With just a touch of defensiveness she said, "I'm starting my own agency. I pitched that account for myself."

"Under the name Millennium Advertising."

"You found the copy." She rolled her eyes, her movements

showing some of her old energy. "So what do you think? Am I crazy? Am I a terrible person?"

"Well, you're not crazy. You're a very good salesperson, and I assume you can handle a business. Austin's growing again; you should do very well."

"But was it wrong to pitch the account before I quit?"

Which was the heart of the matter; or perhaps more honestly, the conscience of it. I allowed myself to think about it. Nola was on straight commission, meaning that if her accounts didn't do business in a given month, she didn't make any money. As far as I could tell, her time was her own. I only had one quibble. "You used Desi to write the copy."

"But not on Rose Sterling time! She did it on her lunch hours, or after five, or at home. Believe me, this was a self-preservation move, not a way to hurt Rose Sterling." But we both knew Audry wouldn't see it that way.

Nola caught her breath and went on again. "And I paid Desi for the time she put in. Now, maybe it wasn't what I'd pay a regular freelance writer, but we had a bonus deal worked out. If I got the account, she got the difference plus some additional. Jolie, I wasn't out to hurt anybody, but I have to take care of myself and my family. You know how that is. Of all people, you should understand."

Nola had been my confidante through more than one crisis in my own life when I had been a single mom, trying to raise Jeremy and in general hold things together. She'd had her problems, too, both personally and financially. More than once we'd brown-bagged it together, pretending we were bringing food from home in an effort to lose weight rather than to save money. And we'd shopped at the Junior League Thrift Shop when we couldn't afford new clothes any other way. I'd cried on her shoulder over men, money, Jeremy, and my career. I'd trusted her with secrets and she'd honored me the same way. If we had to give each other advice, we knew the order of priorities: family came first, then friends, then business. It was a credo that worked, at least for us.

"I do understand," I said. "In fact, if you need help with

copywriting when Millennium takes off, I might suggest some-one. She lives out of town, but her fees are reasonable, and hey, she's just a fax away.''

"Are you serious?"

"Sure."

Nola smiled, flipping her coat back. "I can't tell you how much better I feel. I thought about becoming a Catholic, just so I could go to confession." She sat forward in the chair, then leaned back, letting out relieved breaths. "You know, I'm going to hold you to that promise of writing copy for me."

"I'd love to. When will you know about the account?"

"January third, and I swear to you, I'm turning in my resig-nation the minute I know. I've already written the letter."

"I've got my fingers crossed." I held them out to show her that I really did.

And still something niggled at the back of my mind. Could Desi have written the copy, and then used her knowledge of Mil-lennium Advertising to blackmail Nola? Not that Nola would have responded by killing her; Nola simply wasn't that kind of person. But maybe James had done it to protect Nola—

"You don't look happy about something," she said.

"I keep thinking about Desi's death. And just about Desi, I guess, too."

"What about her?"

"I don't know." Nola watched me patiently until I phrased the question. "You said she was ambitious. Is that right?"

"Yes. Which is why she was so hot about working with Mil-lennium. She figured she could move ahead in a new agency a lot faster than she could at Rose Sterling. She could get around me a lot easier when she wanted something than she could Audry, too." There was some anger in her voice.

"But were you worried about her? You know, did you think she'd push too hard? Maybe try to get your clients?"

The response was succinct. "I didn't say I was going to hire her. I said that's what she wanted."

"Oh."

"I hadn't decided, okay? But it was doubtful. She wasn't honorable. At least I didn't trust her to be." She drank hot chocolate, taking in big gulps as if it were time to go.

"Hold it. Amber says that Desi was straight arrow—absolutely perfect in the honor department. So what am I missing here?"

Nola put down her drink, sat back, and frowned. "Are you serious?"

"One hundred percent. Amber swears that Desi was a straight shooter. And wait a minute, so does Ted Polovy. You know, the security guard in the building."

"My, my, isn't that interesting."

"And Fred thinks she was wonderful, too. Honest, demure..."

"Yes, but Fred still thinks it's 1970. He's disappointed because he went to Town Lake last weekend and couldn't find the love-in he thought they were holding."

I laughed. "Well, he did sound a little out of touch. Okay, so he's always that way, but it was most noticeable when he was talking about Desi. Like maybe she wasn't quite real."

We both sipped chocolate, and finally Nola shook her head. "You'll have to figure out your own truth about it, Jolie. I think Desi was honorable when it suited her."

"Wasn't it Camus who said that every man has a moral code of his own likes and dislikes?"

"The man was ahead of his time—it sure is true these days." She stuffed her napkin in the now-empty cardboard cup and tossed it toward the trash can. When it went in she said, "Two points."

"So what about Desi and men? How was she with them? Half the agency seems to have been in love with her. Male half."

"She said something to me once about her ex-husband. I got the impression he was abusive, and it changed something in her." Nola shook her head with the frustration of not being able to find the words. "Men were like cats or something. She liked them, sort of charmed them, but she just wasn't having any, you know? As if she could control her destiny more easily if she didn't get involved with men."

"Interesting." Not being the athletic type like Nola, I got up and put my cup in the trash. When I was seated at the table again I said, "So you don't think she was sleeping with Michael?"

Nola looked at me for a long moment. "Jolie, I only know for sure of two women who've slept with Michael Sherabian." She raised an eyebrow. "I'm looking at one of them."

I refused to flinch. "And who was the other?"

"His wife."

"Oh." Long pause, while I tried to tough it out.

It was Nola who broke the silence. "Well, kiddo, now we know all of each other's guilty sins."

"Not all," I said. "Let's not mention any more, on the off chance that one of us may have forgotten."

"Good thinking." She looked at her watch. "Guess I'd better run. I can't believe tomorrow is Christmas Eve. Lord, and today's the day my mom is flying in."

"Do you have to pick her up?"

"No. James's new office is closer, so he's going to get her, but I don't envy him. I told her that two days before Christmas was going to be impossible; I'll bet the airport looks like rush hour on the freeway. And it's Friday on top of it. Always a bad day for travel."

Something about Friday and travel hit me unexpectedly. Today was Friday. "What time is it?" I asked.

"A little after three. Why?"

Todd was flying out at 5:50 P.M. on Friday. With tickets for two people. I had assumed it was Friday of next week, but what if I was wrong? What if he was leaving today? That second ticket needn't be for a girlfriend—

Things fell into place with a tiny click.

"I've got to run." I meant that literally, jumping up and running for the parking lot.

IT HAD BEGUN to drizzle and I slid my way along the slick highway with hundreds of other cars, our headlights beaming yellow and barely penetrating the dark and cold afternoon. All the muttered curses, all the promises to God, didn't speed up the traffic as I crawled through the nasty weather at thirty miles an hour.

Just let me get there in time, I prayed.

Between swipes of the windshield wipers, I tried to calm myself. Other people were at the house. Prissy was there, maybe Stephanie. Surely they would stop Todd. Wouldn't they?

The lights in front of me glowed brighter red, and cars slid to a halt. Another car lurched into my lane, and I stepped on the brakes fighting the wheel as the Intrepid slid to the right. I stopped just inches from the car ahead of me.

"Asshole," I snapped.

I put my attention back on the road, and when the exit appeared out of the haze in front of me, instead of relaxing, my constricted muscles remained tight.

The residential streets were easier to traverse. Very few cars were out, and the lights from the big houses in Prissy's neighborhood gave off warmth and hope that everything was as it should be.

"Just let Christopher be there," I prayed silently.

In the wide driveway was a car I didn't recognize and I pulled in beside it, parking too close. My feet crunched on the ice as I made my way around that other vehicle. It had a child's car seat in the back, and that frightened me into hurrying, so that I lost my balance and had to grab the door handle to remain upright.

Maybe the car belonged to a friend of Stephanie's, I told myself, planting my feet more firmly. Someone her age who also had a little one. Surely that was it. Except it seemed very bad weather for a visit.

With quick, careful steps I made my way toward the back of the house. At the corner I turned onto the patio and stopped, stunned.

Christopher was sitting alone, three steps up on the outdoor staircase. He wasn't wearing a coat and his tiny body was wracked with shivers. Tear tracks had dried on his face.

"Oh, my God! Christopher, you'll freeze to death out here."

I ran up the steps, pulling open my own coat so I could envelop him in it.

Just as I reached him I heard another voice behind me. "Stop right there. Don't you go near him."

TWENTY-FIVE

IT SOUNDED like the voice of God—demanding and commanding—but I didn't hesitate. I threw open my coat and reached for
Christopher. The material caught on something behind me and I
fell to the tile on one knee.

Even as I yelped in pain, I thought it was an accident. I jerked
at my coat, and hopped up the step to get hold of Christopher.
"What in the hell—?"

"I told you not to do that." It was Todd.

Somewhere my brain was registering his words, but they made
no sense, as if the real meaning were hidden in code.

"Are you crazy?" I demanded. "He'll die of exposure."

"That boy has been coddled too much by women, and I won't
have any more."

"He's a baby. You don't leave a baby out in this weather." I
pulled Christopher to me. His hands were purple with the cold,
and his body shook. I wrapped him up with me in my coat as
fury coursed through me. "I don't know what your problem is,
Todd, but this is criminal—"

I heard a crack on the tile; it sounded like a baseball bat. I
jerked around, falling to a sitting position.

"Todd—what in the—"

He was holding a set of nunchaku. Two thick, short wooden
sticks attached on one end by a short length of chain. They are a
martial arts weapon, cruel and lethal. He flipped them expertly,
coming up a step so that I could feel the rush of air as one spun
within inches of my face.

He didn't stop even when I flinched backward.

"Todd, cut it out."

The nunchaku landed in his hand effortlessly, as if responding
to my command.

"Christopher is being punished," he said. His voice held resignation, as if this was unpleasant but necessary. "I have the right to do that—I'm his father."

I wasn't a bit surprised. But I was furious. "Todd, you may have some rights where Christopher is concerned—"

"I have *every* right. I am his father." He slapped the nunchaku again, and the contained ferocity of the act shook me out of my anger. It was replaced with a gut-level fear.

Christopher was like a little animal, burrowing against me.

I heard the quiver in my voice, and hoped it was from the cold as I said, "Todd, I know sometimes children can be difficult—"

"He is not difficult, he is spoiled rotten! He does exactly what he pleases no matter what I tell him. That is unacceptable. When I left Phoenix, I left Christopher on the condition that Stephanie would raise him right. Well, she hasn't. I should have known she didn't have it in her."

He didn't mention what else I suspected—that he'd been abusive to both Stephanie and Christopher, and it had all been blamed on drugs. Maybe drugs were in part at fault, but I was beginning to realize that Todd, just Todd, was to blame.

And Prissy never knew the truth, wouldn't hear it. Didn't want to know what her best friend's son was really like. God help them all.

I took a breath. "I'm sure it's been difficult. But now that Christopher's punishment is over, I'll take him inside."

"No! It's not done. You go inside and mind your own business."

A tiny whimper came from Christopher as he pressed himself even tighter against me.

"Christopher is a baby, and this could—" I stopped. I didn't want to frighten Christopher any more than he already was. With great effort I brought my voice under control. "He has to get inside. Certainly you understand about exposure." The gray skies were sending down sleet. I had to get Christopher out of the weather.

I started to stand and the nunchaku whipped around, smacked

against the wall, and flew toward me. I cringed, yanking Christopher with me. My back hit the hard step above and I let out an involuntary cry.

"All of you women are weak. You're ruining Christopher, turning him into a wimp. He has to be tough. Strong, like a man. Don't you, Christopher?" When there was no response Todd leaned closer so that I could smell his breath. "Don't you? Answer me!"

The little voice responded. "Yes, sir."

"And who am I?"

Christopher's lip quivered, but he said firmly, "My fodder."

Now I was the one who was shaking.

Sleet stung us. My jaws barely moved as I forced myself to say calmly, "Todd, I didn't mean to countermand your authority—"

"I wasn't going to press my duties with Christopher. I just wanted to see him," he said, tilting his head with some sick version of pride. "After all, he is my son. But then I saw what was happening to him. How he didn't behave. Coming into my room twice after he'd been told not to! You knew better, didn't you, Christopher? Didn't you?"

"Yes."

"You speak up when I talk to you!"

"Yes, sir."

"Getting away with being a spoiled brat. That's what you are, aren't you? You're a very bad boy, aren't you?"

"Yes, sir."

"No!" The word shot out of me. "He's not bad." The nunchaku flew again, but I went on. "Christopher may have *done* something bad—we've all done some bad things—but he's not a bad boy. He's a good boy. A very good boy."

Todd flipped one of the sticks upward and caught it deftly, so that the two pieces of wood lay in his right hand. Deceptively peaceful. He stood up straight, like a drill sergeant. "That's reverse psychology. Pop psychology. Weak bullshit."

"No. It's fact. As his father, you know Christopher is good, or you wouldn't bother with him." I pulled the coat tighter; it barely closed around Christopher. He was still cold, but the shaking had lessened.

When Todd didn't respond I glanced toward the house. The lights were on, but apparently no one else was there. Todd noticed my look and said, "Stephanie went with Peter, and then Prissy got a phone call from Brackenridge Hospital. She was told Ross was in an accident. I volunteered to keep Christopher so she could go."

The world was spinning too fast. "Is Ross—?"

"He's fine. Probably at his office." Todd glanced at his watch. "It should take Prissy another ten minutes or so to get to Brack, and I'll be gone by then."

Relief made me weak. Christopher almost slid out of my arms; I pulled him closer. "You're going away now," I said.

It was misplaced hope on my part.

"*We* are leaving. Christopher and I. Aren't we, son?"

I could feel Christopher tip his head forward slowly in a terrified nod. His words were a whispered, "Yes, sir."

Friday. I had been right, it was today.

Todd reached out toward us. "Christopher, we're just going to leave your Christmas presents, we don't have time to fool with them now. I want you to stand up and go wait for me at the car."

"No!" I jerked away, the cry like a wound.

The nunchaku flew again. Todd leaned closer and said, "I am not an unkind person, but you are forcing me to do things I'd rather not. You're being unreasonable. Let go of my son."

"Todd, you can't go. It will kill Prissy and Ross—" He jerked Christopher out of my arms, ripping him away with brute strength. "No," I cried. "You can't do this, it's kidnapping—"

With one hand he set Christopher on the ground, and held me at bay with the nunchaku. His eyes still glaring, he said, "Christopher, go. Now."

"Please, Todd, no." I hurt to my soul. "Please, don't—"

"Move, Christopher."

Christopher said quietly, "Good-bye, Aunt Dolie. I love you." He started off.

"You can't!" I jumped up and Todd shoved me back. I slipped on the icy steps and my head smacked the tile. Pain jolted through me and the sky spun. "You can't—"

Todd's face wasn't in focus as he said, "You made me do that; you just remember it was your fault." He started away.

I got to my knees, and my stomach lurched. "No—"

"Wish everyone a happy holiday from me." There was no sarcasm in the words, the last Todd said to me as he hurried toward his car.

My head went forward, until I could feel the freezing railing pressing against my forehead.

In the hazy background a car door opened, and Todd's barked command was lost in the slamming of it. Then a second car door opened and closed.

I gulped in air, and saw that my tears had frozen on the step. A car engine started.

No! He'd have to kill me to get away with Christopher.

This time I tripped on my own coat, then slipped on the slick patio. It didn't matter; I half ran, half slid, falling more than once. The only pain was in my heart. I had to get Christopher back.

The lights of Todd's car raked over me as he swung around on the circular drive and I could see Christopher watching me—straining at the car seat. I could almost hear his cry.

Then Todd reached back and tried to hit Christopher. He missed by inches.

"Son of a bitch," I said, yanking open my car door and jumping in. My eyes were trained on Todd's car as I started the engine, backed around the circle, then swung out into the street. The sleet and rain had formed an icy sheet on the asphalt and suddenly my car broke loose; I was gliding sideways across the street. With stiff fingers I whirled the cold steering wheel, and like a ballet maneuver, the car began to turn again. It slowly straightened.

I frantically looked for Todd. At the end of the block I spotted taillights. God, I hoped they were his.

My knees were shaking, and I forced myself to step down on the gas pedal. The wheels spun and the car didn't move. With another curse I tried again, this time more carefully until the Intrepid started forward. Todd had grown up in the East; he had the advantage of knowing how to maneuver on ice and snow. I had the advantage of a heavier car, and one other thing: I had absolutely nothing to lose.

Todd turned right. I switched on my headlights and started to pray. He was still a block away from me, adding distance with every second that passed. At the corner I braked lightly, looking to my left. A decorated Christmas tree lit the yard beside me. I noticed it as I arced around the corner, the wheels finding nothing solid to cling to. Thank God the street was empty.

My heart almost broke as I realized that Todd was even farther away, and if he got to the freeway, there was no way I could catch him. In the crush at the airport it would even be more difficult to track him down.

In desperation I searched for some way to catch him. I had an idea, and no way of knowing if it would work until I tried it. The windshield was fogging, making visibility even worse in the twilight.

With great care I flipped on the defroster, then turned the steering wheel. The car slid until it hit the curb with a jolt, then the right front tire jumped up and stayed firm on the grass. Perfect. That was the way I was going to drive until I was closer.

It actually worked. I came to a driveway, but I held the car steady. We slid across the concrete and back up the other side. We missed a telephone pole by inches. A mailbox loomed up, and rather than jerk the wheel, I brushed it, the front fender grating against the metal box before it hit the ground.

It shouldn't have been that close to the street anyway.

The important thing was that I was gaining on Todd. I could see him, still on the road, driving at a speed that probably galled him.

I was less than forty feet back.

What I needed now was a plan.

TWENTY-SIX

WE WERE still in a residential area; only two cars had passed me on the icy road, but I didn't want to risk endangering someone else. Unless I had to. I was desperate and it showed in my thinking.

By now Todd had seen me. He tried to drive faster, but even he had his limitations; the car couldn't pull away. I stepped on the gas, bouncing as the tires went up and over a planter edged in brick. I jerked my foot off the accelerator and the car slowed.

"Damn it."

Again I pressed on the gas pedal until I was just a few feet behind Todd. I could see him clearly now, hunched over the wheel like Cruella De Vil. I could see Christopher, too. He was sitting ramrod-straight in his car seat. I hoped he was buckled in.

With a prayer and a hope I pressed hard on the accelerator. The Intrepid bucked forward, began to slide, and just kissed Todd's back bumper.

I honked the horn, waving for Todd to stop. He stared forward, his posture grim and determined. It was clear he was going straight to the airport and nothing was going to deter him.

Out of the gloom and mist rose a stop sign; Todd had to be weighing his options. If he didn't slow down, he had a better chance of reaching the highway without interference from me.

I looked down the cross street as best I could, but by now I was a good thirty feet back, my vision blocked by houses. When I looked forward again I realized Todd's car had picked up speed; he was going to run the stop, which meant I would have to as well. I flicked on my emergency flashers and started honking my horn, then I increased the pressure on the gas pedal. My right foot was shaking. The needle on the speedometer rose slowly, from fifteen to twenty to twenty-five. Out of the corner of my eye

I caught the glare of headlights, coming from my left. They didn't have a stop.

"Don't do this to me!" I laid into the horn, letting it blare a warning.

It might have been my adrenaline pushing the car until we were doing almost thirty. Thirty-five. Todd was beyond the intersection, Christopher was safe on the other side. I continued to honk the horn, I flashed the lights, then closed my eyes and prayed as we went straight through the cross street.

In seconds I was right behind Todd. He was waving me back, but I kept coming. I gestured for him to move over and let me by. Miraculously, he eased to the right. I could see him talking, swearing, as I began to pull around him. My idea would work only if Christopher was strapped in the back on the other side of the car. He was. I drew even with Todd's car, keeping a good ten feet between us. He kept twisting his head to watch me. I waited until I was half a length in front of him, then with stiff movements I swung the steering wheel right. As if in slow motion the Intrepid lurched toward Todd's car. I saw his look of fury, then fear, as the Intrepid rammed into his door.

Metal crunched. Both cars rocked and bobbed. Together they picked up speed, slamming across the icy asphalt until Todd's front wheel jumped the curb. Tenaciously the Intrepid hung on. With one more nudge of the gas pedal I had Todd's car pinned between mine and a telephone pole.

With careless hurry I swung open my door and jumped out of the car. When my feet hit the ice they went out from under me and I grabbed for the door handle, just missing as I went down. The asphalt was hard and slick. I heard an engine behind me, and suddenly I was blinded by more headlights from a car rounding the corner. In a purely reflexive move, I let go of the car door and slid under the frame.

The other vehicle stopped just inches from my half-open door.

"Are you all right? Is anybody hurt?" Only the man's Reeboks and his jean legs were visible.

"I'm fine." As I reached out to grab the frame, his hand clutched at mine instead. He pulled me out and helped me stand.

"There's a baby in the other car," I said, already feeling my way toward the back fender, hanging on to the Intrepid for balance. "My nephew. Please. We have to—"

"Should I call the police?"

"Yes." It was like a miracle. "Yes. Call the police."

He started in the other direction, but I hardly noticed. I was on someone's lawn now so that I could move quickly. Through the rear passenger window I could see Christopher, hear him crying, "Aunt Dolie, we need help."

"I'll get you, little bug. Don't cry." I grabbed the door handle and jerked, but Todd had it locked. Son of a bitch.

I tried the front door; it was also locked.

Todd was screaming at me. "Look what you've done! You smashed my door and I'm trapped. I think my arm is broken."

Frantically I looked around. Not five feet away a bush was covered with a tarp—held down with bricks.

"Get me out of here," Todd yelled. "Now. Do you hear me? Christopher, shut the fuck up! Now, I want out now."

I picked up the brick and planted myself solidly next to the front passenger window. "Christopher, close your eyes and look the other way. Hurry!"

Todd realized what I was about to do. "You could kill me! You can't just—"

I reared back and flung the brick into the passenger window. It bounced off harmlessly.

Todd became even more abusive. "Damn it, you stupid bitch, you can't—"

I grabbed the brick again, only this time I imagined Todd's face where I aimed it. With my adrenaline pumping I smashed the brick into the glass. Millions of glittering shapes scattered around me, a few still clinging to the safety sealant as the glass shattered; it was almost beautiful.

"Aunt Dolie!"

I unlocked the back door and threw it open. Christopher was

strapped in his car seat, his coat lying on the seat beside him; a knit cap poked out of the pocket. I unhooked the strap on the car seat and jerked the restraining bar over his head.

"What about me? Why aren't you helping me?" Todd was flailing, trying to get at us, fumbling to undo his seat belt at the same time.

"He can help." I gestured toward our good Samaritan's car, only to see that he was driving off. "Quick, look at me," I said to Christopher, ramming his cap down on his head.

"You sent him to call the police, didn't you?" Todd screamed. He had his hand on the seat belt, but so far hadn't been able to unhook it. "You're going to pay for this! You're going to jail for kidnapping. Christopher is my son, and you can't take him. You rammed my car on purpose; I'll get you for assault."

"You've got the charges right, but the person wrong."

It wasn't much for a last insult, but the best I could do. With one arm around Christopher's body and one around his head to shield him, I said, "Come on, little bug." As if he could help. With one mighty heave I brought him out and for the first time he was safe, clinging to my neck, almost choking me. "It's okay, baby, you're fine now. Come on." I set Christopher on the ground and reached back into the car for his coat.

That was a mistake.

Todd grabbed my hand and bent it backward at the wrist. I felt the pain to my marrow. "No!" I tried to jerk away, but he increased the pressure and I waited for the bones to snap.

"Not so tough now, are you, bitch?" Todd snarled, almost smiling as he held fast to my wrist. "Now you're going to get me out of here, and then you're going to drive me to the airport."

Any second my wrist was going to break. "Please, no more—" I gasped, and lowered my head as if I could escape the pain. Christopher was clutching at my coat; he'd started to cry.

"Let go!" I begged. My head went down and I saw the nunchaku on the floor behind the passenger seat.

Any port in a storm, any weapon in a pinch.

Ignoring the pain I took hold of one end of the nunchaku with my free hand and flipped them upward.

I knew instantly there wasn't enough power, but the weapon itself had force. The other stick jerked at the end of the chain, hitting the dome light, blacking it out.

This time it was Todd who gasped and flinched. I swung the weapon again, accidently hitting the back of the seat, so that the other stick dropped harmlessly. Todd released my wrist just as I whipped the nunchaku in a third, more powerful, swing. It hit the rearview mirror, then bounced back, catching Todd on the side of the head.

"Goddamn it!" he yelled.

"Watch your language, asshole!" I jerked backward, out of the car, before I realized the jacket was still inside. This time I stayed low until I could snatch it out.

It took more precious time, but I had to get Christopher warm. His face was pale as I struggled to zip up his jacket. In the reflected streetlight we edged around the two cars while I pulled up his hood to cover his ears.

Hand over hand we moved along the back of Todd's car, my frozen fingers barely able to grasp the frigid metal. When we reached the other corner, I realized the Intrepid was five feet away across slick asphalt. It sat in the street like a cold hulk. "Hang on." I slid my feet slowly, taking careful little steps until we could reach the bumper; Christopher was clinging to my hand and my coat. The door creaked ominously as I pulled it open. Todd was still yelling at us, mixing his threats with curses and pleas. I ignored him.

"Get in the backseat. Hurry, Christopher." His teeth were chattering as he scrambled in.

"Thank you, Aunt Dolie," he said, his voice very little.

"Oh, Christopher." I kissed him quickly, trying to secure the seat belt with frozen fingers that refused to cooperate. "I'm sorry Todd got you, but you were very brave, sweetie. Very brave." Finally the lock clicked into place. I tugged at it once for security as I added, "You are good and brave."

"I'm cold, too, Aunt Dolie."

"Here." I took off my coat and wrapped it around him, then slammed the door.

I jumped in the front seat and started the car. "Hang on. And stay brave just a little longer."

With the gearshift in reverse, I gave the car some gas. Tires spun and the two cars remained locked together as if in some battle to the death.

"Are we stuck, Aunt Dolie? Todd will come and get us!"

"No, he won't, because we're not stuck. See?" I opened the door and rocked the car, which did no good at all. "The road is just a little slick, but watch what happens." Once again I tried the gas pedal, only this time I used all the control I had. "Gently, gently, see, we're moving."

It was wishful thinking. The wheels spun, smoke lifted from the front of the car, and neither vehicle shifted more than an inch or two.

Todd's mocking laugh caught my attention. He appeared to have the seat belt undone and was crawling toward the passenger door. Dear God, he was coming.

TWENTY-SEVEN

THIS TIME I prayed. Maybe I didn't deserve to be safe, but Christopher did. "Hang on, now, Christopher," I said. "We're leaving." With one last prayer I touched the accelerator. The car slid back a few inches. In my joy I quit pressing on the gas and the car plunged forward. Again it hit Todd's car, knocking him off balance. A string of expletives mauled the air.

"Okay, here we go." I closed my eyes and tried again. Slowly and with great care we eased backward. Todd was out of his car now. He had to stop because another pair of headlights was coming toward us.

I couldn't think about those things; I let the Intrepid slide to a stop, then I put it in drive.

I CLOSED MY EYES, gave it just the tiniest amount of gas, and without a roar, or even speed, we crept away.

I carried Christopher toward the lobby of the high-rise building that housed Rose Sterling Advertising. The place was beginning to feel like a second home and I was looking forward to seeing Ted Polovy, hoping for a little reinforcement.

Once over the threshold I realized there was a woman at the security desk. "Where's Ted?" I asked her, looking behind me, as if Todd might appear.

"Not here."

"But, I thought—" I guess I'd thought he worked twenty-four hours a day.

"Gone for the night," she said. The fluorescent lights in the lobby made her skin appear a brownish yellow, and her voice held no curiosity at all.

"Oh." I hadn't realized until that instant how much I'd counted on having someone here; someone who carried a gun, and would use it in our defense. Someone who would believe what I had to say without background information. Now we were on our own. But then, we had been all along.

"You want to sign in?" she asked.

"Sure." It was all I could get out without giving away how I was feeling.

I shifted Christopher to the desk and wrote my name. My nose was wet, but that was from the cold, just the cold, I told myself, sniffing hard. In the bottom of my coat pocket I found a linty tissue and blew my nose, before adding the name Rose Sterling to the next line of the sign-in book. The guard leaned toward Christopher and said, "Are you going to do some work?"

He shook his head. "No." By now he was warmer, but his face remained pale and pinched with a bright red nose. That could have been the cold, too. "My Aunt Dolie worts harder."

"Works," I corrected.

The woman nodded. "And, honey, we all do." She reached behind her and came up with a candy cane, which she handed to Christopher. "Here, have you been a good boy?"

Christopher blanched. His eyes fixed first on her, then on me. "I don't know. Aunt Dolie—?"

"Yes, you have. You've been a very good boy. You are a very good boy."

The woman picked up on the seriousness of my tone, and while she probably didn't understand it, she dropped her teasing manner. "A little bird told me that you are a good boy. Here." She handed over the candy. "Merry Christmas."

Christopher took it with the solemnity of someone accepting a Nobel prize. "Thank you."

I tried to smile a thank-you as well, but I doubt I succeeded. She acknowledged my nod and then pointed to the elevator. For once it was waiting, its doors open. I hurried us in that direction.

"Where we going, Aunt Dolie?"

"To my office, it's up on the seventh floor." I was clinging to Christopher, holding him to calm myself, hoping it was all going to be okay. The agency was the only safe place I could think of for the two of us to wait. "You want to push the button?" I stepped closer to the panel so he could press the seven. And the nine and eleven. The doors closed and we started our ascent.

My insides were shaking, just like my outsides had been earlier. At one point during the drive on Mopac my legs had quivered so violently I'd wondered if we'd make it. I had turned up the radio and started singing loudly. "Jingle Bells." I think we sang it seven times on the trip.

And all along I had wondered where Todd was. I knew he'd gotten help; another car had stopped as we drove off. I was fairly sure he wasn't hurt badly, but beyond that, there was a chance that his car was drivable, and he was capable of doing the driving. It was that thought that had frightened me most and followed us like a specter.

He could have come after us, and I didn't dare go to the police station because I couldn't ask for help without getting Child Protective Services involved. Their mission is to safeguard the child in any situation, and when things are unclear, as they certainly would be in our case, Christopher would be whisked away and it might take hours, even days, to get him back.

"When are we gonna see my mommy?" Christopher asked. His staunch efforts to remain brave were becoming harder to maintain.

I hugged him tighter. "In a little while. She's at a party right now, and I don't want to take you back to your grandma's until we know that your mommy's home. And I want your grandma and grandpa to be there."

"Can Todd find us?" he asked, sliding one arm under my heavy coat collar to hang on a little better. I kissed his cheek.

"No, sweetie, he can't. Todd doesn't know where I work." Or did he? Someone could have told him. And if he knew the name of the agency, he could look it up in the phone book to get a location. He could be here now, he could have arrived ahead of us—

My heart started hammering.

I took a deep breath to calm myself. Todd was behind us. It didn't matter what magic he worked, he couldn't be in this building or in these offices. It simply wasn't physically possible. "We're safe here," I said to Christopher. "We'll have something warm to drink, and then in a little bit we'll go home, when we know everyone is there."

"And Todd is in jail. Or dead."

Even three-year-olds know about dead these days.

I held on to his hands, warming them. "Everything will be okay. The police will take Todd and he will never come to hurt you again. Never." Only I couldn't be sure that Todd would never come back. In our world there are no such assurances.

The elevator stopped and I attempted to smile. "Here we go." I set Christopher down and ushered him out.

While Christopher was walking on his own, I noticed that he was so close his feet kept brushing mine. I reached down and took his hand.

It was only a little after five, but the place was locked, the lights dim. I used the key I'd forgotten to return to let us in.

Once inside, I stopped and listened. There were only the creaks of cold window glass on a blustery night. "See the Christmas tree? Isn't that beautiful?"

"Who are the presents for?"

There were only three, and I'd hardly noticed them before. "I think those are for the people who own this company. Or maybe they're just empty boxes, you know, wrapped up for decoration." I urged him down the hall. "Let me show you my office, okay? We have lots of fun things."

We went cubicle to cubicle, checking each one for signs of a stranger. I knew Todd wasn't there, knew he couldn't be, but I had to peek behind the desks and peer around the plants.

"Look at the toys," Christopher said, pointing to the top of Ralph's computer. "Are those your toys, Aunt Dolie?"

"No, those belong to a friend, but I know he'd like you to play with them."

I scooped up all the little plastic figures, handed a dalmatian to

Christopher, and we moved on. It was Donna Katherine's office that Christopher liked best. "It's Christmas!" All the decorations seemed to bring a little color back to his cheeks, or maybe it was just the glow from the lights around the waving Santa and the tiny ceramic village. "This is my friend Donna Katherine's office. Pretty, isn't it?"

"Is she a elf?"

I thought of Donna Katherine's tall thin body. "No, not an elf. Just a lady who likes Christmas."

"Aunt Dolie, look!" He pointed to the tiny rail cars. "There's a elf on the train. I like elves."

"Come on," I said, swooping him up into my arms and heading for the break room. "How about something nice and warm to drink?"

"Okay. Hot chocolate? I like hot chocolate. And whit cream, too."

I had been thinking more of chamomile tea, but that was out and hot chocolate in.

Once I had it fixed, with some tea for myself, and we were seated at the tiny table, it was time for me to do something. All the way in the car I had focused on getting here—getting Christopher in a place that was safe and warm, with something hot to drink. Our physical safety had been my only thought, but now there had to be a next right step. Unfortunately, my mind was still too revved up with fear for me to think.

"This is good, Aunt Dolie." Half a cup was already gone; I hoped it was helping.

"I'm sorry there wasn't any whipped cream," I said.

Christopher leaned closer and patted my hand. "It's okay." He looked around. "How do you work, Aunt Dolie?"

"I write commercials. Like you see on TV."

"I see TV."

"I know."

"Once there was a dragon on TV. A big one. With green eyes." He sat up on his knees and I grabbed his arm to keep him steady. "If I was a dragon, you know what I could do?"

"Be careful. What could you do?"

"When I see Todd, I could fire him!" He breathed what he imagined to be hot air toward me. A low growl accompanied it. "And then I'd fire him again. And again."

"Honey, you won't see Todd anymore."

"But if I do," Christopher said, climbing down from the chair, "you know what I could do? I could punch him, and kick him, and sock him hard!" He reared back and did a karate kick, then two quick chops with his little hands. "See, Aunt Dolie, I could get him."

"Yes, you could." Was I helping him get past the fear or increasing the likelihood of nightmares? "And you were already incredibly brave. Incredibly.

"Now let's go make some phone calls." I took his cup and mine, then marched toward Donna Katherine's office. On the off chance that someone came in, I would be able to hear them, and she had all the Christmas paraphernalia for Christopher to look at. "Follow along, do what I do. Hup, two, three, four."

"Are we bein' soldiers, Aunt Dolie?"

"Nope, we're just marching."

"I could be a marching elf." He strutted beside me, lifting his knees as high as they would go. "Up two, three, four. Up two, three, four..."

WHILE CHRISTOPHER PLAYED with the miniature train, I got busy calling numbers, trying my best to track down some reinforcements. Prissy was not home, nor was I successful with my calls to Brackenridge Hospital to see if she was still there. The icy front had caused a rash of accidents which overloaded the emergency room capacity, and on top of that, Brackenridge was designated to care for the indigent and homeless who were streaming in suffering from cold and exposure. The woman on the switchboard had been sympathetic but unable to help. The nurse on the floor had no sympathy left.

"I think I saw the woman you described, but I have no idea where she went. I don't think her husband was here—wait! You can't go down there, sir, and I've told you that twice. Look, I'll be right with you!'' I'm sure she didn't intend to sound so vicious. "You might try the other hospitals," she said to me.

I barely got my thank-you out before she hung up.

Christopher stood up and said, "Can I go look at the tree?"

My first reaction was to say no. I didn't want him out of my sight, not even for a moment, but common sense reminded me of the futility of that.

"Sure, you can see the tree."

I followed him to the front office, double-checked the front door to make sure it was locked, and then used the phone at Amber's desk.

I tried Ross's office first only to get a recording that referred me to his home, and an additional number, which I wrote down and called immediately. It belonged to his assistant, but she was out Christmas shopping, according to her teenage daughter, who wasn't sure when her mother would be home. Dead end. I hung up and tried Austin Edge hoping to reach Matt. There I got a jolly holiday greeting, with no other numbers mentioned. Next I attempted to remember Ross's cellular number, which was another exercise in futility. It wasn't listed in the phone book either, and Southwestern Bell doesn't have cell phone numbers. I was straight out of luck and feeling bereft.

I dialed Nola's number. "Hey, kiddo, what are you doing?" she said.

"I'm having a bad day, Nola. A very bad day."

"You want to tell me about it?"

I desperately wanted to tell someone. I needed sympathy and if someone didn't get home soon, I was going to need help. "Hold on a second." I put the line on hold and turned to Christopher, who was walking around the tree touching all the bulbs he could reach. "I'll be in the room with all the Christmas things, okay? Then I'll be right back."

He nodded, and I raced into Donna Katherine's office, pulled out the chair, and picked up the phone at the same time. "Nola?"

"I'm here."

"The most horrible thing happened." And then I told her. In detail, letting the anger come up again, along with the fear. When my words caught in my throat, I put her on hold, ostensibly to listen for Christopher, who was singing "Jingle Bells."

"Look, I don't like you two being there alone," she said when I came back on the line. "I'm coming down there."

"Absolutely not! Not in this weather—it's horrible out there. Are you crazy?"

"No, but you shouldn't be by yourself." She paused. "Look, you can come here. We'll have dinner, it's safe, it's—"

"And it's south," I said. "Way in the other direction from Prissy's house. Thanks, Nola, but with the roads icy, I think we're better off where we are. Somebody is bound to get home soon." Christopher came into the office and leaned against me, resting his head on my lap. "Look, I'd better go. Just hold a good thought for us, okay? And say hi to your mom for me."

"I will, but I may show up there."

"Please don't. We'll be fine."

When I had hung up Christopher said, "Aunt Dolie, I have a microwave."

"A what?"

"In my head. You know, like my mommy gets. A microwave."

A migraine.

As mothers have done for decades, I rested my palm against his forehead, but there was no fever.

"I'll get you something for it, and then you'll feel better."

"Yes, please."

He was running out of energy and bravery—it was long overdue.

"There's a first aid kit with all kinds of wonderful things to make you well," I said, trying to sound cheerful, "and it's right in the break room. Will you walk with me?"

He nodded, but didn't speak. A very bad sign.

Unfortunately, it wasn't in the break room. Probably because the police had confiscated the damn thing. Instead of swearing, I smiled, a heroic effort. "Not to worry, it's someplace in this building."

Surely that was true.

Christopher sniffled. "Aunt Dolie, my head hurts too bad."

"I know, sweetie." I picked him up and held him tightly as he started to cry. I made no effort to stanch the tears or to shush him. If anybody deserved a good cry, it was Christopher. No child should have to suffer what he'd been through, both physically and emotionally. His body heaved with the sobs.

"I want my mommy."

"I know, baby, I know." I rocked him back and forth, fighting my own tears, humming a lullaby that I had sung to Jeremy when he was that age.

TWENTY-EIGHT

EVENTUALLY Christopher hiccuped to a stop. I rocked him a little longer, then said, "Here," reaching for a paper towel. "Here, blow." He did. "Good boy. Maybe a cool cloth will help your head."

"Yes, please."

And maybe the release of his tears would help, too.

I wet several paper towels, folded them up, then carried Christopher back to Donna Katherine's office. "How about if I make you a pallet with my coat?" I asked, folding the heavy wool. "I'll bet you didn't get your nap today, did you?"

"No."

"Here, come and lie down, and I'll put this on your head."

He stretched out, his eyelids already drooping.

I bent over and kissed his forehead, then gently placed the wet towels on it. "How is that? A little better?"

"Yes."

Seeing Christopher like this and knowing what he had endured was almost overwhelming. Children should be protected from abuse, from all abuse. Christopher was too little to protect himself; it wasn't fair that adults were allowed to brutalize our babies. And there should be a very special hell for people like Todd, hell with a one-way door so that adults who prey on children never get out. Ever.

My own head throbbed as I bent down to tuck Christopher in to his makeshift bed. As the shock wore off, the parts of my body that had made contact with ice, cement, or asphalt were needing the relief aspirin could give. It was on the agenda, although first I picked up the phone, hit the redial, and waited for Prissy's number to ring. It did, but again the answering machine came on. The first time that had happened, I'd left a message saying I had

Christopher with me, we were fine, and I'd call back later. I'd been careful not to leave a number in case Todd had returned to the house. This time I just hung up.

"Is my mommy still gone?"

"Yes, she is. But don't worry, she'll be home soon. Just rest."

"Don't go away, Aunt Dolie. Please?"

"I'm not leaving. I promise."

"Okay." He closed his eyes, then said, "Can you turn down the light?"

"I'll see what I can do."

"And when I finish resting, may we go home?"

"Yes we may."

I found the switch that turned off the short row of fluorescents over where Christopher was sleeping, then I sat beside him on the floor, rubbing his back until he fell asleep.

Once he was deep in slumber, I got up, my knee joints creaking and every muscle complaining. I wanted to stretch out on the floor along with Christopher and sleep away this nightmare, but our prolonged absence would cause a panic for Stephanie and Prissy. Probably for Matt and Ross, too. Jeremy might even worry.

I started through the offices on a quest for a pain reliever, and while my movements were weary, my search was more thorough than it had been earlier when all I'd needed was a recorder. Not that the recorder had done me any good.

Or had it? Maybe the tape would prove premeditation on Todd's part. Premeditated kidnapping? I pressed my palm to my forehead. I needed help. I needed aspirin.

The one thing I was almost positive of was that Stephanie had installed the little recorders. None of the conversations on the tapes were prior to her arrival. Was she using them to get some kind of evidence against Todd? She wouldn't need it now because I would be a witness to his abuse, and I would be happy to testify in any court we could get him in.

By now I was rifling Nola's office, but she had nothing medicinal in her desk. That was a sure sign she'd already been cleaning it out in anticipation of leaving.

Ralph's cubicle was next and it contained new packs of chewing gum and Gummi Life Savers, neither of which could cure a headache. Fred, our graphic artist, didn't have a desk, just a drafting table, and the cabinets he used for paper and tools didn't harbor anything edible.

I inspected the copy room with extra care, since that would be the next logical place to put a first aid kit, but it wasn't there. After that I moved into Audry's office, and noticed how I stayed as far away as possible from the windows. I'd also turned on very few lights, as if someone could see me from the street seven stories below. It wasn't possible, at least I was sure I couldn't be recognized, but even convinced of that, I couldn't make myself get closer to the glass.

Audry's office didn't appear to contain anything personal. No chewed-on pencils, no little sticky notes with scribbled messages, not a nail file or vitamin. Finally, in the very back of a credenza drawer I found a small makeup bag with a hairbrush, a lipstick, a lip pencil, and some Tampax, but no aspirin.

Michael's side drawer held a brand-new bottle of antacids, the giant economy size, still full. Unfortunately there was nothing for pain. I went next door and discovered that Chester had one small prescription bottle in his desk. Lanoxin. I noticed it was dated yesterday. Another new bottle.

Several thoughts struck me at once. First, that during their search the police had taken far more than just Desi's trail mix. They must have confiscated all the medicines, drinks, and foods that were in open containers. Sergeant Bohles and his crew had probably needed trucks to carry all the huge bottles of aspirin, ibuprofen, acetaminophen—the whole gamut of pain relievers—as well as sinus pills and allergy medicines. And antacids; after all, in ad agencies people thrive on pressure and die of heart attacks in their early sixties.

Heart attacks?

Heart attack. Digitalis. Lanoxin.

They'd all been mentioned in the articles on mistletoe! Unfortunately, I couldn't remember exactly what had been said. I actually reached for the phone to call Prissy before I realized she wouldn't answer. Then I remembered: The faxes she'd sent me were still here at Rose Sterling. I had inadvertently left them in Desi's desk.

The wind howled outside the glass walls, and the lights flickered.

Within seconds the power came back on, but the momentary blackout jolted me enough that I went to check on Christopher. He was sleeping soundly, and after pulling the corner of my coat a little higher on his shoulders, I hurried to my old office.

I remembered folding the faxes and sticking them in a drawer.

Without hesitation I pulled open the center drawer and reached for them. Now they were lying open and facedown.

Someone had read these faxes and left them unfolded.

I felt a moment of heartsickness; someone had gone snooping in my desk. Then I took a breath and put it in perspective. I had left the agency permanently. This was no longer my desk, and any of the Rose Sterling staff might have had a legitimate excuse to look through the drawers. They could have read the material, as could Sergeant Bohles or one of his people. Whoever it was hadn't taken the faxes, and might not have even known what they were.

Only the person who murdered Desi Baker would understand their significance. The odds were seven to one in my favor it wasn't the killer who had found them.

In light of everything else that had happened, I didn't have the energy to worry about it.

Instead, I scanned the papers in my hand, homing in directly on the technical information on the chemicals. Lanoxin was mentioned along with Digitoxin, Crystodigin, and several others. "...slowed the heart and were especially dangerous when taken by a person who was already low in calcium or potassium. This could include persons who were dieting and exercising heavily." That might well describe Desi Baker.

"This family of drugs can act almost instantly, depending on the amount of food in the stomach, dosage, and susceptibility of the person ingesting it.'' It was basically like digitalis, the same drug used by Agatha Christie in *Appointment with Death*. The first reaction to a drug overdose of Lanoxin would be increased heart rate, which Desi would have assumed was a normal reaction to waiting to give her speech about Chester. By the time she'd left the dais she'd have been sick to her stomach, then she'd experience vomiting and diarrhea. Then death.

Was Chester capable of giving Desi Lanoxin? I sank into the chair, feeling as if someone had sucked the marrow from my bones. I couldn't believe such a thing. Wouldn't.

Damn.

I folded the articles carefully, my brain whirring as fast as a locust's wings. The Lanoxin had been in an unlocked drawer that was accessible to anyone in the agency. So why all the articles on mistletoe? Could Desi have ingested both, increasing the symptoms and hurrying death?

Perhaps she had been drinking mistletoe tea for several days with only slight effects, then at the party as a last-ditch effort the murderer slipped some Lanoxin into her food. The high level of the chemical would make death almost instantaneous, and without a very clever medical examiner, it might have passed for accidental. All the murderer had to do was remove the mistletoe articles from Desi's office.

And Nola had searched Desi's office.

But that had been on Tuesday. Who had been there Monday morning? And what was the motive? Men or money? The faltering fortunes of Rose Sterling Advertising...and who had access to Chester's pills...

I rubbed my throbbing forehead. Better to think of aspirin first, and the only places I hadn't checked were Amber's desk and Donna Katherine's; I moved to the front office. When I flicked the light switch, I discovered a pile of torn wrapping paper against the far wall and a scattering of Styrofoam peanuts on the gray carpet. Apparently the unopened presents had been too much for Christopher to resist.

With an involuntary groan, a response to bruises, not Christopher's actions, I bent down to clean up. It appeared the packages had been nothing more than decorative empty boxes, but to make sure, I ran my hand through two of them; I found only a few more of the lightweight Styrofoam peanuts. The third box was also empty, but I spotted one small item on the floor, almost hidden by the scattered peanuts. It was a computer disk with a fresh, bright blue label.

There was no writing on it, and I put it on the desk with the faxes. Just in case. After that I scooped the remains of the presents into Amber's wastebasket.

I was on the far side of the tree making one last inspection of the rug when I heard the key in the front door. I looked toward Donna Katherine's office where Christopher slept. The outer door began to open. If I ran toward the other office I would give away Christopher's presence and put him in danger. I had to stay here and hide.

I was completely behind the tree before I realized how foolish I was being; only office personnel had keys. It couldn't be Todd at the door. But even knowing that, I didn't leave the safety of my concealed spot. Instead I waited, tense and alert. The door opened with a whoosh of air, and then I heard soft footfalls on the carpet that stopped at the front desk. After that there was only silence, a listening silence.

I wanted to step out and see, but I couldn't. The tension from the dangers we'd already faced clung to me and held me rigid. Even as I chided myself for being foolish, the overhead lights went out, leaving a thick blackness.

Power failure? Ice buildups somewhere?

I noticed a ray of light from under the front door and a haze of color from the direction of Donna Katherine's office. Very clearly, whoever had come into the office had turned off the lights and was now standing in the dark. Waiting. Just as I waited.

My throat tightened. Who was this intruder? What did they want?

My biggest fear was for Christopher. I would endure anything before I would put him through another minute of pain. And still I didn't move.

A jumble of thoughts struck me as I crouched in the darkness. I could confront this person, whoever it was, and somehow get him or her out of the suite. But even if I accomplished that, how would I alert the guard to Christopher's presence? He couldn't be left here alone.

I didn't have much bravery or adrenaline left.

With a resolve that came only from my love for Christopher, I stood up and, in doing so, brushed the tree, setting off a rattle of ornaments. A flashlight beam arced across the room and caught me in its light.

TWENTY-NINE

THERE WAS one heart-stopping moment of light blindness, then a voice in the dark said, "Jolie?"

I blinked several times, but still couldn't see. "Who is it?"

"Oh, damn. Darn."

"Ralph?" I said. "Is that you?"

"Yes, sorry." He shifted the flashlight until it cast a shadowy upward beam on his face so he looked like a monster. "But what in the world are you doing here in the dark?" he asked.

"I wasn't in the dark until you turned out the light," I said. I sounded testy. "And what are you doing here? And why the light?"

"It's a long story."

In the blackness with only a flashlight illuminating the space between us, I began to see possibilities. Frightening possibilities.

Had Ralph been in love with Desi? Or perhaps just enamored of her in a schoolboy way that never touched on reality. Had he heard the rumor of her affair with Michael, true or not, and reacted with murder?

I didn't believe it.

"Ralph—"

Another key sounded in the door. Ralph jumped, flicking off the light and hitting the side of the desk in a way that sounded painful. "Damn! Quick!"

Even in the dark he found me; his hands grabbed at my shoulder and he pushed me farther back behind the tree.

"Wait, what—"

"Be quiet! Nothing. Trust me."

Then the door was open and a switch was flicked, but instead of turning on the overheard, it merely lit the tree where we were hiding. Even with the glow of the tiny colored lights we remained invisible.

It had all happened too quickly for me to think. Who was the good guy here, and who the bad? How should I have responded? I never got to choose, I merely reacted, tucked silently at the rear of the tree.

The new arrival paused near the door, then shut it firmly and made a movement toward the desk. Then silence. Too much silence.

It stretched on and on, and in that time I flashed to the faxes and the computer disk sitting on Amber's desk. There was the Lanoxin, too. Solid evidence of the person who'd killed Desi Baker, and now I was pretty sure I knew who that person was. At that moment it did me no good.

With a tiny shift I could see the desk through the fir branches and tree decorations; it was merely a shape on the edge of the darkness. I shifted again and Ralph's grip became harder. His expression was fierce. I twitched my arm to get some relief and he scowled at me.

I mouthed, "Let go," ready to scream if necessary.

He eased his grasp only a fraction.

What in the hell was going on?

I heard a shuffle of paper, but I still couldn't see anything.

What was this new person doing? Reading messages? Picking up mail?

Then I heard the words, "Son of a bitch!" The thick accent told me it was Donna Katherine.

She moved and I could see her red hair as she whirled around and started for her office.

I couldn't hold back any longer—she would find Christopher, and I couldn't let any more happen to him. I shoved at Ralph and in the same moment called out, "Wait! Donna Katherine, stop!"

She jerked around so quickly her heavy purse hit the wall. "Damn!"

Donna Katherine had every right to be here checking her messages, regardless of the time of day.

"Hi," I said, exhaling mightily and stepping even farther away from the tree. Ralph remained in his hiding place, and despite my conclusions, I still didn't understand all that was going on. "What are you doing here?" I asked.

"I might ask you the same thing." Her usual flippancy had been replaced by an intensity that could have been the result of my sudden appearance.

"Well, it's kind of a long story."

She waited, staring at me. "You've been following me, haven't you?"

"What? No, not at all." That made no sense. "Following you? Why? And how would I get here ahead of you?"

"By going the wrong way on a one-way street."

"I didn't do that. I—" I rubbed my forehead again, hoping to ease the knot of pain, or at least give me time to think. "It's been a very long day."

She stared at me, her jaw stiff with distaste. "You've got some faults, Jolie, but stupid isn't one of them." She waved my faxes and the computer disk in the air, her gold bracelets jangling. "How'd you figure it out?"

I remembered Donna Katherine wrapping packages as the police did their search of the building; right under their noses she had hidden the computer disk. And the hell of it was, I wasn't sure what was on it—I only suspected.

I nodded toward the things she was holding. "That's the proof."

"Oh, you think so?" With that she gripped the disk in both hands and did a quick jerk that cracked it in half. One more hard twist and the metal labeling popped off. A fragile, thin gray circle, the disk itself, was revealed.

Ralph leaped out from behind the tree. "No!"

Donna Katherine cocked her head. "Well, well, look who's joining the party! Mild-mannered Ralph." She didn't slow her movements, she simply crumpled the disk.

"Damn!" He lunged toward her, but I was in the way. It gave Donna Katherine time to tear the disk with her teeth, and by the time Ralph reached her, there were two rents all the way through it. Donna Katherine stepped smoothly back out of his grasp, but handed over the shattered remains of the computer disk.

With a sweet smile at me she said, "I don't know what got over me just now, I can't believe I did such a thing. I can't think why I would."

"Maybe they can save some of the information," Ralph said, staring with disbelief at the broken pieces in his hands.

"Now, darlin', that's just not possible; you know that. But don't be upset. Why, it's almost Christmas, and now we can all go home. Or wherever."

"I have copies of two invoices from Desi's files," Ralph began. "And copies of the articles on mistletoe you gave her. Jolie, you found those, didn't you? And now the police have them. Donna Katherine, they'll prove you doctored the information and got Desi to—"

Donna Katherine cut him off with a wave of her hand. "You know, when you work with computers as much as we have, you figure out folks can create anything they want with the right software. Even false evidence. Like those invoices you were talking about and the articles. I'm not sure why you think they're so important, but I'll bet Miss Desi made them. Can't prove otherwise."

"They're real," Ralph said. "And the money. The police will find the money you embezzled."

In all my years at Rose Sterling, Donna Katherine had always worked alone. Then Desi Baker came along. She had obviously found discrepancies in the financial records and had kept invoices as evidence of it.

"Ralph," I said, "how much did you say Rose Sterling charged the clients at those fairs?"

"The bank deposits show a thousand dollars per client, but the invoice I found in Desi's desk was double that."

So Desi had discovered the embezzlement, and then what? Had Donna Katherine placated the younger woman, getting her transferred into copywriting? No, that wouldn't have been enough.

Had Donna Katherine promised to make restitution? Yes, that must have been how it worked, only Donna Katherine had no intention of giving the money back, and so Desi had to die.

I'd never thought of Donna Katherine as clever. I'd believed she was hardworking and a little ditzy, but I'd been wrong. She was a very resourceful woman, and it showed in the way she'd covered herself.

When I'd come around looking for a bathroom, it was Donna Katherine who'd sent me, Michael's ex-lover, downstairs to find the body. That little bit of quick thinking implicated me.

No doubt Donna Katherine had also sent Desi down to that bathroom, or maybe she'd taken her there, promising to bring help.

I looked at Donna Katherine, wondering how she could live with herself. "You really are a piece of work."

The many fabrications were coming to mind, like the comment about Michael wailing in the bathroom, and the convenient rumor that Desi and Michael were lovers. That had thrown suspicion on both Michael and Audry, when in truth, neither one had a motive to kill Desi.

And there was the note slipped under the bathroom door.

"You wrote the note, too," I said. "The one signed M."

Donna Katherine merely raised one eyebrow.

It was Ralph who put it all in perspective. "Right from the start you've lied and stolen, and then you did murder to cover it all up. I don't understand how anyone could do that, especially not steal from Chester." He stopped and shook his head as if sickened. "And then to kill Desi..."

Donna Katherine chose to ignore the last part. "I did not hurt Chester," she said firmly. "I love Chester Sterling—he is the kindest, gentlest, most wonderful man in the world, and I would never hurt him. Never."

"You embezzled a hell of a lot of his money—"

"If, and let me repeat, if I took money, which I did not, it would have been for Chester. It would be his retirement fund to protect him from his bloodsucking daughter."

"With a little left over for you?"

"You know, Ralph," she said, "I think you've missed some things."

"Oh?"

"Do you have any idea how many hours I have spent here at Rose Sterling? Do you? I have put in at least ten hours of overtime every week of my career. Get out your calculator and figure it out—that's over four thousand hours of overtime. Overtime!" She was on very solid ground here, her analytical mind spitting out the figures she had obviously brooded over as she carried out her personal plan for vindication. "At least Chester used to give me some kind of bonus at the end of the year, but not Missy Tight Pockets. No, sir. She'd just tell me to go home if I mentioned how many hours I was putting in; she didn't have any idea how long it took to do my work."

"And so you embezzled. And then to cover it up, you killed." Ralph hit the word hard.

Donna Katherine glared. "Let me repeat one more time for your feeble brain that I did not do any of those things. But if I had taken money, it would have been my money. Do you understand? Money owed to me. You start figuring out how much money I was due, plus interest, plus all those vacations and sick days I never took."

Just as Matt had told me, when people are stealing money, they don't dare take a minute off; they can't because someone else would discover the thefts.

But surely Donna Katherine had to know she'd be caught eventually. One good audit would have done it, and once the police suspected her of Desi's murder, there were a hundred ways they could prove that the embezzlement was her motive. Bank accounts, purchases above and beyond her income, invoices that didn't match—all manner of evidence would convict her. It didn't seem very smart for a woman like Donna Katherine.

Ralph leaned against the front desk. "Come on, Donna Katherine, just between us, you stole the money, didn't you? And when Desi found out, you promised to pay it all back—she was just naive enough to believe you'd do that. Except you changed your mind and killed her to make sure she wouldn't talk."

There was something odd about the way he stood, with his hip thrust out and his right leg forward. I couldn't understand why he was in such an awkward stance until I spotted the bulge in the front pocket of his corduroy pants. It was rectangular and small. Ralph had the voice-activated recorder in his pocket.

Donna Katherine realized it the same time I did.

With a laugh she reached into her big black leather purse. Very expensive black leather purse, I noticed. "You can take the tape recorder out of your pants, Clark Kent." She brought her hand out of her purse; it was holding a small revolver. "And I need you to give it to me. Then I can leave this place and never come back."

"You have a ticket to Rio?" he asked.

"Darlin', let's just say that where I'm going, you can't find me. And neither can anybody else." She glanced at her watch. "Now, hurry it up, Ralph. Jolie's got to tie you up, and then I'm out of here. I wouldn't have come back at all, except I wanted that stupid disk. I'll be taking the pieces with me, just in case."

"What about the hard drive on your computer? I'll bet there's evidence there."

"Darnedest thing," she said. "My hard drive crashed today. There's not a solitary thing on it. Nothing."

I had to look away so she wouldn't see my expression. Prissy had said even information that had been erased could be retrieved from a hard drive. No telling what the police would find on Donna Katherine's computer, perhaps even the fake stories on mistletoe.

"Okay, Ralph," Donna Katherine said, growing visibly impatient. "Hand over the tape recorder. Now."

"The police usually find fugitives from justice," he said, not moving. "They'll catch up to you somewhere, you wait."

"That's not your concern; just give me the recorder. If you don't, I'll shoot you; I mean it!"

Stone-still and smiling, he said, "I think I'll just keep it for myself."

"Ralph!" I snapped. "Give her that damn thing." The man was even upsetting me, and I didn't have the extra tension of a gun in my hand.

"Relax, Jolie," he said. "This may be the last time you ever see Donna Katherine as a free woman. The police will find her—"

"No, they won't," she snarled. "Give me the recorder."

"You have a phony ID?" he asked. I was hardly breathing. "Fake passport?" he went on. "Swiss bank account?"

She pulled back the hammer of the gun. "I'm fixin' to shoot your sorry ass if you don't do exactly like I tell you. First, give me the recorder!"

He didn't budge.

I stuck out my hand. "Ralph, stop acting stupid!" I had no intention of dying so he could play hero. Besides, Christopher was in the other room. "Hand over the tape recorder."

"Listen to the lady," Donna Katherine said.

I was afraid to take my eyes off her, afraid I wouldn't see her squint, or stiffen her arm, or do any one of the things that would come right before pulling the trigger.

Out of the corner of my eye I saw Ralph slide his hand in his pocket and bring out the recorder. I started to relax, then realized he was moving awkwardly again. Oh, God...

Donna Katherine stiffened.

Ralph lifted the recorder and, with a flick of his wrist, threw it at her.

I hit the floor just as the hammer came down.

The bullet whined over my head, and a Christmas ornament shattered. Ralph leaped the distance to Donna Katherine, knocked the gun from her hand, spun her around, and flattened her against the wall. His military training stood him in good stead.

As he pulled out handcuffs he said, "Jolie, we need the police. Sergeant Bohles. Call nine-one-one."

Once I could stand, I ran over to the two of them, my breathing ragged. I didn't know who I was angriest at, Donna Katherine for killing Desi, or Ralph for endangering all of us. "Listen to me," I whispered savagely, "Both of you, keep it down! There's a baby asleep in Donna Katherine's office, and he doesn't need to hear any of this!"

The two of them turned to stare at me as if I'd lost my mind. Then I ran to call the police.

THIRTY

CHRISTMAS MORNING started with the little voice once again outside my door. "Aunt Dolie! I need you!" Only this time Christopher was so thoroughly bundled up against the cold only his eyes were visible. Even his nose was hidden in a scarf. Jeremy was right behind him, saying they needed us because Prissy wouldn't let them touch the presents until we arrived.

"Puts everything in perspective, doesn't it?" Matt said with a grin once we had shooed the boys out and were getting dressed.

"Now we're just needed to give out presents." I pulled on a sweater. "I like that better."

We arrived at the big house within five minutes to find Prissy in the kitchen.

"Merry Christmas," I said, giving her a hug.

"Merry Christmas." She bent down to pull sweet rolls out of the oven. The coffee was already brewed. "Want some tea?"

"I'd love some. You know, I've never told you this," I said, "but you set a standard the rest of us can never live up to. You're too perfect."

She laughed. "It's only because I'm too insecure to just kick back and let myself go. If I had your self-confidence, it would be different."

"My self-confidence?" I had started toward the cupboard for a cup, but I stopped and turned to look at her. "I think we need to talk."

"Oh, your tea is already made." She smiled. "But I nuked it this morning."

"There's hope for you yet."

Then Stephanie was in the kitchen pouring coffee, and Christopher arrived, demanding that we hurry. "It's getting too late!"

We all moved into the great room as Jeremy, who was standing near the tree, announced, "I'll play Santa Claus."

"And I'll help!" Christopher added, tripping over a huge present that Matt had brought down from the apartment. "That's a big one," he said, righting himself.

"It's something special for Jeremy," Matt said, winking at me.

It was a duster, just like the one Jeremy had borrowed from Matt. This one differed slightly in that, against my feeble protests, Matt had stuffed the pockets with money. Big money. Not enough to buy the new pickup Jeremy had been openly hinting for, but enough for a decent used one. He would have to get an after-school job to support it and make the insurance payments, which I thought was a good idea.

"Cool! I love big presents." Jeremy grabbed the box and put it beside the couch. "This will be my pile," he said, turning to Christopher and holding out a square present. "Here, Christopher, put this one over there. It's for you."

"For me? Oh, thank you."

As the two boys divvied up the packages, making stacks all around the room, Ross started a fire in the fireplace and Prissy handed out napkins. Stephanie came to sit beside me.

"Merry Christmas," she said.

"Same to you."

"And thank you again." Her dark eyes seemed much older and much wiser, but she also looked peaceful.

"You'd have done the same if it was Jeremy," I said.

I had spent so much of the last two days at the police station and courthouse I'd decided if I ever got back to Purple Sage, I'd never leave again. I'd given a statement that would be used against Donna Katherine, who was in custody and being indicted on murder charges. Formal charges also had been filed against Todd, including kidnapping, assault, and endangerment of a child. There were others, but I'd lost track. Unfortunately Todd had flown out by the time the police began their search, and now he was believed to be someplace on the East Coast. They did know that he'd arrived at Baltimore Airport, so they were tracking him from there.

It had not been easy telling the story to the police. Especially for Stephanie, because, as I had suspected, there was a great deal more to tell, and much of it was unpleasant.

Todd and Stephanie had dated during her second year in college; when she'd discovered she was pregnant, Todd had waved good-bye and headed East. However, all the oohing and aahing he heard from his mother and his "aunt" Prissy about the adorable Christopher started him wondering if he'd made the right choice. It was his mother's death that spurred him into action, searching for what he then considered his rightful family, Stephanie and Christopher.

Todd had arrived in Phoenix shortly after Stephanie, and had settled into the apartment next door just as if he belonged. While Stephanie had been wary, Todd had set out to woo both her and the son he didn't know. Those first few weeks had been wonderful, and Stephanie had even told her mother the truth about Christopher's parentage. It was shortly after that when the not-so-subtle shifts in Todd's behavior started. Todd became the abuser. Primarily it was emotional abuse and most was directed at Stephanie. It was then she realized he was doing drugs and began pulling away, but Todd refused to budge. He began to *discipline* Christopher, just as his own father had disciplined him. Peter Javitz entered the picture, convincing Todd, in a very civilized way, to move on.

And while I still didn't like the relationship between Pete and Stephanie, I couldn't help but think more kindly toward him.

All the problems might have ended there had Todd not called Prissy and played on her sympathies to get an invitation for Christmas. She didn't know the full extent of what had gone on in Phoenix, and had only slight doubts about the plan. Even when Stephanie arrived and tried to tell her mother the truth, she hadn't wanted to listen. After all, Todd was her best friend's son, and Prissy had a hard time separating her feelings for the two.

During the last two days there had been many tears and recriminations. Thank God the worst was in the past, and while we did have to live with the past, and in some cases make restitution, there were better times ahead.

"Have you decided if you're going back to Phoenix?" I asked Steph as she accepted a package from Christopher.

"Yes, I am."

"Oh." That wasn't what I'd expected to hear.

Then she smiled. "And Mom is going with me. We'll pack up everything and get us moved back here probably by next week."

"That's wonderful! And Matt and I will take care of Christopher while you're gone." I glanced over at Matt, who had turned his head when he heard his name.

"I don't know if you want Christopher for a whole week," Stephanie said. "He can be a lot of work."

"Obviously," Matt said, leaning forward to better see Stephanie, "you don't remember what you were like at that age. He is easy compared to you. We'll take him."

Christopher was just walking in front of me and I grabbed him. "Did you hear, little bug? You're coming to my house!"

"Goody."

"And you're going to stay for a whole week!" I scooped him onto my lap, but he wriggled down.

"Aunt Dolie, please. I'm givin' presents."

"Well, pardon me."

He held up a six-by-three-inch box with red wrapping paper and a green ribbon. "It's for you. And you're s'posed to open it right away."

"I am, huh?" I shook the heavy little box, then looked at the tag. It was from Jeremy and Matt, both of whom were grinning at me. "Okay," I said, ripping open the paper. The box came from a print shop. "What in the world?" I pulled off the lid and discovered business cards. My business cards with a pale ivory card stock and black script that said: *Jolie Wyatt. Author.* "I don't believe it! These are wonderful, thank you." I leaned around Steph to hug Matt.

"What do they say?" Ross asked.

I picked my way around the presents to hand him one. "My card." Then I gave Jeremy a hug. "Thank you."

"You're welcome. Merry Christmas, Author."

I tried to thread my way back through the maze of packages, but stopped midway. "This is unbelievable. Would you look at all these presents."

"Look at mine, Aunt Dolie!" The mountain beside Christopher was taller than he was. Every one of us had gone overboard and we knew it, but after the past week, we'd indulged. Next week he started therapy.

"You sure got a lot of packages," I said.

Christopher's face grew serious. "Does this mean I'm a good boy?"

"It doesn't matter whether you got a lot of presents or not, you're still a very good boy," I said.

"Very, very good," Prissy added.

"And what about me?" Jeremy demanded. "Am I good, too?"

"You're perfect," I said.

He grinned. "That's nice to hear; of course, I had to pry it out of you."

Christopher waved his arms at the packages. "It's time for presents!" He hopped toward a large box but tripped on Jeremy's feet, knocking him off balance. The two of them began to fall. Jeremy reached out to save them and hit the Christmas tree. It teetered, the stand tipped, and the tree began to list crazily. With a tinkling of ornaments it started over and came to rest against the far wall, its lights twinkling merrily.

There was a stunned silence. Slowly we all turned our eyes to Prissy.

She was staring at the tree, blinking in disbelief. Her mouth opened.

A giggle came out. It rolled into full-fledged laughter. After a moment she took a breath and said, "Not perfect; just wonderful."

RANSOM FOR A HOLIDAY
Fred Hunter

For Barbara Hopper

PROLOGUE

NATHAN BARTLETT hadn't thought of boots, or gloves, or even his coat, though the temperature was below twenty, and the snow was almost a foot deep, and the barn was over two hundred yards from the house. He hadn't even thought to bring the flashlight, though he realized it would have done little more than illuminate the falling snow. As he'd stolen out into the night, all he'd been able to think about was the welfare of his sister.

He bent forward into the strong wind that blew the wet, heavy snow into his face, stinging his eyes and blinding him further. After trudging on in this fashion for a few minutes, he stopped and turned his back to the wind in an effort to quell the rising confusion caused by the driving storm that buffeted him. The thought of the recent discovery he'd made performed the same service on him mentally. He hoped that all his questions would be cleared up when he reached the barn. He hoped the situation was not as dire as he believed.

Looking back in the direction from which he'd come, the house was barely visible. They had no guests this weekend, so the two-story building stood like a darkened mass looming in the background, further obscured by the gauzelike curtain of snow. The only light visible was a dim glow from the front parlor reflecting off the snow. His sister was probably still sitting in there reading. Nathan hadn't told her where he was going or even that he was going out at all. He had slipped, as quietly as possible, out the back door. As he watched, a gust of wind swept across the light, causing a momentary rift in the sheet of white. Nathan blinked at the gravel driveway that ran along the side of the house. Though the parlor light didn't provide enough illumination to be sure of anything, he could have sworn that there was only one car in the drive when there should have been two. He sighed and thought, with some dismay, that the person that he was meeting must be late, and that he'd be forced to wait in the cold barn, which was something he hadn't counted on.

Nathan took a deep breath and turned back into the wind, throwing his left arm across his brow in an effort to shield his eyes. There was nothing to guide him: no lights coming from the barn itself, and no lights in the apartment above it, leaving the barn discernible only as a slight interruption in the snowfall. The wind whipped around the sides of the building, causing the snow to swirl sideways around it and making the huge wooden structure look like little more than an eddy in the eye of a storm.

It wasn't until he was upon it that the building itself became apparent. The bright red paint looked black in the night. He stopped for a moment, hugging himself against the cold before retreating into the barn, and listened for signs of life. He couldn't hear any human movement, only the steady howl of the wind and the occasional creak of wood as the barn protested against its treatment. Finally, Nathan shivered and grabbed the handle of the door. With one strong pull, he slid the door open.

He stood in the doorway for a moment. The stillness within the barn made the darkness seem even more deep, and he spared himself a nervous laugh at the idea of different shades of dark. He reached for the switch mounted just to the right of the door and flipped it, but the expected light failed to materialize. He repeated the motion several times, but nothing happened. He thought for a moment that perhaps they'd had a power failure during his short trek from the house to the barn. He glanced back toward the house, but the snow was falling so thickly now that it was a wasted effort. Even if the light was still on, he'd be unable to see it.

He turned back to the interior of the barn and took a tentative step inside.

"Hello? Are you here?" he called into the blackness.

His voice rang in the emptiness like the last vibrations from a muffled bell. He waited for a moment, then called again, "Hello? Are you here?"

He was met with a silence so defiant that Nathan almost jumped out of his skin when, after a lengthy pause, a voice returned from the darkness, "I'm here."

"The lights have gone out."

"Only in here."

Nathan could feel his brow furrowing. He looked from left to right, peering into the darkness and trying to discern from which direction the voice was coming. After a long pause, during which he wasn't quite sure what they were waiting for, Nathan said, "Well?"

"You were the one who wanted to see me." The voice stopped, then after a moment added with a slight laugh, "I don't know why you couldn't have waited for better weather."

"I don't expect you to still be around when the weather's better," Nathan replied. He paused for a moment, then put his right hand on his hip, and said, "I know who you are."

"I figured that much."

"And I want to know what you're doing here."

"Did you tell your sister you were meeting me?"

Nathan sighed. "I didn't tell Sara anything about anything."

"You didn't tell her who I am?"

"I didn't want to tell her until I found out what the hell you're doing here. I don't want her to be hurt."

"I don't want to hurt Sara."

"But that's exactly what you're going to do, isn't it? That's the only reason I can think of that you would come here. If you weren't up to something, then why the hell pretend to be somebody you're not? Why didn't you just tell us who you were to begin with?"

"That wouldn't have served my purpose."

There was a slight movement in the darkness, as if the person to whom the voice belonged was shifting to a more comfortable position.

Nathan breathed deeply. "And what would your purpose be?"

No response came from the darkness.

"Answer me!"

Nathan could hear movement again: the sound of shoes crunching on the ground, and a small *tink*, as if a can of some sort had been set down. After a brief pause, there was a click, and Nathan was instantly blinded by the bright light of a high-powered flashlight. He threw his hands up over his eyes.

"Jesus! Switch that damn thing off or get it out of my eyes!"

"You want to know what I'm up to?" the voice demanded with a sneer.

Nathan was angry now. He had discovered the identity of the masquerader on his own, and, despite the cold and wet and the dazzling light, he knew he had the upper hand in the situation and took exception to the tone of voice with which he was being addressed.

"I know what you want," Nathan said, his voice dripping with disdain. "It's the money, isn't it? Of course. You're after my sister's money."

There was a loud "Huh," from behind the light, as if the owner of the voice was greatly amused. The slightest beat went by before the reply came.

"No. I'm after yours. Catch!"

Without warning the light came hurtling toward Nathan, just above his head. Instinctively his hands flew up to catch it. As the light swirled around the room, the figure advanced on the unsuspecting brother, appearing to come forward in quick jerks like a dancer in a strobe light. Nathan caught the flashlight and fumbled to swing it around, sweeping the light across the tines of a pitchfork just before they plunged into his chest.

His scream was abbreviated by the suddenness of the attack and the deadly accuracy with which one of the tines was driven through his heart. Whatever was left of the sound he made was smothered by the blanket of snow that continued to fall unabated, as if its only purpose was to deaden the end of a life.

ONE

"THE ARRANGEMENTS have all been made," said Lynn Francis as she came into the kitchen. She was carrying a sturdy Samsonite suitcase, light blue in color, which belonged to Emily Charters, the elderly mistress of the house. "Sara has made arrangements for Emily to have a room on the ground floor, so she won't be climbing up and down stairs. And you'll have one of the usual guest rooms on the second floor."

Jeremy Ransom was sitting with his elbows resting on top of the small kitchen table. His blond hair, which he'd cut very short for the summer, had now grown out to a businesslike length, which had the unfortunate side effect of making the increasing gray more prominent. On occasion, when he spent a little too much time scrutinizing it in the mirror, he'd hear a creaking, ancient voice in the back of his mind singing the phrase, "silver threads among the gold." He could only shake the words out of his head and dispel any misgivings by reminding himself that he was still just on the brink forty. He rose when Lynn entered the room.

"I'll take that."

"She'll still be a couple of minutes," Lynn replied, motioning for him to sit back down. She went to the sink and started to fill it to wash the breakfast dishes. "You know, she protests about the whole thing, but she really is excited about going away, I think."

Ransom smiled. In the short time he'd known Emily, he'd come to greatly admire her. She was sharp as a tack, with a keen eye and a shrewd mind that could put information together with an alacrity that Ransom found almost astonishing. She had demonstrated this time and time again over the past year, proving instrumental in solving one case of murder and offering insights into others as Ransom plied his chosen profession as a homicide detective for the Chicago Police Department. But even though she was never reluctant to share her views on the professional matters at hand, she still maintained a natural reticence when it came to personal matters that Ransom found very appealing. As a confirmed loner, Ransom regarded with abhorrence the idea of anyone intruding into the sanctuary his life had become, and, as a result, he had kept his life private from everyone. One of the main reasons that a filial warmth had developed between Ransom and Emily, and that he'd unofficially adopted her as his grandmother, was the tacit agreement between the pair that love existed but was never to be spoken of.

"Do you think I'm doing the right thing, taking her away?" said Ransom with an uncharacteristic touch of self-doubt.

Lynn glanced at him and smiled. She found it agreeable but somehow a little disheartening to find the normally overconfident detective a bit unsure of himself.

"A change of scene might be good for her," she said, flipping her tawny hair back off her shoulder by way of punctuation. Then she added with only a hint of coyness, "It's good for everyone."

"She's doing too much."

"How much is too much?"

"It's only been a couple of months since her bypass. She should be resting."

"Emily's not the type of person to take life lying down."

Ransom's expression displayed the fact that he wasn't pleased. He'd been shaken by Emily's near miss with death, not only at the thought of losing her but at the thought that, after all of his years of independence, he'd allowed someone into his life only to find his foundation deeply shaken. And the fact that he was now capable of being so shaken, shook him even further.

"That doesn't mean she doesn't have to take care of herself," he said at last.

Lynn glanced at him again. She pursed one side of her mouth and said, "I know it doesn't. And you're probably right. But you know Emily."

"Yes," Ransom replied wryly, "she's not going to rest unless I get her off by herself."

"Is that so?" said Emily with a twinkle in her eye. She'd appeared so quietly in the doorway that Lynn almost dropped the dish she'd been wiping. Ransom immediately rose and gave Emily his seat, holding her hand as she lowered herself onto the chair.

Lynn cocked her head sideways at the old woman and smiled. "You know it's true. Your friend here has me come in to clean for you twice a week, and still I find you've been doing housework when I'm not around."

"Things have to be done."

Lynn folded her arms across her chest. "I could take it as an insult, you know. Don't you think I do a good enough job?"

Emily's forehead, already wrinkled with age, creased with concern. "Of course you do, my dear. And I appreciate the two of you wanting to take care of me, but dust does settle all the time and one does need a reason to live."

Ransom laughed. "Emily, if dust is giving you a reason to live then I can't get you out of town soon enough."

Emily sighed wistfully. "I wasn't meant to be idle. I *enjoy* doing things."

"I know you do," Ransom replied more seriously, "and you can do as much as you want once you've fully recovered. But as long as you're here at home I can't get you to do that, so maybe a little holiday, somewhere where you'll be waited on, will help."

Emily's shoulders elevated slightly in what, for her, passed for a shrug. Despite her protests, there was a gleam in her eye that showed Ransom she was looking forward to the trip. Maybe a little more than he thought was healthy for her. He shook his head again at his own folly. In his present state of anxiety, Emily couldn't win: If she was reluctant to go, he was worried, and if she was anxious to go, he was worried. He tried to put these thoughts aside.

"You'll have a wonderful time, Emily," said Lynn as she resumed washing the dishes. "My friend Sara has a nice room for you on the main floor of her bed-and-breakfast, so you'll only have to go up an incline to get into the place. And, even though they usually only serve breakfast, she's also planned to serve all your meals so you don't have to worry about going out for them.''

''She sounds very accommodating.''

''She's a really nice woman, and a good friend.''

''How do you know her?''

''She used to work for the same company that I did, before I started doing for the likes of you,'' Lynn replied, giving a playful flip of the dishcloth in Emily's direction. Lynn Francis had once been the right-hand woman to the CEO of Harris Assurance, and had given up her exalted position to become what she cheerfully referred to as ''charwoman to the rich and famous.'' She had chosen this path because it made her, to a great extent, master of her own time. Time had become one of the most important things in Lynn's life since her lover had become terminally ill. The freedom her chosen profession afforded her allowed her to take care of her lover at home. ''Sara's mother died a while back and she used her inheritance to do what she'd always wanted to do, buy a B and B. I guess the two of us were just nice, simple girls at heart who happened to get snagged up in the corporate world. It was a great relief to get out.''

Emily smiled knowingly at the young woman. ''I believe there's a lot more to it than that.''

''So, anyway,'' said Lynn, shying away from the hint of praise, ''everything is taken care of and there's nothing for you to worry about—your room, your meals, everything. I'll be stopping in here every day for the week and checking on Tam, just as I promised.''

As if in response to her name, the large, bottom-heavy calico shifted in her basket beside the stove, raising a pair of sleepy green eyes to her mistress. Tam was completely white except for a perfect circle on the top of her head that was half orange and half black. She'd been named for this circle, which made her look as if she were wearing a small hat.

''Well,'' said Emily with a dramatically resigned sigh, ''I feel as if I'm being commandeered.''

"Don't think you aren't," said Ransom.

"You'll love it," said Lynn with casual enthusiasm, "LeFavre is a pretty little town, and there's hardly anyone around at this time of year."

"But are you sure we won't be inconveniencing your friend? Most people like to spend Christmas alone with their families."

"I think Sara will be happy to have the company. Both her parents are gone."

"She was an only child?" Emily asked, raising an eyebrow.

Lynn glanced at Ransom. "Um...no, she had a brother. She lost him two years ago."

Emily clucked her tongue. "That's a shame."

"She hasn't had the house open to guests since that, so this'll be good for her, too. The two of you will be sort of a maiden voyage for her, getting her back in the swing of things. It'll do her good."

"It sounds to me," said Emily with a renewed twinkle in her eyes, "that you may have missed your calling."

Lynn stopped in her tracks and blushed attractively. "I don't know what you mean."

Emily smiled at her benignantly, and replied, "Of course you do!"

"It's time for us to be on our way," said Ransom with a glance at his watch.

He picked up Emily's suitcase as Lynn helped her on with her navy blue coat, lined with wool for extra warmth during the winter. Emily then covered her voluminous gray hair, that she kept piled in a bun at the back of her head, with a light blue knit hat. Ransom could never resist mentally noting thankfully that Emily's hat was devoid of the shiny little plastic dangles that he believed to be in favor with elderly women.

Emily and Lynn waited on the front porch while Ransom ran down to the car and stowed her suitcase in the trunk alongside his. During his brief absence, Emily turned to Lynn, and said, "Will you be all right over Christmas?"

"Sure I will," said Lynn, "Maggie's out of the hospital and back home, even though it may not be for long."

"She's home? My goodness! I thought she had tuberculosis."

Lynn wrinkled her nose. "So did her doctors. But it was a false positive. That happens too often with people with AIDS." Lynn stopped for a moment and sighed, as if remembering the relief she'd felt on first hearing the news. "We know something will get her one of these days, but at least it looks like we'll have another Christmas."

Emily's fingers gently tightened on Lynn's arm. Lynn smiled in return.

"So, I'll be fine," Lynn said brightly, "you just go and have a good time."

"I do appreciate you making the arrangements for us. Like most people my age, I don't go away very often. I don't really like to."

Lynn shot her a curious glance. "Then why are you doing it now? Did we really push you that much?"

"Oh, no, not at all," said the old woman. "No. But Jeremy has been very distressed, and I really think he needs a rest. It'll be good for him."

Lynn's eyes opened wide. "You mean you're going away for a week because *he* needs a rest?"

Emily leaned toward her, and said confidentially, "Well, you know, my dear, I don't think he's ever had one."

Ransom returned and offered Emily his arm, carefully leading her down the steps and along the walk. The air was crisp and fresh, and there'd been enough new snow overnight to at least temporarily cover the grimy slush that is a staple of Chicago winters. Once Emily was safely secured in the seat belt on the passenger side, Ransom climbed behind the wheel.

Tam had silently stolen onto the porch and brushed up against Lynn's leg. Lynn reached down and picked up the cat, which then rested in her arms as she watched Ransom and Emily drive away. Tam even suffered her right paw to be waved in the direction of her retreating mistress, though the look she gave Lynn afterward clearly indicated she doubted the sanity of the woman in whose care she'd been left.

Ransom turned on the radio, which he kept tuned to one of the two local classical stations, but found to his dismay that they were devoting an hour to Mozart. He could never understand why so many people found Mozart so soothing while the frenetic nature of his works only served to jangle Ransom's nerves. He felt sure that a steady diet of Mozart while he was behind the wheel would eventually cause an accident. He quickly switched to the second station.

They'd left late enough in the morning to miss the brunt of the rush hour, but traffic was still heavy enough that it took over forty-five minutes for them to pass the Loop, reach the Skyway, and get beyond city limits. As they passed through the center of the city, Ransom marveled anew at how, even with a layer of clean snow, as well as clear skies and a bright sun, Chicago could still manage to look dingy. But even that dinginess was somehow endearing. The city had formed his hearth and home for almost four decades now, and though he had, on occasion, vacationed away from it, he had never gone away without a pang of regret. As they approached the city's border he found himself already entertaining the yearnings of a frequent traveler who longs for the comforts of home the minute he's away. He tightened his grip on the steering wheel, reminding himself of the importance he felt this trip had to Emily's health. A quick glance at her showed him that he'd been right in his estimation. Merely being outward bound seemed to have added more spark to her weary countenance.

Emily sat quietly by his side, her eyes moving back and forth, taking in her surroundings as if she were seeing them for the first time. Ransom had long since ceased to be surprised that Emily could find so much of interest at a time of life when he would have thought she'd seen it all. But Emily had once told him that her philosophy of life could be summed up very simply: only dull people find the world dull.

They descended the Skyway onto I-94, leaving Chicago behind

for the brief stint through Indiana before reaching Michigan. The chaos of the city gave way to rolling drifts of snow, which, after a while, lulled Emily to sleep. It wasn't long before Ransom realized that, rather than relaxing in this serene setting, his grip had tightened on the steering wheel. He could feel the tension in his shoulders radiating up his neck and down his back. He took a deep breath, released it slowly, and found to his amazement that his jaw was beginning to unclench. He wasn't surprised by the action so much as by the fact that he hadn't known he'd been clenching it, and wondered if he'd been holding it that way only for a matter of hours, or if it had been that way for years. He smiled at himself.

He settled back against the seat and flexed his hands a couple of times on the steering wheel, making a brave attempt to get in the spirit of things. A calm, rational voice inside his head told him that he'd become too set in his ways, that if the prospect of a few days away from home would cause him further anxiety, then it had been much too long since he'd been away. But the conscious part of his mind wondered just how hard a week of peace and quiet would be on his nerves.

SARA BARTLETT sat distractedly over a mug of coffee at the table that occupied one corner of the kitchen. The table was made of oak with the legs painted white and the surface dark green, which apparently was all that was needed for it to be certified a "country table" in the catalogue from which she'd purchased it. She'd had the kitchen completely redone with modern appliances, large and dependable enough to provide for the needs of ten guests, the maximum for whom Hawthorne House could provide at any given time. She'd retained the latticework cabinets that hung at eye level across two entire walls, although she'd had them stripped, sanded, and painted white. Yellow curtains with white lace trim covered the windows over the sink and on the two doors, one to the backyard and the other to the driveway.

Though Sara was barely thirty years old, the cares of the past two years had taken their toll: tiny, downward-sloping lines marked the corners of her mouth, making her look as if she were slightly frowning when she was displaying no particular emotion at all. Likewise, the corners of her eyes were marked by barely visible crow's feet which, at a short distance, looked almost like tears. She had dark, wavy, shoulder-length hair, and light blue eyes that would have been considered lovely had they not been dulled by circumstance.

Millie Havers, the middle-aged woman who worked mornings for Sara preparing home-made muffins for the guests and performing the general cleaning duties, stood at the sink finishing the last of the breakfast dishes. Though the kitchen appliances included a good-sized dishwasher, without guests there were hardly ever enough dishes to warrant using it. Sara had kept Millie on while the house was closed to guests more out of a need for company than a need for help. She'd recognized very early on that, left to herself in the large, isolated house, she would have gone mad. And there was always enough work to be done in a place the size of Hawthorne House. Millie never openly questioned Sara's decision to keep her on, hoping that the young woman, of whom she'd grown quite fond, would eventually be able to reopen the house and move on with her life. She was more than pleased that that day seemed to have arrived.

"It'll be nice for you to have a tree up again," said Millie, thinking it best to rescue Sara from her thoughts with some everyday conversation.

"I guess," Sara replied, lifting the mug to her lips and taking a sip.

"It's best," Millie pursued in her matter-of-fact way, "best to get things back to normal. It's been a long time."

"I've been planning to reopen for some time," Sara said halfheartedly, "I just never got around to it."

"Oh, I know that. It's good you're doing it now."

Sara laughed ruefully. "I don't think I'd be doing it now if my friend Lynn hadn't been so insistent. She asked me to have them—at the going rate, of course—because they need to get away. The elderly woman has been ill and can't travel very far."

"That's not all I meant, though," said Millie. "It's best to get back to recognizing the seasons and letting everything kind of...I don't know, kind of go on the way it should."

Sara didn't look at the woman. She liked Millie and saw her as something of a mother figure, more from Millie's matronly manner than from the fifteen-year difference in their ages. But although Millie was pretty wise and was usually right, Sara didn't believe that anyone could understand what she'd gone through.

"Well..." Sara said slowly, setting the mug on the table but keeping her hands around it as if needing the warmth, "well, you know that Nathan was... Nathan died just before Christmas."

"Two years ago," Millie assented quickly, trying to hurry Sara past this.

"That first Christmas I was just in shock. I don't think I even knew...that I was aware of the day. Then last Christmas...the second...was worse—because I wasn't in shock anymore."

"I know."

Sara sighed and smiled at the woman. "So now you might get your wish."

Millie frowned and brushed a stray strand of gray back from her forehead. "What do you mean?"

"This year I can feel life going on, I think. I don't like it, but I know it's happening. And you're right, it's probably for the best."

Millie's face slowly broke into a warm smile. "That's good, Sara. That's real good. It'll get better. You'll see."

"I'm still not sure I can face the tree, though."

"Then why have one? You don't need to."

"Of course I do. I'm having guests for the holiday and they'll be expecting the place to be decorated. After all, this is a business."

Millie shook her head. "Mmm, I don't know that I'd like spending the holidays with strangers." The moment it was out of her mouth she quickly turned her head away and muttered "Damn" at herself.

Sara swiftly alleviated her embarrassment. "They're friends of friends, and Lynn said it's important for them to get away. Anyway, Christmas is supposed to be a time of giving, isn't it? Let's just say I'm finally getting back into the swing of the holiday by giving the one way I know how."

Their conversation was interrupted by the sound of wet rubber boots smacking on the tile floor as Hansen Crane thudded into the kitchen. Hansen was in his early sixties and looked as if he were purposely trying to earn the label of a "character." He was somewhere over six feet tall and heavy-set, made to look heavier by the plaid wool coat that covered him from shoulder to thigh. He had frizzy hair, the color and consistency of steel wool, that ran down the back of his neck and a matching beard so scruffy it looked almost as if a tumbleweed had lodged on his chin.

"Welp," he said in his booming bass voice, "the tree's up and ready."

"Thank you, Hansen," Sara replied. "Would you like some coffee?"

"Warm you up," Millie added.

"No, thanks. You got anything else you want me to do now?"

Sara hesitated a moment, looking down into her mug as if the future might reveal itself to her in the brown liquid. "Yes. There's some boxes in the basement I'd like you to bring up and put in the parlor by the tree."

Hansen blinked. "What kind of boxes?"

"Ornament boxes. They're in the southeast corner of the basement. There's three of them. They're large and red with leaves of holly printed on them in green. You can't miss them."

"Doesn't sound like it," Hansen replied as he headed out the back door and down the basement steps.

"Honestly, that man can't do anything without making a commotion out of it," said Millie without rancor.

Sara smiled and shrugged. "He's big. Big men make noise."

"I 'spose," said Millie with a laugh as she retrieved a towel and began drying the dishes. "My Herbert's a big man, and you should hear him coming up the back stairs! He sounds like a herd of buffalo! I wouldn't trade him for a quiet man, though. I like always knowing where he is in the house. I wouldn't like having one of those husbands that pop up on you unexpected and scare the life out of you."

Sara laughed. "That's one thing you never have to worry about when you grow up in a city. There's usually so much noise that I don't think you can ever be surprised by something like that. That took some getting used to out here...the quiet. You can be..." Her voice trailed off and she seemed to sink again into reverie. It still amazed her how many things could bring back so vividly the loss of her brother. She'd been about to say that you could be startled quite easily in the country, when suddenly the last time she'd been truly startled flew back into her mind with such graphic clarity that her stomach did a slight lurch.

"You can be what?" Millie asked.

Sara came back to attention and shook her head. "Oh, nothing."

Before Millie could pursue this further, Hansen's distinct, heavy tread could be heard starting up the wooden steps from the basement.

Millie smirked and shook her head. "Just like in that movie—the scary one about the dinosaurs."

Hansen appeared in the back doorway carrying three large, identical boxes, each piled on top of the other.

"These the ones you were talking about?"

"Yes, thank you. Would you put them in the parlor?"

"Sure."

He trod loudly through the kitchen, sending the glassware in the cabinets rattling in protest.

The two women fell silent for a moment, Millie cheerfully drying the last of the dishes and Sara trying not to think of anything while finishing her coffee. After a moment, Johnnie Larkin came into the kitchen. Johnnie was about twenty-five years old and had managed to pass through the gangliness of youth without any negative residual effects. He was fairly poised for his age, with straight brown hair, bright brown eyes, and an ingratiating smile that some of the townspeople found a little too ready.

Johnnie had moved to LeFavre a little over three years earlier and had taken a cheap room in the apartments over the town's one drugstore. He'd quickly made friends with most of the year-round residents in his age group, and it became generally known not long after his arrival that he'd "run away from home to live life the way he'd always wanted to," namely by living in a resort community where he could work more or less on his own, and spend his plentiful free time at the beach. He made a good enough living doing odd jobs for the locals, from pruning trees and bushes to cutting up felled trees for firewood and mucking out barns. He'd been an increasing presence at Hawthorne House since Nathan's death, partly from Sara's need for help with heavy work, and partly because (as Millie often told her husband in the evenings) Johnnie had a rather obvious crush on Sara.

"I brought the little dresser down and cleaned it up," he said to Sara, "and I moved the bed frame down and put it together."

Sara smiled at him. "Thanks, Johnnie."

"I'll bring the mattresses down, but I'm afraid I'm going to need some help for that. They aren't too heavy, but they're awkward, you know what I mean?"

"Hansen will help you."

Johnnie's face clouded slightly. "Is he here?"

"In the parlor. Hansen?" She called his name and waited. After a moment he clomped into the kitchen. "Would you help Johnnie bring a mattress and box spring down to the den?"

"Sure." He looked at Johnnie and the mass of hair on his face formed into something resembling a smile. "Come on, young man." With this he left the kitchen. Johnnie followed with a hint of reluctance. After a couple of seconds, they were heard ascending the stairs.

Sara rose from the table, went to the sink, and rinsed out the mug, giving it a cursory wipe with the dishrag. She handed it to Millie, who dried it and placed it in the dish drainer.

Sara sighed heavily. "I guess I'm going to have to face it sometime."

She headed for the parlor. Millie followed her, wiping her hands on her apron as she went.

Sara stopped in the archway that separated the parlor from the hallway, laying her hand against one side of it as if she needed to prop herself up. The seven-foot pine stood tall and dark in the center of the front picture window, blocking out a good deal of the morning light and making the atmosphere in the room seem more than a little gloomy. To Sara, the tree seemed like a shadowy, unwelcome stranger, casting a cloud over her mood that she didn't believe would lift until the tree was removed and the holidays were over.

"Well, there it is," said Sara.

"Don't worry. It'll look better after we get it decorated," Millie said with forced cheer. "Just like old times."

Sara glanced at her over her shoulder. "I haven't owned the place long enough to have old times."

Millie pursed her lips and thought a second, then said, "Well, just like not-so-recent times, then. In you go."

They went into the room and Sara steeled herself for a moment before removing the lid on the top ornament box. Inside was a tangled mess of green wire and Italian lights in a variety of colors.

Sara sighed ruefully. "Nathan always put these away and he never took the time to store them properly. Honestly, we go...we went through this every year."

Millie looked over her shoulder. "Don't worry, I'll straighten them out."

She picked up the box and took it to a wing chair in one corner of the room. She sat down, laid the box at her feet, and began to carefully pull out the strands, twisting and turning them around and through each other, as if she were playing cat's cradle with barbed wire.

Sara placed the second box on the love seat in the center of the room and sat down beside it. She removed the lid tentatively as if she thought something might leap out of the box at her, then laid the lid aside and began to take out the ornaments one at a time, gingerly unwrapping them from their tissue paper and considering each item in turn.

Millie managed to get the end of one strand of lights separated and draped over her shoulder and was in the process of trying to locate the opposite end when she heard a single choking gasp from Sara. She stopped what she was doing and looked up to find Sara staring down into her palm, tears streaming down her cheeks.

"What is it? What's wrong?"

Sara sniffed a couple of times and sat still a moment, then slid two fingers between a tiny thread and held up the ornament she'd found for Millie to see. It was a tiny unicorn. The body was of clear glass, and the horn was tinted pink.

"It was a gift from Nathan. He bought this for me our first year here."

Millie's forehead creased with concern. "I know it's hard, sweetie, but you knew you'd have to go through these things someday."

"Yes, I know." Sara retrieved a piece of wrapping tissue and used it to dab her eyes.

It was then that they heard the sound of a car coming up the gravel driveway beside the house.

"Oh, damn! Don't tell me they're here already!" She finished wiping her eyes quickly and stuffed the used tissue in the pocket of her skirt. Then she got up from the love seat and went to the side window that overlooked the drive. The moment she looked out the window, her back stiffened, her normally pale skin reddening.

"Who is it?" Millie asked distractedly as she fought with the mass of wire.

"Jeffrey. Jeff Fields."

Millie stopped and looked up. "Really?"

"Um hm."

With more resolution than she'd yet demonstrated that morning, Sara strode from the parlor to the front door. It was near enough that Millie could hear what was said.

Sara opened the door before Jeff had climbed the last step to the porch. He was around Sara's age but had a solid, sturdy build that made him look a little older than he was. He had broad shoulders and a straight back that looked perfectly at home in his sheriff's uniform. His long, sandy hair was perpetually falling into his eyes, which were approximately the same shade of blue as Sara's. When he saw Sara, he smiled uncertainly, as if he knew it was the right thing to do but didn't know how it would be received. Sara didn't return the gesture.

"Hi, Sara. How're you doing?"

"Fine, Jeff. How are you?"

"I'm all right."

They stood staring at each other in the attitude of former lovers who come upon each other unexpectedly and don't know how to proceed. It was clear that Sara wasn't willing to give him any encouragement, and it was equally clear that Jeff wasn't going to allow himself to be cowed so easily. He continued to smile at her as if almost defying her to resume the conversation. She didn't.

"Aren't you going to ask me why I'm here?" he asked.

She shrugged. "I figured you'd tell me."

He glanced down at the wooden floor of the open porch and appeared to be lost in thought. If Sara could have read his mind, she would have seen that he was mentally kicking himself for his manner of approach, as if her very posture were telling him that he'd already blown it.

Finally he looked up into her eyes, and said, "I just thought...with Christmas coming I wanted to come out and make sure you were all right...and invite you over if you didn't have anyplace else to go. I don't like to think of you being alone at Christmas."

Sara folded her arms just below her breasts. "You don't have to worry about that. I have company coming."

"Company?"

"Guests."

"Paying guests," Jeff said, wishing he'd been able to make it sound less disdainful.

"This is a business, Jeff."

"I understand that." There was a slight beat before he added, "I just wanted to make sure you were all right." He turned and started back toward the steps, and added, "That's all."

Sara hesitated for a moment, caught in a confusing morass of emotions. She didn't want to give him any reassurance, but she couldn't stand the thought of being impolite to him, either.

"Jeff," she said a little too eagerly once she'd found her voice.

He stopped and turned to face her.

"Thanks for stopping by."

Jeff put two fingers to his forehead by way of salute, and said, "Any time." He continued down the stairs and across the paving stones that formed a path along a flower bed to the driveway. As Sara went back into the house, she heard him start the car and pull hastily out into the road.

Sara stood with her back against the door for a while before rejoining Millie. From where she stood, she was looking directly into the dining room. Though the sideboard was empty, in her mind she could see it piled with muffins, plates of butter, the coffee urn, and the tea kettle. She pictured the warm summer breezes stirring the tan chiffon curtains over the windows, and the guests as they came down alone or in pairs, impressed by the spread and happily helping themselves to food, then finding places at the table. She had successfully created a family atmosphere among disparate strangers.

Then there was her real family. Her brother, Nathan, helping her with whatever needed to be done around the house, particularly the books and the bills, and handling the rare complaint that came their way with a sense of tact that one would have expected in a much older man. It had been her dream, and that dream had come true, until one day when in the blink of an eye the dream was destroyed. What she was left with, these two years later, was not a nightmare, but something more like a trance. A static deadness that threatened never to go away.

She was startled from these thoughts by the sudden appearance of Hansen Crane thudding into the dining room from the den, followed closely and more quietly by Johnnie Larkin. Hansen continued into the kitchen and out the back door while Johnnie came into the dining room, apparently looking for Sara.

"Was that Sheriff Jeff?" he asked, his tone not-so-gently mocking.

"Yes."

"What did he want?"

"Nothing."

Johnnie looked at her for a moment, then said, "Well, is there anything else that needs doing before I go?"

"Um...yes. Hansen cut some firewood yesterday. He piled it in the barn. Could you bring some in?"

"Sure thing," Johnnie replied. He sounded as if he were anxious to be particularly ingratiating. He started out of the room but paused and turned back to her. "Sara, is everything all right?"

"Yes, of course. Go on, now."

Johnnie hesitated for just a second before heading out to get the wood.

Sara went back into the parlor without a word, sat on the love seat, and resumed the business of unwrapping ornaments. Millie was staring at the archway when she entered as if she'd been frozen in that position ever since Sara had gone to answer the door.

After a few moments, Millie said, "When are you going to forgive that young man?"

"Who?"

"You know who I'm talking about. Jeff."

Sara didn't look up. She merely scrutinized the glass country church she'd just removed from a piece of red tissue. When she realized that Millie was still looking at her, and not likely to stop until she'd received an answer, Sara set the ornament aside and pulled another from the box as she said simply, "There's nothing to forgive."

TWO

EMILY AWOKE after a nap of over an hour, refreshed and with only a slight feeling of disorientation, which passed quickly.

"You shouldn't have let me sleep," she said with a little cough.

"It seemed like you needed it. And besides, you're supposed to relax, remember?" Ransom replied.

"Did I miss anything important?"

Ransom smiled and shrugged. "It's an interstate. Only miles and miles of 'amber waves of white.'"

Emily returned his smile, a playful twinkle in her eye. "If they were indeed amber, then you should have woken me."

With only one stop to have a light lunch and refresh themselves, it was just over three hours after beginning their trip that they came to the exit for LeFavre. Ransom pulled from his pocket the small hand-drawn map that Lynn had given him. At the end of the exit ramp, he turned left and drove for about a mile, where he came to a crossroad marked 130th Street.

"I wonder where the other hundred and twenty-nine are," he said wryly.

At the stop sign, there was a sign for LeFavre with an arrow pointing west, indicating that a left turn was called for. Ransom turned right.

"Shouldn't we be going the other way?" Emily asked, wrinkling her forehead.

"Not according to the map. Hawthorne House is actually about five miles outside the town proper, but it's still considered part of the town's jurisdiction."

"I see."

They had driven for a few more minutes when their destination came into view on the left side of the road. Though Lynn had told them that the place was big, they were not prepared for the actual size of the house. It was a huge two-story wood-framed building painted a pleasant, muted yellow, with ornamental shutters, porch railings, and all the woodwork painted white. Situated as it was atop a small snow-covered hill, Hawthorne House looked like a decoration perched on the uppermost tier of a cake.

Emily said "Good heavens!" as Ransom steered the car up the incline of the gravel driveway.

"Indeed," said Ransom.

He climbed out of the car, feeling the stiffness and weariness that comes with driving for so long. He stretched for a moment, then walked around to the passenger side and opened the door for Emily, carefully handing her out of the car. Sara was on the porch to greet them even before Emily was fully upright.

"Hullo!" she called to them. "I'm Sara Bartlett."

Emily gripped Ransom's arm as he led her across the paving stones, which had been swept free of snow.

"Hello," he replied, "I'm Jeremy Ransom. This is Emily Charters."

"Of course," Sara said with as much cheerfulness as she could muster. She came down the stairs to meet them. "Miss Charters, do you think you can manage the steps? If not, there's a ramp at the side door."

"Oh, no, no. There's only four steps. I'm sure I can manage."

Emily took hold of the railing with one hand while Sara took her other hand.

"Ah," said Ransom. "Well, if you're all right, then I'll get the suitcases from the car."

"I'll be fine, Jeremy," Emily replied lightly.

Sara led Emily into the front hall, and Emily stopped there for a moment to get her bearings.

"My goodness, this is lovely," said Emily. "Is the house Victorian?"

"Hmmm...maybe a little later than that. But it still shows signs of the period," Sara replied. She hesitated for a few seconds, then said, "Would you like me to show you the house, or would you like to rest for a while?"

"Oh, no, my dear, I like to see my surroundings before I bed down in them."

"Should we wait for Mr. Ransom?"

A knowing smile spread across the old woman's face. "No, I think we should probably go ahead. He might be a while."

Sara's dark eyebrows knit closer together. "But he was just going to get your luggage."

"So he said," Emily replied with a great deal of amusement, "but I suspect he's going to smoke, also."

Sara smiled. "Really?"

"It's one of his few vices. I don't approve of it so he doesn't do it in my presence. But I daresay that three hours in the car was quite trying for him."

"Ah," said Sara, her smile becoming a bit more conspiratorial, "then maybe I'd better start by showing you the parlor."

Sara gave her arm to Emily and led her around the corner into the aforementioned room. With the help of Millie Havers and Johnnie Larkin, Sara had managed to get the tree fully decorated. Now, with the lights glittering in the recesses of the branches, the tree no longer looked dark and foreboding, but instead was fulfilling its purpose as a colorful reminder of the season.

"That's a handsome tree," said Emily.

"Thank you," Sara replied absently.

"It's beautifully decorated. Did you do it yourself?"

"No. Millie Havers—she's the woman who helps me out here—she helped me, along with Johnnie Larkin. He helps out around here, too." Sara said all this a little hurriedly, as if trying to politely rush to another subject. The peculiar tone was not lost on Emily, who noted it without a word.

Sara directed Emily's attention to the fireplace in front of which stood two comfortable-looking wing chairs. Logs had been laid on the grate ready for the evening's fire, which Sara had thought would be a nice welcome to her holiday visitors. Then she led Emily to the side window.

"There's a view from here that I thought you'd be interested in," said Sara with a smile as she drew back the curtain.

This was the window that looked out onto the driveway. There was Ransom, resting against the side of the car and smoking a small plastic-tipped cigar as if he was drawing his life from it.

"It is a nice view," said Emily, "and not exactly unexpected."

Sara showed her the rest of the first floor, which consisted of a large living room with bay windows that looked across the lawn into a wooded area, a dining room, and a large library just off the living room and next to the den. The library had floor-to-ceiling shelves, which were lined with musty volumes that showed signs of age and multiple readings. The only furniture consisted of two mock-leather chairs, beside which were small smoking tables.

"If you don't like the smell of smoke," said Sara, "you might not like this room."

"Oh, no," Emily replied as she gazed admiringly at the shelves, her ancient eyes conveying the closest thing to envy that Emily ever demonstrated, "this is splendid. There's something about the atmosphere of a library that lends itself to smoke. I always think libraries should be a bit close."

Sara smiled. "It probably lives up to that. It's been a while since anyone's been in here, except for when I come in to get a book. And that's only for a second. I like to read in the kitchen. I don't know why."

"I imagine it's a bit friendlier there," Emily said absently.

Sara found her mind wandering again as she considered this. She hadn't realized it before, but she didn't really like the library. Possibly because of the stuffiness, and partly because when the door was closed the room was so quiet and removed. And lonely. She needed nothing to accentuate the loneliness. She became so lost in her thoughts that she didn't hear Emily speak.

"Miss Bartlett?"

"Oh, I'm sorry," said Sara, regaining herself.

"I was just saying this house is very large. I thought Lynn mentioned that it had been a farmhouse at one time."

"Oh, only in a manner of speaking. It wasn't really a farm. It was built by a man called Zebediah Hawthorne, if you can believe such a name, who owned a vineyard. A lot of wine is produced in this area, you know. He built this house for his family, which was very large, but so was his business, so I guess he had the money to do it."

"What happened to the vineyards?"

"They're still there, just north of us—behind the house. Twenty years or so ago, Hawthorne's children...or grandchildren, I'm not sure which, sold the vineyards to a big company, which of course didn't need the house. So they sold it off with a generous plot of ground. It had two other owners before me."

Emily clucked her tongue. "I suppose that will always be the way. The children knew the value of the business that their father had built, but they didn't know the value of the family home."

Sara paused. The subject of family was one that would often catch her unawares and cause her pain, even when it wasn't in reference to her own. The mere mention of someone not valuing their family unexpectedly cut to her heart. She could feel tears beginning to well in her eyes.

Emily immediately noticed the change in the young woman's demeanor, and laid a hand gently on her arm. "My dear, is anything the matter?"

"No...I...no..."

"Hello!" Ransom called from the front door.

Sara almost sighed with relief at the interruption and exited the library without a word. Emily followed her. They found Ransom by the door holding Emily's suitcase, along with his own serviceable plaid cloth bag.

Sara closed the door behind him, and said, "Come right in. Oh, Miss Charters, I haven't shown you your room yet. It's right through here, next to the library."

She led them back through the living room and opened the door to the right of the library, then stood aside to allow her guests to precede her.

The room was fairly large and painted a very light shade of

tan. There was a window facing east, looking out over the side lawn and wooded area, and another facing north with a view of the back of the property. The barn stood prominently in the near distance. The windows were covered with sheers of a darker tan than the walls, and there were white shades that could be pulled down for privacy.

The dresser that Johnnie had carried down earlier had been placed beside the east window, and directly across the room from it was a queen-sized pencil-post bed made of maple. The bed was covered with a huge, inviting comforter encased in a cover printed all over with tiny cornflowers. Beside the bed was a nightstand on which rested a boudoir lamp. In the corner of the room, between the windows, was a chair with a soft cushion and a straight back, perfect for reading in, and next to it was an antique floor lamp with a large, fringed shade.

"It's not as bright and cheery as I'd like, Miss Charters..." said Sara as she pulled back the sheers.

"Please, call me Emily."

Sara smiled. "And please call me Sara."

Emily inclined her head by way of acknowledgment. "The room is lovely."

"Thank you. It was originally a bedroom. I used it as a den, or a reading room, as I like to call it, since it communicates with the library." She gestured to a door on the left side of the bed. "But we've made it a bedroom again in honor of your stay."

"Oh, I hope you haven't gone to too much bother."

"Don't be silly. It wasn't a problem. Lynn told me you needed to be on the first floor. She also gave me strict instructions that you were to be treated like the family jewels."

Emily's right hand went up to the neck of her dark blue wool dress. "That was very kind of her, I'm sure."

For the first time, Sara's smile took on a degree of warmth. "I knew if she said it, it had to be true. Lynn is a very hard person to win over. If she says you're a jewel, then I believe it."

"Thank you," said Emily primly, as if she thought it was

faintly indecent to be praised so directly. But her eyes sparkled in a way that betrayed her pleasure.

"The door on the other side of the bed is the bathroom. I think it was the last owner who added a shower. It's not very big, but it's the best we have on this floor."

"I'm sure it will be fine."

Sara stopped for a moment and glanced around the room, then turned back to Emily, and said, "Now, is there anything I can get you?"

"I think I'd like to unpack my things. But afterward I might like a little tea."

"That would be fine. I'll show Mr. Ransom up to his room, and then have tea ready for you in the dining room in about twenty minutes?"

"The dining room?" said Emily hesitantly.

Sara glanced at Ransom, then back to Emily. "Yes. If that's all right. Would you rather have it in here? I'd be glad to bring it to you."

Emily smiled indulgently and shook her head. "There's really no need to be oversolicitous of me. No matter what Jeremy and Lynn may think, I'm not a bit of fine china. I'm not in imminent danger of shattering to pieces."

Sara smiled and brushed her hair back with her hand as her cheeks turned a slight pink.

Emily continued. "I was just thinking that…if it's just the three of us here for the holiday…we should probably stay a bit more informal. Would you mind if I had tea in the kitchen?"

"Oh!" said Sara with a laugh, "No, not at all. I'll have it for you there in just a little while."

"Thank you," said Emily as she turned to her suitcase, which Ransom had put on a stand at the foot of the bed.

Sara turned to Ransom, and said, "Now I'll show you your room, if you like."

"Thank you," he replied. Sara preceded him out of the room, and he paused in the doorway for just a moment. He looked back at Emily and said with a sly smile, "Don't kid yourself. You *are* a bit of fine china."

Once he'd left the room, Emily stood looking down at the contents of her suitcase. After a moment a sigh escaped her lips and she gently closed the case. She then crossed to the chair by the window. She reached down and pressed the cushion a couple of times with her hand, and once satisfied as to its firmness and height, she lowered herself onto it. Despite her claims to the contrary, she'd found the trip fatiguing, and found that fact a little distressing. As she sat there with her eyes closed, she assured herself that she would have found a three-hour drive a bit tiring even before having the operation for what she called her "little problem," the heart attack that had necessitated a quadruple bypass.

She took a few deep breaths to relax herself and sank back into the chair. She was surprised to find that cares and worries, of which she hadn't been consciously aware, seemed to be melting off her in the quiet of this room and the comfort of the chair. For the first time she realized that Jeremy might just have been right, that she had needed to get away from the normal routine of her life in order to properly relax, and it might not have just been Jeremy who needed a vacation.

SARA LED RANSOM to a large bedroom at the top of the stairs. It was furnished in much the same way as Emily's room, except for the addition of a large reproduction of an antique wardrobe.

"Hm," said Ransom as he opened the wardrobe and inspected the interior, "very nice."

"Very practical," Sara emended. "When they built a lot of these old houses they didn't think much of closet space. Now, the bathroom is just to the left of this room. With no other guests you'll have it pretty much to yourself. And there's a small room just down the hallway that you'll find particularly useful."

"Hm?"

"It's a smoking room. You're welcome to use it. There's an

exhaust fan in the window that keeps the room, and the rest of the house, fairly clear.''

Ransom raised his right eyebrow. ''You seem to have thought of everything.''

''We...I like my guests to be comfortable.''

Ransom smiled and laid his suitcase on top of the dresser.

''Tell me, Mr. Ransom...''

''Most people just call me Ransom. Except Emily.''

Sara gave a single nod of acknowledgment. ''Tell me, exactly how is Emily? I mean, she says she doesn't need special care, but Lynn seemed to think she was quite weak.''

Ransom sighed. ''It's hard to tell with Emily. When I first met her, I mistook her for a frail old woman. She straightened me out on that point very quickly. As for today...to look at her you wouldn't think she'd had open-heart surgery just a couple of months ago. She's always been strong and she's not the type to give in to weakness or to like a fuss being made over her. That doesn't necessarily mean that it doesn't need to be made.''

Sara stood looking at him, her head tilted to one side and a questioning expression on her face. ''What does all that mean, though?''

Ransom shrugged. ''It means if you're going to watch out for her you'd better not let her see you doing it.''

THREE

JOHNNIE LARKIN strolled the aisles of Macklin's Supermarket, the largest of its kind in the area. Although there was a small grocery store in LeFavre, when the locals had any sizable purchases to make they usually drove the fifteen miles to the neighboring town of Mt. Morgan, in which Macklin's was located. Johnnie pushed his shopping cart along with two index fingers and whistled as if he didn't have a care in the world. He wore a blue plaid shirt and a pair of overalls with the shoulder straps unfastened and tied around his waist. The bib hung down below his waist like a denim loincloth.

"Hello, Mr. Crabtree," Johnnie called in his friendliest manner to an elderly man who stood with a hose spraying a fine mist over the vegetables.

Mr. Crabtree turned around slowly, his arthritis precluding any more rapid movement. His unblinking eyes stared dully at the young man.

"Hullo, Johnnie," he said with formal cordiality after a pause. His tone was unsure enough to make it sound as if he didn't particularly care for Johnnie, but couldn't remember the cause.

"You have any sweet potatoes?" Johnnie said, enjoying the old man's discomfiture.

"Uh-huh. Over there. Right in front of you."

"Thank you, sir," Johnnie replied, touching a finger to his forehead.

He selected several potatoes from the bin, eyeing them carefully as if he really knew how to tell a good one from a bad one, then tossed each in turn into his cart. He then selected some baking potatoes in the same manner, and retrieved two bags of fresh cranberries from a shelf above the bins.

"Looks like you're doing an awful lot of shopping," said

Crabtree with feigned disinterest, his natural curiosity getting the better of his reticence. "You having people in for the holidays?"

"It's not for me, it's for Sara. Sara Bartlett," Johnnie replied happily, knowing that anything he told the old man would probably be common knowledge within the hour.

"She opening up Hawthorne House again? For the holidays?"

"Just for a few select people," said Johnnie. Implicit in his tone was the idea that he was one of the select.

"Well, I'll be," Crabtree said as he turned the hose on a bin of celery. Then he added, more to himself than for Johnnie's benefit, "Used to be people stayed home at Christmas."

"Sara tries to make Hawthorne House as much like home as possible," Johnnie said, giving the old man a gentle, friendly pat on the back. He could feel Crabtree stiffen at his touch.

Johnnie paused for a moment and withdrew his hand, wasting an indulgent smile on Crabtree as the old man walked away muttering, "...still nothing but a glorified hotel."

Johnnie tried not to begrudge Crabtree's coolness. He knew that although LeFavre, Mt. Morgan, and many of the surrounding towns catered heavily to the tourist trade, most of the locals jealously guarded their small-town spirit, entertaining a mild distrust of anyone who hadn't been born in the area, or lived there for several generations. They also regarded the tourists as a necessary evil, treating them like spoiled children who needed to be relieved of their excess money lest they spend it foolishly—somewhere else.

But, although he knew that the gentle snubbing wasn't reserved for him alone, Johnnie couldn't help feeling the injustice of it. He liked to think of himself as thick skinned but, in the arrogance of his youth, he believed he should be accepted at face value on the strength of the character he exhibited, rather than on his place of birth or the length of time he'd lived in the area. He shook his head in mild disgust at the thought.

With a sigh, Johnnie reached into his side pocket and withdrew the lengthy list with which Sara had provided him. After checking it over to make sure he'd gotten everything he needed from the produce section, he resumed his whistling and headed for another part of the store. He rounded the corner into the baking goods aisle and literally ran into Amy Shelton. He caught sight of her just in time and turned his cart aside at the last moment, just grazing the side of Amy's cart.

Amy Shelton was pretty if a little on the plain side. She had light blue eyes and long blond hair that she held in place with a pink headband. Her white blouse and navy blue skirt were both very clean and pressed, and a sweater that matched the color of her headband hung across her shoulders. Her winter coat, which was unstylish but serviceable, was stuffed in the child seat of her shopping cart. Though her appearance was decidedly starched, there was a softness about Amy that made most people treat her as if she were a porcelain doll.

"Oh! I'm sorry!" she exclaimed as the carts collided.

"My fault," said Johnnie.

When Amy realized who it was she'd bumped into, she blushed a deep red.

"Oh!" she said again. Her hand flew to her heart and fumbled with a button on her blouse as if she had just discovered she wasn't dressed. "Oh. Hello, Johnnie."

"Hi. Long time no see."

"Yes," she stammered. "Yes. How have you been?"

"I've been just great. How about you?"

"I'm fine. Just fine."

There was an extremely awkward silence during which Johnnie continued to look at Amy while she studied shelves lined with bags of sugar as if she were convinced that there really must be a difference between the brands.

"How's your mom and dad?" Johnnie asked in an attempt to break the silence.

"They're fine. The same as always."

Johnnie started to say something else, but Amy headed him off.

"We're having my brother and his family in for Christmas. We haven't seen them in a long time. It'll be nice. We're all looking forward to it."

"That's nice. Look, I just wanted to say—"

"I really can't stay and talk. I just ran in to get some things we need. Some last-minute things. I know there's still a few days till Christmas, but I don't want to have to be running back and forth to the store while my brother's here. Excuse me."

She pulled her cart back and started to push it around Johnnie, but he laid a hand on the side to stay it.

"Amy, I just wanted to say—"

"No!" she said loudly, then shot an embarrassed glance up and down the aisle to make sure she hadn't attracted anyone's attention. She then lowered her voice, and said, "There's no need to say anything. It's all right." She stopped and looked up into his eyes for the first time. "Please don't say anything."

Johnnie looked at her with a sad smile and removed his hand from her cart. Without another word she wheeled the cart away and disappeared around the corner.

It took him another half hour to finish his shopping. He paid for the groceries and was waiting for the cashier to finish bagging them when Jeff Fields came up and laid a handful of frozen dinners and a carton of Coke on the counter. In an apparent effort to ignore Johnnie, he turned his full attention to a rack of tabloids hanging next to the cash register.

Johnnie glanced down at Jeff's groceries and smiled. "Whoa! The staples of a bachelor's diet."

Jeff returned the smile reluctantly, more to conceal his emotions than from any desire to invite further conversation. "I guess."

"I hate when I have to buy frozen dinners," Johnnie pursued. "It makes me feel like such a stereotype."

"Well, there's some of us that don't care what people think."

"I suppose."

There was a momentary silence interrupted only by the sounds of the brown paper bags rattling as the cashier filled them. Jeff would have liked nothing better than for the silence to continue, but thought it best to take the initiative in directing the conversation rather than let Johnnie continue.

"You look like you're stocking up there," said Jeff, jutting a thumb in the direction of the rapidly filling bags.

"We're having people in for Christmas."

"We?"

"Up at the house," Johnnie explained with a smile that indicated he was choosing his words purposefully. "Oh, then of course, you know that. You stopped by earlier, didn't you?"

"I stopped by Hawthorne House," Jeff replied, the remnants of his smile freezing on his face.

The tone of this exchange wasn't lost on the cashier, who shot a glance at Jeff, catching his attention before she rolled her eyes.

"Sara's put up a tree this year. We decorated it this morning."

"Sounds like you're making yourself pretty useful."

"Yeah. Of course, Sara needs a man around the house since her brother died."

Jeff folded his arms across his chest and leaned against the counter. "Hm. Maybe she'll find one."

There was a slight glitch in Johnnie's ingratiating smile, something like the blink of a computer screen in response to a flash of lightning. But it was only fleeting. His smile returned full force as he said, "By the way, I don't guess there's been any breaks in finding out who killed her brother?"

"There's nothing new, no," Jeff said, trying with difficulty to stem the flow of blood to his face. Given the fact that he could feel the temperature of his skin rising, he knew he wasn't being successful.

Johnnie heaved a dramatic sigh. "I don't suppose there's much chance of finding out who did it...after all this time."

Without visibly changing his expression, Jeff's smile seemed to become more menacing.

"Well, you never know what may come up."

"Yeah, right," said Johnnie.

The cashier had finished packing the bags at this point and Johnnie tossed them into the cart and rolled it out the front door, whistling as he went. Once he was gone, the cashier leaned halfway over the counter and said to Jeff, "You know, if this was that Angela Lansbury program on TV, that guy would be dead before long.''

Jeff's smile melted. ''Well, we can always hope.''

''DO YOU MIND if I go on working while you have your tea?'' Sara asked.

''Not at all,'' Emily replied with a smile as she took a sip. Although Sara had a large collection of mugs for the coffee that was the preference of most of her guests, she'd thought Emily would prefer a normal cup and saucer. Sara had also set out a plate of brightly decorated Christmas cookies in the center of the table.

''I could fix a sandwich for you if you'd like.''

''Oh, no. We had lunch on the way. This is fine.''

''I thought maybe a meat loaf would be all right for tonight. With lots of vegetables on the side. I didn't know whether or not you'd given up on meat,'' said Sara, wiping her hands on the brown-checkered towel that hung from the refrigerator handle.

''Not entirely,'' Emily said as she replaced the cup in its saucer. ''Of course, doctors would have you give up anything pleasurable, but it's difficult to change a lifetime of eating habits, and at my time of life there hardly seems any point.''

''Oh, don't say that.''

Emily sighed. ''None of us go on forever.''

Sara smiled sadly and hesitated before opening the refrigerator door. ''Yes, I know.''

Emily watched Sara with a keen eye as she removed two packages of meat and placed them on the counter. Her movements were slow but precise, as if whatever had just clouded her thoughts made her afraid that she might forget something important.

''This is a very lovely house,'' Emily said, hoping to take Sara's mind off whatever was troubling her.

''Thank you,'' Sara replied with a gratified smile.

''It must be terribly difficult to keep it up.''

Sara looked at her and blinked. "Not really," she said with forced matter-of-factness, "I'm financially very secure."

She'd laid the slightest stress on the word "financially." Emily was surprised that, although money didn't appear to be a problem for Sara, it would be the first concern to pop into her mind. Emily's eyes widened and her lips formed an apologetic frown. "Oh, my goodness! I'm sorry, I wasn't referring to money. You see, my own house is fairly small—little more than a bungalow, really—and I find it difficult to keep it properly on my own anymore." She stopped and smiled to herself, adding, "At least that's what Jeremy tells me. That's why he hired your friend Lynn to come in and clean for me."

"Oh!" said Sara with an embarrassed laugh, "I misunderstood you. Yes, this place really is a lot for...for one person, but I have plenty of help. Millie Havers comes in in the mornings. She prepares breakfast—usually fresh muffins. She's a terrific baker. And she helps me clean. You'll meet her tomorrow morning. And there's Hansen Crane. He lives out back in the apartment over the barn. He does work around the place, and I pay him a little and give him a place to live. He keeps the grass cut and does most of the gardening and whatever else I ask him to do. He's getting on in years, so I don't like him to do the real heavy work—but you know how some men are, he'll do it anyway. And I have a young man, Johnnie Larkin, who comes in whenever I need him to do the heavier things."

"Well, it sounds as if you're pretty much taken care of," said Emily as she lifted the cup to her lips again.

"Yes, I'm not...I have enough help."

Sara had put the meat into a large bowl and paused in the process of cracking a pair of eggs into the mixture. Her gaze traveled out the window over the sink. From there she could see the blanket of snow covering the yard, and the woods beyond it. The leafless trees stood crowded together, their branches straining upward like a riot of naked arms reaching to the sky for help.

"Is there anything the matter, Sara?" Emily asked gently.

"What? No. No..." She cracked the eggs into the bowl and

dropped the empty shells into the garbage can. "I was just thinking how pretty this area looks during the summer. I don't know, somehow when everything's blooming it doesn't seem so...so..." Her voice trailed off.

"Lonely?" Emily offered.

"I was going to say isolated. Isn't that funny? We're exactly the same distance from town no matter what the season, but during the winter it seems more isolated."

Emily lightly laid her fingers on the sides of her cup and sat silently watching the young woman with concern. She was reluctant to bring up a painful subject, but at the same time felt that it was preying on Sara's mind and talking about it might help her.

Emily cleared her throat, and said, "Sara, Lynn told us that you lost your brother a couple of years ago. I'm very sorry."

"Thank you," Sara replied as if by rote. She paused for a beat in the process of mixing the contents of the bowl.

"Was his death very unexpected?"

"Very," said Sara, a touch of irony in her voice. Then she added before Emily could ask the next obvious question, "He was killed. Murdered."

"Oh, how awful," Emily said with feeling. But despite the sympathy she felt, her interest was piqued. "Did the police apprehend whoever did it?"

"No. No, they didn't."

Emily's eyebrows elevated at this. "You mean they have no idea who did it?"

Sara shot an annoyed glance at her. "They have ideas, all right," she said with an edge. When she saw the surprised look on Emily's face, she immediately relented. She gave Emily a halfhearted smile, and said more softly, "They had ideas, but nothing panned out. Everything came to a dead end."

"I'm really very sorry," said Emily. "It must leave you feeling very much at loose ends."

Sara stopped and looked at Emily with mild surprise.

"Yes. Yes, it does," she said. Then, adopting a more professional tone as she wiped her hands on the towel again, she added, "Now, what kind of vegetables would you like with your dinner?"

While the vegetable menu was being discussed inside the house, outside Johnnie steered his old but reliable hatchback up the wide driveway and parked next to Ransom's Nova. He switched off the ignition and jumped out of the car in a single motion, then strolled to the back of the car and popped the hatch. He was no longer whistling, but his satisfied smile served as an indication that he was still entertaining his own pleasant thoughts.

It was because of this that he didn't hear the approach of Hansen Crane until he was almost upon him.

"Hi, there, Johnnie boy," said Crane with a jocular tone that had just a touch of sarcasm about it.

Johnnie paused in the act of pulling the first grocery bag from the back of the car. He was glad that his face hadn't been in view when he first heard the voice, because it never would have done to give Crane the satisfaction of seeing the smile disappear, any more than it would have done for Crane to have seen it to begin with.

"Hello, Crane," Johnnie said with elaborate deference as he straightened up, bag in hand.

"You the one that messed up my woodpile?"

"'Scuse me?" said Johnnie, feigning confusion. "How can you mess up a woodpile?"

"By pulling wood out willy-nilly, lettin' the stack fall all over the place, and not piling it back up where it belongs."

"Is that what I did? You sure it didn't just fall over on its own?"

"I don't know why, I see a mess and I just think you had something to do with it."

The smug look on Crane's face almost forced Johnnie into saying something he was sure he'd have been sorry for later. He had to remember his position, plus the fact that Sara, for reasons he could never understand, actually liked the old man. He heaved a sigh meant to let the older man know he was being indulged, and said, "I'll go restack them as soon as I get the groceries inside."

"That woodpile's been messed up since this morning," said Crane, laying a hand on the upraised hatch of the car.

Johnnie paused for a second, then said, "At least it can wait till I get these inside."

"It's plenty cold out here," said Crane, his smile remaining in place as if a testament to how cold it was, "the food'll keep."

"Look, Crane," Johnnie began, but one glance at the unmoving older man told him it was no use. Instead, with an attempt at grace that was visibly costing him a struggle, Johnnie said, "Oh, all right! I'll take care of it."

He dropped the bag back into the car and marched off toward the barn. Crane smiled after him as if he'd achieved some sort of victory.

It was almost twenty minutes before Johnnie brought the first load of groceries through the back door into the kitchen.

"My goodness!" said Sara as she took one of the bags from him and set it on the counter. "You took your time about coming in. I thought I heard you drive up ages ago."

"That was your Mr. Crane," Johnnie replied with an apologetic smile that didn't quite hide his annoyance, "Don't blame me if anything's defrosted!"

"I hardly think that's possible in this weather," said Sara, glancing into the second bag as she took it from him. "Oh, Johnnie, this is Emily Charters, one of my guests for the week."

Johnnie beamed his most ingratiating smile and doffed an imaginary hat at Emily. "Hello, I'm pleased to meet you, ma'am!"

"Good afternoon," Emily replied, her eyes fixed on Johnnie appraisingly.

"Now," said Sara, "what was this about Hansen?"

"Who knows?" said Johnnie. "He got a bee in his bonnet about the woodpile. He said I left it in a mess, as if there was such a thing as a neat woodpile."

Unnoticed by Johnnie, Emily nodded to herself as if her appraisal had been verified.

"Honestly," Johnnie continued, his tone taking on an amused exasperation, "that old man is nuts!"

"And did you mess it up?" Sara asked with a smile.

"Well, yeah," Johnnie replied sheepishly, "but cleaning it up could've waited until I had the groceries in, but no, he insisted I do it right away."

"Well, no harm done. And you know that Hansen likes to have things done a particular way."

"Yeah, I know," Johnnie replied with a knowledgeable nod. "I'll get the rest of the bags."

Sara gave a little laugh when he was out of earshot. "There's always been a little tension between Hansen and Johnnie. It's so typical. Hansen doesn't seem to think Johnnie knows anything because he's young, and Johnnie doesn't think Hansen knows anything because he's old."

"Oh, yes," said Emily, "quite understandable."

Sara began to unpack the groceries. "It's been worse the past couple of years because with...well, I've needed more help around here so I've had Johnnie around more, and that's caused more friction. To tell you the truth, I tend to be a little indulgent when it comes to Hansen. He can be a bit quirky, and he's set in his ways, but he does know what he's doing. I've been trying to get Johnnie to understand that since Hansen's old—" She stopped suddenly and glanced at Emily, her cheeks turning pink. "I mean, that he should..."

Emily smiled as she rescued Sara from the faux pas in which she'd become mired. "If you were going to say you've been trying to convince that young man that he should respect his elders, you'll get no argument from me. It's one of the ironies of life that by the time you learn to respect your elders, quite often you no longer have any elders left to respect."

Sara laughed genuinely for the first time. Emily couldn't help thinking how pleasant it sounded coming from her, and how sad it was that circumstances prevented her from doing it more often.

Johnnie returned with the remaining sacks of groceries and set about helping Sara to unpack them and put them away.

"You'll never guess who I ran into at Macklin's," he said.

"Who?"

"Jeff Fields, for one."

There was a beat before Sara said "Oh?" She removed some cans from a bag and put them on the shelf above the refrigerator.

"Yeah. He seems to be getting around today." Johnnie's face hardened as he added, "He should do less visiting and shopping and do more investigating."

Sara stopped. "You didn't say that to him."

"No," Johnnie replied slowly, "no, of course not."

Sara stared at him for a moment, then went back to unpacking. Johnnie continued, "But...well, never mind. He wasn't the one I was surprised to see. Guess who else I saw."

"Tell me," said Sara, her tone intimating that she wasn't in the mood for guessing games.

"Amy Shelton."

Sara paused with her hand on top of the refrigerator. "Really?"

"Yeah."

"How was she doing?"

"She seemed to be doing okay. She said they're having family in for Christmas."

"That's nice." Sara retrieved a couple of more cans from the bag and slid them onto the shelf. With her back still turned to Johnnie she said, "What else did she have to say?"

"Nothing, really. She was in kind of a hurry...so she said. I...I got the feeling she didn't want to talk to me too badly."

Sara turned around and looked at Johnnie, her expression anything but pleased.

"Why would you think that?"

"Because she knows I work—" He stopped abruptly and cast a glance over his shoulder at her. His face paled a little, and he couldn't have looked more apologetic if he'd tried. "Well, you know how she is. She's always been kind of an odd one."

"No, she hasn't," Sara said firmly. "I remember her as being a very nice person."

"Okay, okay," he said resignedly, raising his palms as if to repel an invisible assailant, "but you know how some people are."

Sara didn't respond. Johnnie looked down at the floor for a moment, then back up at her. "I guess when she saw me there were just too many connections. I'm sorry."

Sara shook her head ruefully as she went back to the groceries. "I just hate to think of her not doing well, that's all."

"She's all right. She said she was looking forward to the holidays."

As he said this he gave Sara a light rub on the shoulder from which she didn't recoil. Emily watched this entire exchange silently with slightly raised eyebrows.

Johnnie placed one of the bags on the floor, dropped to a crouch, and began to transfer the baking potatoes and sweet potatoes into separate bins in the bottom drawer next to the sink.

"It looks like you're going to be making quite a spread," said Johnnie, trying not to sound too obviously as if he were changing the subject.

Sara glanced at Emily, and said, "Well, I have very special guests for Christmas."

"You're going to be really well taken care of," Johnnie said to Emily, "you should see all the food."

"I'm looking forward to it," Emily replied.

"Yeah," said Johnnie as he stood up and proceeded to fold the bag. "You really have something to look forward to. Sara's a great cook. Christmas dinner should be something really special."

Sara was not so far lost in her thoughts that she missed the none-too-subtle hints.

"Where are you going to have Christmas dinner, Johnnie?" she asked, casting an amused glance at Emily.

"Oh, I don't know," he replied with practiced nonchalance. "I suppose at my apartment. I can make something."

"Why don't you have Christmas dinner here?"

"Oh, that's all right. I appreciate it, but I don't mind being on my own. If I did, I never would've left home!"

Sara placed a hand on her hip, and said, "You can go on being polite just so long before I'll take you at your word."

Johnnie laughed, and said, "Okay, okay! I accept. Thank you very much! Oh, before I forget it, I should give you your change." He reached around toward his back pocket and his face suddenly went white.

"What's wrong?" Sara asked.

"My wallet's gone!"

"It's right there." She pointed to where his wallet was lying, on the floor by where he'd been crouching. Sara started to reach for it, but Johnnie quickly snatched it up off the floor as if he was afraid that one of the two ladies might want to abscond with what little he had.

"Damn!" he said with an embarrassed smile. "I've gotta stop doing that! I don't make enough to lose anything."

He gave Sara the change from the shopping and slipped the wallet into his back pocket, giving it an extra pat as if that would hold it in place. "Now, do you need me to do anything else? I don't have anything planned for the rest of the day. If you need me, I'm available."

"No, that's all right. Thank you."

"Oh. Okay." He sounded disappointed. "I'll be going, then. 'Bye, Miss Charters. Nice to meet you."

Emily smiled in response.

"He's a nice boy," said Sara once Johnnie had gone.

"He's hardly a boy," Emily replied as she took a sip of tea.

Sara laughed gently. "I suppose you're right. He's only about five years younger than me."

"He seems interested in you."

Sara glanced at Emily. The look on the young woman's face was a mixture of what Emily took to be admirably modest embarrassment tinged with something a bit darker. Though she had no way of knowing what the cause might be, Emily could have sworn that Sara found the idea of Johnnie's interest somehow distressing.

"I don't think...well, maybe he is. But I'm...I'm not really interested in anyone. Not now."

Emily looked at her quizzically for a moment, then set her cup back on its saucer. "I'm so sorry. I didn't mean to be so personal."

"Oh, no," said Sara, recovering herself and waving the matter off, "I just never think of Johnnie that way. He seems so young."

Emily nodded thoughtfully. "Yes, he does."

FOUR

RANSOM WOKE with the curious but not unpleasant sensation of being swathed in a floating cloud with an angel hovering somewhere overhead. It was a few minutes before he became fully cognizant of his surroundings. The cloud was nothing more than the combination of an extremely comfortable mattress and a soft, white comforter. The angel he'd sensed in his half-waking state was the slowly rotating ceiling fan meant to help keep the heat circulating.

Though Ransom had never been one to sleep late, as he lay there he thought how easy it would be to stay peacefully wrapped in the warmth of the bed, lolling in and out of sleep, for the better part of the day. But it wasn't long before he became aware of the inviting aroma of freshly brewed coffee and muffins apparently just coming out of the oven. With only a modicum of reluctance, he pushed back the covers and slid out of bed. He retrieved his black satin robe from the back of the chair over which it was draped and slipped into it. As he tied the sash, he went to the window.

The view was only partially obscured by a massive oak tree, denuded for the winter and spreading some of its more spindly branches across the window like a spider web. Through the branches he could see the front yard and the road. Far in the distance he could make out a farmhouse, which sat like the fixed point of a triangle from which the property on the opposite of the road spread out. There was something unreal about the scene, as if he were seeing a painting of farmland in winter rather than the farmland itself, and he experienced the same curious sensation one sometimes feels when looking at a painting, of wanting to be drawn into it. It was his first glimpse of how hypnotically seductive this type of tranquility could be, and he made a mental note of his need to resist it.

Though it was after eight in the morning, there was very little in the way of activity outdoors. There wasn't much in the way of traffic, either, which he attributed to the fact that this wasn't exactly a main thoroughfare. But as Ransom gazed languidly out the window, he saw a car appearing over a ridge in the distance on the left. He didn't find anything particularly surprising about this, or in the fact that as it came nearer, he could make out the sheriff's emblem on the passenger door. The car passed the house with the same steady pace with which it had approached, neither too fast nor too slow, and continued on at the same rate until it had disappeared. The driver's head hadn't turned as he passed.

Ransom marked the seemingly innocuous event with a simple "Hm."

After he'd showered, shaved, and dressed, he came downstairs to find Emily already seated in the dining room and eating a fresh muffin as she talked with Millie Havers.

"The blueberries are frozen, of course," Millie said. "You should taste them during the season. You can get beautiful blueberries at roadside stands in these parts."

Emily swallowed a bit of muffin, then said, "Oh, I'll bet they're wonderful. But these muffins are very, very good."

"They can't be half as good as I can do in the summer," said Millie. Despite her self-effacement, her beaming smile showed the pride she took in the praise. "Those frozen ones don't hold a candle to the real things. I guess we have to sacrifice a little taste to have them all year round."

"That's true," said Emily with a tinge of wistfulness, "but taste isn't the only thing we sacrifice, you know. We sacrifice all sense of time as well."

Millie paused in the process of wiping her hands on her apron and furrowed her brow. "What's that, miss?"

"Time. I remember when I was a little girl how we looked forward to 'strawberry time' and 'blueberry time' and so on. But these days we have to have everything all the time. We've lost the sense that there's a time for everything." She took another bit of muffin and chewed thoughtfully before adding, "Then of course, it *is* nice to have them."

"You're right there, Miss Charters."

"Am I late for the sermon?" said Ransom from the doorway, where he'd paused to listen during this exchange.

"Oh, Jeremy! Good morning. This is Millie Havers. She made these lovely muffins."

"Pleased to meet you," said Ransom.

"Help yourself," Millie said with a smile as she gestured to the covered basket in the center of the table.

"Miss Havers has been telling me about all the things to do in the area."

"We have a lot of nice little shops in town," said Millie, "and antique stores here and there. They're usually only open weekends off season, but 'most everything will be open this week. And the Presbyterian church on the north end of town has a Nativity play they're doing on Wednesday night and a carol service they do on Christmas eve. It's usually pretty good. Always gets me in the mood of the season."

"That all sounds very nice," said Ransom, "but remember, Emily, you're here for a rest."

"Oh, I remember," said Emily in such a perfect travesty of a little old lady that had she been any younger one would have thought she was doing an imitation of herself.

Millie laughed, and said to Ransom as she exited to the kitchen, "I'll get you some coffee."

"They're so nice and accommodating here," said Emily, "I can't believe that they normally wait on people like this."

"You just naturally bring out the domestic in people," Ransom replied as he spread butter on half a muffin.

As they finished breakfast they discussed their plans for the day. Emily said she thought she'd like to visit some of the shops, and Ransom agreed, with the proviso that they have lunch in town to avoid having to come all the way back to the house.

Sara appeared for the first time that morning as Ransom and

Emily were preparing to leave. She looked a little more haggard than the day before. There were small, light gray crescents under her eyes serving as evidence of a poor night's sleep. She gave Ransom a map of the local antique stores, which were scattered around the area. Ransom transferred a doubtful glance from Emily to the map before folding it and sticking it in his pocket. He thanked Sara and told her they wouldn't be there for lunch.

"I worry about that young woman," said Emily as she and Ransom headed toward LeFavre.

"How so?"

Emily gave him a gently reproving look as if she thought he might just be having her on. The right corner of her mouth slid up into a half smile. "Now, Jeremy, I'm sure you must've noticed that Sara seems to be troubled."

Ransom shrugged. "It hasn't been all that long since her brother died."

"It's been two years."

"That's still not that long."

Emily said "hmm" and sat silently for a few moments.

"He was murdered, you know."

"Was he?"

"And the murderer was never caught."

"That could make it harder to get over the loss," said Ransom in a matter-of-fact tone that seemed to indicate that he wasn't interested in pursuing the topic.

"Yes, that's true, I'm sure...." Emily said musingly as she turned away from him, letting her gaze travel to the landscape. "But I can't help believing there's more to it than that."

The town of LeFavre sat in a semicircle around a small bay fed by Lake Michigan. It was accessible by a two-lane street off the main highway. The street inclined downward into the town then continued along the waterfront. The last turn before reaching the water was Main Street, onto which Ransom steered the car. He parked in one of the many empty spaces and they sat there for a few moments taking in their surroundings.

There were rows of shops in a variety of styles and sizes, all of them old, on each side of the street. The absence of newer architecture made it look as if, at some point in the past, the townspeople had decided that any further progress would upset the ambiance of the place and had simply stopped. What they were left with was a Main Street that was unself-consciously quaint.

The sidewalks were lined with trees spaced at regular intervals, carefully maintained and kept trimmed to approximately the same size. Each of them was decorated with hundreds of white Italian lights, which, although they couldn't be seen to their full effect at that time of day, even in the sunlight lent a pleasant, glittering effect to the scene.

Once out of the car, they made their way very slowly up one side of the street with Emily supported on Ransom's arm. The store windows displayed a variety of home-made wares, ranging from hand-dipped candles to oil paintings. They passed by shops selling clothing, candies, and pottery, and one that appeared to sell nothing but cotton throws on which detailed maps of the town had been printed in the customer's choice of colors. There was also an ice cream parlor called the Soda Shoppe, which was closed and shuttered for the winter. Despite his fondness for Emily, the pace was maddeningly slow for Ransom, who compensated by setting his jaw and concentrating on each step they took as if he were dissecting the components for further study. His efforts did not escape Emily's notice. At one point, she wordlessly patted his hand in acknowledgment of his effort.

The first store that they actually went into was a small wood-framed building that had obviously been converted from a house. The bulk of the front was made up of a large convex lattice window through which they caught glimpses of hand-made jewelry displayed on huge, rough rocks scattered about the floor.

When they entered, they found the proprietor—and artisan—of the store behind the counter by the cash register, working with some small bits of silver and beads. She was a very large woman who was probably in her fifties but looked a good deal older. She had very long, multitoned gray hair and leathery skin that bore signs of too much time spent in direct sunlight. She wore a faded cotton peasant dress and a strip of matching fabric tied around her forehead as a headband. There were rings on each of her fingers, oversized hoops from which small feathers dangled on her ears, and a necklace of large turquoise stones for which her ample breasts served as a display rack.

"Welcome to The Silver Eagle," the woman said, spreading her arms wide as if delivering a benediction.

"Hello," Emily said primly, hoping to stem any potential effusiveness.

"Feel free to look around."

Emily wandered to a glass case that held some of the simpler items: small silver crosses and geometric figures designed to be suspended from a chain around one's neck. A miniature metal tree on which gold and silver chains in various weights and lengths had been hung sat at one end of the case.

"I didn't know you liked jewelry," Ransom said quietly, as if there were some chance that the proprietor wouldn't hear any conversation being held in this tiny store.

"Oh, I don't really, other than my earrings," Emily replied, absently giving the small pearl in her left lobe a tug, "but I was thinking of getting Lynn some token to thank her for taking care of things for me while we're away."

"Here?"

"Not necessarily. We've just started."

"Hm," Ransom replied. He left her scrutinizing the things in the case while he wandered around looking at some of the trinkets arrayed on the rocks. On one he found a pair of onyx earrings in the shape of turtles, their heads stretching toward the sky. On another, there was a small, unpainted bit of clay cleverly shaped to look like an adobe hut with a ring through its chimney to allow for a chain.

"There's a price tag on everything," said the proprietor, "but if you got any questions, all you have to do is ask."

"Thank you," Emily replied. "Do you make all of these things yourself?"

"Sure do," said the woman, joining Emily by the case. "With my own two little hands. Well, maybe not so little!"

She thrust her hands out to show Emily. They were, indeed, very large, the skin was dried and cracked and the nails bitten down to stubs.

"You do some very delicate work," said Emily with a note of surprise in her voice that wasn't lost on the woman.

"Don't seem possible, does it?" she said, rubbing her palms against the sides of her dress. "But if you're delicate here"—she thumped her chest with her index finger—"it comes out in your work."

"Well, I must say that these things are very lovely."

"Thanks," said the woman proudly. There was a slight pause, then she asked with the interest of someone who spends a great deal of time alone, "You folks just in for the day, or in for the holidays?"

"We'll be here through Christmas."

"Ah. You got relatives around here?"

"No, we just came to the area for a little vacation."

"Really? Where're you staying?"

"Hawthorne House."

The woman didn't exactly recoil, but the change in her attitude was apparent. It was as if she had retreated behind an invisible iron door, promptly and defiantly slammed shut. Though neither Ransom nor Emily had been facing her when it happened, the abrupt shift in the atmosphere was so acute that they both turned, almost in unison, and looked at the woman.

"Is anything the matter?" said Emily, her thin gray brows knitting together.

"No. No, 'course not," said the woman, brushing her hands on her dress again as if she were having trouble getting something off them.

"Are you quite sure?"

"'Course I am," said the woman. She crossed back to the counter at which she'd been working when they'd come in.

"Forgive me," Emily pressed on with a glance at Ransom, "it

just seemed to me that the mention of Hawthorne House had some effect on you."

"No," said the woman, making an attempt to recover the warmth she'd shown them earlier. "When you said it, it just reminded me about...well, no, I don't tell tales out of school." When she added this last she looked from Emily to Ransom and back again, her expression giving them both the idea that not only did she tell tales out of school, she probably told them everywhere else, as well.

There was a slight pause before Emily said, "We know about the murder."

"You do?" The woman eyed Emily with something resembling wariness, as if she thought it highly suspicious that someone would stay in a place where they knew a murder had been committed. "Okay. You know. Well, all I was going to say was when you mentioned that place it reminded me of the murder. I didn't mean anything against anybody."

Emily's eyes narrowed and her mouth formed a smile that on anyone else would have been called wicked. "I'm sure you didn't."

"It's just that we don't have that kinda thing happen here often. It don't bring back to mind pleasant thoughts...." She stopped and glanced down at the materials with which she'd been working, then muttered, "...past or present."

"They investigated the murder, didn't they?" Ransom cut in, "And they didn't find anything."

"No, *they* didn't find anything." The woman's emphasis of the word "they" dripped with acid, and a smug smile spread across her face. Ransom thought that if he could have done it with impunity, he would have lifted one of the heavy rocks and hurled it at her.

They let the matter drop and spent a few more uncomfortable minutes looking at the jewelry before leaving the store, Emily having decided that she didn't think anything there would quite do.

Once outside, Emily said, "Well, that was certainly curious. Whatever could've made her act so strangely?"

"Do you mean when we came in or later?"

"You know very well what I mean. Why, she seemed almost angry."

"Hm."

Emily remained lost in thought as they continued down the street, barely giving her attention to any of the windows they passed. They reached the first corner at which they found an establishment aptly named The Corner Drug Store. It was a two-story red-brick building, the only one on the street that actually looked as if it had been meant to be a store. The second floor was a row of nondescript apartments.

As Ransom and Emily paused in front of the store, a door to their right, which led up to the second floor, was carelessly thrust open and out came Johnnie Larkin. He barely seemed to give them a glance as he went by, but suddenly stopped in his tracks when he recognized Emily. He wheeled around.

"Hello! Hello, Miss Charters!"

"Hello," said Emily with the formality she reserved for people she found a bit too boisterous. "I don't believe you've met my friend, Mr. Ransom."

"No, I didn't." Johnnie stuck out his hand and shook Ransom's vigorously. "Please to meet you." He turned back to Emily, and said, "So, you made it into town today!"

"Yes."

"Well, I'm gonna be out to the house later. I got some work to do at the Darcy farm, but Sara usually has stuff for me to do, too, so I'll probably see you later!"

Without waiting for any reply, he hurried off down the street and around the corner, leaving Emily and Ransom staring after him.

"A very energetic young man," said Emily.

"Humph," was Ransom's reply. "Do you want to go in the drugstore for anything?"

Emily peered in through the window, and after a few moments

her interest seemed to be caught by something. "I think so. I think I should like some postcards."

Ransom held the door open for her, then followed her in. They stopped just inside the door, and Emily said quietly, "I think it would be better if I did this myself."

Ransom gazed at her with a puzzled look. He glanced from the counter and back at Emily, raised his right eyebrow, and smiled. "I'll look around."

Ransom paused at the end of the aisle where they'd been standing and watched her. To his trained eye, he thought he could see her growing more frail as she approached the counter. He disappeared down the aisle.

A tall carousel of postcards stood on one end of the counter, and behind the counter an elderly man sat on a stool reading a book. He was wearing old black jeans, a white shirt, and a bolo tie clipped at the neck with a small silver moose head. Inured as he was by years of exposure to casual browsers, he gave no sign of noticing Emily's approach.

Emily turned the carousel slowly, occasionally exclaiming at the beauty of the cards. There were pictures of the bay, the beach, Main Street, and some of the historic or more distinctive houses in the area.

"You have some very beautiful cards here."

"Um hm," said the old man without looking up.

Emily continued to turn the rack, letting out a sporadic, disappointed "Oh, dear." When she still hadn't managed to wrest the man's full attention, she took a faltering step backward and put her right hand to her cheek. She said absently, "I was hoping...oh, dear."

The old man sighed and set his book aside. "Help you find something?"

Emily gave him a relieved smile, and said, "Well, I don't know. I noticed that you have postcards here of some of the local houses. And I was hoping to find the one at which I'm staying— I have a friend, you see, who likes postcards and is always nice enough to show some interest in what I'm doing. It's always nice for someone to show interest in what you're doing, don't you think? But as I was saying, I don't see a picture of it here. I don't suppose you have any cards that aren't on display.''

"Not really," he said, not unkindly but not apologetically, either. "Sometimes we run out of a particular card and have to reorder. We might have it coming in later. What house are you staying at?"

"Hawthorne House."

"Hawthorne House?" the man echoed blankly. "No, we never did carry one of that."

"Really?" said Emily with feigned surprise. "I understood it to be a very old house—it's certainly very well maintained—and from what I've heard, it's had quite a history."

The old man nodded his head, and replied, "It has a history, all right."

Emily's eyes widened and her voice took on a quaver. "What do you mean?"

He returned a condescending smile that Emily took as a sign that he enjoyed making timid women uncomfortable. "I don't mean anything. Just that some people might be afraid to stay there."

"Afraid?" said Emily, her eyes growing even wider. "Do you mean that the house is...is *haunted?*" Her voice became low and hollow as she spoke the last word, as if she thought that merely saying it might draw the spirits of the dead from the very floor around her.

"Pah!" said the old man, "I don't think there's nothing to worry about from the dead. It's the living you have to worry about."

"What do you mean?" Emily asked, clutching her purse more tightly.

The man leaned toward her, cocked his head sideways, and lowered his voice so that he sounded just as if he were telling a ghost story to a group of children around a campfire. "That woman that owns the place—Sara Bartlett—her brother was murdered two years ago. Pitchfork was driven right through his chest. And they never *did* find who did it!"

"Oh, my!"

The old man sat back on his stool and folded his arms across his chest, his satisfied smile indicating he was pleased with the reaction he'd elicited.

"Of course, some of us have our own ideas on that score."

"I don't understand."

He counted off each reason on his fingers as he said, "Only one person had any interest in his death, only one person gained by it, only one person really *knew* the boy well enough to kill him."

Emily put a hand to her heart and looked as though she might give in to a faint. "You don't mean Sara? That nice young woman? Why would she kill her own brother?"

"Who knows?" said the old man with a shrug. "But I'm not the only person 'round here that thinks Sara Bartlett might've got away with murder."

I'm sure you're not, thought Emily sharply as she struggled to maintain her timid visage.

Ransom collected her not long after that and led her out of the store. A degree of her frailty seemed to disappear once they were out on the sidewalk.

"Are you feeling better?" Ransom said, a sly smile playing about his lips.

"I beg your pardon?"

Ransom shot a glance at the drugstore window. "I thought for a minute in there that you'd gone a little weak."

"Well, you know, Jeremy, there is a certain type of person who likes to play on the credulity of others...."

"Are you referring to him or to you?"

She smiled but didn't comment. "...and it is sometimes possible to use that to your own advantage."

"And was he one of those people?"

"Oh, yes," Emily said with a tinge of sadness, "he was rather of a type. I wouldn't be surprised to learn that he spent his youth setting fire to cats."

"Good Lord, Emily!" Ransom laughed. "Did you learn whatever it was you wanted to know?"

Emily frowned. "Local sentiment appears to be that Sara killed her brother."

Ransom's eyes narrowed. "Why?"

"Apparently for no other reason than she knew him better than anyone else."

Ransom grunted in response to this.

They spent a few more minutes browsing the windows of the shops before deciding it was time for lunch. They stopped at the Red Lion, a pseudo-English restaurant in which the ambiance and the food were equally pleasant. It was also one of the few restaurants open year-round. Still insistent on Emily's complete rest and relaxation, Ransom made it a point to stay off the subject of the unsolved murder. For her part, Emily shied away from the topic for fear that her continued interest would increase Ransom's anxiety on her behalf. She chose instead to ruminate on the matter to herself. The end result of this concerted effort to avoid the subject was that, despite the light conversation in which they engaged over their Caesar salads and trifle, the murder was the foremost thought in both their minds. *Rather like trying not to think of spotted elephants,* Emily thought as she spooned the last bit of the dessert into her mouth.

After lunch, they spent a little more time sight-seeing, then, though they hadn't completed their circuit of even one side of the street, decided to put off doing any more until the next day.

WHEN THEY RETURNED to Hawthorne House, Emily retired to her room for an afternoon nap, and Ransom retrieved an ancient, dog-eared book and his cigars from his room and went to the smoking room. He switched on the exhaust fan and settled into one of the Naugahyde chairs, then he extracted a cigar from the pack, stuck the plastic tip between his lips, and lit it.

He closed his eyes as he drew in the smoke, then slowly released it. He hadn't been aware of how much tension he was experiencing until he felt it dissipating with the smoke into the air. He took another drag, feeling his shoulders relax and his muscles loosen as he released another stream of smoke. After a few more puffs in the self-imposed darkness, his eyes slid open and he looked out the window. The snow spread out across the landscape like a blank page on which nothing would ever be written. Accustomed as he was to the excess sensory stimulation provided by the crowded view from his Chicago high-rise apartment, the relative nothingness of his new surroundings left his nerves hungry. He smiled to himself at the thought of his disquiet being caused by all this peace.

Ransom was interrupted in this reverie by the sound of the door opening. He started to rise when he saw it was Sara, but she quickly motioned for him not to bother. She looked less haggard than she had that morning, and Ransom suspected she had napped while they were gone. But the circles were still under her eyes and her face was ashen. Even if she'd been able to get some rest, it hadn't helped her very much.

"I didn't see you when you got back from town. I just wanted to make sure everything was all right."

"Everything was fine," he said, trying his best to sound more congenial that was his norm.

"Did Emily do all right?"

"She got along fine. We tried not to overdo it."

"Good."

A silence fell between them. Ransom took a puff of his cigar and scrutinized the young woman, who still stood hesitating in the doorway, looking at the floor. From her intense, frustrated expression, Ransom decided that she desperately wanted to ask him something more, but either didn't think she should or didn't know how to proceed.

After a moment, he said, "Miss Bartlett, you're letting the smoke out of the room."

"Oh," she exclaimed, looking up. She smiled at him and stepped inside, closing the door but not letting it latch. She stood with her hand on the doorknob, as if she still wanted very much to talk to him but didn't want him to think she was going to be a bother.

"Well, what did you think of our little town?"

Ransom continued to eye her for a beat before answering. He had a feeling he knew what it was she wanted to know, and he was trying to decide on how to relay the information without causing her embarrassment.

"The town was very nice," he said, then narrowing his incisive eyes at her added, "I can't say that I find the people overly friendly."

The anxiety on Sara's face increased noticeably. "Did anyone say...was anyone rude to you?"

"No. Just reserved." Ransom paused for a moment, then without sounding the least bit as if he were trying to draw her out said, "We chalked it up to the usual small-town bias. That's all it is, don't you think?"

Sara looked for a moment as if she were going to confide in him, but instead she cast her eyes back to the floor. The sadness in them made it abundantly clear that she knew the real cause of any reticence that might have been shown her guests. "Yes, I'm sure that's all it is."

Ransom sighed inwardly. She was certainly making it difficult.

"I imagine you experienced much the same thing when you first moved here. But that must've changed by now."

Sara's cheeks flushed and her hand tightened on the doorknob. "It takes people a long time to forget," she said softly.

"Forget...?" Ransom replied, raising an eyebrow.

She looked up at him and her voice quavered when she said, "To forget...that you're new. That's all I meant. You can't get lost here the way you can in Chicago. There's not enough people. And the ones that're here don't have a lot of other things to think about." She glanced at her watch, then back at him, and said, "It's getting late. I've got to get dinner started." She opened the door and paused just long enough to add, "I'm glad you had a good time in town."

With this she disappeared, closing the door behind her.

Ransom sat for a few minutes taking thoughtful puffs from his cigar and considering Sara's plight. After a while he shrugged and turned to his book.

He'd brought with him a volume of Dickens's Christmas books that included *The Haunted Man,* which he intended to reread over the holiday. It was one of his favorites: the story of Redlaw, a man haunted by painful memories of his past. Redlaw encounters a ghost who is "the awful image of himself," and pleads with the apparition to erase his painful memories so that he might have some peace. The ghost complies, but the blessing turns into a curse when Redlaw discovers that it's the painful events and memories in our lives that give us compassion and humanity.

As Ransom opened the well-worn book and settled back into the comfortable chair, the sorrowful expression on Sara's face still uppermost in his mind, he wondered if perhaps Dickens, for once, had been wrong.

EMILY WOKE in the middle of the night with the sudden alertness of someone whose sound sleep has been interrupted by an unexpected noise. She lay there for a minute, listening intently for a recurrence of the sound, but there was nothing but the crackling silence of the still night air.

She slowly turned her head and looked at the luminous dial of the travel alarm she'd placed on the bedside table. It was a few minutes after two. She rested her head back on the pillow and stared at the ceiling for a few moments, but she heard nothing, not even the settling noises so common to older houses.

Emily closed her eyes and sighed. She was just about to drift back off to sleep when she heard it again, a sob so muffled it might have come to her from another world rather than somewhere in the house. She pushed back the comforter and shifted her legs over the side of the bed, pulling herself up into a sitting position at the same time. She slipped her feet into a pair of soft house slippers, and pulled on the cream-colored cotton robe she'd laid across the foot of the bed. With a little effort she stood up and stayed there for a moment trying to decide from which direction the sob had originated. It occurred to her that it had been so faint it might have come from the library. She went to the commuting door and pressed her ear against it. Hearing nothing, she turned the knob and pulled the door open as quietly as possible.

The moon cast enough reflected light through the library window for Emily to see at a glance that the room was unoccupied. She went through the library and opened the door to the living room, still trying not to make any noise. She stood in the doorway for a moment and was just about to step out into the room when she heard another choking sob, still muffled but this time clearly audible and coming, she thought, from the kitchen. She rounded the corner and looked in.

Sara was sitting in the darkness on the chair at the far end of the table. She had one leg drawn up under her floral flannel nightgown, her right arm was hanging over the back of the chair and she was covering her mouth with her left hand. The tears on her cheeks glistened in the moonlight.

Emily was standing very still in the archway trying to decide whether to advance or retreat when Sara chanced to look in her direction.

"Oh! Miss Charters!" she said, jumping up from her chair and wiping her eyes with the sleeve of her nightgown. She remained by the chair. "I didn't see you there. I'm sorry, did I wake you?"

"No," said Emily. She thought for a second about what might be the best way to proceed, then said, "No, I was having a little trouble sleeping. That happens sometimes. I'm afraid it's one of those things that comes with age. I didn't know you were up— but I was wondering, would it be much trouble if I had some tea?"

There was a pause during which Sara looked quite confused, as if she thought she might not have understood Emily correctly. Then she said, "Sure, it's no problem."

She switched on a small light over the stove, which illuminated the room just enough to see but not enough to be startling, then set about heating the water for tea.

Emily took a seat on the opposite side of the table. She hadn't really wanted any tea, but she thought the best thing for Sara at that moment might be to keep busy.

"You'll have to forgive me," said Sara, making an effort to regain her composure. "I don't usually...I'm not usually up in the middle of the night. I don't usually fall apart like this."

"Sometimes it helps," said Emily quietly as she watched Sara.

"I've just been...there've been a lot of things lately."

"My dear, I know it's none of my business, but don't you have someone you can talk to about your troubles? Lynn told us that both of your parents were deceased, but surely there must be someone...."

Sara shot her a surprised glance. "I don't know that both of them are dead. My mother died about six years ago, but she and my father divorced when I was very young, and I never saw him again." She paused for a moment, then as if in answer to an unasked question added, "It was a very acrimonious divorce."

"But surely you have someone—"

"I have some friends, I suppose," Sara replied with an awkward shrug, "but no relatives. Nobody like..." Her voice trailed off.

"I understand."

"Do you?" said Sara as she laid cups out. She then put a couple of tea bags in a ceramic teapot and set it in the center of the table.

"I think I do. I know that your brother was killed and that the murderer was never caught. And I was in town today. It's a small town, and in a small town, if you talk to people at all, you're bound to hear the local gossip."

"I know what they think," said Sara with feeling, "and I don't care about it."

"You don't?" Emily replied with some surprise.

"No, I don't. I realize I seem..." She stopped and thought for a moment, then shook her head dismissively. "No, I don't know how I seem. But I really don't care what a bunch of local busy-bodies think. I realize some of them say that I killed my brother, but I know I didn't. Their thinking it isn't going to change the facts."

"That's very sensible of you."

Though the kettle had not yet begun to whistle, the water was making enough noise to indicate it was ready. Sara switched off the burner as she removed the kettle. She filled the teapot on the table and replaced the kettle. Emily continued to watch her intently, waiting for her to continue.

"The thing that I can't...the thing I can't get beyond is that even though I didn't kill Nathan myself...I *know* I was responsible for his death."

With this she crumpled into her chair and buried her face in her hands. Emily's eyebrows slid upward, sending creases across her forehead. She reached into the cuff of her robe, pulled out a clean linen handkerchief, and handed it to Sara, who accepted it with a nod and dabbed her eyes.

"Forgive me," said Emily, "but I don't understand. If you didn't kill your brother, how could you be responsible for his death?"

Sara gestured limply around the room. "Because of this."

"Yes?"

"This was my dream. *My* dream, you see? It was me who wanted to own this place...to have a place like this. If it wasn't for me and my stupid dream, we never would have been here and Nathan never would've been killed."

"But you don't know that," Emily remonstrated softly.

"Yes, I do!" Sara said. Her tears were flowing more freely now, and she kept Emily's handkerchief pressed against her nose. "It doesn't matter who killed him, really. Whether he was killed by one of the locals for some reason, or if he was killed by somebody who was just passing through, any way you look at it, he was killed because he was *here!* And he was here because of me."

"Sara," said Emily gently but firmly, "I understand how you

might feel that way, but I really do believe that, without knowing why your brother was killed, you cannot know for sure that it had anything to do with his being here.''

Sara's watery eyes blinked at Emily over the top of the wadded-up handkerchief. "What else could it have been?"

"Oh, I don't know. Any number of things, I suppose. But when we don't have all the facts it's very easy to jump at the most obvious conjecture as being gospel truth. But I can tell you that the older you get, the more you find the obvious can be very deceptive."

Sara hazarded something of a smile. "You know, Lynn warned me about you. She said you could be pretty deceptive yourself."

"I beg your pardon?" said Emily, though there was a twinkle in her eye.

"She said that you pretend to be a little old lady, when you're really as sharp as Solomon and straight as a die."

"Well, I don't know about that," said Emily, her pleased smile betraying the pleasure she took in the secondhand compliment.

A silence fell between them, during which Sara lifted the pot and poured out the tea. She put a spoonful of sugar in her cup and stirred it pensively. After a moment, she said, "It doesn't really matter, you know...I mean, why Nathan was killed."

"But of course it does," said Emily.

"No, I mean it won't change things. No matter why he was killed, when Nathan died, my dream died with him. Nothing will ever be the same."

"Well, if I may ask a question, under the circumstances don't you think it might be better if you didn't stay here? Why not sell Hawthorne House and start fresh somewhere else?"

"Because it wouldn't make a difference." Sara put her hands around her cup as if to warm them and straightened herself in her chair. "You see, when Nathan was killed and nothing...nobody was found, my life was sort of thrown into...a void, I guess you'd call it—one that just never goes away. I wander around and around as if I'm only half-awake, looking for a way out, but nothing has ever seemed right since Nathan was killed. And I don't think that void will be closed until there's...some solution. Do you have any idea what I mean?''

"Of course. I would think it's the most natural way to feel under the circumstances. There is a rather large mystery there, and the human mind wants all mysteries to be solved. But sometimes the world has other ideas.''

"What do you mean?''

"Only that not all mysteries *can* be solved, at least not in this life. And sometimes the only way to go on is to shut the door on that void on your own.''

"I wish I could," Sara replied sadly. "I really wish I could.''

They sat in silence for a moment, with Sara staring disconsolately into her teacup as Emily watched her, a compassionate smile spreading across her face. "On the other hand," she said at last, "perhaps the best thing for us to do would be to solve the mystery.''

"Jeff did all he could," Sara replied, her voice ringing hollow.

"Well, I happen to know someone who is rather adept at solving puzzles.''

"You do?" said Sara, sounding as if she were afraid to entertain any hope.

"You know him, too: Mr. Ransom is a homicide detective. He might be persuaded to look into this for you.''

Sara hesitated. "Oh...I couldn't ask it. He's supposed to be enjoying himself.''

"That's true," said Emily, her smile becoming more mischievous, "but I don't think he is.''

Sara looked stricken, and before she could say anything Emily continued quickly, "Oh, no, Sara, you mustn't think it's because of you. You've provided a perfectly lovely place for us. I'm afraid that Jeremy is used to a great deal of mental activity. He's not the type of man who can rest easily." She lifted the cup to her lips, and added, "Yes...a little puzzle might be the best thing for him.''

FIVE

THE FOLLOWING MORNING, Millie had pots of coffee and tea waiting on the dining table for Ransom and Emily when they came to breakfast. Piles of scrambled eggs lay ready in a food warmer on the sideboard, and Millie told them she was just about to pull some country biscuits out of the oven for them.

"What makes them 'country' biscuits?" Ransom asked.

"I'm making them in the country," Millie replied over her shoulder as she bustled out to the kitchen.

Ransom prepared a plate of eggs for himself and for Emily, put them at their places on the table, and took his seat. Once he was situated, Emily said, "Jeremy, there's a little matter I'd like to discuss with you."

"Yes?" he said distractedly as he scooped a forkful of eggs into his mouth.

"There's something I'd very much like you to do for me."

"What's that?"

"I'd like you to look into Nathan Bartlett's murder."

Ransom stopped abruptly in the act of taking a drink of coffee. He set the mug on the table with a light thud, sat back in his chair, folded his arms, and raised an eyebrow. "Whatever for?"

Emily's eyes became more incisive as she leaned in toward him. "Because that young woman, Sara, needs to know what happened to him. She's living under a very dark cloud—you noticed that as well as I did yesterday when we were in town. And the only way to dispel that cloud is to find out once and for all who killed her brother."

Ransom gazed at her for a moment before answering, "I'm sure the local authorities looked into it when it happened. I'm also sure they're very capable people."

"That may be, but they didn't *solve* it, and in this case it's the results that matter rather than the effort. Because it wasn't solved, Sara lives under constant suspicion. In a town such as this, if the matter is never resolved then the suspicions will always be with her. People may be polite to her, they may treat her courteously, even kindly, but there will always be that wariness and doubt toward her.''

"There may be that, anyway. That's the way it is with gossip."

"But that's just the thing," Emily replied earnestly. "You know, Jeremy, gossip is very often true. That's why when the gossip is false, it's so damaging."

"Which leaves me to wonder," said Ransom, "if Sara didn't kill her brother, why are people so willing to believe she did?"

"Because people are poison," said Millie hotly as she banged into the room through the kitchen door. She was carrying a small basket full of biscuits over which she'd laid a cloth napkin to hold in the warmth. "'Scuse me. I'm sorry, I didn't mean to listen in. I just heard the tail end of what you were saying. Anyone with an ounce of sense in their heads would know Sara would never kill anybody, let alone her brother! And anybody that says different is just spreading poison. And I tell you something else, too: Jeff Fields did his job, no matter what anybody tells you!"

"I beg your pardon," said Emily, the shine in her eyes showing the admiration she felt at the woman's defense of her employer, "but who is Jeff Fields?"

Millie set the basket in the center of the table and brushed her hands on her apron. "Jeff's the sheriff. And he *did* investigate that murder, he just didn't find anything. That's all there is to it, no matter who tells you different."

"Why would anyone tell us 'different'?" Ransom asked, apostrophizing the idiom wryly. Emily shot him a glance.

Millie looked at the palms of her hands, then their backs, as if checking for traces of whatever she'd been trying to brush off. She faltered when she answered him as if she thought she might be betraying someone. "Well, because Jeff and Sara, they were going together when it happened. They were...well, I would've said they were in love. But then Nathan had to go get murdered and Jeff had to investigate, and when nothing came of it..." She shrugged as her voice trailed off.

"When he didn't bring anyone in," Ransom said, narrowing his eyes, "the local people thought maybe he didn't exactly do his job."

"That's right!" said Millie, nodding angrily.

"And if he didn't do his job it was because Sara was the guilty party, and he was in love with her."

"But he wouldn't do that," Millie protested. "He's a good man. And the fact that he was the one...well, I don't think Sara ever got over it. I don't know that she'll ever forgive him."

Millie's eyes began to tear up, and rather than stand there and cry in front of them, she said "Oh, hell!" and fled to the kitchen.

"A rather convincing testimonial," said Ransom.

"Jeremy, you're not to be cynical," Emily said, coming as close to severity as she ever had with him. She folded her hands on the table. "I *know* that Sara didn't kill her brother."

"How do you know that?"

"Because she thinks she's responsible."

He smiled at her. "Emily, you're going to have to explain that."

She related to him the entire midnight conversation she'd had with Sara. When she finished, she added, "You see, Jeremy, it's bad enough that the people of this area blame Sara for Nathan's death, but if this case remains unsolved, Sara will go on blaming herself for it, too, simply because she was the reason he was here in this town."

Ransom sat back in his chair and considered this soberly, never taking his eyes off Emily's. After a few moments he said very pointedly, "You realize, of course, that in all probability—I'd almost go so far as to say in all possibility—she's right. Whether he was killed by someone from the area or whether he was killed by someone who was just passing through, whatever the motive, it's most likely her brother would be alive today if they hadn't moved here. You may be asking me to prove that Sara's fears are true."

Emily sighed. "That's a chance we'll just have to take. I believe that for Sara the uncertainty is worse. Maybe in time she'd be able to come to terms with it, if you're right. But if you can solve the case, at least some of her questions would be answered."

"A two-year-old trail is likely to be very, very cold."

"I have the utmost faith in your abilities."

"Even *I* need something to work with."

Though she might have been discouraged by his mild protest, the degree of interest in his voice told Emily she was on the right track.

"Well, Jeremy, if nothing else you can prove that the solution is simply unattainable."

"I suspect, my dear Emily, that you've been taking lessons on the sly from Sergeant Frank Newman."

"Whatever do you mean?" said Emily with elaborate innocence.

Ransom eyed her for a few moments, absently tapping his index finger on the tablecloth. At last he sighed, and said, "Well, perhaps I can ask a few questions."

He said this with as much reluctance as he could possibly muster and still be thought gracious. But it didn't escape Emily's notice that, for the first time since they'd arrived in town, he didn't seem bored.

"Thank you," she said with so little emphasis one would've thought she'd asked him nothing more than to pass the biscuits.

"MISS BARTLETT, at Emily's request, I thought I'd do a little checking into the death of your brother."

Sara nodded her head silently as she took a seat. Ransom had sought her out directly after he and Emily finished their breakfast. He ushered her into the smoking room, closing the door behind them. He pulled a chair up and sat facing her.

"I'm not sure that's a good thing," Sara said, giving a nervous tug to the hem of her skirt, which immediately slid back up over her knee. "I'm not sure it's very wise to stir it all up again."

"It would seem that it's never completely settled down for you."

Sara averted her eyes from him, appearing to be intently studying something just beyond his right shoulder. "Well, that may be...maybe it's just my imagination...."

Ransom gently drummed his fingers on the arm of his chair, a sure sign that his professional impatience was returning. "Do you really believe that?"

She brought her eyes back to his, and after a beat she quietly said "No."

Ransom gave her his most ingratiating smile. "Then why don't you tell me what happened the night your brother was killed?"

It was, of course, a very painful topic for Sara, but there was something so reassuringly direct in Ransom's manner that she felt as if she'd been asked to relate the story to a disinterested third party.

She started slowly. "There was a very bad storm that night. A blizzard. I was...I spent the evening...the late evening...in the parlor. That's the front room, where we have the Christmas tree. Nathan had gone up to his room..."

"When was that?"

"Um...about nine o'clock, I think. He said he was going to watch TV or something. When I went up to bed..." Ransom looked as if he were about to inject another question, but she beat him to it. "That was about eleven. I went up to bed. I stopped by his room on my way and he wasn't there."

"Why did you do that?"

"What?" said Sara, looking almost startled.

"Why did you go into his room? Did you usually do that?"

She shifted in her chair. "Well, yes. I usually stopped in to say good night if his light was still on."

"And was it?"

"No. But his door was slightly open, and that wasn't usual. So I went in, and he wasn't there. I called to him, but he didn't answer, and I started to look all over the house...and then I started to get scared. I'm not...I don't usually get scared like that, but there was the storm and everything, and I couldn't imagine where he'd gone.''

"It was perfectly natural," said Ransom kindly.

Sara gave him an abbreviated, self-deprecating smile, which seemed to be the best she could manage. "It was like he had just...vanished from the house...like he'd been spirited away."

"Hmm..." said Ransom. He continued to study her face intently, and from her vacant expression, he felt it was apparent that she didn't realize the irony of her choice of words. "What did you do then?"

She absently twined a strand of her dark hair around her index finger as she answered. "Well...I knew he hadn't driven anywhere—the storm was so bad, I didn't think he could've if he'd wanted to—but I knew he hadn't because the driveway is right by the side window to the parlor. I would've heard a car. But I knew he wasn't in the house, and the only other building near here is the barn. I thought he might've gone back there to talk to Hansen about something. Hansen Crane, our handyman, lives over the barn."

"You didn't hear him go out?"

She shook her head. "No, I didn't."

"Wouldn't you ordinarily?"

She hesitated for a moment, looking as if this were the first time she'd ever thought of this. "Yes..." she said slowly. "Yes, I suppose I would. But the wind was making a lot of noise, so if he went out the back door, I might not have heard him...if..."

Ransom completed this for her. "If he was being quiet. What happened next?"

As she continued, she unwound the strand of hair from her finger and re-coiled it in the opposite direction. "I went to the back door and looked out. I couldn't really see the barn at all through the blizzard. I couldn't tell if the lights in Hansen's apartment were on. But I still thought that was the only place Nathan could've gone, so I put on my coat and took the flashlight we keep by the back door, and went to the barn. When I was just about there, I could see that Hansen's lights were out, so I went into the barn itself to check there. And I found him...." She let go of her hair and her hand dropped into her lap. She was staring at the floor next to Ransom's chair, looking as if she were seeing it all again. Her eyes began to well with tears as she continued with some difficulty. "He was there...in the center of the floor...lying on his back...with that thing...that pitchfork... sticking out of his chest." She stopped and flicked the tears off her cheeks with her fingers. "I'm sorry."

"That's perfectly all right."

"I screamed when I saw him...and ran out of the barn and up the side stairs to Hansen's apartment and banged on his door. He let me in and we went back to the house and called the sheriff." She shrugged sadly as she said this last to indicate that was all there was to her story.

Ransom stared at her a moment through narrowed eyes, holding the tip of his right index finger to his lips. At last he laid his hand back on the arm of his chair, and said, "Did it take him long to answer the door?"

"What?" said Sara, once again as if he'd startled her.

"Hansen Crane. Did it take him long to answer the door?"

"Oh," she said, her expression clearing, "yes, it seemed like it took him forever. But I was...so upset, I can't be sure. But yes, I think it took him a long time. Why?"

"I was just wondering if you had to wake him."

"Oh, yes. I think so."

Ransom considered this for a moment, then recrossed his legs and said, "Did you see anything on your way to the barn?"

"Anything? No. I could barely see anything at all for the storm. Anything like what?"

"Footprints."

"Footprints? No, I didn't see any footprints."

Ransom raised an eyebrow. "Not even your brother's?"

Sara shook her head slowly. "No. Not even his."

Ransom sat completely still for a few moments, processing the information. At last he cocked his head, leaned in toward her, and said, "One last thing, Miss Bartlett. Do *you* have any idea who killed your brother?"

Sara raised her eyes from the floor and met Ransom's. "My brother was the kindest man alive. He didn't have any enemies."

"What about friends?"

"He had lots of friends."

"Anyone special?"

Sara averted her eyes again and shifted in her chair. "I don't know what you mean."

"Of course you do," Ransom countered without emotion. "Miss Bartlett, if you really want this matter resolved, it's important that you're completely honest with me."

Sara's cheeks flushed as she replied, "I have been." She stopped and adjusted her skirt, which apparently hadn't come along with her the last time she'd moved. With the fidgeting and the redness of her face, she couldn't have looked more uncomfortable if she'd tried. "Well, Nathan had a girlfriend. They were very close. Her name is Amy. Amy Shelton."

"She lives in town?"

"Yes," Sara said, looking almost as if she thought she'd just betrayed her best friend to the Gestapo. She added quickly, "Amy couldn't possibly have had anything to do with Nathan's death. She loved him. She couldn't have killed him."

"Then who did, Miss Bartlett?"

Sara threw her hands up in frustration. "I don't know! I haven't got a clue!"

WHEN RANSOM had finished with Sara, he found Emily in the parlor standing by the Christmas tree, admiring the ornaments from close range.

"There are so many beautiful things on the tree," she said. "Some of them are like ones I remember from my childhood." She lovingly fingered a delicate German glass ornament that looked worn enough to be an original. "Some of these must be family heirlooms."

"Very nice," said Ransom, his mind obviously on something else.

"Did you have your talk with Sara?"

"Yes, and it was quite interesting." He filled her in on what Sara had said. "If she's giving me an accurate account of what happened that night, I can almost see why popular opinion is against her. The whole of the story rests on her version of it alone. Nobody else was on hand."

"Hansen Crane was," Emily reminded him.

"Apparently he was asleep."

"Apparently?" Emily echoed with an amused smile, enjoying his dogged refusal to accept any statement at face value.

Ransom replied, "Somehow I can't imagine that being killed with a pitchfork is a very quiet business."

"That's true," said Emily thoughtfully, "and as he was stabbed in the chest, one would think he would've seen it coming and cried out."

"Or even if he hadn't seen it coming, he'd probably cry out on impact. People rarely 'go gently,' unless they do it at home in their beds."

Emily nodded. "And sometimes not even then."

They fell silent, both of them lost in their thoughts. Finally Emily said, "Well, how do you propose to proceed?"

Ransom sighed. "Would it be all right if we postponed our second junket into town? Do you mind being left here?"

"Oh, no," said Emily, "I shall be quite all right. I've brought *King Lear* along to keep me company."

Ransom gazed at her in disbelief. "You brought *Lear* to read on a Christmas trip?"

"'A sad tale's best for winter,'" Emily quoted with a smile.

"That's not from *Lear*."

"Very good, Jeremy. You're correct. But it was appropriate to the moment, none-the-less."

Ransom laughed. "Then if you don't mind staying here, I'll go to the sheriff's office and have a talk with him. Maybe he'd be willing to tell me what he found when he investigated."

"Oh, I'm sure he will," said Emily with elderly gusto, "I'm sure he'd do 'most anything to see this matter settled."

"Why do you say that?"

"Because," said Emily with a twinkle in her eye, "he was in love with her."

EMILY WATCHED the parlor window as Ransom drove away, pleased not only that he was looking into Nathan Bartlett's murder, but also with the expected side effect: he hadn't been over-solicitous of her all morning.

Once his car was out of sight, Emily left the parlor and went to the kitchen, where she found Millie giving the pots and pans a hearty scrubbing. Though it was a chore that most would probably find tedious, Millie seemed to be enjoying herself.

"Hello, miss," said Millie. She wiped the back of her hand across her forehead and gestured to the sink full of water. "Even with guests, to my mind there just doesn't seem enough dishes to bother with that electric thing."

"Yes," said Emily wistfully, "and there's something about cleaning that's very satisfying to one's soul, don't you think?"

Millie laughed. "There's some wouldn't say so."

"Do you mind if I join you for a little while?"

"Suit yourself. I'd be glad for the company."

Emily took a seat at the kitchen table. "I always think that the kitchen is the most inviting part of any house."

"It's the heart of the home. That's what they say."

Millie was silent for a moment while she scrubbed out the pan she'd used to scramble the eggs. Then she said, "I thought I heard Mr. Ransom drive off. Didn't you want to go into town with him?"

"He had something he wanted to do on his own."

Millie paused in the act of rinsing off the pan and turned to Emily. "Is he really going to look into Nathan's murder?"

"Yes," Emily replied, "he's already started."

"Well, thank God for that," said Millie, resuming her tasks, "and good luck to 'im."

Emily cleared her throat. "You know, you might be of some help to us in that respect."

Millie shrugged. "Don't see how. I wasn't out here that night. Truth is, I'm almost never out here at night."

"It's not necessarily that night that I'm interested in. It's difficult to believe that Nathan could've been killed without something leading up to it."

"I don't find it hard to believe at all."

"Really?" said Emily, emitting an aura of innocent interest in the woman's opinion.

"Sure. I don't think it's all that mysterious. I just think he was killed by a tramp. No other explanation for it. Nobody didn't like Nathan. There must've been some tramp out there, taking refuge—like they say—in the barn—just a place to sleep for the night. Nathan caught him, and the tramp killed him." Millie shrugged with her palms up, as if she truly believed she'd explained everything.

"Yes, but *why* would Nathan have gone out to the barn in the middle of a storm?"

"Who knows? Maybe he just remembered something he forgot to do."

Emily pressed on, trying to gently direct Millie away from what Emily felt was a rather shaky theory in an attempt to elicit some more pertinent information. "And why would a tramp have killed him? Surely Nathan, if he was as nice as everyone says he was, wouldn't have been a threat to him."

Millie hesitated, casting a doubtful glance at her hands. "Well, I don't know about that. But who's to say what some vagrant will do if you come on him unexpected."

"That's very true," said Emily, "but suppose...well, let's suppose for a moment that there was some other reason for the murder. Tell me, what was going on back then?"

"How d'ya mean?"

Emily adjusted herself in her seat, an unconscious sign that she was getting down to business. "What I mean is, can you give me the lay of the land?"

Millie rested her hands on the sink and pursed her lips, lost in thought. "Well, the place had been open to the public...three years then. Everything was going pretty well. There's never a lack of business around here during the summertime. And Sara has a knack for this sort of thing. Um, she hired me on right off the bat, and about a year later, Hansen showed up and she hired him, though I don't think Nathan was too happy with that at first."

"Really?"

"Oh, that's nothing to think of!" said Millie. "Nathan was from the city and I don't think he ever heard of such a thing as a drifter before. He asked all kinds of questions about him. Even to me. He asked me if I knew anything about him or about his past or where he'd come from. But I didn't know anything. He's just a typical drifter. I'm surprised he's stayed here this long."

"That's very interesting," Emily said. "And did this happen just before Nathan died?"

"Oh, no!" said Millie, waving her hand in the air as if the idea was a gnat that needed to be brushed away. "It couldn't have anything to do with this. That was way back almost two years before Nathan was killed."

"I see," said Emily. "And when did Johnnie Larkin appear?"

"Um...around about the same time as Hansen, maybe a little later."

"Did Nathan have any objection to Johnnie?"

"Oh, no," said Millie, her face breaking into a smile. She seemed to find the thought of Johnnie amusing. "Johnnie's young. You don't expect young people to be as settled as somebody Hansen's age. And you gotta remember that Johnnie works for a lot of people. Hansen was moving here onto the property."

"That's true," said Emily thoughtfully. "Now, what about Sara's and Nathan's social life?"

"Well," Millie said a bit reluctantly, "well, they were both pretty busy with running the place."

"Surely they wouldn't have been as busy off season?" said Emily coaxingly.

Millie smiled. "Oh, okay! Just about everyone seemed to like Sara back then. But she was seeing Jeff Fields, especially. He came out to welcome her and check to see that everything was all right out here after she got her license to open the place. I think they hit it off right away. They started going together and got pretty serious...at one point. They were quite a pair.''

''And Nathan?''

''He didn't socialize much, so people didn't know him as well as they knew Sara. But them that knew him liked him, especially Amy Shelton.''

''Amy Shelton?''

A fond smile spread across Millie's face. ''He was sweet on her. And she was sweet on him, too. They probably would've ended up married if it hadn't happened.''

''Can you tell me if anything unusual was happening back then?''

''Like what?''

''Well, was Nathan acting completely normal before the murder? Did anything seem to be on his mind?''

Millie pursed her lips as she cast her mind back over the expanse of two years. ''I don't know...I suppose he might've been a little preoccupied.''

''In what way?''

''Oh, I don't know,'' said Millie, frowning with consternation at her own inability to articulate what she was thinking, ''I'm just saying it. Don't know that I ever thought it before. I can't say I know why I thought of it.''

''So it was nothing specific that you could put your finger on,'' Emily offered, her gaze intensifying.

''Nope. Like I said.''

''He didn't say or do anything that was out of the ordinary?''

''Not that I can think of,'' Millie replied, setting about washing a baking sheet.

Emily folded her hands on the table, let out a frustrated sigh, and lost herself in thought. After a few moments, she said, ''Millie, if Nathan wasn't killed by Sara, and he wasn't killed by a tramp, that leaves someone else...presumably from the area.

Don't you have any idea of anyone who might've wanted to kill him?"

Millie pursed her lips again, and said, "Well, there's many around here who'd cut you with a word, or kill you with a look, but I don't know if anybody'd take a pitchfork to you."

"And yet, someone did," said Emily pointedly.

Millie paused and glanced at her. "Yeah, that's right." She went back to her washing. "If it hadn't happened, it wouldn't seem possible."

Emily nodded her head, though she didn't appear to be paying attention to her.

"I wonder..." she said reflectively.

"What's that?" asked Millie.

"I wonder why they didn't get married."

Millie stared at her for a moment as if she thought Emily might just have slipped a cog. "Well, Miss Charters, they didn't get married because Nathan was killed."

"Oh, no," said Emily, "I didn't mean Nathan and Amy, I meant Sara and the sheriff."

Millie's expression transformed into a deep frown. "I don't know for sure, but it's a damn shame. That murder seems to have soured everything."

"Yes," said Emily, "it did."

SIX

THE COUNTY SHERIFF'S OFFICE was on the main highway, halfway between LeFavre and Mt. Morgan. It was a small building of pale yellow brick with a disproportionately large parking lot. As Ransom pulled into a space near the front door, he couldn't help thinking that the place looked more like a rest stop on the interstate than a sheriff's office.

The interior was no more prepossessing than the exterior. There was a long, cheap counter spanning almost the entire length of the room. Behind it were three desks, none of which were in use at the moment. The floor was covered in wide tiles that had been white at one time, but were yellow with age and heavily scuffed with usage. Several hard, straight wooden chairs sat in a line against the wall. They were so thickly varnished that they didn't just look wet, they looked as if they would ripple if anyone sat on them. On the right-hand wall behind the counter was an office door with a glass window etched in an intricate enough pattern to keep the interior of the office obscured.

Standing behind the counter was a young blond man who Ransom took to be a deputy. He was dressed in a khaki uniform which, in his case, was an unfortunate choice of colors, since, with his Aryan looks, the uniform made him look uncomfortably reminiscent of Nazi youths. Then again, Ransom thought, that might have been the point.

"I'd like to see Jeff Fields," said Ransom.

"Is there anything *I* can help you with?" replied the deputy without so much as a hint that he was willing to comply with Ransom's request.

"It's a personal matter," Ransom said without emotion.

"That right? You a friend of Jeff's? I don't remember ever seeing you."

Ransom closed his eyes and sighed. When he opened them again, he said, "Is he here?"

The deputy smiled broadly, apparently feeling he'd achieved the desired effect, and called out, "Jeff! Gentleman here to see you!"

There was movement in the office on the right. Ransom could see a blob of color approaching through the etched window. As it neared, it increased in size, fragmented into jagged pieces, and splayed apart like a cubist painting come to life. When the door opened with a loud groan, the shards of color congealed into the person of Jeff Fields.

Ransom had tried on occasion to subdue his penchant for making snap judgments about people he was going to question for fear that these impressions, if too steadfastly adhered to, might cause him to disregard or miss important information. However, his failure to stem the flow of first impressions was mitigated by the fact that his initial assessments were, more often than not, highly accurate. So it was with dismay that he realized that his first glance at Jeff Fields yielded absolutely nothing. He might as well have been looking at a wall. It might have been from being on vacation, or from his unofficial standing in this community, the closeness of the holiday, or any of a hundred other things. He preferred to believe that it was because Fields really was a wall.

Fields stared at Ransom for a moment with such practiced inscrutability that Ransom couldn't help but admire the technique. It gave him a minor glimpse into what it must be like to be on the other end of one of his own investigations.

"You wanted to see me?"

Ransom gave a single nod. "On a private matter."

Two creases cut wide swaths across Fields's smooth forehead. "A private matter? I don't know you."

"Yes, I know. My name is Ransom," he said with a coy smile, "I'm staying at Hawthorne House...." He let his voice trail off suggestively.

If he'd been hoping for some sort of reaction on the part of the sheriff, he was disappointed. There wasn't so much as a twitch. But Ransom could sense a change in the atmosphere of the room, not so much from the sheriff as from his deputy, who paused in the act of shuffling some papers on the counter and looked first at Ransom, then at Fields. Fields didn't budge for a moment, then pushed his door open and said "Come on in." There was no warmth in the invitation.

The inner office was as unimpressive as the rest of the place: the same drab yellow walls and the same overzealously varnished furniture. As Ransom took a seat in front of the desk, he thought the impression of his posterior would probably remain there until someone else's reformed it.

"So you're staying at Hawthorne House," said Fields without preamble. "So what's the problem?"

"I've been asked to—unofficially, of course—look into the murder of Nathan Bartlett."

Although Fields could not have been described as being animated, this news seemed to turn him to stone. "Sara asked you to do that?"

"The request came from her, yes," said Ransom, seeing no reason to bring Emily into it.

"You a detective?"

"I'm a homicide detective, from Chicago."

"And Sara brought you in to find out who killed her brother, huh?"

Ransom rested his elbows on the arms of the chair and pressed his fingers together. "As a matter of fact, I'm one of her guests for the week. She was told I was a detective and I agreed to look into this for her. The matter seems to be causing Miss Bartlett a great deal of distress."

"She doesn't think I did everything I could?" There was no hint of recrimination in his tone, nor did he appear to be hurt by the prospect. But Ransom thought his choice of words might indicate a measure of remorse felt by the sheriff.

"She didn't mention it," said Ransom with a smile he hoped might widen the chink in the sheriff's armor. "However, I'm sure you did everything you could. I have no desire to interfere with an ongoing investigation, but I'm assuming that after two years, the investigation is...not ongoing."

Fields looked at him for a moment, then replied, "There's nothing to investigate, Mr. Ransom."

Ransom cocked his head sideways, and said, "I don't want to get in your way. I know what I would think if someone came barging into my area and stepping on my toes."

Fields folded his arms across his massive chest. "What would you think?"

Ransom smiled. "I would think they were barging in and stepping on my toes. But that's not what I'm trying to do here. The only thing I'm trying to do is help that young woman, if I can."

"You think you can do better than I did?"

Ransom sighed and sat back, resting his arms on the chair's. "It's been suggested that you might have had an interest in not solving the case."

Fields's face began to flush, then almost as if he'd become aware of betraying some emotion, the redness quickly ebbed as though he'd recalled the blood from his face.

"When did you get to town?" he asked.

"The day before yesterday."

Fields whistled. "You've been busy already, haven't you?"

Ransom put his palms up and shrugged eloquently. "Just sightseeing."

"Damn sight more than that." Fields heaved a deep sigh before continuing. "Look, I know what the people around here say, because, even though none of 'em have had the balls to say it to my face, it still gets back to me. I know they say Sara did it and I let her get away with it. I'm sure you've heard I was going with Sara. Hell, I'll go even further than that—I loved her. Still do. But I'm a good cop, first and foremost. If I could've proved that Sara killed Nathan, it might've killed me to do it, but I would've brought her in." Here he stopped, dropped his head down and added half under his breath, "Damn near killed me as it was." He drew his head back up and faced Ransom. "What most people don't know is that it's not enough to think somebody did it. It's not even enough to know in your heart that they did it. If there isn't any hard evidence, as far as the law's concerned, they *didn't* do it. You know that.''

Ransom nodded. He did know that, and there wasn't a cop in the country who didn't have to grit his teeth when he thought of it. But he thought he knew something else, too. From the vehemence with which Fields had delivered this declaration, Ransom felt there was something really troubling to the sheriff about this case—something that went beyond merely not having it solved.

"So you didn't have any hard evidence?"

"We didn't have any evidence at all," Fields replied.

"Would you mind telling me what you did have?" Ransom asked, rejoining his fingers.

Fields didn't reply right away, choosing instead to stare stone-faced at the detective for a moment, looking, Ransom thought, not unlike someone had pulled his plug. Ransom leaned in toward him. "Sheriff, it might surprise you to know that you're not the first person to tell me since I arrived in town that you're a good cop.''

Fields looked as if he would have liked to brighten, but restrained himself.

"And no, it wasn't Sara who told me that. I have no reason to believe otherwise. I know that any law enforcement agent worth his salt, whether sheriff, cop, or desk clerk, wants to see a murderer apprehended''—he paused for effect, and added pointedly—"by any means necessary. Perhaps in my unofficial capacity I can find out things that you couldn't in your official one. But either way, I have to believe you want the murderer found."

Fields looked uncertain for the first time, though that uncertainty flickered across his features for barely a second.

"Yes, I do," he said at last.

"Then will you tell me what you had back then?"

"All we had was Sara's statement—that she didn't know Nathan had gone out, that she went to look for him and found him dead in the barn, and that she went up, got Hansen, and called me."

"She called you personally?"

"I don't see anything surprising about that. I was on duty that night anyway. She knew that."

"Sara *knew* you were on duty that night?"

Fields paused. "'Course she did. If I wasn't, we would've been together. So?"

"Nothing, I just wanted to make sure I understood you. You questioned Hansen Crane, of course."

"Of course," Fields echoed. "Said he was asleep and didn't hear anything until Sara came pounding at the door."

"There wasn't any reason to think Hansen might've killed Nathan?"

Fields shook his head. "Only because he was on the premises. But Hansen didn't have anything against Nathan that anybody knew of, and so far's we know, he'd never seen or heard of him before he came here."

"Hansen just showed up one day? That would've been about a year after Nathan and Sara moved here."

"Yeah. But there's nothing in that, either. People drift into town here and there, stay a while, and go. It happens in places like Chicago, too, Mr. Ransom, except you got so many people there you don't notice them."

"So he just showed up on the Bartletts' doorstep one day and asked for a job?"

"Yeah, but that wasn't the first place he went. He stopped by several places asking for work before that. I'm sure half the people knew he was looking for work before he ever made it out to Hawthorne House. Just happened they were looking for help."

Ransom thought about this for a moment, then said, "So it would appear that he wasn't specifically seeking out Sara and Nathan."

Fields paused, then said broadly, "Well, he could've been stopping other places first just to give that impression, but we have no reason to believe he's anything more than what he appears to be."

Ransom narrowed his eyes, and said, "If someone other than

Sara Bartlett killed her brother, then *somebody* in this town is not what he appears to be.''

What little there was of a smile on Fields's face disappeared. He clearly didn't enjoy being bested.

"Hansen's like Sara, there's no hard evidence against him," said Fields soberly, "but unlike Sara, he didn't have any known motive."

"What would Sara's motive have been?"

"She got her brother's money."

"Did she need it?"

"She not only didn't need it, if she'd wanted it, he would've given it to her. That's how close they were."

"That's not much of a motive," said Ransom, looking off in the distance as he ruminated. "And there was no other evidence?"

"Nope," said Fields with an abbreviated shrug. "The storm was so bad that there wasn't even any footprints by the time I got out there."

In a way, this verified what Sara had told him.

"And there weren't any fingerprints on the pitchfork," Fields added.

"Not surprising."

"No, it wasn't. If there *had* been, I might've had to bring Sara in, but the fact of the matter is, her fingerprints wouldn't have proved anything, because they *should've* been on it, 'cause she's used it once or twice. So's Hansen. But it was wiped. And there was no reason for either of them to do that."

The two lawmen sat and stared at each other, both aware that there was one reason that either Sara or Hansen, if they'd been clever enough to think of it, might have wiped the handle of the pitchfork: so the sheriff would reach the exact conclusion that he had. But that still left them with no evidence, so whatever their motive might have been, it had the desired result.

At last Fields said, "So you can see what I mean. We have no evidence, and no other suspects."

"What about Amy Shelton?"

"Amy!" Fields exclaimed with a deprecating laugh. "You ever seen Amy?"

Ransom shook his head.

"She could barely wield a table fork, let alone a pitchfork. She's a weak little thing."

"Hmm," said Ransom with elaborate consideration, "I understood she was in love with Nathan."

"So?"

"Sooo," Ransom said slowly, "love, hate, they both can lead to murder for one reason or another."

Fields sighed heavily. "Look, Mr. Ransom, no matter what you think, I did do my job. Just because I don't think Amy could do it doesn't mean I didn't follow her up. As it happens, she was supposed to have had a date with Nathan, but they called it off because the weather was so bad. She has an alibi. She stayed in all evening and all night, verified by both her mother and father."

Ransom raised an eyebrow. "I would hardly expect her parents to do anything other than back her up."

"Neither would I," said Fields, his mouth turning down at the corners, "but I have no reason not to believe them, either. Hell, the weather was so bad, *nobody* went out that night unless they had to. Why do you think people are so dead set on Sara as the killer?"

Ransom paused for a second, then replied, "For the same reason you are."

A silence fell between them during which they continued to stare at each other across the sheriff's desk, both of their expressions nearly unreadable.

Finally Ransom said, "Sara told me that she knew Nathan hadn't driven anywhere that night because she would've heard the car."

"Yeah?"

Ransom smiled. "So I assume that means she would've heard someone else's car as well—if someone had driven out there."

"That's right," said Fields with a nod to show that he already knew all this.

"Is there any other way out there—some way that somebody could get to the barn without driving up to the house?"

"There's an access road to the vineyards about two hundred yards behind the barn."

"Were there any tracks there that night? Any sign of a car?"

Fields heaved a bored sigh. "Mr. Ransom, you don't know what it's like to live in the country. Out here, when we have a storm like that it isn't just tracks that disappear, it's the whole damn road."

"So there was nothing there?"

"Not that was still there by the time we got out there."

"Hm. Then it doesn't look good for Sara, does it?" he said with a smile.

"And at the same time," Fields replied with a superior smile, "that's why Sara wasn't arrested. Someone else *could've* gone out there. But whether or not that's likely..."

He let his voice trail off and they fell silent once more.

"Well," said Ransom, suddenly rising from his seat. The bottom of his pants hesitated a second before following him. "I appreciate your time. Thank you very much."

"Mr. Ransom," said Fields as he rose from his desk. Ransom stopped and faced him. "No case is closed in this county until I say it is, whether or not the investigation is active. If you find out anything, I expect to hear about it."

Ransom smiled. "Certainly." He crossed to the door, opened it, and paused in the doorway, looking back at Fields. "By the way, Sheriff, I was wondering if you were...for some reason...expecting more trouble out at Hawthorne House."

The deep furrows returned over Fields's brow. "Why would you ask that?"

"Because I could have sworn I saw you drive by there yesterday morning. It seemed to me that you...just might have been keeping the place under surveillance."

Fields allowed a flat smile to spread across his face. "Just cruisin' the area, Mr. Ransom. Just doing my job."

After a beat Ransom returned a much broader smile, and said, "Of course."

WELL, GERALD, thought Ransom as he started his car. He stopped before putting it in drive, brought up short by the fact that this was the first time in two years he'd headed into an investigation without the aid of his full-time partner and part-time Boswell, Gerald White. Ransom had always found White able and unassuming, and more importantly, unlike others with whom he'd been partnered over the years, White didn't get in the way. He readily accepted the position of second banana, doing a lot of the leg work and allowing himself to be used as a sounding board for Ransom's deliberations, while not shrinking from offering his own ideas. It wasn't until this moment, when Ransom was ready to let the ideas fly, that he realized just how important a position his partner held. It was a role that Ransom knew Emily could never fill, not because she was incapable of being a sounding board, but because, despite Ransom's faith in his own abilities, he harbored the notion that she just might be even more clever than he was. With all these thoughts in mind, as well as the information imparted by Jeff Fields, Ransom pulled a plastic-tipped cigar from the pack in his pocket, lit it, and headed back to Hawthorne House.

He found Emily quietly reading *King Lear* in the parlor.

"You look like you haven't budged since I left," he said.

"Oh, no," said Emily as she laid the book aside, "I've only just come back here. I've been doing a little investigating on my own."

"Have you?" said Ransom, taking a seat beside her.

"I had a little talk with Millie Havers." She told him what she'd learned.

"So basically," said Ransom with a sigh, "everything was fine between everybody, and the murder came completely out of the blue."

Emily nodded. "The only thing at all out of the ordinary was that Nathan seemed a little preoccupied, but Millie was quite unspecific about that.''

"Well, that could have been anything. He could have been worried about business, or he could have been thinking of proposing to Amy.''

Emily considered this for a moment, then said, "Now, tell me, what did Jeffrey Fields have to say?''

When Ransom had finished telling her, Emily sat back in her chair and gazed at him, her eyes alive with interest.

"It seems very significant to me that it was known that Jeffrey Fields would be on duty that night.''

"It did to me, too. It meant that he would almost certainly be the one to get the call about the murder...assuming that it was discovered that night.''

"Oh, it meant much more than that, it meant that most likely it was generally known he wouldn't be *here* that night.''

"That's true,'' said Ransom, "and with the weather as bad as it was, the murderer could also be fairly certain there wouldn't be any casual visitors here.''

They fell silent. Ransom stared into the unlit fireplace, while Emily's gaze was fixed on the Christmas tree as if she thought she might divine some insight from amidst its branches.

"The problem, as I see it,'' said Emily at last, "is *why* would someone want to kill Nathan Bartlett? Everything seems to have been innocuous enough. I don't see any sense in it at all.''

Ransom smiled ruefully. "I think that's why people are so willing to believe that Sara did it. With the lack of any motive anywhere else, her money motive is the most obvious. And barring that, she's the most likely person to have had a motive nobody knew about.''

Emily straightened herself in her chair, folded her hands, and adopted the schoolmarmish attitude she so often displayed when taking matters in hand.

"Jeremy, I really believe that Sara wants this case solved. I can't imagine her doing that, or agreeing to let you look into it, if she was the murderer. Now, how do you think we should proceed?"

Ransom sighed heavily and fingered the pocket that held his cigars. "Well, I think we have to proceed on the assumption that Sara is telling the truth. And, if she is, then there are some other assumptions we can make."

"Yes?" said Emily.

"Sara told me one thing that I think was very important: she didn't hear Nathan leave—and ordinarily she would have—and this was after telling her that he was going to his room. This tells me that he didn't want her to know where he was going."

"And that he was going to meet somebody, and didn't want her to know about it."

"Exactly. Also, I think we can assume that Nathan was killed not long after he left."

"How do we know that?"

"Footprints," Ransom replied simply.

"I beg your pardon?"

"When Sara went out to the barn, there were no footprints in the snow—they'd been wiped away by the wind and the storm. That had to have taken some time. The last time she saw Nathan was around nine, she went looking for him shortly after eleven. I think he was killed shortly after nine."

"That's very interesting," said Emily slowly, her eyes narrowing. "You know, it occurs to me, Jeremy, that the most likely person for him to be going to meet was Hansen Crane."

"Possibly," said Ransom, tapping his upper lip with his index finger, "except why wouldn't he have told his sister that he was going to talk to Hansen? After all, he talked to Hansen all the time. Sara wouldn't have thought anything of it. Why would their meeting have to be clandestine?"

Emily considered this for a moment. "You know, I think it's very interesting that Nathan asked so many questions about Hansen Crane."

"Yes," said Ransom with a thoughtful nod, "but I have to

agree with Millie about one thing. It seems to have taken place much too long before the murder to have anything to do with it.''

"Perhaps...but there's always the possibility that Hansen Crane found out about Nathan's interest much later. And he was on the premises that night.''

"Hm,'' said Ransom. "But according to Jeff Fields, there was no reason to believe Crane killed Nathan.''

"When it comes to that,'' said Emily, "we have no reason to believe *anyone* killed Nathan, except that he's dead.''

Ransom laughed. "Well, you have me there, Emily.'' His expression grew more sober. "This is the problem with taking up two-year-old threads—they fall apart so easily.''

Ransom stared into the fireplace for a few moments. "You know, I got the uncomfortable feeling that Jeff Fields doesn't want this case solved.''

"Really?'' Emily replied with genuine surprise, "Why?''

"I can think of a couple of reasons. No matter what he says to the contrary, he really does think that Sara did it, and he doesn't want to put her away.''

"I suppose that's possible,'' said Emily rather doubtfully.

"The other possibility is worse. Jeff Fields could be the murderer.''

"The *sheriff?*'' said Emily, her expression absolutely scandalized.

"Why not? If they were, as we've been told, on the road to being married, then maybe he was the one that wanted all the money and not her.''

"But Jeremy, they didn't end up getting married.''

Ransom shrugged. "He didn't count on the effect Nathan's death and the investigation would have on Sara. It wouldn't be the first time that someone committed murder for gain and ended up with nothing. *And* it would explain why he didn't 'solve' the murder, and why he's not happy with having me look into it.''

Emily's eyebrows slid upward, her expression one of mild amusement. "That all may be true and, I admit, it's quite plau-

sible, but I can think of another, less sinister, reason for not wanting your intrusion."

"What's that?" he asked, his tone slightly irritated at being
referred to as an intrusion, especially by the person who'd asked
him to intrude.

She leaned forward a little in her chair. "Because he wants to
be the one who solves it."

Ransom stared at her for a moment, letting this sink in. Although he'd told Fields that any lawman would want a murderer
apprehended, no matter what the means, Ransom had to admit—
if only to himself—that he would prefer to be the one who did
it. It hadn't even entered his mind that the sheriff might feel the
same way.

He replied reluctantly, "I suppose he could feel the same way
about it as I do."

"Oh, no, that's not what I mean at all, Jeremy. I mean he might
want to do it *for Sara.*"

"*For her,*" said Ransom slowly rolling the words around in
his mouth.

"So," said Emily, "what will we do next?"

Ransom sighed. Despite Emily's faith in him, he couldn't get
past the feeling that they were chasing the wind. Though they'd
questioned three of the people involved with Nathan, they'd
turned up nothing more than Jeff Fields had at the time, and he
didn't exactly share Emily's confidence that they would ever find
more. The one thing that made Ransom want to pursue the case
was the renewed enthusiasm he saw in Emily's eyes. This was
the first time since her operation that she was really showing signs
of returning to her old self. Ransom felt it incumbent upon himself
to encourage this.

"Well," he said, "no matter how little he appears to figure
into it, we keep coming back to Hansen Crane, so I should talk
to him. If nothing else, he can confirm what we've learned so
far."

"Hmm..." said Emily, looking down at the floor reflectively
and pursing her lips. "You know, people keep referring to him

as a typical drifter with one exception. Millie Havers pointed out that she was surprised that he's stayed around so long.''

"Maybe I'll ask him about that," Ransom replied with a smile.

"And there's one other person it would be very important to talk to."

"Amy Shelton."

"Exactly!" said Emily. "If Nathan was, indeed, preoccupied before he died, she might be able to tell us why."

SEVEN

THE LAUNDRY ROOM was a small, square space, not much bigger than a pantry, located just off the kitchen. Sara was in the process of transferring a load of linens from the washer to the drier when Millie came down from the second floor.

"Well," said Millie, brushing a stray strand of gray hair back over her right ear, "I got the beds made and the bedrooms clean, though there was hardly any more to do but dust. Miss Charters is neat as a pin and that Mr. Ransom is maybe the cleanest man I've ever seen in my life."

Sara glanced at her over her shoulder and managed a weak smile. "Thank you, Millie."

"So, I guess I'll be getting along." She grabbed her coat from the peg by the back door and slipped it on. She hadn't taken her eyes off Sara. She paused in the doorway, looking as if she wasn't quite sure whether to go or stay. "Sure is nice having guests again, isn't it?"

"Yes, it is." Sara set the timer on the drier and pushed the start button. Millie stepped out of the way so she could pass back into the kitchen.

"And you couldn't hope for a better way to start up again than with those two. They seem to be as nice as they can be."

"That's true." Sara retrieved a handful of potatoes from the bin below the sink. She placed them on the counter and looked at them for a moment as if she couldn't remember what she'd intended to do with them.

"Sara," said Millie gently, "you all right?"

"Yes. Yes, of course. It's just..." She turned her plaintive eyes to her older friend. "Do you think I've done the right thing?"

Millie's brow furrowed, sending across her forehead a web of creases that seemed to spread out in all directions. "What do you mean, honey?"

"In letting Mr. Ransom open up this can of worms again."

Millie shrugged, an action she hoped would convey that the situation wasn't as bleak as Sara seemed to think it. "Don't know. He might be able to help. And he couldn't hurt."

"If only I could be sure of that."

Millie frowned, causing a further set of wrinkles to shoot away from the corners of her mouth like drooping fireworks. "Sara, do you know something about all this that you never said?"

Sara looked at her for a moment, her expression blank. "No. Of course not." She stopped and frowned, trying to think of how to put what she was feeling. Millie, who had always been rather direct, continued to watch her unflinchingly, which only added to Sara's discomfort. At last Sara sighed, looked back up at Millie, and said, "Do you know what foreboding is?"

"Yeah."

Sara slowly shook her head as she said, "I just have this feeling something terrible's going to happen."

Millie smiled warmly. It was a gesture that erased all the creases from her face except those time had put there. She crossed to Sara and laid a matronly hand on her shoulder. "That's just jitters," she said in her usual matter-of-fact tone. "Probably all that'll happen is nothin'!"

There was a sudden loud knock at the back door that so startled both the women that Millie dropped her hand to her side and spun around to look, and Sara let out an involuntary "Oh!"

The door popped open and Johnnie Larkin stuck his head in and said, "Sara? You there?"

Sara and Millie heaved relieved sighs. Millie said, "Johnnie, you just about scared us out of our shirts!"

"Oh. I'm sorry," he said, coming in and up the stairs. "I didn't mean to."

Sara laughed, feeling the tension in her body ebb a little. "It's all right. We were just talking and you startled us."

"Sorry," said Johnnie with a smile so puckish that he looked exactly like a schoolboy who'd just stuck a frog in the face of a little girl and made her scream. "I just came out to see if you had any work today."

"No, I'm sorry. Nothing that I can think of."

"Okay."

"You didn't have to drive all the way out here. You could've just called."

"Oh. Well…" He looked down at the floor and ran a hand through his long, dark hair. "It's okay. I was driving by this way, anyway, so I just thought I'd stop in and ask."

"What brought you out this way?" said Millie with a mischievous grin.

"Huh?"

"You said you were out this way."

"Oh. Yeah. I just had some work this morning."

"Where at?" said Millie as conversationally as she could.

"Um…" He glanced from Millie to Sara. "At the Darcy farm."

"The Darcy farm?" said Sara, recounting the potatoes as if for some reason she were having trouble retaining the total. "That's way on the other side of the highway."

Johnnie's normally ruddy cheeks grew redder and his eyes went back to the floor. "I didn't mean I was going right past here. But I was out in the car and thought I might as well stop by instead of going all the way home and maybe having to come back, you know?"

Millie's smile broadened and she thought it best to beat a hasty retreat before Johnnie noticed the look on her face. She was sure it would have told him how transparent he was, and though she didn't mind teasing him a little, being a basically kindhearted woman she wanted to spare him any real embarrassment. She tied her plaid scarf around her neck, and said, "Well, I better get going," then trundled down the back steps as they called goodbye to her.

Sara watched Millie go with feelings that were a mixture of amusement and abandonment. She turned a smile to Johnnie.

"Well, as long as you're here, would you like a little lunch? I've got some ham."

"Oh, I don't want to impose," he replied, though the way his eyes had lit up at the invitation his eagerness to accept it was obvious.

"You're not imposing. I wouldn't have asked."

"Oh. Okay then."

Sara took a fresh loaf of bread from the bread box and some leftover ham from the refrigerator. She unwrapped the ham, set it on a cutting board and started to cut off a few thick slices. Johnnie watched her for a moment, then eager to be helpful retrieved a couple of plates from the cabinet and set them on the table.

"So, how's it going, having guests again?"

Sara shrugged. "Not as bad as I thought it might be."

"Good. Then do you think you're gonna reopen permanently?"

"Maybe. We'll see."

Johnnie opened the refrigerator and peered inside. "So...if you're going to reopen, maybe you'll need more help around here."

With her back to him, Sara allowed herself to smile. "That's about it. 'If' and 'maybe.'"

Johnnie located a jar of mustard, straightened up, and closed the refrigerator. "Well, that's good, 'cause I'm always available."

"I know," said Sara lightly.

He put the mustard on the table and went to the drawer by the sink to get a knife. Instead of going back to the table, he leaned against the sink and watched Sara, his eyes full of anxious expectation.

"Sara..." he began tentatively.

She quickly handed him the loaf of bread, and said, "Would you put this on the table for me?"

She silently cursed her own good nature as she arranged the ham slices on a plate. She knew she should never have asked Johnnie to stay for lunch, but, even though he'd driven out to the house of his own accord, it wasn't in her nature to let someone go away completely emptyhanded. And Johnnie was one of those men who looked as if he would never have a proper meal if left to himself.

Although Sara had been in a mental fog for a long time, she hadn't been completely oblivious to Johnnie's attention, though she'd hoped it was something that would remain unspoken. Johnnie's rather obvious crush was just another cause of mental confusion. In her rare moments of clarity she couldn't see any reason for not returning his affections: after all, there was nothing inherently wrong with him. In fact, he had many good qualities. He was helpful, he was eager (maybe a little too eager), he was dependable, and he was something of an outsider in the community, like herself. Unlike most of the people in the area, Johnnie seemed to have absolute faith in her innocence of any wrongdoing. She might go so far as to say that he wore his faith in her like a badge of honor. She chalked it up to the natural perversity of human nature that it was his unwavering faith that made her uncomfortable. It reminded her of religious zealots who cling blindly to their beliefs as if entertaining any doubts will cause the object of their admiration to shatter.

She shook her head as she rewrapped the rest of the ham. If she were completely honest with herself, any discomfort she felt around Johnnie was not being caused by him, but was coming from within herself. It was because of Jeff Fields, who stood as another issue from her past that might never be resolved. For the first time since Ransom had agreed to investigate she realized that she was holding out hope not only that she'd be able to close the door on Nathan's murder, but that she'd be able to close it on her relationship with Jeff as well. The problem was that she didn't know on which side of that door she wanted to end up. She let out an involuntary shudder.

"Is anything wrong?" said Johnnie, his voice rising with worry.

"Oh, no, I just had a little chill," Sara replied as she replaced the ham in the refrigerator. She then transferred the plate of ham slices from the counter to the table and took a seat.

"My God!" said Johnnie with a laugh. "You never do anything by half, do you?"

"What do you mean?"

He pointed to the plate on which the ham was tastefully arranged, the slices overlapping in a circle.

"Force of habit, I guess," she said with a rueful laugh. "I always feel like I'm preparing for the guests."

Johnnie grinned. "Well, I'm not company, I'm family."

Sara tried to return the smile. "Yeah, you are."

Johnnie slapped a couple of slices of ham on a slice of bread, spread mustard on another slice and closed the sandwich while Sara nibbled at a piece of ham. He was lifting the sandwich to his mouth when his gaze traveled over Sara's shoulder. He stopped with the sandwich in midair, his eyes widening.

"What in the hell is he doing?"

"Who?" Sara turned around to see what Johnnie was looking at. Through the window in the back door they could see Ransom, bundled up in a down coat and long black scarf, trudging through the snow toward the barn.

"Oh," said Sara, "Ransom. Mr. Ransom. He's probably going out to talk to Hansen. He's a detective. He's looking into Nathan's murder."

Johnnie gaped at her in astonishment. "You've got to be kidding!"

"No."

"I thought he was a guest! You mean, you actually hired a detective?"

She shook her head. "No, he really is a guest. But he's a homicide detective and he offered to see if he could find out anything. I should've mentioned it to you, I guess. I don't know whether or not he'll want to talk to you."

"To me?" Johnnie's face did a quick transformation from disbelief, to wariness, to perplexity, as if each new idea was flashing across his face like a slide show as he rapidly considered all the possible ramifications of this. Finally he screwed up his face in question, and asked, "Do you think that's a good idea?"

Sara gave her characteristic shrug. "It couldn't hurt."

He tapped his sandwich against his plate a couple of times as if he were trying to get its contents in order, then said, "You're right. It's probably a good thing." He took a bite of the sandwich and chewed it as if it were an idea he was mulling over with his teeth. "I never did think Jeff Fields had enough brains to take on something like that. I mean, sure, he's all right for giving out traffic tickets and maybe bringing in a drunk or two, but beyond that, I don't know." He paused and looked at Sara for a reaction, but she just continued to pick at the piece of ham, absently sticking bits of it in her mouth. Johnnie continued, "And I don't think I could ever forgive him for treating you like you had something to do with it. That's crazy. Just goes to show he doesn't have his whole brain working."

Sara dropped the ham on her plate and stared down at it. "He was just doing his job. And I was the obvious...I don't think he could avoid it."

Johnnie smacked his lips derisively, and said, "Oh, well, maybe it can all get settled now."

"Let's hope so."

Johnnie ate in silence for a few moments, glancing at Sara occasionally as if hoping to find some sign of acceptance. After a couple of minutes he said, "And you know, Sara, maybe once this is all behind us, you and me could—"

Sara suddenly glanced up at him, stopping him in midsentence. He found it disheartening that, rather than looking surprised or unaccepting, she just looked pained.

He sighed. "Well, maybe we could do something together some time. Go to a movie or something. Maybe get to know each other better."

The wild rush of emotions flooded in on her again. In the mass of conflicting thoughts, she remembered Emily's admonition that sometimes you had to fight your way out of the void on your own. With no faith in the outcome of the investigation, she thought just maybe it was time for her to pull herself up by her bootstraps and try going forward on her own. But the idea was still unappealing.

"I can't think about that now," she said out of the blue. She suddenly realized she'd said this aloud in answer to her own thoughts. She looked at Johnnie, whose face had fallen, apparently from having taken this as her answer to him.

Sara decided it was best not to correct this for the time being.

RANSOM CLIMBED the rough wooden staircase up the side of the barn to Hansen Crane's apartment. Though it wasn't very cold by the standard of a lifelong Chicagoan, it was still cold enough to slow his movements a bit. These days it seemed to him that the cold made his joints congeal. Ransom shook his head in disgust, taking this increased sensitivity to the temperature as just another sign that he was getting older. When he reached the top of the stairs, he knocked on the window of the cracked wooden door and waited. Across the inside of the window was a worn curtain, and as he waited he tried to decide if the barely visible pattern on it had been sun faded into obscurity or was just bleeding through the other side. He was about to knock again when the curtain twitched slightly, then was abruptly swept aside. The effect of the face appearing in the window was startling. Despite the general heartiness of Crane's face, there was something about the bushy beard and long, stiff gray hair that immediately brought to Ransom's mind the idea of Santa Claus in the last stages of dissolution. But even without the unsettling mental image of the patron saint of children in decay, the wariness in Crane's eyes would have been enough. Ransom didn't trust him.

Crane let out a muffled grunt at the sight of Ransom, then opened the door.

"You're that detective, aren't you?" he said, blocking the doorway.

"Yes."

"Sara told me you were snooping around. Can't say I like the idea."

Ransom raised his right eyebrow. "Sara said 'snooping'?"

The bush around Crane's mouth twitched. Ransom assumed he was smiling. "She said something nicer, but it boils down to the same thing, don't it?"

"Do you think I might talk to you?"

"I don't have anything to say I haven't said already, to the real police."

Though Ransom didn't change expression, he bridled inwardly. He was fully aware that he was operating outside of any official jurisdiction, but, up until now, nobody had questioned his authority. It was a blow to his pride to realize that people had been answering his questions more out of their love for Sara than out of any respect for him. But it was apparent that for someone like Hansen Crane, usually wary of strangers, whether or not he had any affection or loyalty to Sara he wouldn't relish being questioned by anyone. Ransom would have liked nothing more than to whip his badge out of his pocket, flash it at Crane, and proceed with all the authority that accompanied it, but that not being possible, he decided to take a different tack.

"I understand that Miss Bartlett has been very good to you."

"Do you?" said Crane, his ability to emit words apparently not depending on lip movement.

"She gave you a job when you needed one," said Ransom with a shrug that implied that anyone should understand this, "and a decent place to live."

"What if she did?"

Ransom sighed. "Then I wouldn't think it would be asking too much for you to answer a few questions that might help her. What harm would that do?" Ransom paused for a moment, then narrowed his eyes slightly and added as simply as before, "Unless, of course, you have something to hide."

Crane seemed to harden in place, giving Ransom an inkling of how sudden and thorough a process it must have been when Lot's wife made her ill-fated mistake. Ransom was just beginning to think they'd reached a standoff when the handyman suddenly inhaled deeply, then slowly exhaled.

"That strikes me as being what they call a 'cheap shot.'"

Ransom smiled. "Did it work?"

The curve in the center of Crane's beard deepened. "The part about Sara did," he replied, stepping aside to let Ransom enter. "I guess I do owe her. Come on in."

Crane's flat delivery belied his words, making it clear to Ransom that he still didn't believe he owed anyone anything. Ransom stepped past the old man and into the apartment. It consisted of one medium-sized room, fairly dark due to the fact that there were only two small windows at either end of the room in addition to the one in the door. The ceiling sloped downward on both sides and the walls were bare wood and completely unadorned. A very small section of the far end of the room was partitioned off with paneling into what looked like a small shed, which Ransom assumed fit the description of a water-closet.

The room was completely devoid of personal items, except for a few bits of clothing hanging from a short makeshift rod jutting out from one wall and a can of tobacco and a pipe that lay on the table. The table was small with chrome legs and a blue plastic top, and had two matching padded chairs. The set looked as if it dated from the fifties. There was a tattered braided rug in the center of the floor, a twin bed pushed up against one wall, and a small, ancient refrigerator that chugged noisily in one corner. Next to the refrigerator was an electric stove so old it could have actually been the prototype. Everything looked like it had been hastily purchased at resale shops to accommodate someone whose tenure was unsure, although Ransom reminded himself that for all he knew these things really could have been sitting here since the fifties.

The meager heat was provided by a set of electric floorboard heaters that looked as if they'd been installed in the not-too-distant past.

"So, what do you want to ask me?" said Crane, dropping his bulk onto one of the chairs, which let out a loud squeak in protest.

He hadn't invited Ransom to sit down, which the detective chalked up to a lack of manners rather than a desire for him not to stay long. Ransom crossed to the table, pulled out the other chair and sat down as purposefully as he could. The bush around Crane's mouth formed a slight crescent, which Ransom found particularly irritating at the moment.

Crane slid a dirty fingernail under the lid of the tobacco can and popped it open. Since the can was almost full, a bit of tobacco sprayed onto the table, which Crane ignored. He stuffed some tobacco into the pipe, cramming it down tight with his thumb. He then stuck the pipe in his mouth, his teeth biting down on it with a pronounced click. He pulled a pack of matches from his side pocket and made a great show of lighting the pipe, puffing in and out rapidly several times and sending bursts of smoke upward as if he were signaling Indians. Ransom sat with his arms folded throughout this display, making it clear that he could wait until he had Crane's full attention before continuing.

"Well?" said Crane at last with some irritation.

"I just want to ask you a few questions. You've probably heard them all before."

Crane inclined his head, a gesture that told Ransom that the handyman was sure that was true.

"I've already been told that you were here when the murder took place."

"Uh-huh."

"Can you tell me what happened?"

Crane leaned a bulky elbow on the top of the table, and said, "Well, you oughtta know that already, too."

Ransom smiled. "Only one side of it. I'd like to hear..." He started to say "your version," but decided it might be best to use less confrontational terminology. "I'd like to know how it looked from your perspective."

Crane huffed. "Didn't look like nothin'. First thing I knew, Sara was pounding on the door and yelling out my name."

"What were you doing at the time?"

"Sleeping. Just like I told the sheriff. What else would I be doing that time of night?"

"Isn't that a little early for bed?"

"Maybe in the city," said Crane with a grunt, "not for hard-working folks."

"Hmm," said Ransom. "When did you go to bed?"

Crane blinked. "Huh?"

"It's a simple question. What time did you go to bed?"

"Well…" Crane hesitated. He stuck his thumb and forefinger inside his beard and scratched at his chin. Ransom tried not to grimace. The motion made it look as if there might be something residing in Crane's beard that he was trying to pick out. Finally Crane gave an abbreviated shrug, and said, "Well, hell, that was two years ago! How the hell should I remember what time I went to bed?"

Ransom pursed his lips. "We might be able to make a rough estimate. Sara said that you took quite a while to answer the door. You must've been sleeping pretty soundly."

"Nothin's wrong with my conscience."

"I simply meant that that would mean you'd been asleep for some time. Could it've been two hours?"

"Don't know," said Crane with another shrug.

"Well, let's try it this way. Would it be common for you to go to bed before, say, nine o'clock?"

"It's common for me to go to bed whenever I get tired," Crane replied, his tone mocking Ransom's.

The detective stared fixedly at him for a moment, then said, "No matter, I'm sure the sheriff has it in his file."

Crane's eyes narrowed slightly and his bushy eyebrows slid toward each other. He looked as if he didn't like the idea of something he'd said being written down somewhere. "What's so important about when I went to bed, anyway?"

"You say you were asleep when Sara knocked."

"I was," Crane interjected a little testily.

"But Nathan was killed earlier. I suspect that he might have been killed a little after nine."

Ransom paused. He could have sworn the handyman had stiffened slightly, but he didn't give any visible signs of movement until a thick stream of smoke poured out of the side of his mouth.

It was an action so calculated to be startling that Ransom almost laughed.

"So, I was wondering if maybe you heard anything unusual earlier...maybe a couple of hours before Sara came to your door."

Crane snorted. "Only thing I heard was the storm, and that wasn't unusual."

Ransom gazed at him for a moment, but the handyman's expression remained stoic.

"So," said Ransom at last, "what did you do when Sara came to the door?"

"She told me what she found. I took her back to the house and she called the sheriff."

Ransom's face became a picture of puzzlement. "You didn't look in the barn?"

"Why should I?"

"To check to see if Nathan was really dead."

Crane emitted a "Humph." "I had no reason to doubt Sara."

"You weren't curious at all?"

"I seen enough death."

Ransom cocked his head. "Have you?"

"I'm sixty-three years old. You haven't seen death by then, you haven't been living."

He made it sound as if death by pitchfork were a common occurrence. *Then again*, thought Ransom, *for all I know it might be out here.*

"And that was all there was to it?"

"That was it."

Ransom closed his eyes for a moment and sighed. "Do you have any idea who might've wanted to kill Nathan?"

Crane shrugged. Ransom was beginning to find the motion annoying. "Sorry."

"Did anyone dislike him?"

"Not that I know."

Ransom sat back in his chair and folded his arms. "What about you?"

"What about me?"

"Did you dislike Nathan?"

"Nothing to dislike. He was pretty much the same as everybody else."

"Hmm," said Ransom as if he were pondering this thoughtfully. "I suppose you would know. You've probably met a lot of people in your time."

"You're bound to if you live long enough."

"I mean in your travels. I understand you've been a sort of nomad."

"I get around."

"Have your travels ever taken you to Chicago?"

There was a slight hesitation before Crane responded. He took the bowl of his pipe in his finger, adjusted the stem between his teeth, and another cloud of smoke poured out of the corner of his mouth. Finally he said, "Can't say I remember."

The two men stared at each other for a few moments like two animals from different breeds of the same species, challenging each other for territory. After a while, Crane looked down at the tabletop, drummed his fingers on it once, then looked back up. "Why?"

"I was just wondering if perhaps you'd chanced to meet Nathan Bartlett sometime."

A broad smile made itself evident beneath Crane's beard. "Nope. I never set eyes on him before I came here." He announced this proudly, as if that one statement formed the bedrock of his honesty. Ransom wondered if it was the only absolute truth he'd spoken. After a pause Crane asked hesitantly, "Why d'you ask that?"

"Well.." Ransom replied with a coy smile, "people seem to think that Sara murdered her brother because she was the only one who knew him well enough...."

Crane let out a disdainful snort, and said, "Well, sorry to tell you, but I didn't know him before I came here."

Ransom continued as if he hadn't been interrupted. "...And because she was the only one out here...beside you, of course. You have to understand it would be natural to suspect you since you were the only other person on the premises the night Nathan was killed.'' Ransom let that hang in the air between them for a few seconds before he added, ''Weren't you?''

'''Course I was,'' said Crane, ''anybody else had come out here I would've seen 'em.''

Ransom didn't allow his expression to change. He merely waited a bit, then said lightly, ''But you were asleep.''

The few inches of visible skin on Crane's face reddened, though he didn't avert his eyes from Ransom's. He forced a smile, and replied, ''That's right. I was asleep.''

A momentary silence fell between the two men, then with his characteristic abruptness, Ransom leapt from his chair as he said, ''Well, thank you for your time, Mr. Crane. You've been very helpful.''

Crane rose from his chair tentatively, like a balloon that hadn't been fully inflated. There was a puzzled look in his eyes that showed he dearly wanted to ask the detective how he'd been helpful, but he restrained himself. Ransom moved to open the door, but paused with his hand on the doorknob and looked back at Crane.

''You know, I find you very interesting.''

''Why's that?'' asked the handyman, almost as if responding to this was a compulsion.

''All those years you spent on the road, and suddenly you settle down here. I've never known a real drifter to do that before.''

There was a pause before Crane responded. ''You get used to comfort.''

Ransom glanced around the room rather pointedly. ''I guess that could be true. The *prospect* of comfort could be very enticing.''

Crane froze in place. He looked as if he'd just been hit by a strong gust of wind against which he had had to steel himself.

Ransom smiled, popped open the door, and left Crane behind.

''HE KNOWS SOMETHING,'' said Ransom as he looked out at the barn from the back window of Emily's room. The sky was overcast with dark blue-tinted clouds that threatened to shower the area with more snow.

Emily sat in the reading chair with her hands folded in the lap of her deep purple dress.

"Did he say something to make you think that?"

Ransom shook his head. "No, but it was the *way* he didn't say it. He was a bit too pleased to tell me he hadn't known Nathan before he came wandering onto the scene. It made me feel as if I hadn't asked the right question, and he was glad of it."

Emily's eyes were fixed on the bedpost nearest her as she considered this. At last she turned her incisive blue eyes back to Ransom, and said, "Was there anything else?"

Ransom sighed. "There was one thing I found very interesting. I reminded our Mr. Crane that he had been a suspect when the murder occurred. When I asked him if it was true that he and Sara were the only ones out here that night, he said that if there'd been anyone else he would've seen them."

"That sounds very logical," said Emily, her puzzled expression showing that she wasn't quite sure why Ransom found this of interest.

"But when I reminded him that he'd been asleep, he said, 'Yes, I was'—but his face turned red when he said it. He looked like I'd caught him in something."

Emily's eyes widened and her eyebrows arched, forming two carets over her eyes. "But you hadn't."

Ransom nodded. "That's just the point."

Emily looked at him for a moment, then her face brightened with understanding. "Oh, I see. When you reminded him that he'd been asleep, he blushed because he mistakenly thought you'd tripped him up and caught him in a lie."

Ransom lowered himself on the edge of the bed. "And I suspect that means that he wasn't asleep, and that he either saw or heard something." He paused for a moment, then added pointedly, "And that would explain Millie's puzzle."

"Hm?"

"Millie's puzzle. Why would a drifter suddenly decide to settle down?"

Emily continued to gaze at him for a moment, her hands gently flexing into one another as she silently turned this over in her mind, trying to work it out. Suddenly it came to her, and the corners of her mouth turned downward. "Oh, dear."

Ransom nodded. "Exactly. He's stayed here and hasn't spoken out because he's blackmailing someone."

"Or he's waiting for something," said Emily reflectively, "but...oh, dear!" she said again, her frown deepening. "The implications of that are very distressing. The most obvious person from whom he could extort money would be Sara, *if* she was the one he saw. She's the only one we know of connected with this case who has any money. It would explain more than anything else why she's allowed him to stay." Emily wrung her hands in her lap in a display of frustration so utterly uncharacteristic of her that it worried her companion. She said, "Oh, I do hope that Sara didn't murder her brother. I would hate to think my own brush with death had so sorely affected my judgment of human character."

Ransom was still very much aware of his own fears, which had been fading, that Emily had been seriously altered by her heart attack and subsequent surgery. But those fears had all revolved around the resignation with which she seemed to approach her own death, they were not out of any belief that her unerring insightfulness had been damaged. But he also remembered how quickly she'd regained her vigor the moment she'd become interested in the case he'd been working on at the time, so he refused to accept that there'd been any lasting damage to her sense of perspective.

"Emily, I would still take your impressions over the facts. Even though the facts—or what we know of them—continue to point in Sara's direction."

Emily smiled on him benignly. "Thank you, Jeremy."

He rose from the bed and went back to the window, resting the tips of his fingers against the sash.

"And when it comes to Hansen Crane, there are some good arguments against it being Sara that he might have seen, or that he's blackmailing—if that's what he's actually doing."

"Oh?" said Emily with interest.

"Well, first of all, the apartment over the barn isn't exactly palatial. I would think if he was extorting money from Sara he could do a better job of it."

"Remembering, of course, that he isn't used to very much. It may seem palatial to him."

Ransom glanced at her over his shoulder. "I *hardly* think—" he began in the tone he usually reserved for one of Gerald White's musings. He stopped suddenly, remembering to whom he was speaking, and modulated his tone. "I don't think he could fail to notice the difference between his apartment and this house."

The change of tone wasn't lost on Emily, who couldn't hide the amusement in her eyes. "The point is well taken."

Ransom looked away from her and cleared his throat. "Yes, well...secondly, even if Sara was giving Crane a place to stay because he knows something, it still doesn't explain why he'd *want* to stay here. Sara already has all her and her brother's money. He could've gotten whatever he wanted out of her and been long gone, which would've been infinitely safer."

"Hmm," said Emily thoughtfully. She looked as if she'd like to accept this, but found it a bit doubtful. "But Sara is still the only one we know of who has any money."

"That's right. But we have to remember that this is still pure speculation." He stopped, curled his lip, and added wryly, "If only Gerald could hear me now I would never hear the end of it! I'm forever admonishing him about the dangers of speculation."

"I wouldn't think you could hope to solve any mystery without allowing yourself to entertain various possibilities."

"Agreed. But there's a difference between doing that and letting your imagination run wild without any basis in fact." He paused again, then heaved a deep sigh. "I'll tell you one thing I *believe* to be fact. If we could find out what it is Crane's waiting around here for, we'd probably have the whole thing sewn up."

Emily didn't respond right away, and Ransom turned around to find her pressing her thumbs together as if she were invoking some kind of spell, and her gaze had once again fixed on the bedpost. After a few moments, she said quietly, "Pure speculation..."

"Emily?"

"Maybe that's what it is...pure speculation..."

"Emily, are you all right?"

Emily suddenly wakened from her semitrance and looked at him. "Oh, yes. I'm sorry."

Ransom hesitated a moment, his look of concern giving way to a smile. "All right, what is it?"

"I'm not sure. It's just the phrase you used seemed to set something off in my mind." She shook her head with frustration. "I do wish I didn't feel as if my mind was in such a muddle."

"It seems perfectly fine to me."

As Ransom said this his eyes were drawn back out the window by a sudden movement in the distance.

"Hello, what do we have here?"

Hansen Crane had come out of his apartment and stood at the top of the stairs testing the air. He turned up the collar on his coat and descended the stairs.

"That's funny."

"What is it?" Emily asked.

"Maybe nothing," he replied, not taking his eyes away from the window, "but I barely left Crane five minutes ago and he looked like he was settled in for a while. Now suddenly it looks like he's going somewhere."

"Hm," said Emily with a thoughtful nod, "perhaps our speculations weren't very far off."

"How do you mean?"

"Maybe you lit a little fire under Mr. Crane."

Crane reached the bottom of the steps and with what Ransom took to be a rather determined step headed for the house.

Ransom sighed. "I'm afraid not. He's coming to the house. He probably just has some work to do."

"Ah, well..." Emily said wistfully. She straightened herself up and said, "Now, what do you think our next step should be?"

"*Our* next move," said Ransom with emphasis, "is for you to get some rest."

She blinked at him. "I haven't done anything all day."

"You've been overexercising those wheels and gears of yours," he replied more sternly than he ordinarily would have. "And you need your rest."

"Not quite so much, I should think, as Sara needs her peace of mind."

"Her peace of mind has waited two years. It can wait another day. Besides, this is supposed to be a vacation. If you don't allow for at least a little of that then I'll begin to think it was a mistake for me to agree to look into this case."

Emily eyed him shrewdly for a few moments, though her smile never faded. "I'm not sure I think it gentlemanly of you to threaten an old woman."

He returned her gaze in kind, and replied, "Oh, Emily, I wouldn't dare."

Emily laughed, the renewed twinkle in her eyes a reminder to Ransom that she was on the mend (and that he had, indeed, been right to take on the case).

"So," he said with a return to his professional demeanor, "perhaps we can talk to Amy Shelton tomorrow morning. I think she's the next logical person."

"I agree," said Emily, not unlike a grandmother bestowing her blessing. Ransom couldn't help but smile.

"As for our holiday, tonight is the Nativity play that Millie told us about. I was wondering if you might like to go to that."

"That would be nice," said Emily. "If nothing else, it would be seasonal. And it might prove instructive."

"My dear Emily, I hardly think they'll put a new spin on the story."

Ransom left her resting in her usually unruffled fashion in the reading chair, a hand-knitted throw covering her lap and legs, and continuing her reading of *Lear*. He crossed the short expanse of living room to the kitchen and was surprised to find Sara alone at the table, quietly looking through a small wooden recipe card file.

"Oh," he said mildly, "I thought I saw Hansen Crane come in here."

Sara looked up from her search, and said, "He did. He just came in to borrow the car."

"The car?" Ransom echoed. He silently kicked himself for sounding so surprised, and once again chalked this uncharacteristic laxity up to being on holiday.

Sara looked up at him and blinked, obviously surprised by the reaction. "Yes."

"Does he borrow your car often?"

"Not really. He just wanted to run into town for some tobacco."

A smile spread across Ransom's face. "Did he, now?"

"Yes," said Sara, her expression becoming more quizzical by the minute. Since Ransom continued to stand there without saying anything more, apparently lost in thought, Sara finally asked, "Was there something I can do for you?"

"Oh, no," he replied, "you've done more than enough for me."

Ransom left Sara with a puzzled look on her face and went back up to the smoking room. It looked as if Emily had been right. Maybe their speculations weren't so far off.

EIGHT

RANSOM AND EMILY invited Sara to accompany them to church, but she begged off, claiming to have a slight headache. Emily narrowed her eyes at the young woman, and said, "You know, my dear, I think it's best in situations such as this to face people squarely. Otherwise you simply add to it by making them think you have something to be ashamed of."

Sara looked down at the floor, and replied quietly, "I really do have a headache. But...thank you."

"Very well," said Emily kindly, "you must do what you think best."

The First Presbyterian Church of LeFavre would have been more aptly named the First and Last, since it was the only church actually located within the town's limits, although there were three others in nearby Mt. Morgan. The church had been built between the First and Second World Wars with a sudden influx of money from the more wealthy members of the congregation who seemed to think that a healthy monument to God would stave off any further international conflict. A wide, brightly lit stone staircase, rather ostentatious given that there were only seven steps, led up to two enormous oak doors, curved at the top, each of which was decorated with proportionate wreaths of holly. Inside was a broad narthex surrounded by arches opening into recesses that led nowhere, except for the one directly across from the doors, which served as the entrance into the nave. Ransom felt as if he were entering a Swiss convent.

The narthex was so crowded with people it was easy to see why Sara hadn't wanted to come. It seemed that the annual Nativity play was popular enough that people had come from miles around to see it. Either that or they really didn't have much to do around there, which was the explanation Ransom chose to adopt. There was a slight dip in the general buzz of conversation as he and Emily entered the church, which quickly regained momentum and was accompanied by furtive glances in their direction.

They ran into Millie Havers almost immediately. She was dressed in a deep green skirt and jacket, and a cotton blouse of a contrasting shade. The phrase "Sunday-go-to-meeting outfit" wryly sprang to Ransom's mind, and he tried to dismiss it quickly for fear that, in his newly acquired laxity, what he was thinking would transfer to his face.

"Nice to see you could make it," said Millie a little too loudly. It was apparent that if there was any scandal connected with their having come, Millie was more than prepared to brazen it out.

"Thank you," said Emily. "My, but there's a lot of people here."

Millie nodded. "Lots of folks look forward to this, though you wouldn't know why when you've seen it. It's pretty much the same every year."

"Well, then," said Emily brightly, "it's taken on the aura of tradition."

"Like as not," replied Millie with a brisk nod. A silence fell among the three of them. Millie looked from Emily to Ransom, then back again. "Sara didn't come, I take it."

"No," said Emily, shaking her head regretfully, "she said she had a headache."

Millie's face clouded over. "Damn people, anyway, though I shouldn't talk that way in church."

Her gaze wandered over Emily's shoulder, and her face brightened with recognition. "'Scuse me, Miss Emily, I have to go say hello to Mrs. Parker. This is the first time she's been up and out since having her youngest." With this, Millie disappeared through the crowd, apparently parting it through sheer force of personality.

"Since having her youngest?" said Ransom, curling his lips. "Are we to assume that Mrs. Parker's eldest sprang out of her fully grown?"

"Jeremy..." Emily said warningly. The stern yet amused expression on her face made him laugh.

"Mr. Ransom!" called a familiar voice a little more loudly than Ransom would have preferred. He and Emily glanced around the crowd—a useless reflex on Emily's part since most of the churchgoers towered over her, making it almost impossible for her to see past the surrounding bodies. The voice called Ransom's name again, closer this time, and Ransom spun around to find Johnnie Larkin approaching from the outer door, smiling and waving his hand.

"Hi, there!" said Johnnie as he reached them.

"Hello," said Emily with cordial formality.

"Mr. Larkin," said Ransom.

"Wow! Big turnout," Johnnie went on with youthful exuberance. "Who'da thought they'd pack them in like this?"

Emily gazed at the young man with the kind of expression usually reserved by the elderly for when they suspect that our future generations might be unredeemably lost. She thought it best not to say anything.

"Where's Sara?"

"At home," Ransom replied.

Johnnie's face darkened. "Damn. I was hoping to sit with her."

"You're welcome to join us if you like," said Emily in a tone that caused Ransom to shoot a glance in her direction. Her eyes remained trained on the young man.

"Oh, thanks," he said amiably, "but I got a lot of friends here, and I'll probably hook up with one of them."

Emily smiled at him.

"You know most of the people around here, don't you?" Ransom asked.

"Sure I do. I been here long enough."

"Is Amy Shelton here?"

Johnnie's face went blank. "Amy? I...I thought I saw her. Why?"

"Miss Charters and I need to speak with her, and I thought perhaps you could point her out to us."

A smile spread across Johnnie's face. "Oh, yeah! Sara told me what you were doing. I hope you can help her."

Johnnie stopped speaking, and Ransom continued to look at him until the young man suddenly realized he hadn't answered Ransom's question.

"Oh! You wanted me to point her out." He laughed at himself, then craned his neck and rolled up on his toes to scan over the crowd. After a few moments, he said, "There she is! Come on! I'll introduce you."

Johnnie led the way through the crowd like a human cow-catcher parting the way for Ransom and Emily. Johnnie came to a stop by a timid young woman who stood with an older couple that Ransom took to be her parents. Amy hadn't noticed their approach.

"Hey, Amy! Hi!" Johnnie nodded a greeting to the couple but didn't speak to them.

Amy turned when she heard her name, but when she saw Johnnie her eyes darted away from him. She looked at her hands, then her shoes, then off to the side as if she'd just seen the last remnants of a vanishing spirit.

"Amy, I got to introduce you to somebody. This is Mr. Ransom and Miss Charters." He leaned in toward Amy, who leaned backward slightly. "Mr. Ransom is a detective, and he's looking into Nathan's murder."

Amy glanced at Ransom, her expression a mixture of curiosity and wariness, and a touch of something else Ransom thought he noticed in Sara when he'd first offered to investigate: hope.

Ransom's first impression of Amy Shelton was that Jeff Fields's assessment of her had been right. He couldn't imagine a young woman who seemed so diminutive and insignificant being able to wield a pitchfork with enough force to penetrate a man's heart. Then again, he couldn't imagine her generating enough force to penetrate a man's heart in any other way, either. He wondered if she had seemed this insignificant before the loss of her prospective fiancé.

"I'm Amy's mother," said the woman standing behind Amy.

Mrs. Shelton was an excessively angular woman with high, jutting cheekbones, close-set eyes, and a pointed nose. She looked like a clay figure that had been pinched in the center of the face by its creator. She stepped forward, between Amy and Johnnie, in a way that cut him out physically if not emotionally. She waved a hand over her shoulder in the general direction of the man standing behind her who was so nondescript as to be almost invisible. "And that's Amy's father."

Ransom stared into the woman's eyes for a moment before transferring his gaze to Amy.

"Miss Shelton, would you mind if Miss Charters and I stopped by tomorrow morning and asked you a few questions?"

"We're very busy," said the mother. "It's almost Christmas, and we have a lot to do."

Ransom didn't even bother to glance at the woman. His eyes remained on Amy, who continued to look at the floor.

"Miss Shelton?" he said with kind insistence.

There was a pause of the type in which one imagines the earth is holding its breath in anxious anticipation of the answer. Without looking up, Amy replied very quietly, "I don't mind."

"Amy..." said Mrs. Shelton with overt disappointment. She then clucked her tongue loudly and glanced over her shoulder at her husband, who looked as if he wouldn't have dared to interfere, even at his wife's entreaty.

"Would ten o'clock be all right?"

"Yes," said Amy, barely audibly.

"Well, there you are!" said Johnnie brightly. Mr. and Mrs. Shelton both looked at him so coldly that even Johnnie couldn't ignore the drop in temperature. He cleared his throat and muttered something about going off to find his friends, which he did immediately without looking back.

Whether or not Mrs. Shelton would have gone further in protesting the intrusion of the detective, any more discussion was interrupted by the church organ beginning to boom a seasonal hymn from the sanctuary, which Ransom took to be the church equivalent of blinking the lights in the lobby. Mr. and Mrs. Shelton hurriedly led Amy away, with Mrs. Shelton furiously whispering in the poor girl's ear, as the crowd began to pour into the nave of the church.

Emily slipped her arm through Ransom's as they followed the crowd.

"You don't care for our Mr. Larkin, do you, Emily?"

"I don't dislike him," said Emily in a tone that implied she would never actively dislike anyone, "I just wonder about his upbringing. It's amazing how many people, despite what they may wish for themselves, end up like their parents. Look at Sara and Nathan. They were brought up by their mother who by all accounts was quite a responsible woman, and without the influence of their father, they turned out to be quite responsible themselves."

"Unlike Johnnie Larkin."

"I fear not. Still, he's young."

They entered the cavernous nave with the stifled reverence usually reserved for unfamiliar places of worship. Even to the casual observer the interior of the church would have been impressive: the ceiling was extremely high and curved with exposed rafters that gave Ransom the feeling of being in the belly of a whale. On each side, there were seven towering windows of intricately designed stained glass depicting the stations of the cross.

The chancel was festooned with a controlled riot of poinsettias arranged as a circular frame around a small wooden replica of a stable, the centerpiece of which was, of course, the manger.

As usual, Emily's eyes were alive to everything around her. She surveyed the scene with admiration, letting out an occasional "Hm" to signify her approval. Ransom, on the other hand, was more aware of the curious unity that seemed to form among the congregation, the type of unity common to any large group of people who gather together for a common purpose, whether it be to worship or to stone someone. But a gathering in a church was usually imbued with a positive energy that was hard to resist, and, added to that, the fact that they were there to celebrate the apex of the Christian religion the atmosphere was doubly charged.

As Ransom helped Emily into her seat, he glanced back to the entrance and saw Jeff Fields coming into the church alone. He was wearing a black suit with a white shirt and black tie, but his straight posture managed to make him look as if he were still in uniform. He took a seat on the aisle in the last pew.

Appropriate Christmas hymns were provided by a children's choir that filed into pews on either side of the chancel with childish solemnity suitable to the occasion. The Christmas story was then read by a young boy of about ten years who seemed undaunted by the task, and actually seemed to understand some of what he was saying. His words were acted out by children of various ages to the accompaniment of the usual ooohs and aaaahs and reminiscent chuckles of the adults of the congregation. The minister gave a brief sermon on the importance of each section of the Christmas story, after which the congregation joined in singing several of the more familiar carols. Emily sat quietly during the proceedings, an unreadable smile on her face and the trademark sparkle in her eyes.

When the service was over, the congregation filed out of the church. The organist provided a steady stream of carols as they left. If anyone had paid extra attention to the sleuthing duo on their arrival, nobody seemed to take notice of their exit. The members of the congregation were much too caught up in their delight over the success of the children's performance.

"You seemed to have enjoyed yourself quite a bit," said Ransom as he ushered Emily to the car.

"Oh, yes," said Emily, "it's always nice to see traditions being passed on to the next generation. And they acted it nicely, don't you think?"

"I suppose," said Ransom, his mind going back to when he'd first met Emily in a case involving what she would always refer to as "a rather unfortunate production of *Love's Labors Lost*." She seemed to have a talent for adjusting her assessment of a production to the specific situation, making allowances for the children's performance that she never would have allowed for the more mature actors who had adulterated her Shakespeare.

"You know," Emily continued, "just being in a church reminded me of *King Lear*."

Ransom couldn't help stopping in his tracks he was so surprised by this.

"*Lear*? You're joking!"

"Oh, not because of the service, but because of the horrible muddle of Nathan Bartlett's murder. I don't know...being in church made me think that—just perhaps, mind you—being a detective is a sacred duty, a duty to put things right."

"I'm sure I've never thought of it that way," said Ransom, his tone more sardonic than he normally would have allowed for Emily.

She patted his arm for emphasis. "No, I'm not putting it correctly. What I mean is that it brought to mind that line from *Lear*: 'We'll talk with them too—Who loses and who wins; who's in, who's out—And take upon's the mystery of things, As if we were God's spies.'"

Ransom stared at her incredulously. "You got that from the Nativity play?"

"My mind wandered a little."

"That quotation is hardly appropriate to the season."

"Perhaps," Emily replied lightly, "but entirely appropriate to the situation."

WHILE the childish shepherds were watching their stuffed animal flocks by night in the sanctuary of the First Presbyterian Church, Hansen Crane lay on the narrow bed of his rough apartment watching nothing in particular on the small black-and-white television Sara had "loaned" him years ago, telling him at the same time that she didn't want it back.

The promise of snow Ransom had noticed earlier in the day had been realized in the form of a light flurry that had been falling for about an hour. The evening was very quiet and very dark, the only light being provided by the images flickering across the television screen that Crane had perched on the foot of his bed.

He was just beginning to doze off when he heard a loud rumble from the lower part of the barn. The sound started suddenly and stopped just as abruptly. Though Crane believed he knew what had caused the noise, he thought it best to go down and check it out, to make sure it wasn't anything more serious.

He hoisted himself out of bed with a grunt, retrieved his bulky wool coat from the back of the chair over which he'd slung it, and as he slipped it on he patted the pocket, feeling for the penlight he usually kept there. He then headed down the stairs on the side of the barn. He slid open the barn door and reached for the light switch and flicked it. But as with Nathan two years earlier, the action was not accompanied by the expected flood of light. He extracted the penlight from his pocket, and flicked on.

Though it didn't provide a lot of light, it was enough to see that it was just as he had thought—the woodpile had toppled over again.

Crane cursed at the sight and stepped closer for further inspection, all the while thinking of just what he was going to say to Johnnie tomorrow about his inability to perform even a simple task correctly.

He let out a satisfied "Humph" and straightened up, and it was at that moment he heard a step behind him.

He wheeled around but was so startled that he was unable to focus either the light or his attention on the assailant who had so quietly stolen up behind him. The only thing he saw in a quick flash was the block of wood just before it came in contact with his head.

The penlight fell from his hand with a soft clattering noise, and Crane was not far behind it in reaching the ground. For a few seconds after he sprawled out, immobilized by the blow, he was unsure whether the light had gone out or he'd suddenly been blinded. A flood of thoughts poured into his mind, the uppermost of which was the fact that he should have known this would happen. It was his last thought before the second blow fell.

NINE

RANSOM AND EMILY set off for Amy Shelton's house at about nine-thirty the next morning. Sara gave them explicit directions that were easy enough to follow given that the Sheltons lived in town, and there wasn't exactly a maze of streets in which to get lost.

As Sara helped Emily on with her coat, she said, "Please be gentle with Amy. I haven't seen her since the murder, but I understand that it...well, that she took it very hard."

"Of course," said Emily with a questioning look on her face.

Sara smiled sheepishly. "I know you will be...but could you caution Mr. Ransom as well?"

"I can assure you that Jeremy will adopt whatever attitude he finds suitable." As this didn't appear to placate Sara, Emily laid a thin, pale hand on the young woman's arm, and said gently, "I know that he can seem abrupt at times, but I've never really known him to be unkind."

Sara's cheeks turned pink, and she looked away from Emily's penetrating eyes as she replied, "Thank you."

The Sheltons' house was located on one of the more residential streets in LeFavre. Butler Drive was approximately the length of three city blocks and lined on both sides with large wood-framed houses, each centered on its own generous plot of ground. A few of the houses had their windows shuttered for the winter, indicating that they were owned by summer dwellers, but most of the houses were still occupied, as testified to by the presence of plentiful but tasteful Christmas decorations. It crossed Ransom's mind that this was what Chicago had probably looked like at the turn of the century, before multigenerational family residences became too costly or too cumbersome to be maintained and were either divided into ill-shaped apartments or demolished altogether and hauled away along with the trees that had sheltered them to make way for modern apartment complexes.

The Sheltons' house was an ample two-story structure painted a muted tan with decorative shutters in brown. A wide veranda surrounded the front and left side of the building.

Ransom helped Emily out of the car then up the walk to the five steps that led to the veranda. Emily's right hand held the railing and her left tightened on Ransom's arm as they made their way up the steps, which were lightly dusted with snow. It appeared that someone had shoveled before it had completely stopped snowing and hadn't returned to remove the remainder. When they reached the door, Emily loosened her grip and Ransom pressed the lighted doorbell. The door was opened before the second tone of the bell had completely faded. They were confronted by the stony countenance of Mrs. Shelton, who looked as if she might have raced for the door to beat all comers. Her face was red and she was making an effort to breathe evenly. She'd opened the door just far enough to fit her body in it as a blockade, and stood with her left hand gripping the outer doorknob with enough strength that her knuckles whitened. Ransom half expected the knob to bend in her hand.

"I thought I made it clear to you last night that we were too busy for this sort of thing!" she said without preamble.

"You made your feelings quite clear," said Ransom with calculated calmness, "as did your daughter."

Mrs. Shelton set her jaw and grasped the doorknob even tighter. Unattractive red blotches appeared on her fingers. "We have company, you know. We can't have our holidays upset like this."

"We'll only take up a few minutes of her time."

There was just a beat before Mrs. Shelton spurted out, "It's bad enough we all had to go through it once without Sara Bartlett dragging us all through it again."

Throughout this brief exchange Emily stood with her arm through Ransom's looking at Mrs. Shelton as if she were an unfamiliar creature that Emily feared might not be entirely responsible for its actions. "Surely you don't blame Sara for wanting to know who killed her brother?"

Mrs. Shelton transferred her glare to Emily, and said, "I blame the Bartletts for bringing this whole mess down on our heads."

"Really?" Emily replied incredulously.

Ransom sighed and cocked his head at the woman. "Mrs. Shelton, I realize that my investigation is purely unofficial, but the matter might very easily become official again."

"What?" the woman said sharply.

Ransom smiled, clearly aware of the effect his next words would have on her. "I mean that the case is not closed. The sheriff can ask your daughter to come to the station at any time to be questioned."

"Questioned!" Mrs. Shelton replied venomously. She began to sputter, apparently so stunned that she was unable to find exactly the right words with which to tell the detective exactly what she thought of him. She sounded like a motor boat that couldn't quite get started. Ransom was just about to interrupt the performance to ask her point-blank whether or not she was going to let them see her daughter, when he was saved the trouble by the young woman herself.

"Momma," Amy's voice came from behind the door.

Mrs. Shelton started and ducked her head back behind the door, twisting the knob in her hand as if she had hold of Ransom's head and was trying to snap it off.

"Gladys wants to know what you want for dinner."

"Tell her I—"

With uncharacteristic assertiveness, Amy cut her off. "I think you should go talk to her yourself."

"You what?" the mother snapped.

Amy gently pulled the door open the rest of the way as she repeated calmly, "I think you should go talk to her yourself." There was a slight pause, then Amy added much more meekly, "I won't remember. I'll probably get it wrong. It would be much better if you did it."

Mrs. Shelton glanced from her daughter to Ransom, who she

remembered to face with a scowl, then she heaved a world-weary sigh designed to let everyone within earshot know that she was always being sorely tried.

"Oh, all right!" she said as she marched down the hallway, her wooden heels thumping noisily. For all her ferocity, Ransom thought her exit made her look more like a petulant child than a protective mother.

"I'm sorry," said Amy, her eyes downcast so that she appeared to be apologizing to the floor. "Won't you come in?"

They followed her into the hallway, the floors of which were heavily varnished hardwood. The most prominent feature was a staircase, curved at the bottom, with an ornately carved mahogany banister. In the curve of the staircase stood an enormous Christmas tree decorated entirely in white lights and tiers of gold garland so carefully arranged that they might have been done by an interior designer. The tree stood very straight and erect, not as if it were proud to be displayed in such a stately home, but more as if it were afraid to droop. Ransom wouldn't have been surprised to find the branches trembling.

All of the visible wood had been polished to within an inch of its life, which elicited a muffled "Oh, my" from Emily. Just to the left of the door stood a big, sturdy coatrack with hooks that reached out threateningly—as if it would snatch the coats off the backs of the passing guests and not be terribly circumspect about whether or not the guests came with them. A spacious living room was visible through an archway on the right. It was antiseptic and the carpeting and furniture all looked as if they'd never been touched, let alone used. Ransom thought with an inward chuckle that there should be a red velvet rope stretched across the entrance.

Amy led them through the second doorway on the left, closing the door behind them and inviting them to sit on the leather couch under the window on the far wall. A glass display coffee table flanked the couch and two matching chairs were opposite it. Displayed beneath the glass of the table were a fishing reel and a variety of brightly colored lures.

Amy sat across from them in one of the chairs. She was wearing a dark blue knee-length skirt, a white blouse, and had a white angora sweater draped over her shoulders. To Ransom, the ensemble made her look like an overaged teeny-bopper. She folded her hands neatly in her lap and crossed her ankles in the most ladylike fashion.

"Your father is a fisherman, I take it," said Ransom.

"It's a quiet sport," Amy replied in a forlorn tone that suggested that she didn't think further explanation was necessary. "I really have to apologize for my mother."

Emily breathed a gentle tut-tut to let her know that she didn't need to do this.

"Oh, yes," Amy said, lifting her eyes to Emily's for the first time. "I'm afraid my mother...my mother is a bit sensitive when it comes to 'the family name.'" She apostrophized the phrase with some distaste. "Any hint of scandal sets her off. So you can imagine what bringing up Nathan's murder does to her."

"No," said Emily kindly, "I can only imagine what it does to you. And we're the ones who should apologize. I'm sorry if we've made things more difficult for you."

"No. No, you didn't," said Amy, looking down at her hands. Emily took this as a sign that Amy couldn't look her in the eye while telling a lie, no matter how politely that lie might be meant. "It doesn't matter. I only want you to find out who killed Nathan," Amy said more forcefully than she'd spoken before. Then she faltered. "It's just that..."

Her voice trailed off and Emily attempted to complete the thought for her. "It's just that you're afraid the killer may be someone of whom you are fond."

With tears welling up in her eyes, Amy responded with a nod of her head.

"I think you can rest easy on that point," said Emily. "We don't believe that Sara killed Nathan."

Amy looked up suddenly, the look in her eyes showing that she was grateful she hadn't had to say it. The tears had started to run down her cheeks.

"It's just that everyone seems to believe it."

"Well, we don't necessarily," said Ransom slowly, "but I'd be interested to know why *you* do."

Amy looked startled for a moment, her eyes darting back and forth from Ransom to Emily as if beseeching their forgiveness for something.

"Me? I don't believe she did it!" There was a slight hesitation before she continued. "But everyone seems so sure and..." Her voice trailed off again.

Emily smiled at her. "You like Sara Bartlett, don't you," she said, making it a statement rather than a question.

"I did," said Amy. A tear that had been sliding straight down her cheek had its course altered when it was caught in the small crease caused by the slight smile she exhibited. The tear disappeared in the corner of her mouth. "I do," she amended, "it's just..."

"I understand," said Emily. Ransom glanced at her and raised an eyebrow. Emily continued more for his benefit than for Amy's. "You *want* to still like Sara but you don't know what to think."

"Yes," said Amy, nodding her head eagerly as if greatly relieved that someone really *did* understand.

"Well," said Ransom, taking charge of the conversation from which he felt he'd been excluded long enough, "perhaps if we can clarify the matter things will be able to get back to normal."

Amy looked at Emily as if in mute appeal for further consolation. Emily noticed a curious similarity to the desperation that often appeared in Sara's eyes: a silent cry for help dulled by the belief that no help was to be found. She gave Amy a single nod, which seemed to signify that she could trust the detective.

"All right," said Amy.

Ransom cleared his throat. "Miss Shelton, I understand that you had a date with Nathan on the night he was killed."

"Yes, but it was canceled. The weather was so bad."

Ransom raised his right eyebrow. "You say that as if you don't quite believe it."

Amy lowered her head but not before Ransom noticed her rueful smile. "The weather *was* very bad. I suppose it's just...vanity. I guess I thought—at the time—that if he really cared he would have come over despite the snow, but that's just silly. I wouldn't have wanted him to risk his life or anything." She raised her head and blinked away a fresh onslaught of tears. "It's just I loved him so much."

"Had he ever broken a date before?"

Amy responded with a shake of her head.

"Did you think there was another reason for it, other than the storm?"

"Not really," she replied with a pronounced lack of conviction.

Ransom studied her for a moment. He crossed his legs, laid his right hand on his uppermost knee and began to silently drum his fingers across it.

"Did you notice anything different about Nathan just before he was killed?"

She looked up at him. "Different?"

"Yes. Was he acting differently at all?"

Amy had been looking at Ransom. She slowly turned her head toward Emily. Ransom sighed and his drumming fingers stiffened and slowed. "Miss Shelton, we've heard that Nathan was a bit preoccupied just before the murder."

Amy lowered her eyes to her lap. "Yes, he was."

She stopped and Ransom struggled to retain his rapidly diminishing patience. Emily shot him a concerned glance, then turned to Amy and said, "Do you have any idea what was on his mind?"

The peculiar half smile returned to Amy's face. "I thought it was because of me."

"I beg your pardon?"

Amy looked up. "I thought it was because of me. I thought he was working himself up to asking me to marry him."

The slight quaver in Amy's voice caused Emily's eyebrows to slide upward and Ransom's fingers to pause in their steady rhythm. "And were you proven wrong?" Emily asked. Despite the lightness of her tone, Emily's eyes had narrowed and were trained on the young woman as if she were trying to see into her mind.

"After a few days I thought it couldn't be what I'd been thinking. Nathan was usually very up-front. I'd never known him to be timid. And"—she paused and glanced from Emily to Ransom, her cheeks flushing red—"and I'd given him every reason to believe I'd accept." Amy stopped and pressed her fingers against her forehead as if admitting this had caused her physical pain. The three of them sat in silence for a few moments. When Amy finally moved her hand, it was to wipe away her freshly flowing tears. "But like I said, after a few days I realized it wasn't that he was worried about proposing."

"Did you ask him what was bothering him?" asked Ransom.

"Many times. Many times. At first jokingly, because...but he didn't tell me—he said it was nothing. Then I began to think maybe what was bothering him was that he didn't want to...that he wanted to stop seeing me. So I pressed him about it."

"What did he say?"

"I asked him if he was unhappy with me."

She stopped for a beat and smiled as the scene came back to her. "He put his arms around me and hugged me and told me I was just being silly."

"But you didn't let it go at that," said Emily, giving the young woman a benevolent, understanding smile.

For the first time, Amy gave a little laugh which was checked quickly by a demure cough into her hand. "Of course not. I kept pressing him to tell me what was wrong—once I knew it wasn't me I wasn't so afraid—and he finally...after a lot of...well, he finally told me."

She stopped again, and Ransom fought the desire to finally let go of his temper and yell "And?" He was spared this by Emily putting the word to Amy much more gently than Ransom could have managed at that point.

Amy gave another little cough, and said, "He said he thought he'd seen a ghost."

"A ghost?" said Emily with perfectly Victorian amazement.

Amy smiled. "I know. I thought he was putting me on because I'd been pestering him. But that's what he said."

Emily leaned forward slightly in her chair. "Did he say anything further?"

"Well, I asked him if he meant he'd seen it at Hawthorne House, because there's always stories about old houses, and that's when—" She paused again and looked at Emily and Ransom in turn. "That's when he said something even more strange."

"Stranger than that he'd seen a ghost?" said Ransom wryly.

"Yes. He said he'd seen it all around."

Both Emily and Ransom emitted a "Hmm" in unison, sounding so much alike one would have thought they really were related.

"He changed the subject after that, and I didn't pursue it. He tried for the rest of the evening to act perfectly normal...but I could tell there was still something wrong."

Ransom uncrossed his legs. "Did you tell all of this to the sheriff at the time?"

Amy shook her head blankly. "Why would I?"

"Because it might be important."

Amy mustered enough spirit to wrinkle her forehead and stare at the detective as if she thought he might be pulling her leg. She shook her head as she answered, "A ghost can't stab somebody, Mr. Ransom."

Ransom sat back in his chair and folded his arms, a smile spreading across his face.

"Some of them can."

Ransom and Emily didn't stay much longer after that. There wasn't much more Amy could tell them, and Ransom didn't feel the need to ask her about her own alibi for the time of the murder—that had already been checked by the sheriff.

Amy led them from the room, pausing by the door to glance down the hallway before proceeding, presumably to check for the presence of her mother, though Ransom didn't know what difference her mother's presence would've made to their exit. She showed them to the door and went with them out onto the veranda. Just as Ransom and Emily were about to descend the stairs, Ransom stopped and turned to Amy.

"Miss Shelton, one last thing. Last night I thought I noticed a certain...coolness on your part toward Johnnie Larkin...."

Amy lowered her eyes to the ground, her face turning beet red, "Not really. Not..."

"I was wondering what the cause of that was."

Amy didn't answer. Though Emily had stopped along with Ransom, she hadn't looked back at Amy until Ransom asked this. Amy's reaction created a great deal of interest in the old woman.

"I don't mean to embarrass you," Ransom continued, "but the relationship between all the people who were here at the time of the murder is very important."

Amy lifted her head just enough for them to see her lower lip was trembling. "I didn't have a relationship with Johnnie then."

Emily's eye widened and she inclined her head just slightly. "*After* Nathan was murdered?"

A fresh flood of tears streamed down Amy's cheeks and for the first time she seemed in danger of breaking down completely.

"I was so lonely, you see...and I needed someone to talk to. And so did Johnnie. He and Nathan were...friends. And I guess Sara was so upset she couldn't talk to anyone. So Johnnie sought me out. And we spent most of the time talking about Nathan. Most of the time."

Emily had slipped an arm around the young woman. She patted her arm, and said, "There, now. There's nothing to be ashamed of. It was a very difficult time for you."

Ransom stood staring at Amy through thoughtfully narrowed eyes. "Did Johnnie break it off?"

Amy shook her head. "There was nothing...serious to break off. He just drifted away. But...I should've expected that, because I'm sure Sara needed him eventually, and he's always had a crush on her. I think I was just..."

Emily patted her arm again, but Amy broke away from her and ran into the house, shutting the door behind her. As Ransom led

Emily down the steps he said, "It seems our little Johnnie isn't above 'comforting the widow.'"

Emily clucked her tongue, her eyes trained on the walk beneath them as she replied, "Oh, I hope Miss Shelton is right. I hope he wasn't just taking advantage of the situation." From the tone of voice in which she'd said this, Ransom gathered that this strand of hope was very tenuous.

Inside the house, Amy paused by the door and made an attempt to wipe away her tears with the tips of her fingers, succeeding in little more than smearing the salty streams across her face. She listened intently for a moment for any sound of her mother's approach. Though the interview had been short, it had been exhausting, and the last thing she wanted to do at that moment was face another interrogation from her mother.

Hearing nothing, she started for the staircase. She hesitated when she reached the tree, looking at it with no discernible expression. After a moment, she reached up and unhooked a part of a gold garland from one of the branches over which it was draped and released it, letting it droop down unattractively and leaving a gaping dark space on the side of the tree.

She smiled and went up the stairs.

IT WAS SHORTLY after Ransom and Emily had left for their meeting with Amy Shelton that Sara made her circuit of the bathrooms, collecting soiled towels and replacing them with fresh. She loaded the used towels in a round laundry basket and headed downstairs.

"Have you seen Hansen this morning?" Sara asked as she came into the kitchen.

Millie looked up from the bowl in which she'd been mixing the ingredients for pumpkin pies. She'd already made the crusts and fitted them into four pie plates, which she had sitting on the counter. She swiped a loose strand of hair off her forehead with the back of her wrist and sighed. "Not hide nor hair," she said in answer to Sara's question.

"The front walk hasn't been shoveled yet from last night. I swept off the porch. I suppose I can do the walk...."

"Nonsense," said Millie, "you let Hansen do it. Lord knows he should earn his keep."

Sara pursed her lips and looked down through the back-door window. "He usually does it without being asked."

Millie went back to mixing the pie filling. "He's probably out there sleeping it off."

"Oh, Millie! Hansen doesn't drink. At least, not that I know of."

"He's a man," said Millie with a shrug.

Sara laughed. "Does your Herbert drink?"

Millie shrugged again. "He's a man, too. But Herbert doesn't do anything to excess. Lord knows there's some things I wish he would!"

"Well, I'd better go check on him and tell him there's work to do," said Sara with a definite lack of enthusiasm.

She crossed the kitchen and reached for her coat, which was hanging on one of the pegs by the back door, pausing for a moment with her hand resting on the sleeve. If Millie had been facing her, she would have seen the black shadow that passed across Sara's face, a shadow caused by a sudden, sickening sense of déjà vu. She shook her head briskly as if physically attempting to cast off the cloud, plucked the coat from the peg, and slipped her arms into the sleeves. Then she went out the back door, letting it close behind her with a soft thud.

Millie continued to blend the pie ingredients in the bowl until they reached a consistency that met with her satisfaction. She popped the blades of the mixer into a bowl of water she'd left in the sink for just that purpose and pushed the mixer to the back of the counter out of her way. Then she took a long-handled wooden spoon, picked up the bowl, tilted it, and began to push the filling into the crust-lined pans with the spoon.

She had just finished filling the second and was about to start the third when the back door was flung open with such violence that it banged loudly against the wall, startling Millie so badly that she dropped the bowl onto the counter. She rushed over to the steps leading to the back door and looked down. There was

Sara, half collapsed with her back against the door and her eyes closed. To Millie she looked like a deflated accordion.

"What is it? What's wrong?" she said anxiously.

Sara's eyes popped open and she turned her face to Millie. She looked at first as if she didn't quite recognize her, then suddenly her expression changed, as if a curtain had fallen from her eyes, revealing her surroundings as familiar.

"Oh, Millie!" she exclaimed, racing into her arms. She buried her face in Millie's shoulder and began to cry.

"What is it?" said Millie, who was becoming greatly alarmed.

Sara lifted her head and tried to focus her bleary eyes on Millie's face.

"What is it?" said Millie again, almost shaking her.

"Oh, Millie! It's happened again!"

JEFF FIELDS arrived soon after receiving the call. He went out to the barn to view the body. Even with the barn doors fully open there was not quite enough sunlight to take in the scene in detail. He flicked the switch to the right of the door and the work lights sprang on. He crouched by the inert form of the handyman and surveyed the damage, paying special attention to the head. When he rose, he was shaking his head. He didn't need a coroner to tell him what had happened, but he'd have to call him just the same.

Fields went back to the house and made the necessary calls, then had a brief talk with Millie, who seemed to be more aggravated than shocked by the situation. She told him what she knew, which amounted to little more than explaining that she was in the kitchen when Sara ran in as if she were being chased by the devil and said "It's happened again." Fields then asked her where Sara had gone.

"She's waiting in the library," said Millie, pursing her lips and rolling them sideways as if she were moving a particularly vexatious plug of tobacco around into her cheek.

"Thank you," said Fields as he started to leave the room.

"Wait," said Millie, catching him by the arm, "you listen here, Jeff. Sara's really shaken up by this, so you go easy with her."

Fields stared at her a moment, his expression unchanging. "I always have," he said with meaning, "you know that."

Millie wouldn't relent. "Then you be easier than easy."

Fields hesitated as if he would have liked to say something more, but without so much as a shake of his head he left the room.

Though Sara didn't usually like the closeness of the library, she was finding it oddly comforting at that particular moment, like a cat who retreats to a small space for an imagined sense of security. She glanced up as Fields entered the library. She closed a book that was lying open and unread in her lap and set it on the table by her chair. A blue-and-white cup of tea that Millie had provided to settle her nerves rattled in its saucer as the book reached the table. She absently smoothed back her hair, then dropped her hands to the arms of the chair and turned away from him.

"He *is* dead, isn't he?" she asked quietly.

"Yes."

"Was it an accident?"

There was a barely perceptible beat before Fields said, "No, he was murdered."

Sara's head snapped up, her expression full of dull shock. "Murdered? But the woodpile...I thought...he was warned..."

Fields shook his head. "Someone tried to make it look like an accident, but it wasn't."

"Murder..." said Sara in disbelief.

There was another pause during which Fields stared at her as if he were studying her face for a sign of something, while at the same time worried that he might find it. Finally he asked with quiet firmness, "Sara, what did you mean when you said 'It's happened again'?"

"What?" she replied, her face screwed up with confusion.

"After you discovered the body you came running back into the house and said to Millie, 'It's happened again.' What did you mean?"

She answered falteringly. "I meant...only that...I guess that I'd found another body. That's all."

"You're sure."

She nodded.

"You're sure you didn't mean there'd been another murder?"

She looked up at him. "Well...I might have assumed...I don't know, it was such a shock to find him like that...what difference does it make?"

Fields continued to stare at her as ideas ran through her head, until suddenly the difference became clear. Instead of looking shocked or angry, all strength and emotion seemed to drain out of her at once. Her limbs went slack and her head drooped as if she simply no longer had the power to hold it up. Rather than defeat or sadness, her expression seemed to be one of complete and utter hopelessness.

"Oh, I see," she said vacantly. "That would've been a slip. It would've meant I knew he'd been murdered."

For the first time there seemed to be a chink in Fields's armor. "Sara, I don't want to have to question you, but you know I've got to."

"I know."

"When was the last time you saw Crane alive?"

"Just before Mr. Ransom and Miss Charters left for the play last night. About six-thirty, I guess. I saw him closing up the barn."

"The play. You didn't see him after that?"

"No."

There was a long pause, then Fields asked, "Was there anyone out here with you last night?"

She turned her dulled eyes up to him and shook her head. "No. Nobody was here but me. And no, I didn't see or hear any cars or anyone come to visit Hansen. I spent the evening watching *White Christmas* on the television up in my room, and then the news, and after that my guests came home. I didn't hear anybody or see anybody or talk to anybody in all the time they were gone. And yes, I know how that looks. I know it looks like I was the only one out here again when somebody got murdered, and I know what everyone will say. They'll say the same thing you're thinking. But I didn't kill Hansen, and I didn't kill my brother.'' She buried her face in her hands and wept audibly.

Fields slowly moved to her side in fits and starts, his tentative approach at odds with his granitelike expression. Once he was by her side he reached out a hand toward her shoulder, but withdrew it just before making contact. A few seconds went by, then he tried again, successfully bringing himself to lay a sturdy, comforting hand on her shoulder.

Sara bristled slightly at his touch, then seemed to relax a bit, though she continued to cry quietly.

With hand in place, Fields crouched down beside her, and said, "Sara, I don't believe you killed Hansen, and I never believed you killed Nathan, either."

She turned her face, wet and distorted with crying, toward him and said, "Yes, you did."

Fields closed his eyes and exhaled. "I had to proceed...I had to go on what evidence there was. I had to go on the facts. That doesn't mean I believed them."

"Of course you did," she said sadly. "Don't you think I can tell?"

His normally impassive face looked pained. He had worked for years to cultivate an unreadable countenance, and was now distressed to find that the one time he'd needed most to remain a blank page, when Nathan was killed, he'd somehow betrayed himself.

He sighed. "Sara, I've been trained to look at the facts and only the facts—it's the most important part of my job—to look at the facts and no matter what, not let my emotions get all tangled up in what I can see, because that's the easiest way to screw up a case."

She shook herself loose from him, stood, and crossed to the window, keeping her back to him. "I could see it in your face, you know—back when Nathan was killed—I could see it in your face that you thought somehow I'd done it."

Fields had remained crouched by the chair. He rose slowly. "All you saw in my face was frustration. I couldn't believe you would kill anyone, let alone Nathan, and I couldn't prove you hadn't done it."

Sara stared out the window, tears hovering on the rims of her lower lids as if they'd been arrested there by his words. There was a glimmer of understanding in her mind that she knew hadn't been there before, and she couldn't quite bring herself to focus on it. But in her mind she could see Jeff as he was when he'd come there in response to the call about Nathan's murder. He'd seemed gruff and cold, and as the investigation wore on he grew even colder and more irritable, to the point where she knew that he thought she was guilty. For the first time she began to have an inkling that his actions may have had a completely different meaning, one she'd misunderstood. But if she was mistaken, it was now too deeply rooted to be swept away in only a minute.

"And what do the facts tell you now? That I'm guilty again?"

"Circumstances don't look good," he said, "I know how it looks."

"So do I," Sara said dully.

Fields crossed to her, this time without hesitation, and stood close behind her, his hands on her upper arms.

"Sara, just because I've taught myself not to listen to my emotions, that doesn't mean that my heart's stopped talking to me. I know you wouldn't kill anyone."

There was a long silence. At last Sara reached up and covered his right hand with her left. "I was right. It's happened again. Only this time it's worse."

TEN

AFTER THEIR INTERVIEW with Amy Shelton, Ransom walked Emily back to the car in silence. He saw to it that she was safely buckled into the seat belt on the passenger side, then rounded the car and climbed in behind the wheel. Emily stared at him as he stuck the key in the ignition, held his hand there for a moment without turning it, then released the key and sat back in the seat, his eyes gazing all the while through the front windshield.

"Jeremy, what is it?"

"Hm? Nothing," he replied. He made an abortive reach for the ignition then sat back again.

"It must be something," said Emily.

He sucked in his cheeks for a moment, then exhaled and turned to her. "It's this unbridled speculation we've been indulging in."

Emily hesitated for a second, then said, "Well, I said before—"

"No, it's not that," he said, gently cutting her off as he turned his gaze back to the windshield. "Emily, I've just had the most peculiar idea, and I don't know if I finally have let my imagination run wild with me."

Emily looked at the side of his face, her eyes playful. "And are you going to tell me what it is?"

Ransom could feel his face flush. Once again he'd forgotten that Emily was not his partner, Gerald, and unlike him would be far less inclined to accept the role of Boswell. He cleared his throat, and said, "Sorry. If I hesitate it's because the idea seems crazy...and yet, it fits what we've learned so far." He turned to her and explained more forthrightly, "It's everyone's insistence that Sara must've killed Nathan, and money being the only possible motive."

"Yes?"

"Well, what if they're right?"

"Jeremy, I refuse to believe—"

He raised his palm, signaling her to wait. "I don't mean about Sara, I mean about the money."

There was a pause during which Emily's eyebrows knit very close together. "You mean that someone else killed Nathan for the money? But who?"

He sighed very deeply. "It was what Nathan said about seeing a ghost. First of all, from what we've learned of Nathan Bartlett, does he strike you as the type who would imagine things?"

Emily considered this for a moment, then said matter-of-factly, "No. He kept the books for Hawthorne House, and I'm inclined to believe that you won't find a fanciful bookkeeper outside of your Mr. Dickens."

"*Hardly* fanciful," said Ransom, with slight annoyance.

Emily smiled. "But what is your point?"

"Just this: When he said he saw a ghost, he meant it almost literally."

"Almost?"

"I think what he was saying was that he saw someone either that he didn't expect to see *here,* or that he didn't expect to see at all." He paused for a moment, turning a significant glance toward Emily as he said, "Perhaps someone he didn't even know was still alive."

Emily gazed at him for a few moments, her lips pursed and her eyebrows arched. Suddenly her eyes widened and the furrows over her brow deepened so much it almost made her look cross. "Their *father?*" she said, her voice rising so high at the end that it practically disappeared.

"Um hm."

"But Jeremy, even supposing you're right about what Nathan meant when he said he'd seen a ghost, it could've been anyone. He could've seen someone from school, someone from Chicago, an old friend. Even an old enemy. What makes you think it was his father?"

Ransom shook his head ruefully. "I admit it's purely conjecture. Very thin conjecture. And you're right, it very well could've been anyone. But it's also an educated guess based on some rather uneducated gossip.''

"Yes?"

"Well, assuming that the 'ghost' he saw was someone from his past, whoever it was caused him some distress—two different people noticed he was preoccupied.''

"That still could've been anyone," Emily interjected.

"Except for one thing. A few days after he said it, he was dead. And we keep coming back to the money. If Nathan was murdered for his money, and Sara didn't do it, it had to be some-one else who stood to inherit.''

"But Sara was the only one to inherit, wasn't she?"

"That's right. But their father has been estranged from them for years. He couldn't know how their money would fall out.''

Emily thought for a moment. "Assuming their father could possibly be the murderer, how could he inherit? He divorced their mother ages ago.''

Ransom sighed. "I can tell you, but you're not going to like it. The only way he could inherit is if neither Nathan nor Sara had made wills, and they both died. At least, I believe their money would go to their father, divorced or not, if they had no other immediate family.''

Emily blinked. "You're quite correct. I don't like it at all. If that's true, then Sara's life is in danger.''

"Well, if it'll ease your mind any, this conjecture of mine is probably just a bunch of rot. It's been two years since Nathan was killed and Sara's still alive. It's just as likely that Jeff Fields really is the murderer and his plans to marry Sara just fell through.''

"That's true...there's only one problem with that: Nathan had seen Jeff Fields for three years before being killed. Why would Fields *suddenly* have needed to kill him?"

"Maybe he learned something about Fields that wasn't to his advantage.''

Emily clucked her tongue. "That still wouldn't explain why

Nathan said he'd seen a ghost so late in the game. Oh, Jeremy," said Emily with frustration, "the timing is all wrong. It doesn't work with Fields, and if what you're thinking is true, then Sara would've been killed long ago. But she's still alive. Why all the waiting? Why all this time in between events? It's all most irritating. And I can't see why their father..."

"You're right," said Ransom with a degree of self-disgust as he sat up and turned the key in the ignition, "it's a perfectly ludicrous idea." He drove to 130th Street and headed back toward Hawthorne House.

Emily clenched her right hand into a frail fist and rubbed it into the open palm of her left, all the while gazing out the window as she mulled over all they'd said. Suddenly her face brightened.

"Oh, how perfectly stupid of me! *King Lear!*"

Far from expecting this response, Ransom was completely bewildered. "What?"

Emily shook her head and clucked her tongue with disappointment. "How unbelievably stupid I've been! I should have seen it before. And what makes it worse is that I've been rereading it, and never once made the connection."

"Emily, what are you talking about?"

Emily turned to him, and explained. "*King Lear,* the father who was cast off by his daughters and then turns to them for help. And all that tragedy happens after he has been spurned." Emily suddenly turned away from him, looking out the windshield as if a fresh idea had just sprung up in front of the car. "Oh, dear! I wonder if that really happened?"

"What?" said Ransom, his exasperation increasing. It was the first inkling he'd ever had of what it was like for Gerald to be his partner.

"Of course," she continued as if turning her thoughts over aloud, heedless of Ransom's presence, "I don't suppose he really would've had to contact her. Then again, one would think he would have tried that first before resorting to murder...."

Ransom's expression had changed from exasperation to concern. "Emily, I think I've been running you around too much. I brought you up here for rest, and I've been the one that's keeping you from it.''

This broke in upon her reverie. She shook her head, and said, ''No, Jeremy. I think I've had quite enough rest already. That's the only reason I can see for my muddled thinking.'' She shifted very purposefully toward him in her seat. ''Now, there are some things we need to know: First of all, we need to know whether or not Nathan and Sara made out wills, and we need to find out if it's possible for their father to be here without their recognizing him.''

''Well, we can assume that Nathan *did* recognize him.''

''But not readily,'' Emily said correctively, ''or else he would've acted on it.''

''Maybe he did. That could be what got him killed.''

Emily folded her hands in her lap. ''I suppose that could be true...but still...that wouldn't explain why Sara didn't recognize him as well.''

''How old were they when their father and mother divorced?''

''I don't know,'' Emily replied, elevating her shoulders in a slight shrug. ''All Sara said was that her mother and father divorced when she was a child, and that the divorce was acrimonious. I wonder just how acrimonious it was.'' She paused for a moment, then posed a question more to herself than to Ransom, in a tone of utter disbelief. ''*Could* Sara's father be around here without her recognizing him?''

Ransom narrowed his eyes and began to drum his fingers on the top of the steering wheel. ''You would think that even if she didn't recognize him outright, there would be something familiar about him.''

''Yes, but that's just it,'' said Emily with renewed vigor, ''you'd also think that if Nathan had known their father was in the area, he would've said something to her. And yet she's never said a word about her father, except when she told me of the divorce. I can't believe she would've held that back if she knew. So the most important thing we need to do is locate Sara's father!''

"Well," said Ransom with a heavy sigh, "I have another bit of conjecture for you that you're going to like even less. If their father really is here, I have an idea who he might be."

"Hansen Crane," said Emily vacantly, almost as if she hadn't been listening to him.

"I give up," said Ransom, laughing, "I might as well turn my badge over to you and retire to Sussex and keep bees. Or do whatever Dr. Watson did when he retired."

Emily smiled appreciatively, but replied with a simple tut.

"And how did you arrive at Mr. Crane for the role of Mr. Bartlett?"

"The same way you did, Jeremy, simply arithmetic. He's the only one we know of who's involved in this case who's old enough to have been Nathan and Sara's father. Of course, I *suppose* it doesn't have to be somebody connected with Hawthorne House...and in that case, it could be anyone in the area."

"Except it would have to be someone who came here in the past five years, since Nathan and Sara came here."

"Not necessarily. You have to remember, Jeremy, that we have no idea where this father has got to since he left their mother. He could've settled here long ago."

"I suppose so," said Ransom with a heavy sigh, "but I really do like Hansen Crane in the role."

"Why?"

"Because he's hiding something. I'm sure of it."

Emily sighed with frustration. "But even if it were true, and Hansen Crane was their father, it still leaves us with more questions than it answers."

"Yes," Ransom interjected, "the first and foremost being why did it take Nathan so long to recognize him? Crane was here for quite a while before Nathan was killed. Which would mean that Nathan didn't recognize him at first...or..." His voice trailed off as he mentally went through the possibilities. Emily picked up the thread.

"Or...somehow Nathan discovered who Hansen Crane really

was. Remember, Millie told me that Nathan asked a lot of questions about Crane when he first showed up.''

"Yes, but that could have been nothing more than natural worry on his part.''

They fell silent for a few moments, each lost in their own thoughts as they sped on toward Hawthorne House. Finally Ransom shook his head. "I still have trouble believing that they wouldn't have recognized their father somehow.''

"Hmm," said Emily, giving this due consideration. "Mr. Crane seems to be a very credible character…very much of a type. Maybe it's simply a very credible disguise.''

Ransom looked at her, returning the playful smile she'd given him earlier. "A lost relative showing up in disguise? How perfectly Shakespearean.''

Emily could not help but laugh at the struggle he seemed to be having to keep the smugness out of his tone. She refolded her hands, and said, "Well, Jeremy, I believe you would say touché, wouldn't you?''

Hawthorne House had just come into view when Emily uttered an involuntary "Oh, my!" Ransom saw immediately what had drawn her attention. In the drive alongside the house were several cars, two of which were readily identifiable as belonging to the County Sheriff's Department, along with Johnnie Larkin's beat-up hatchback.

Emily's hand went up to the side of her face as she said, "Jeremy, you don't think…"

"It could be anything," Ransom replied with an assurance he didn't really feel.

Ransom applied additional pressure to the gas pedal so that they covered the short distance that remained to the house in record time. He turned the wheel, slowing down just enough to keep Emily from flying into the passenger door, and sped up the driveway sending a shower of snowy gravel onto the road. Emily seemed completely unperturbed by this, her attention set on the house as if she could pierce its mysteries through the sheer intensity of her gaze.

Johnnie was standing in the parlor window, his hands resting on either side of the frame as if he were holding himself back from diving through the pane. His face was ashen and blank, and even at this distance Emily could tell he'd been crying. His body jerked in a sudden spasm, apparently startled by their arrival. Emily noted with interest that it had taken him an inordinate amount of time to notice their approach, given that the road was visible from the parlor window. She feared that his distracted state didn't bode well.

Ransom pulled the car up on the left side of the sheriff's cars and switched off the ignition.

"You wait here," he said peremptorily as he pulled the keys from the ignition and popped open his door.

"I'll do nothing of the sort!" Emily said so firmly that Ransom was checked in the act of climbing from the car.

"Emily, we don't know what's happened."

"And do you think for a moment that I'm going to wait out here, nibbling my fingernails and waiting for you to come back and break the news to me? I'm not as frail as all that!"

Ransom paused just long enough to shoot her a half smile, then jumped from the car and went around to her side and helped her out.

"You've never nibbled your fingernails," he intoned.

They crossed the paving stones, from which someone had cleared the snow, and entered the house through the front door.

Johnnie was on them before Ransom had even managed to close the door. "Thank God you're back! That damn sheriff is gonna screw this up, just like he did the last time! I *told* him," he whined, tears welling up in his eyes, "I *told* him!"

Ransom looked at the young man sternly. "You told who?"

"I told him it was dangerous! You can ask anybody! Oh, God! I can't believe it!"

"I don't know what you're talking about," Ransom said, his voice hardening in an attempt to quell Johnnie's rush of emotion and bring him into focus.

"Is Sara all right?" Emily said.

"Sara?" said Johnnie, his face going blank again. "Of course." He turned back to Ransom and said, "I came out here—just like I do most days—to see if there was any work for me to do and I found all this!" He waved his arms in the direction of the kitchen as if the movement were somehow sufficient explanation.

At that moment Jeff Fields came into the living room and saw them. "Larkin, I told you to wait in the parlor."

"I've told you everything I know," said Johnnie with no hint of the bravado with which he usually addressed Fields. "Just ask Millie and Sara...I warned him."

Fields's expression remained closed, his jaw set solidly. "Wait in the parlor."

Larkin stared at him doe-eyed for a beat, then turned and went back into the parlor like a dog that hates its master but is afraid to disobey.

"Well," said Fields, turning his stony gaze on Ransom, "I must say you sure know how to stir things up. We haven't had a murder out here for two years, then you show up and poke your nose in and first thing you know we got another body."

Emily stiffened her spine until she seemed to tower in her tiny frame and demanded in her harshest tone, "Is Sara all right?"

Fields barked a single "Huh" at her, and said, "She's fine."

"Then who's been killed?" Ransom asked.

"Hansen Crane."

"Hansen Crane?" said Emily, her voice hollow with disbelief, "Hansen Crane?"

"Yeah," said Fields. He turned back to Ransom, and said, "And I want to talk to you."

Emily shook her head as if the action was necessary to get her brain back into working order. She looked at Fields, and said, "Where *is* Sara?"

"She's waiting in the library, and nobody's going to see her until I'm finished with her." He jerked a thumb at the door to the library, in front of which stood a young deputy whose arms were folded across his chest. He seemed to stand just a little straighter when attention was directed at him.

"You need to guard her?" Emily asked disapprovingly.

"I was talking to her and we got interrupted when everybody else showed up. The coroner's out back now. I want to keep her from talking to other people until I'm done questioning her. She preferred waiting in the library." He paused and folded his arms. "And there isn't a guard on the door to keep her from coming out, it's to keep others from going in. This is an investigation and I'm not going to be accused of not carrying it out right." He stopped just short of adding, "Not this time," but all three felt it was implicit. Fields looked at Ransom, and said, "You, in the kitchen."

Ransom gave Fields one of his most infuriating smiles, and said, "Yes, Officer."

Fields marched into the kitchen and Ransom followed him at a more leisurely pace, pausing in the doorway just long enough to shoot a glance at Emily. He raised an eyebrow and gave a slight nod, then turned away and disappeared into the kitchen. If Emily could have managed a smile in these circumstances, she would have done it for Ransom's uncanny talent for terse, expressive nonverbal communication.

She headed for her bedroom door, a certain frailty being added to her gait as it had been when she'd approached the clerk in the drugstore.

"Where're you going, ma'am?" asked the deputy with all the severity of a youth in authority.

"I'm going to my room...Sergeant," said Emily, faltering noticeably over his rank and giving a little nod in the direction of the door to her room.

He flashed a superior smile and corrected her. "That's Deputy, ma'am."

"Oh, yes, of course," said Emily. "I have to lie down. I've been ill, you know, and this has all been very upsetting. You see, I have a heart condition...."

The deputy's eyes showed signs of beginning to glaze over.

He cut her off with a "Yes, ma'am," and carelessly waved a hand in the direction of the door she'd indicated.

"Thank you," Emily said meekly.

Emily went into her room, closing the door behind her. She crossed to the communicating door to the library and paused with her hand on the knob, putting her ear close to the door and listening for the sound of voices. Satisfied that Sara wasn't being questioned, as quietly as she could Emily turned the knob and opened the door just a crack and peered through the space to make sure Sara was alone, then stepped into the room.

"Emily!" Sara exclaimed.

Emily quickly put her finger to her lips. "Quietly, Sara. I'm not supposed to be in here."

The admonition was almost unnecessary, since the hundreds of books that lined the shelves of the little room seemed to swallow sound the moment it was emitted, but Emily wasn't taking any chances.

Sara had risen to her feet and rushed to Emily. Her eyes were red and swollen and her face looked puffy and wet. There were damp stains on her white blouse from where her tears had fallen. She said in an anxious whisper, "I didn't do it! But it's like Nathan all over again. My God, what am I going to do?"

Emily took Sara's trembling hands in her own and gave them an encouraging squeeze. "First, you're going to have to calm yourself. I have some questions to ask you and I don't know how long we have."

Sara stared at Emily through eyes bleary with tears. Something about the matter-of-factness in Emily's tone seemed to stem the young woman's rising panic. She squeezed Emily's hands in return and took a deep breath, which she released slowly.

"Could we sit down, please?" said Emily.

As they took their seats, Sara explained, "I found Hansen, dead, in the barn. Just like...just like before. Only I thought it was an accident. The woodpile fell over. I'm sure it was an accident. I don't know why Jeff thinks otherwise."

"I'm sure he has his reasons," said Emily, adjusting the hem of her dress. "But I need to ask you about something quite different, and it may be a bit difficult for you."

"What?" Sara said after a slight pause, looking exactly as if the last thing she wanted was for things to get more difficult.

Emily cleared her throat. "First of all, how old were you when your parents divorced?"

"My parents?" Sara said, her complete surprise diverting her from the problems at hand. She cast a glance at the door, half-afraid that she had spoken too loudly.

"Yes."

"Well..." Sara continued slowly. "I was a little less than two, I think. Nathan would have been about four. Why?"

"You *think?*" Emily said, her eyes narrowing. "You don't know?"

Sara shook her head.

"Less than two..." Emily said vacantly, "yes, that's very curious."

"I don't understand."

"Well, if you were that young at the time of the divorce, how do you know that it was, as you said, acrimonious?"

"From my mother. She didn't...exactly put him down all the time, but she didn't make any bones about him being...unreliable. From what I could gather over the years, he didn't do a day's work from the minute they married. How he'd been struggling along before that, I don't know. But according to my mother, once they were married he was in and out of jobs all the time, never holding one for very long and it was never his fault that he was fired, if you know what I mean. Mother just thought he was a deadbeat."

Emily gave a single nod, meant to convey both that she understood and that she wanted Sara to continue. "And what did you think of him?"

"My father?" said Sara, drawing back as if she wanted to physically withdraw from the subject. Her right hand went up to her hair, one strand of which she fiddled with absently as she continued. "I was so young...I don't remember anything about him. I do know that he never made any effort to see us after the divorce, so I have no reason to...so I think my mother must've been right." This was said in a tone mixed with regret and bitterness, and Sara averted her eyes as if despite the abandonment she'd suffered, she was ashamed to speak ill of her absent parent.

Emily considered this for a moment, then leaned forward in her chair and said, "Did you hear from your father recently?"

Sara's eyes opened wide with astonishment. "How did you know that?"

"It was just a guess on my part," said Emily with a shrug, "but I thought it likely."

"But why?"

"I'll explain that when we have more time. Now, when did you hear from your father?"

"It wasn't exactly recently. It was..." Her voice trailed off. She looked down at her hands. A flood of memories brought the blood to her cheeks in red splotches, as if it couldn't decide which emotion it wanted to convey.

Emily looked at the young woman, her eyes filled with compassion. She tried to help her along by offering a possible answer. "Was it after your mother died?"

Sara moved her hand from the button with which she'd been playing to her forehead and a choked sob escaped her lips.

"Mother was right, you know," she said haltingly, her voice catching after each word.

"About what?" Emily asked gently.

Sara looked up at her. "About my father. When she was sick she said if anything happened to her, he would come out of the woodwork. And that's what happened."

"He contacted you."

Sara nodded, sending a tear flying onto the front of her blouse. "About six months after she died—that would've been about six years ago—he wrote to me."

"Do you remember where the letter came from?"

Sara sniffed, then wiped the tears away with her fingers and cleared her throat in an attempt to regain her composure. "San

Francisco. It was...he started by saying how sorry he was about my mother, and how sorry he was about the divorce, and how much he wanted a relationship with me and how much he regretted not having been there when we were growing up. But it ended with an appeal for money.''

Emily let out a mild "Tsk."

"Not overtly, you understand, just telling me all about how he'd fallen on hard times and how his health wasn't as good as it used to be, and how he'd heard that I was doing well, and was very glad of it. He didn't come right out and ask for money, but I think it was there between the lines.''

Sara stopped and Emily didn't reply, her attention apparently being taken up by the middle-most shelf of books directly across from her. Sara was confused, thinking perhaps that Emily's lack of response was in fact a form of silent condemnation. She said quickly, "I don't think I was imagining it...I mean, because mother had warned me about him ahead of time. I was actually surprised at how right she was.''

Emily turned to her, and said, "Oh, I'm sure you were right. I'm sorry, my dear, I didn't mean to let my mind wander, it's just you set me to thinking about how difficult it is to change one's nature. I assume that each time your father went out and got a job, he was trying to change his nature, and each time he failed. It would seem that your mother knew him *very* well.''

"Yes,'' Sara replied quietly.

"Now,'' said Emily, shifting in her seat as if preparing to get on with business, "how did you reply to your father's letter?''

"I didn't.''

"Oh?'' For the first time Emily registered genuine surprise. Her eyebrows slid upward and her eyes widened. "Not at all?''

The red blotches, which had begun to dissipate during the previous exchange, began to deepen and spread until Sara's cheeks were in full flush.

"I didn't know what to say. Part of me wanted to lash out at him for not being there, and for hurting my mother, but part of me...well, he was my father, and part of me wanted to know him...or at least, not to hurt him. As much as my mother had come to dislike him, I couldn't help thinking...how sad it was.''

"The divorce?"

Sara shook her head. "No. To be so irresponsible."

An approving smile spread across Emily's face. "You're quite wise for your age."

Sara looked away from her. "I wasn't wise enough to know what to say to my father. I kept putting it off and putting it off until...it wasn't forgotten, but I didn't think of it any more."

Emily's gaze had gone back to the books. "'I cannot heave my heart into my mouth,'" she quoted vacantly.

"What?"

Emily shook her head and smiled. "Just a little quote from *King Lear*. Something that somehow seemed pertinent. Did you never hear from him again, or see him?"

"See him?" Sara seemed horrified at the thought. "No, of course not. I don't think I'd recognize him if I did see him. I wasn't even two years old when he left, remember. And mother was bitter enough that she didn't keep any pictures of him."

"Would Nathan have known him?"

"I...I don't know. He might. He was a little older. I don't know. Why?"

"We're just trying to look at every possibility."

"Every possibility..." Sara repeated slowly. Suddenly the color left her cheeks. "You mean you think that my father might have had something to do with all this?"

Emily gave a single nod.

"But that's impossible."

"Oh, no, my dear. It's simply difficult to believe. But we think that Nathan saw somebody here in town just before he died— someone who he didn't expect to see. Did he say anything about this to you?"

Sara shook her head vigorously. "Nothing. No. And he would have."

Emily paused before saying, "Unless he was trying to protect you."

Sara stared at her for a moment, then said, "Yes, that could be true. It would be like him."

Emily shifted in her seat, and said, "Sara, is it possible...is it at all possible that Hansen Crane could have been your father?"

"Hansen?" Sara said loudly, recoiling slightly. "No! Of course not! I would have known!"

"But you said you wouldn't have recognized him."

"I...I wouldn't. But I think that somehow I would've known. Besides, Hansen's been here a long time. If Nathan had recognized him, wouldn't he have done it a long time before he was killed?"

"Possibly," said Emily, "that's what we thought. But you knew that Nathan asked a lot of questions about him."

"Oh, that," Sara said with a smile, "that was just because Nathan was so suspicious. He didn't understand how anyone just drifting around like that could be up to any good. He felt the same way about street people back in Chicago. He didn't understand how a grown man could be rootless like that. It reminded him of—" She broke off and looked away from Emily.

"It reminded him of your father?" said Emily gently.

Sara shook her head.

"Is that why you let him stay?"

Tears streamed down her cheeks. "I felt sorry for him. I couldn't believe he could be happy living the way he did."

"Of course you couldn't," said Emily kindly, "his kind of life was too foreign to you."

Sara made an attempt to recover herself. "But I know he wasn't my father. The only contact I've had with my father since the divorce was that one letter."

Emily thought for a moment, then said, "That does strike me as strange. Given the fact that you didn't respond to your father's letter, I'm surprised that he didn't try again."

Sara looked down at her hands. "I suppose I really should've answered him one way or the other."

"Yes...yes...I suppose that might have made a difference...." Emily spoke so abstractly that Sara thought her mind might be wandering in more ways than one. "I suppose it might have *fore-stalled* what happened, but I can't imagine the outcome wouldn't have been the same." She stopped. Her eyebrows knit together and she stared off at nothing.

"Emily?" Sara said with concern.

"Now, there are a couple more things I need to know," said Emily, suddenly reanimating. "Did you and Nathan make out wills?"

"Oh, yes, even before mother became ill, she insisted on it. She was very concerned that her money not end up in my father's hands. She worked very hard, you see, making a living after he left. She saved every penny she could. And she inherited a little from her parents. She couldn't bear the thought that my father might somehow end up with it. So Nathan had a will leaving everything to me, and I did the same for him. Of course, that would've changed if either of us had gotten married, but..." Her face clouded over and there was a catch in her throat, but she went on. "But as it turned out, that never happened. There was a provision in both our wills that all of our money would go to charity if we died at the same time."

"Ah," said Emily, moving forward in her chair so that she was sitting almost on the edge, "and when Nathan died, did you make out a new will?"

Sara rose from her seat, smoothed her green skirt, which had wrinkled rather markedly from so much sitting, and walked to the bookcase, resting her arm on one of the ledges. "Almost immediately. I know it sounds...it may sound awful, but I had this overwhelming feeling that something might happen to me."

Emily smiled at the young woman's back. "That is not an unusual reaction in someone who has just experienced a tragedy as you had." She took a deep breath, and added, "At the risk of seeming impertinent, may I ask about the contents of the will?"

Sara emitted a short, rueful laugh. "You mean because I had nobody left?"

"Oh, no, because the contents of your will may be very important."

Sara sighed and dropped back into the chair. "I guess because I'd just lost Nathan I was thinking...I thought a lot about my friends...all the people I'd been close to throughout my life...."

"And?"

Sara heaved a heavier sigh and ran the fingers of her right hand through her long, wavy hair. "And I finally decided to leave everything to the best friend I'd ever had—Lynn. Lynn Francis."

"Really?" said Emily in undisguised amazement.

Sara was somewhat taken aback by the overt surprise on Emily's face. She said, "Was that such a strange thing to do?"

"Not at all," said Emily, laying a hand on Sara's wrist, "it was a very thoughtful thing to do. And very wise. Did you tell anyone about your will?"

"I...well, Millie witnessed it, so she knew about it." Here Sara smiled and her cheeks turned pink, rather than the blotchy red they'd exhibited before. "And if she knows, then everyone else does, too. I love Millie, but she's not...necessarily...discreet."

"Oh, I wouldn't speak a word against her," said Emily firmly, "she may have saved your life."

Sara blinked. "Saved my life? What do you mean?"

"I'm not exactly sure, because there are still so many questions. But you've managed to throw some light on some very important matters."

Sara sat back in her chair and stared at Emily, looking exactly as if she didn't think she'd been any help at all. Emily didn't return her gaze. Instead, she stared straight ahead as if she were looking at an optical puzzle the solution to which, with some uninterrupted conversation, she might be able to divine. They had sat in silence so long that Sara was just about to ask if there was anything else Emily wanted to know when Emily suddenly said, "I wonder how he knew?"

"What?" was Sara's startled reply.

Emily turned to her. "I wonder how your father knew that your mother had died."

Sara smiled ruefully. "Oh, that's easy...."

WHILE EMILY AND SARA were having their quiet talk in the library, a much more electrified discussion was taking place in the kitchen. Ransom sat with his chair pushed back from the table, his legs crossed and his hands folded on his uppermost knee, an attitude so casual and unconcerned one would have thought it was designed to further rankle the sheriff. Jeff Fields sat with his forearm resting on the table. It seemed to be costing him an effort not to drum his fingers on its top. His face was as set and expressionless as always, save for the pulsating vein on his temple that bore witness to his agitation. Despite these minor flaws, which would have escaped the notice of a less practiced eye, Fields was doing well at maintaining his unreadable facade. Ransom thought with an inward smile that the only thing Fields lacked was a pair of mirrored sunglasses to complete the picture.

"I want to know what you've learned," said Fields without preamble.

"I haven't learned a single thing that's new," Ransom replied.

"Look, I told you that if you were going to go poking around in this business that I expected you to report back to me. I don't hear anything from you, and the next thing I know, Hansen Crane's murdered."

"When did it happen?"

"So far as we know, last night. That'd be the *logical* time, don't you think?" He hadn't modulated his voice much when he said this, just enough to let Ransom know he was being sneered at. "Sara found him a little while ago, out in the barn, half-buried by the woodpile."

"You're sure it wasn't an accident?"

Fields produced an unamused smile. "We were meant to think so is my guess. But from the looks of his head, I can tell you no log would've gashed him that bad just by falling. Somebody cracked his head open pretty good—more than once from the looks of him."

"Hm."

"Sara says she saw Crane not long before you and Emily left for the play. Of course, we only have her word for that."

"There's no reason for her to lie. Surely she wouldn't want to account for his being alive right up to the time she was left alone with him if it wasn't true."

Fields slapped a palm on the table, then held it there a moment, apparently trying to regain his composure before speaking.

"So we know he was alive just before everyone went to that damn Nativity play. I wish to God Sara had gone, too! She was the only one here *again!* Before the play you were here, and I suppose you came back right after. So that'd make the best time to kill him while the play was going on."

Ransom nodded. "I agree."

Fields shot him a glance designed to let him know that his agreement was not only unnecessary but unwanted. "And everybody in the whole damn territory was *at* the play, including the people connected with this house. That leaves Sara."

Ransom shrugged. "The service went on for quite some time. Anyone could've slipped out, come out here and killed Crane, then slipped back into the crowd at the church." Ransom paused for a moment, then added significantly, "Anyone."

Fields stared at him, the expression on his face showing that he didn't at all like the emphasis Ransom had placed on the word. His voice was hollow when he said, "Someone could've slipped out of the church without being seen?"

Ransom elevated his right eyebrow. "Would you have noticed someone leaving?"

"I would think so," Fields said doubtfully after a long pause, "but there were three aisles and I was watching the play. I suppose somebody could've gotten out without being seen. It would've been an awfully big risk, though."

"Unless whoever it was sat way in the back," said Ransom with a smile.

There was a very long pause during which Fields sat glaring at Ransom, his breathing becoming heavier. Finally he said, "You seem to be going out of your way to let me know you suspect me of something."

"It's not out of the way at all," said Ransom coolly, "but with everyone so ready to accuse Sara, I felt it was important to point out other possibilities.''

"Including me."

Ransom shrugged. "You're as good as anyone else."

For a moment it looked as if Fields might actually smile. He leaned in slightly, and said, "Then it's too bad I'm the one doing the *official* investigation, isn't it?" He sat back and after a pause added, "Now, what we got is that Sara was left out here alone when somebody got killed. I don't do something about it this time and there's gonna be more than just *talk* about her in town."

Ransom waited a beat before saying, "I thought you did something about it last time."

It looked to Ransom as if the effort it was taking Fields to hold his temper might just make the top of his head blow off. "I *did*," he said loudly. "There was no *evidence*."

Ransom smiled. "There's none this time, either. Is there?"

Fields took a deep, silent breath that he never visibly released. "Look, I brought you in here to ask you questions, not the other way around. You still haven't answered the first thing I asked you."

"Which was?"

"I want to know what you learned. No matter what you might think, I'm not stupid, Mr. Ransom. You must've dug something up, or I think Hansen Crane would still be alive."

Ransom stared at Fields for a moment. He didn't like being questioned, and he didn't particularly like Fields, though he could feel for him. Ransom had to admit that he wouldn't like it if someone interfered in one of his cases, let alone if there was the possibility that that interference had caused another death. Under such circumstances, it was tempting for Ransom to take pity on his fellow officer and go against his usual closed-handed nature by sharing with Fields all the speculations in which he and Emily had indulged. But Ransom reminded himself that no matter what professional empathy he might feel for Fields, the sheriff actually could still be considered a suspect.

"I assure you," said Ransom civilly, "that I have learned nothing more concrete than you did. Everyone I've questioned has told me the same stories they did two years ago. Including Crane.''

"So why the hell do you think Crane's been murdered?"

Ransom shrugged. "Coincidence?"

"You don't believe that!" Fields spat back with something approaching venom.

"No, I don't," said Ransom, narrowing his eyes meaningfully, "but it wasn't because of anything he told me, either." He paused, allowing his features to soften, then said in his most conciliatory manner, "He didn't say anything more to me than he had to you."

Fields seemed somewhat mollified by this affirmation of his judgment. "I tried to tell you you'd be wasting your time."

Ransom smiled. "Oh, but it hasn't been wasted."

"What?" For the first time in their brief acquaintance, Fields looked unsure of himself.

Ransom leaned in toward him. "I'm sure that you must've thought—just as I did—that since Nathan was murdered two years ago and nothing has happened since then, that the murderer had either left the area, or was still here but had some reason for killing Nathan that we could never discover and was fairly certain of his safety."

"Yes..." said Fields warily.

"Well, since you believe—and I'm in complete agreement with you on this point—that Nathan's and Crane's murders are related, then it would appear that the case is more active than either of us thought, wouldn't it?"

"Obviously," said Fields, folding his muscular arms across his chest and sitting back in his chair. "So?"

"So," Ransom continued with measured patience, "if you're correct, and my looking into the case has caused Crane to be murdered, then it would also appear that the murderer has something to fear. And if he—or she—is fearful enough of discovery at this point to risk another murder, then there *must* be something that can be discovered, wouldn't you say?"

With this, Ransom folded his own arms across his chest in a conscious mirroring of Fields's posture. They stared at each other for a while in this rather countrified version of a Mexican stand-off, when Ransom had an idea. He thought it just possible that he could manage to get Fields to do a bit of work for him, while at the same time convincing him that he was willing to share. Ransom sighed, trying to convey that he was giving in to the superior will of the sheriff. "Maybe you're right. Maybe my investigation has caused Crane's death. I'll tell you something that may help verify that. Right after I had my talk with Crane, he made an unexpected trip into town—at least that's where he said he was going—supposedly to buy tobacco. If my talking to him actually caused his death, then it might be worth finding out where he really went yesterday."

Fields eyed him suspiciously. "Why couldn't he have just gone into town for tobacco? What would be so strange about that?"

"Only that he had a full tin of it when I talked to him not five minutes before he left to buy some."

Fields grunted. "I suppose I can check to see if he really did," he said reluctantly, "it should be easy enough. The only place to get tobacco in town is at the drugstore. But I don't see what difference it makes if he went someplace else."

"It could make all the difference in the world," said Ransom with a coy smile. "Where Hansen Crane went yesterday after I talked to him might be the answer to all of our questions."

ELEVEN

BEFORE GOING to join Emily, Ransom went to the parlor to see if Johnnie Larkin was still there. Johnnie had gone back to his place by the window, though his hands were no longer resting on the frame.

"Mr. Larkin," said Ransom, "I would like a word with you."

Johnnie wheeled around. His long dark hair was unkempt and his eyes were bloodshot and open wide. "Jesus! You scared me!"

Ransom fought the urge to retort with "And well he might one day."

"That old fool!" Johnnie continued, "I told him that damn woodpile was too high! But he had to have it his own way. He made me repile it, you know. Halfway up to the damn roof!"

Ransom considered the boy for a moment. Before this he had only seen Johnnie in passing, but now that he was face-to-face with him, what had seemed at first to be youthful exuberance or excess energy now seemed like barely masked anxiety. The problem was that under the circumstances, anxiety would be understandable, so Ransom was left wondering if Larkin's went any deeper than the norm.

"You can set your mind at ease on that one," said Ransom without inflection. "The woodpile didn't just fall on Crane, he was murdered."

Johnnie's mouth dropped open in a picture of surprise. He looked as if he half suspected that Ransom was playing a trick on him.

"Murdered?" he said breathily. "How do they know that? Are they sure?"

"Yes. Now, tell me, you said you told *him*. What did you mean?"

"Hansen," Johnnie replied vacantly. "I told him it was dangerous to pile the wood so high. I..." He faltered and looked to the floor, then back up. "He yelled at me the other day. He accused me of knocking over the pile when Sara sent me out for more wood. I mean, I *did* do it, but it wasn't my fault. The thing was just too high. And that's when I told him that. And he made me pile it back up, just like he had it."

"Was anyone else present when this conversation took place?"

Johnnie face went blank for a moment, as if recalling this was difficult. At last he said, "No. We were out in the driveway. Nobody else was there."

"Did you tell anybody about it afterward?"

"I—" Johnnie stopped as quickly as he'd started. The blood drained from his face and he stared openmouthed at Ransom. "I told Sara, 'cause she asked me why it took me so long to bring in the groceries."

"Anyone else?" Ransom asked, his expression unchanging.

"Your friend was there. Miss Charters."

"I mean anyone else...outside the immediate household."

There was a sudden rush of color back into the young man's cheeks. "I told a couple of my friends the other night. We went out for some beers, and I was telling them about the old—" He stopped suddenly, apparently realizing that it was not considered proper to speak ill of the dead, then continued meekly, "Yeah, so I told a few people."

"Hm," said Ransom, looking at Johnnie through narrowed eyes, "So, basically anyone in town might have known about the 'woodpile incident.'"

"I suppose," said Johnnie sullenly. "What's it matter?"

"It could matter very much if you made it common knowledge."

Johnnie frowned as if he didn't quite know whether this was meant as encouragement or an insult. Then his face suddenly brightened with understanding. He said excitedly, "Oh, I get it! Yeah, I did tell people about that old crock and the damn woodpile! I told lots of people."

"Good," said Ransom with a perfectly opaque smile. "Thank you."

Ransom started to walk from the room, but paused in the archway and turned back to Johnnie. "Oh, by the way, we had a chat with your girlfriend yesterday."

"My what?" Johnnie exclaimed, looking so alarmed that it took an effort for Ransom to refrain from raising an eyebrow. "I don't have a girlfriend."

"You don't?" Ransom said lightly, then with elaborate signs of recalling something, he added, "Oh, that's right. I should've said your ex-girlfriend. Amy Shelton."

"Amy?" Johnnie said vacantly, his previously raised spirits now noticeably deflating. "Oh, Amy. She wasn't...she never really was my girlfriend. She was just..." His voice trailed off. He was silent for a brief interval, then looked up at Ransom and crossed to him. He whispered haltingly, "She was just...everything was so bad here when Nathan was killed. I needed someone to talk to...."

"Talk?"

Johnnie stopped for a moment, then continued with additional embarrassment. "I was lonely. And so was she. And almost everyone else...Sara...was so screwed up at the time." He raised his eyes to Ransom and said somewhat more defiantly, "Amy needed someone as much as I did."

"I see."

Johnnie looked down at the floor again, and said quietly, "But Sara has always been my—she's always been special to me. And after a while things got back to—well, not normal, but...you know what I mean. And me and Amy drifted apart." There was another pause, after which Johnnie looked into Ransom's eyes and pleaded quietly, "*Please* don't tell Sara about it. Please. She really is special and I wouldn't want to do anything to hurt her. Please."

Ransom eyed the young man for a moment, resting his chin in one hand and tapping his lips with his index finger.

"It shouldn't be necessary," he said as he turned from Johnnie and left the parlor.

Johnnie stood for several minutes, staring after the detective, wondering exactly what he'd meant by that.

NEXT, RANSOM CHECKED on Emily and found her lying on her bed, her eyes firmly closed and her breathing even. Her expression was a mixture of contentment and calculation, as if she were happily doing sums in her sleep. He smiled, then quietly closed the door and retreated to the smoking room with his pack of cigars and his well-worn copy of *The Haunted Man*.

As he settled back into the Christmas story, reading as he filled the room with a cloud of heavy smoke, his own measure of contentment fell just short of that being enjoyed by Emily, due primarily to the fact that he was longing for the additional pleasure of indulging in his favorite pastimes while soaking in a hot tub. He sighed at the thought, but dispelled any further dissatisfaction (however little) by immersing himself in the book.

He had reached the point in *The Haunted Man* where Mr. Redlaw, robbed of all compassion by the loss of his painful memories, seeks solace in the company of a feral child. The child had remained in his greedy, animal-like state from a life in which he'd never been touched by kindness or compassion. This part of the story always reminded Ransom of the admonition given to Ebenezer Scrooge by the Ghost of Christmas Present: "This boy is Ignorance. This girl is Want. Beware them both...but most of all beware this boy...." It was another one of the very few passages that would, on occasion, cause Ransom a moment of doubt as to the infallibility of his beloved author. In his many years as a homicide detective, Ransom had seen a lot of people who could be termed ignorant, most of them truly happy. He'd also seen a lot of want and it almost always had the same effect that it had on the feral child—it caused insatiable greed. Ransom knew that many people, no matter how intelligent, had destroyed their own lives and the lives of others through their greed. This all led Ransom to believe that Want was the child of which one really had to beware.

He closed the book, his mind too consumed by these thoughts to concentrate on the story. He gazed out the window and lit another cigar.

RANSOM AND EMILY met shortly after four o'clock to compare notes. By that time Emily had had a long nap and Ransom had finished four of his small cigars. Both of them had achieved a sense of rejuvenation from their solitary pursuits. They met in Emily's room for privacy, and Ransom related the results of his interview with Jeff Fields.

"Do you think it was wise to tell Mr. Fields about Hansen Crane's hasty departure after you questioned him?" Emily asked.

Ransom lifted his shoulders. "It probably made Fields feel that I'm not entirely holding out on him, and from a purely practical standpoint, he can surely find out where Crane went a lot more quickly than I can." He paused, then added ruefully, "Assuming, of course, that Fields didn't kill Crane himself."

Emily then reported on her conversation with Sara. After that they fell silent for a while, each digesting the new information.

"Well, this is most vexing," said Emily at last, bouncing her folded hands in her lap to emphasize each word. She said this with such delicate vehemence that it almost made Ransom laugh.

"Emily, I did warn you that trying to solve a two-year-old murder would have its difficulties."

She looked at him and pursed her lips. "Jeremy, you failed to mention that one of those difficulties might be another murder." She dropped her hands with finality and sighed. "Oh, well, I suppose when you stir up a hornet's nest—even an old one—you should expect to find hornets. But one doesn't expect to lose the chief suspect directly after selecting him. Oh!" She shook her head as vigorously as she was able, her eyebrows knit and her frown so deep it made the lines around her mouth droop. She looked almost as if she thought Hansen Crane had proven rather ill mannered to get himself murdered so inconveniently. After this temporary, and quite mild, loss of control on the part of Ransom's adoptive grandmother, she laid her hands calmly in her lap and gathered herself together with renewed resolve.

"Now, it seems to me that Sara has provided us with at least one important piece of the puzzle."

"Hm?"

"She accounted for the lapse of time—the reason that no further calamity happened after her brother was killed."

"How's that?" said Ransom, raising his right eyebrow.

"She changed her will immediately. If her father had been planning to kill both Nathan and Sara in hopes that all their money would revert to him, then Sara foiled that plan by making out a new will so quickly. It was an act that probably saved her life. The murderer has most likely been lying in wait, trying to figure out how to get his hands on the money."

Ransom was sitting in the reading chair, resting his head on his right hand. His legs were crossed and he was drumming the fingers of his free hand on his knee.

"Emily...if that's the case there's another problem. Sara has been implicated in both murders. If her father hopes to inherit, why implicate Sara? Wills aside, if she was jailed for murder he still wouldn't get the money."

From her perch on the corner of the bed, Emily allowed her gaze to travel out the window to the barn, which had twice been the scene of violence. Even in the late afternoon light, its roof framed by gathering clouds, it was hard to imagine such sinister goings-on in such a placid setting.

"That's true...." Emily replied at length in answer to Ransom's objection. "But I think I can account for that."

Ransom smiled fondly at her. "Somehow I knew you could."

Emily returned the smile in kind, and replied, "Jeremy, you're making fun of me."

"Never!" said Ransom, laughing. "What's your idea?"

"Well, it's supposition, of course, but it's based in part on what Sara told me and what you yourself have supposed. If"—she laid great stress on the word as if it were a reminder that this was all conjecture—"if I am correct and the murderer was forced by Sara making a new will to wait to make his next move, then it would explain why Hansen Crane stayed on here instead of drifting along his way."

"It would?" said Ransom. He sat up and leaned forward.

"Yes. Again, *if* you were right in your belief that Hansen had actually seen or heard something the night Nathan Bartlett was killed."

Ransom stared at her for a moment, the wheels and gears in his mind turning so rapidly as to be almost audible. At last he shook his head, and said, "I'm sorry, Emily, I don't follow."

Emily shifted in her seat. "Well, you remember when you were talking about how Sara's father might be the killer, you referred to this idea as 'pure speculation.' That term struck a chord with me, only I couldn't quite put my finger on why. But now I do. It's because the term has two meanings: the way you meant it, and then..." her voice trailed off suggestively.

Ransom's face brightened. "Gambling on something."

"Exactly!" said Emily, sitting back triumphantly. "You see, if Crane's object was to blackmail the murderer, and the murderer doesn't yet have the money, then he would have to hang on, waiting for the day when the murderer *gained* the fortune, which he couldn't do immediately because of Sara's will." Emily spread her palms expansively. "Pure speculation!"

"Rather impure," said Ransom wryly. "Which means that whatever we thought before, Crane couldn't have been Sara's father."

"It doesn't appear so now that he's dead," said Emily, her head tilting slightly upward as she punctuated her reply with a single stroke of her index finger.

They fell silent again for a few moments, Emily looking on intently as Ransom continued to ruminate on all of this. Ransom stared into the air in front of him with an intensity that made it look as if the very air might split from the force and reveal all the mysteries of the universe to him. Finally he took a deep breath, and said, "None of this would explain why Crane was killed now, after all this time."

"Who knows?" said Emily with a shrug. "Perhaps he grew tired of waiting." Her eyes grew more incisive. "Perhaps he grew afraid. Perhaps the renewed interest in the case, after an interval that would have led him to believe all was safe, made him think he should put whatever pressure he could on the murderer to move forward."

Ransom frowned and shook his head slowly. "I don't know, Emily, that's an awful lot of supposition."

"Well," said Emily with a smile, "as long as I've gone this far, let me take my little hypothesis one step further. What I have proposed to you would also explain how the murderer came to implicate Sara in the murder, even though it might keep him from the money he wants to inherit."

Ransom couldn't help but smile. "I can't wait to hear it."

There was a sly twinkle in Emily's eyes as she said, "He didn't mean to."

"What?"

"He didn't mean to. You said it yourself to Jeff Fields. The murder of Hansen Crane means that the murderer has something to fear. That being the case he probably killed out of necessity and implicating Sara was probably the furthest thing from his mind."

Ransom gazed at her in wonder for a moment, then said, "I've changed my mind, Emily. You shouldn't be on the force, you should be a prosecuting attorney."

"Thank you," said Emily primly. She refolded her hands and cleared her throat. "Of course, the real difficulty is how exactly Sara's father—if, indeed, the mysterious father has anything to do with it—plans to get hold of the money." She thought about this for a moment, then looked up at Ransom, and said, "Now, Jeremy, it is vitally, *vitally* important that we discover the true identity of Nathan and Sara's father."

"I agree," said Ransom with a weary sigh, "but that's going

to be no small task if he really did disappear almost thirty years ago.''

Emily cocked her head and raised her eyebrows as she flashed him a mischievous smile.

Ransom looked at her quizzically for a moment, trying to read the meaning in her expression. At last a smile spread across his face. "Of course," he said, folding his arms, "if Sara's father knew that her mother had died, and if he knew that she and her brother had moved here...somebody's been in communication with him."

Emily beamed at him like a proud parent. "Exactly."

"And you know who that is."

Emily leaned forward, and said, "I asked Emily how her father could've known these things, and she said two words: Myrtle Girdler."

"Myrtle Girdler?" said Ransom with a laugh. "That sounds like the female commandant at a concentration camp."

"Nothing as overtly sinister as all that, I'm sure," said Emily.

"And how do we reach this woman?"

"Very easily. We can go and see her. She lives in Mt. Morgan."

SARA STOOD at the kitchen counter making an attempt to calmly drink a cup of tea. But no matter how hard she tried, she couldn't steady her trembling hand as she lifted the cup to her lips. She watched through the side window as the van into which Hansen Crane's body had been loaded was driven away, leaving ruts in the snow out to the barn, which Sara knew would serve as a signpost to the scene of the crime until the next storm came and swept them away. The van was followed out by Jeff Fields. As his car pulled out of the driveway, Sara could feel her emotions draining away as if they were being pulled out of her in his wake and dispersed into the air with his exhaust.

This was the first time since Nathan's murder that Sara felt she just might have been too hard on Jeff, that she'd completely misunderstood his own position and his own frustration. But instead of finding some measure of solace in this newfound understanding, she was feeling even emptier than before. She pondered this for a few moments, standing at the sink with the cup poised halfway between its saucer and her mouth, her hand continuing to tremble. At last she realized that the deepening void she was experiencing stemmed from the fact that if Jeff, on whom she'd pinned her hopes at one time, felt so powerless over the situation, then what hope was there for her?

"Are you okay?" Johnnie's voice suddenly broke into her thoughts.

Sara started, letting the cup clatter down into the saucer, splashing tea onto the counter.

"Oh!!" she exclaimed. "I didn't know you were still here!" She grabbed a towel from the sink and quickly wiped up the spilled liquid.

"I'm sorry," he said quickly as he advanced into the room, "I didn't mean to startle you—but I wasn't gonna leave as long as Jeff and his goons were still here. I wanted to wait and make sure you were all right."

"I'm fine," she said as she wrung out the towel and draped it over the center divider of the sink.

Johnnie watched with a concerned look on his face as Sara refilled her cup with her still-shaking hands and then moved to the table.

"You don't seem fine," said Johnnie as he took a seat opposite her.

"All right," Sara said with weary resignation, "I'm not fine."

"I didn't mean...I just meant I'm worried about you."

Sara finished taking a sip of tea, then slowly lowered the cup back into the saucer, never lifting her eyes from it. "I know," she said quietly, "I'm sorry. I know you are. And I appreciate it. And I appreciate you waiting to check on me."

Johnnie looked at her eagerly. "You do?"

She nodded. "But really, I'm all right. Or as all right as I could be under the circumstances."

"I was never worried about *that*," Johnnie said pointedly, "I always knew you'd do fine as far as...mentally, I mean, 'cause you're strong. That's one of the things I admire about you. I meant I'm worried about your safety.''

"I'm not," Sara replied softly, still not looking up.

"Huh?"

"I'm not."

There was a pause, then Johnnie said, "What do you mean?"

"Just what I said. I don't care what happens to me any more." There was no self-pity in her tone as she said this, only sadness.

"Well..." said Johnnie with a slight tremor in his voice, "some of us care what happens to you."

"Thank you."

"And with two murders out here, I'm worried about you being out here alone."

"I'm not alone," said Sara, "Mr. Ransom and Miss Charters are here for the next few days."

"What about after that?"

"After that..." said Sara absently, her voice trailing off as she realized she hadn't thought past the present moment at all.

"Because," Johnnie continued hesitantly, "I was wondering how you'd feel about...maybe having me move out here."

"What?" Sara said, her expression clouding over as she looked up at him for the first time.

"I don't mean into the house, I mean I could even just move over the barn—"

"Oh, no!" Sara said, horrified at the thought of anyone going near the barn again.

"Oh, come on, Sara," Johnnie said earnestly, "I don't mind that stuff's happened out there near as much as I mind the thought of you being way out here all alone."

Sara faltered. "I'll be sure I'm all right. Jeff's going to find out who did it this time, and then everything—"

"Jeff!" Johnnie spat, cutting her off. "Jeff's gonna screw this up just like he did the last time. Jeff couldn't find his own ass if his hands were glued to it!"

"That's not fair. You've just never liked—"

He cut her off again. "Liked him? Of course I don't like him, not the way he's treated you! How could I like him? How could *you?*"

Sara suddenly buried her face in her hands and began to cry. Johnnie shot out of his chair and crossed to her.

"I'm sorry, I'm sorry," he said, rubbing her back gently, "I didn't mean to upset you. That's the last thing I meant to do. But you got to face the facts. Jeff Fields aside, you're not safe. And I want to stay out here and...I want to protect you."

He knelt beside her and laid a comforting hand on her right leg. "Sara, I've never made it any secret how I feel about you. You know that. And I've always tried to respect your feelings. You know that, too. But...this thing with Jeff Fields...I mean, you got to stop putting your faith in the people who don't trust you, and start putting your faith in the people who *do*."

Sara slowly lowered her hands from her face, turning her watery eyes on him. He managed a half smile in her direction.

"Oh, Johnnie!" she said plaintively as she slipped her arms around his neck. He returned the embrace, slipping his arms around her waist and drawing her as close as he could given their relative positions. Sara buried her face in his shoulder and wept for a few minutes. When finally her tears began to subside and her breathing became easier, she released him, but he kept his arms wrapped tightly around her. She gently took his forearms and pushed them away.

"Johnnie, that's so sweet. You're a very sweet boy..."

"'Boy'?" he echoed, obviously not pleased with her choice of words.

"...but I've just made a decision. I'm going to take Miss Charters's advice."

"Miss Charters? What's she got to do with anything?"

Sara sniffed deeply and cleared her throat, trying to more fully regain her composure. "She asked me if I might be better off selling the place and starting over somewhere else. I think she was right. This place is just poison to me. Nothing will ever be right for me here. If I didn't know it before, I know it now. When

Emily and Mr. Ransom leave, I'm going to ask them if I can go back to Chicago with them. I have friends there I can stay with. I'm going to sell Hawthorne House and never look back.''

Johnnie, still on his knees beside her, fell back on his heels. He looked absolutely stricken. "You're kidding!"

"No," she said, shaking her head sadly. "There's nothing for me here now."

"But where will you go?"

"I don't care as long as it's away from here."

"But Sara," he pleaded, taking her hand in his, "don't you understand what I've been trying to say? I'm in love with you."

She tried to withdraw her hand, but he held it tightly. "Johnnie, I'm sorry. There's just too many bad memories. I couldn't stay here now if I wanted to."

"Then we could go together. It doesn't matter to me."

"Johnnie, please!" She tried hard to pull her hand away, but his grip continued to tighten.

"Excuse me. I hope I'm not interrupting," said Emily from the doorway.

Johnnie let go of Sara's hand and stood up. Sara heaved a sigh of relief.

"Well, you are, kinda," said Johnnie anxiously.

"But it was all over, wasn't it, Johnnie?" Sara said pointedly.

He looked down at her, his expression as poignant as if he'd lost his best friend, and said, "Yeah, I guess it was. 'Scuse me."

He walked out of the kitchen, almost knocking into Emily as he passed through the doorway. After a few seconds they heard the front door slam.

Emily turned to Sara apologetically. "I seem to have turned up at an embarrassing moment."

"Yes, it was," Sara said. Emily thought she detected a slight shudder. "But it needed to be interrupted."

Emily raised her eyebrows coaxingly. "Indeed? Is there anything I can do?"

"Yes..." said Sara slowly, the courage of her convictions beginning to gel. "When you leave, when you go back to Chicago, could I ride with you?"

"Well, of course you can," Emily replied, wide-eyed.

"I've decided to take your advice and sell up and move on." Emily nodded sadly. "I seldom advocate retreat, but in this situation it might be the best."

"That's what that little scene was about. I was just telling Johnnie about my decision, and he's...well, I guess he's become attached to me. He was distressed when I told him."

"To say the least," said Emily disapprovingly. "He looked as if he wanted to become attached to you permanently."

Sara shrugged. "He's always had a crush on me. I didn't realize it had gotten so serious. I suppose I'll have to do something about it. But I don't want to hurt his feelings. He's really a nice boy and I suppose I could have been interested in him if it wasn't..."

"If it wasn't for the fact that you're in love with somebody else."

Sara's cheeks reddened attractively. "I'm that obvious?"

"Oh, no," said Emily kindly, "but your anxiety over Mr. Fields is rather pointed. I don't think you could be quite so anxious about someone for whom you didn't care."

"It's ridiculous, isn't it?" said Sara with a rueful laugh. "You'd think I'd hate him. How could I love someone who's actually suspected me of murder?"

"The heart is a very difficult thing to govern," Emily replied with gently twinkling eyes.

Sara was struck by the similarity between this and what Jeff had said to her in his more gruff way, but she made no comment. "I think it would be...best...there's many things I should leave behind."

Emily looked at her a moment, then said, "You know, Sara, I doubt very much that he's ever truly suspected you of murder."

"But he—" Sara began, but Emily cut her off.

"He did his job. And it would have caused much more comment in the community if he hadn't."

Sara shook her head. "I suppose that's true. But he's been so awkward and cool to me since then."

"Has he? I wouldn't think that would be from suspecting you of anything," said Emily vacantly. "Perhaps you should consider what kind of man he is."

Sara blinked. "I'm sorry, I don't understand."

Emily folded her hands neatly on the table and leaned forward as if to give her words more emphasis. "I don't think he's the type of man who would take defeat easily."

Sara's eyebrows knit closely together, and she half thought of pressing Emily for further explanation, but the expression on the old woman's face told her that she'd said all she was going to say on the subject and was content to leave Sara to put the puzzle together for herself.

"Now," said Emily brightly, "if you'll forgive my changing the subject, there's a little call I'd like you to make for me."

TWELVE

SARA PHONED Myrtle Girdler that evening, as Emily had requested, and asked if it would be all right for Emily and Ransom to visit the next morning to pursue their investigation. Sara was very timid and apologetic about the fact that the next day was Christmas Eve, and she was sure that Mrs. Girdler must be very busy. But rather than acting overcome with the responsibilities of the season, which is what Sara had expected, Mrs. Girdler barely allowed a decent pause to elapse before expressing her overly avid interest in helping in any way she could. Her eagerness, in fact, left Sara with a sense of uneasy distaste that remained with her until she retired for the night.

Ransom phoned Jeff Fields the next morning and Fields told him that they'd verified that Hansen Crane actually had gone in to town and bought tobacco, and so far there was no evidence that he'd driven anywhere else. The sheriff delivered this news with enough of a sense of superiority to fill the detective with a strong urge to show him up. Ransom had to remind himself that his and the sheriff's aims were both the same.

It was shortly after breakfast that Ransom and Emily set off for Mt. Morgan. The sky was so thick with dense, dark clouds that the morning of Christmas Eve had barely dawned at all. Emily sat in the passenger seat comfortably swathed in her heavy coat, and gazed out the windshield at the sky. The crowded clouds shifted into and around each other as if engaged in a silent, celestial wrestling match. They weaved patterns whose outlines became clear for a moment, only to fade quickly, leaving nothing but indeterminate masses. Emily thought she knew just how they felt. She clucked her tongue.

"What is it?" Ransom asked.

"I can't help feeling that we're always a day late in this matter."

"Not a day late," said Ransom, curling his lips, "we're two years late."

"You were quite correct in what you said about investigating a case when the trail has gone cold. It's most frustrating."

Ransom smiled inwardly. Although Emily might profess to be frustrated, it didn't take a detective to see just how much she'd returned to herself. Ransom glanced at her as she continued to stare out the window. He could tell from the look in her eyes and the bend of her brow that her mind was keenly and actively engaged in putting the pieces of their present puzzle together. She was still too frail to appear anything like robust, but the color had returned to her cheeks in a way that made her look healthier than she had for months. *All in all,* thought Ransom, *I was right. This little holiday has done her a world of good.* It was with only a slight touch of embarrassment that he remembered that it was her own insistence on becoming involved in this case that was responsible for her return to normalcy.

For her part, even though Emily's mind was occupied with the problems at hand, she was aware that whatever tension Ransom had brought with him to the quiet countryside had dissipated as he'd become interested in the case. *Almost like a bored child whose mind could be fully diverted with a puzzle book,* she thought with grandmotherly amusement. But she amended this thought almost immediately with silent admonishment directed toward herself. She knew that Ransom's desire to solve crime did not stem from a Holmesian need for mental diversion, but out of a deep-seated desire to see justice done. The pleasure he took in bringing criminals to book was merely a happy by-product.

"What exactly did Sara tell you about this Girdler woman?" Ransom asked, putting an end to both their reveries.

"Only that she was a long-time friend of the family. She knew Sara's parents before they were married and kept in touch with them both after the divorce."

"How very nonpartisan of her."

"Yes...yes..." said Emily slowly, adopting the vagueness of

tone that usually indicated she was trying not to think ill of someone. "Let's hope that's all it is." She stopped for a moment, then continued in a much lighter tone. "Anyway, the Girdlers are from Chicago. They had a second home here to which they have retired. It was the Girdlers, in fact, who introduced the Bartletts to this area of Michigan."

"Hm," was Ransom's only reply.

They reached Mt. Morgan, passing Macklin's Supermarket, which was located just inside the town limits, where the main highway became Main Street. They followed Sara's instructions, continuing down Main through the downtown area, or what the locals simply called "town." Though Mt. Morgan was by no means large, compared to LeFavre it was a budding metropolis. Main Street was lined with stores that had none of the unpolished quaintness of the shops of LeFavre. These were glass storefronts of a much more commercial nature that included a dry cleaners, a laundromat, and two different hardware chains. A JCPenney stood like a flagship at the center of the first block.

They had soon passed through the center of town and reached Sycamore, the first cross street after the commercial district. Ransom turned left as indicated in Sara's directions and they found themselves on a street very much like one of the older neighborhoods of Chicago. The left side was lined with houses that were a bit closer together than he would have expected to find in such a rural setting, but the right side was devoted to a sprawling park, studded with leafless trees and scattered snow-covered benches. The importance that the community placed on children was evidenced by the amount of playground equipment that stood inert at one end of the park. There were slides, swings, monkey bars, and even one of the horseless merry-go-rounds that children propel with their feet. Ransom smiled, realizing that he hadn't seen one of those since he was a very small child.

With the address Sara had given him in his hand, Ransom quickly located the Girdlers' house at the end of the second block. He switched off the engine, then he and Emily sat for a moment looking at the house. It was a sprawling two-story building, which had received a fresh coat of bright white paint in the not-too-distant past. There was no veranda, but there was a wide columned porch, the roof of which served as a balcony for the front bedroom on the second floor. The property was hemmed in by a short white picket fence that tilted outward at the top as if it were a belt straining against an expanding waistline.

Ransom helped Emily out of the car, up the walk, and then up the five steps to the porch. The front door contained a large window that looked into a wide, open hall. To the right of the door, just above the bell, was a brass plaque on which *Girdler* was embossed in tight, almost illegible script.

Ransom rang the bell, and he and Emily watched as a thin, pleasant-looking woman of about fifty, clad in an industrial gray dress and a small white apron, appeared through the door at the back of the hall and approached them.

She smiled as she opened the door, which seemed to be so heavy that it took most of the woman's strength to get it to budge.

"Mrs. Girdler?" said Ransom.

"Oh, no," said the woman with a sudden rush of color to her cheeks, "I'm Sophie, the cook. I assume you're Mr. Ransom and Ms. Charters. Mrs. Girdler's waiting for you in the living room."

She said this all with the accomplished grace of someone who's spent a lifetime in domestic service, an image that was slightly tarnished when she led them into the room directly to the left and said simply, "They're here," then disappeared back to the kitchen.

The living room was a study in oppressive opulence. The furniture was all plush and overstuffed to the point that it looked like the couch and chairs were growing and might soon engulf the room. In the front window was a tree at least eight feet tall, its branches so choked with lights and ornaments that they sagged under the weight. The air was so heavily scented with cinnamon that Ransom found it difficult to breathe.

The lady of the house was seated at one end of a huge white sofa facing the Christmas tree. She was, to put it nicely, a large woman. Her hair had been dyed white, and she was wearing a bright red dress that was divided in the middle by a ridiculously thin silver belt. Though she was sitting, the belt gave the only indication of where her waist might be, not to mention her lap. Ransom thought with distaste that she looked like a grossly overfed version of the caterpillar from *Alice in Wonderland*. Several boxes of chocolates lay open on the coffee table in front of her, and in the crook of her arm she held a pomeranian that looked absolutely terror stricken. Though Ransom didn't really like small dogs, he had to feel sorry for this one. If its mistress happened to hold her too tightly to her bosom, the poor dog would never be seen again.

"I think I'll let you handle this one," Ransom said to Emily in a furtive whisper.

"Come in, come in. Forgive me if I don't get up." Her voice was much too light for her girth, and it had a giggly quality to it that would have been more suitable to a woman two thirds younger.

"Please, have a seat," she said with a sweep of her arm in the direction of two chairs grouped together by the side of the couch on which she was seated. The motion set the skin on the underside of her arm wobbling.

Emily looked doubtfully at the excessively fluffy chair that Mrs. Girdler had indicated for her. It was covered in pastel pink with curved arms that put Emily in mind of an overflowing orchid. She hesitantly lowered herself onto it and sank with dismay into the much-too-soft cushion. As Ransom took his seat next to her he shot her a reassuring glance to let her know he was aware of her predicament.

"It's very kind of you to see us on such short notice," said Emily with a little cough, "and at such a busy time."

"It isn't any trouble at all," Mrs. Girdler replied eagerly, "the family doesn't start arriving until after noon, and Sophie has everything under control. Would you like a chocolate?" She waggled her stubby fingers in the direction of the candy.

"No, thank you," said Emily. Ransom shook his head.

Mrs. Girdler leaned forward without appearing to bend in the middle and extracted a piece from the nearest box. The dog gave a little yelp.

"Frou-Frou! Shhh!" she said lovingly as she sat back and

popped the candy into her mouth. "All of my friends back in Chicago send these to me for Christmas. Fannie Mays, you know. They're my favorites."

Emily smiled and nodded.

"I was shocked," Girdler continued, scrunching her face up as if she'd discovered something in the chocolate's center that she didn't quite like, "*shocked* to hear about Hansen Crane. Of course, he wasn't from around here, but that doesn't mean he should die. Honestly, just when you're beginning to think you're safe in your home, something like this happens *again*. LeFavre is becoming more and more like Chicago every day!"

Hardly, thought Ransom, trying very hard not to let the disdain he was feeling become evident on his face. The woman reminded him of a fluttering elephant. Just as this thought entered his mind, Mrs. Girdler swallowed the bit of chocolate with an apparent effort. Ransom noted that her neck didn't move when she swallowed.

"But I couldn't imagine—when Sara called me, I mean—I couldn't *imagine* whatever you'd want to see me about. Good heavens! I couldn't possibly know anything about Nathan's murder, and even less about Hansen Crane's. I don't think I ever even saw Hansen, although, of course, my friends have told me about him because you know this is a rather small place and people will talk."

"Hmm," said Ransom, wondering how it had been possible for her to expend so much oxygen without collapsing.

"But," she said, raising her index finger as if she thought someone might have been about to interrupt her, "*but*, I would do anything—*anything*—to help Sara. I've known her and I knew her brother since they were babies. *Babies*." She repeated the word as if she were inexplicably proud of it.

"So we understood," said Emily with her usual quiet grace, "that is why we came to you. We understood that you knew their parents, and we were hoping you could give us a little information about them."

"*Their parents?*" said Mrs. Girdler, italicizing the words with a mixture of surprise and pleasure. "Whyever would you want to know about them?"

"Just for background," Ransom quickly interjected. "When I'm working on a case, I like to know as much about the participants as possible."

"Oh," Mrs. Girdler said with such palpable disappointment that it was clear to Ransom and Emily that whatever she might have said before, she had hoped that she was to be an important player in the mystery and it was quite a let-down to find that she was merely meant to paint the scenery. She heaved a bored sigh and continued, "Well, I knew David and Gina—those were their names—way back in high school, before they'd even met each other. David was a wonderful man! I was quite in love with him myself, you know." She averted her eyes and managed a coquettish blush that Ransom found perfectly revolting.

"Really?" said Emily with enough gusto to convince Mrs. Girdler of her interest.

"Oh, yes! He was very handsome and charming. What they used to call a ladies' man. But, of course, once he met Gina there was simply nobody else for him. I was, in fact, the one who introduced them, and it was the biggest—" Her face turned red again, but this time it was not out of coquettishness. "Well, in light of what happened I suppose I'm justified in thinking it was a mistake to introduce them. I'll never, never forgive myself for it. I could have told David it wouldn't work out, because Gina was simply not the type of woman who could understand him. A man like David required a special kind of understanding. He was a true visionary! That was something that Gina never understood. She was always sooo...*practical*." She curled her lips as if the sound of the word left a bad taste in her mouth. "She was always after him to get a job, get a job, get a job. She didn't realize that a man of David's nature needed nurturing, not *nagging*."

"Yes, well, perhaps she was worried about the welfare of their children," said Emily so lightly that Mrs. Girdler completely missed the implication.

And perhaps she thought two children were enough to nurture, thought Ransom, each passing minute convincing him that he'd been right to pass the reins to Emily on this occasion.

"Oh, but David loved the children. He absolutely doted on them!"

"He did?" said Emily, careful to give the word the proper inflection.

"Oh, yes! He doted on them!"

"But we understood that he never made an effort to see them again, after the divorce."

Mrs. Girdler suddenly lurched forward and selected another chocolate, which she popped into her mouth. The dog used the opportunity to escape her grasp. He ran yapping in the direction of the kitchen as if to complain to the cook about his treatment. Mrs. Girdler didn't seem to notice his departure.

"That was because of Gina. Gina did nothing but poison Nathan's and Sara's minds against poor David once he was gone. What could he do? How could he fight?"

"But surely he could've seen them if he wanted to," said Emily coaxingly.

Girdler shook her head slowly and sadly. "No, it was not to be. He moved out West—to San Francisco—to find his way—he had so many ideas for business, you know, but like so many great men, none of them ever panned out. It wasn't his fault, it was just the way the fates played it. David told me so himself. But he never saw the children again."

"He could've written to them," Emily said with a noncommittal shrug designed to make it clear that she wasn't being judgmental. Ransom shot her an approving glance.

Mrs. Girdler shook her head again, her frown deepening so much that it looked as if it were being branded into her moonlike face. "No, not with Gina around. That would never have done."

Emily cocked her head slightly to the side. "But you kept in touch with him, didn't you?"

Mrs. Girdler looked from Emily to Ransom and back again. From her expression she appeared to feel that she had inadvertently painted herself into a corner. "How did you know about that? Oh, I suppose Sara told you."

"She did mention it, yes," Emily replied.

The woman swallowed again and her eyes became watery. "He wrote to me from time to time, maybe once a year, asking about them. I thought it was very touching, and very sad that he should want so badly to keep in touch with his children, and have to do it through an intermediary, although I was more than happy to be the one to do it. I thought it was only right that their father be kept apprised of how his children were doing. I tried at first to talk to Sara about him, but she wouldn't have any of it, so I stopped trying. That's why I was so pleased when Nathan came around and asked about him."

"He did?" said Ransom so suddenly that he startled Mrs. Girdler. Her head snapped in his direction, which sent a corresponding ripple through the exterior of her body. Ransom felt that he now had an idea of how an avalanche could be started by a loud noise.

"Oh!" she exclaimed, putting her hand to her heart.

"I beg your pardon," said Ransom, "I was just so surprised that after so many years Nathan had suddenly become interested in his father."

"Yes...well..." Mrs. Girdler continued a bit hesitantly, as if she feared Ransom might be prone to outburst. "Well, so was I."

"When did this happen?" Emily asked.

Mrs. Girdler looked pleased to redirect her attention to her older, more subdued, visitor. "Let me see...you know, oddly enough, I believe it was just before he was killed."

Emily leaned in toward the woman, her eyes narrowing insightfully. "Did he tell you why he wanted to know about his father?"

Mrs. Girdler rolled forward and picked out another chocolate. "Yes. I asked him. He told me he just felt badly about never having known him—and I know that's true because you read about that sort of thing all the time, I mean about children wishing later in life that they'd known their parents and such. He was very concerned that his father had had a good life and was happy. He was very, very particular about his father's happiness. It was quite touching, really."

"Yes," said Emily, her tone designed to keep drawing the woman out without appearing to do so. "That's very admirable."

"If a little late," Mrs. Girdler replied with a nod. She turned the chocolate back and forth between two fingers. "I suppose it was guilt, mostly."

"Guilt?" Ransom prompted.

She nodded. "For having deserted him. I mean for not having allowed his father any contact for all those years. It was really, *really* very sad. I like to think that after his mother had been dead for a while, her influence began to weaken and Nathan realized how wrong he'd been to ignore his father. He said he couldn't bear to think of his father being all alone. He asked if he'd ever found anyone else."

Emily leaned in a bit more, her eyes becoming even more narrow. "He asked if his father remarried?"

"Um hm."

"And had he?"

"Oh, yes. More than once, I believe. But that was always the way with David. He could never find the right woman." Her expression became infused with meaning. "But then, of course, people like David usually have their heads in the clouds. They rarely notice what's right under their noses." She gave a little sniff, the implication of which was obvious. "But David was one of those men destined to be unlucky in love, even if he was lucky in other ways."

"What do you mean?"

"Whenever he was particularly low he would meet someone—some woman who he felt could take care of him."

"You mean financially?"

Mrs. Girdler blinked at her. "I mean in *every* way. Being low financially is bound to make you feel low in other ways. I've been very fortunate myself. Mr. Girdler has quite a bit of money."

"Mrs. Girdler," Ransom said, "we were hoping, since you kept in touch with him, that you could tell us where he is now."

She blinked at him, her thick lashes making her look like a mountainous Betty Boop.

"Who?"

Ransom checked himself in the act of a frustrated sigh. "David Bartlett."

"Well, I knew where he was, but I haven't heard from him in years. I don't expect I ever will again, assuming he's still alive." She gave another little sniff that clearly signified how deeply she felt slighted.

"Why do you say that?" Emily asked.

"Because the last letter I sent to him was returned with one of those yellow stickers on it that say the forwarding whatsits has expired. Honestly, you'd think they would send it on anyway since the address is always right there on the sticker!"

"Do you remember the address?" Ransom asked nonchalantly, not wanting to give the woman the satisfaction of knowing that she held any important information.

Mrs. Girdler rolled her eyes up to the ceiling and stuck her pudgy index finger into her cheek, for a moment lost in trying to recall it. Just when Ransom was about to repeat the question, she looked back at him and said, "No, I'm afraid I don't. But I remember the name of the place. It was the Crestview Nursing Home, San Francisco. I sent the letter there, but I never received a reply."

There was little left for Ransom and Emily to do then but to extricate themselves from Mrs. Girdler's company as quickly as they could without appearing to be rude, a social nicety that Ransom would easily have forgone were it not for the presence of Emily. When they had exhausted such topics as mutual acquaintances in Chicago and holiday menus, when Ransom felt he had reached the last thread of his patience, Emily said brightly, "Well, I think we'd better be going and leave you to your preparations."

"I hope I've been of some help," Mrs. Girdler said languidly as she made an abortive attempt to get to her feet.

"Don't get up," said Ransom without inflection. He helped Emily from the chair, the cushions of which had so swallowed her that he was almost forced to lift her bodily from its clutches.

"Oh, yes, you've been most helpful," said Emily as she slipped her arm through Ransom's.

He led her to the entrance to the living room where she applied a gentle pressure to his arm, signaling her desire to stop for a moment.

"By the way," she said, turning back to Mrs. Girdler, "who was it that put David Bartlett into the nursing home? His wife?"

"His wife?" Mrs. Girdler echoed, blinking her large eyes. "Oh, no, she's long gone. I assume it was his son."

Ransom's interest was arrested by this revelation, and Emily's eyebrows rose half an inch as she cocked her head. "Nathan? I didn't think Nathan knew anything about his father."

"Oh, no! Not Nathan," Mrs. Girdler returned with her underaged giggle, "David's other son. The one he had by his second wife. Or was it his third? I don't remember which. It's hard to remember family ties any more."

"Yes..." said Emily slowly, "and yet some remember them very well."

As they stepped outside onto the porch Ransom turned up his collar. The promise of snow was being realized in the form of a light shower that looked as if it might become a blizzard with little provocation.

"What a perfectly odious woman," said Ransom as he walked Emily back to the car.

"I *suppose* she's managed to delude herself into believing that all of her motives have been altruistic, but she is foolish enough to have been used by David Bartlett."

"You think that's what it was?"

"One way or another. Sara's father strikes me as the type of man who wouldn't stick at keeping contact with this woman for the express purpose of keeping track of the family money. And she's credulous enough about him that his true motives would never occur to her."

"Hm..." said Ransom abstractly. He grew pensive as he helped Emily into the car, then climbed behind the wheel. He sat for a moment, staring out the window without saying a word.

"Is anything the matter?" Emily asked.

Ransom sighed disgustedly. "I've been guilty of the fuzziest thinking, which has succeeded in doing nothing more than leading us around in circles."

Emily's forehead creased in reply.

"This is what comes of unbridled speculation. And I'm not

happy to think I'd indulge in it after all the times I've warned others against it.'' He paused, sighed again, and his lips curled as he added, ''I don't suppose I'll ever be able to look my partner in the face again.''

''Jeremy, I wish you would speak more plainly.''

''We've wasted all this time on the Bartletts' father—who couldn't possibly have anything to do with these murders—on what now look to me to be the flimsiest sort of notions I've entertained in the whole of my professional career,'' he said in a burst of temper that he rarely—if ever—had displayed in front of Emily. ''I suppose I could blame it on the fact that I'm on vacation and my brain isn't functioning properly, but it's impossible to excuse any way you look at it, especially in light of the fact that my stumbling around has apparently cost Hansen Crane his life.''

Emily gave him her most benignant smile. ''Certainly you can't believe that. Hansen Crane's death was caused by whatever Hansen Crane was doing, not by your investigation of it.''

''That doesn't alter the rest of it. I've approached this case as a fishing expedition—something I was forced to do because the murder happened so long ago—as if I was on some sort of busman's Christmas. And all I've proved is that you should never *play* at solving murder.''

''Well,'' said Emily somewhat grandly, ''you'd do as well to put the blame on me. I was in full agreement with you on what you call your 'unbridled speculation,' and it was I who got you involved in this business to begin with.'' She said this lightly, not from any desire to second his opinion of their investigation, but to get him to snap out of it. To a certain extent, it had its desired effect.

Two red patches appeared on either side of Ransom's jaw, as if this was as close to his cheeks as he would allow the blood to rush. It nettled him that as usual Emily had caught him out. He wouldn't allow her to take the blame for something for which he truly felt responsible, any more than he would ever be willing to admit that he'd allowed her to influence him into handling the case in the first place.

"I will, of course, call the nursing home to see if David Bartlett is still there, but I hardly think that he left a nursing home and came halfway across the country to kill his nearest relations. Assuming he's even still alive."

"Well, what about this other son of his, the one who put him in the home?"

"What about him?"

"If Sara is killed, and her father is dead, wouldn't that make this other son the next in line to inherit?'

"It won't wash, Emily!" Ransom exclaimed with exasperation. "Even if this nameless son had anything to do with this, he couldn't inherit if his father was still alive—and if he's still alive and in a nursing home all the money would probably end up transferring to the state for his care, so neither of them would get the money. And if the father's dead, the son *would* be the next in line, but what's he going to do? Go back to San Francisco and suddenly put in a claim for the inheritance? That might have worked in *The Hound of the Baskervilles,* but it would never work in this day and age. With an inheritance based on three deaths, Jeff Fields would be on a plane to San Francisco in a minute to see this guy, and if he didn't then I would, and the game would be up. And all of this money passing from mother to son to daughter to father to half brother? I'm sorry, I just don't buy it. The chain of inheritance is too long and far too complicated, and too many things could go wrong. And then there's still the matter of Sara's will. Neither the father nor his son would inherit, anyway!"

He fell silent again and stared out the window. Though he had not yet turned the car on, he seemed to be generating enough heat on his own to keep them both warm. Emily sat with her gaze transfixed on a huge oak tree in the park on her right. Something Ransom said had caused something else to click in her mind.

"The chain of inheritance..." she said very slowly and very quietly. "The chain of inheritance...yes, it is too long and too complicated. Yes...yes, you're right about that, I suppose...."

"What?" said Ransom, her words only half breaking through his own confused meditation.

He looked over at Emily and was alarmed at the look of utter astonishment on her face. Her jaw had dropped open and her eyes were as wide as they would go. But the most alarming aspect of her expression was that all the blood had drained from her face, leaving her as pale as a ghost.

"Emily! What is it?"

She shook her head slowly, which at least had the effect of bringing a little of the color back into her cheeks. "Oh, Jeremy, I've been such an utter and complete fool! It's been there all along, and I never saw it!"

"What?"

She faced him. "*King Lear*. 'Let me, if not by birth, have lands by wit....'"

"Emily, I don't understand."

"Oh, dear Lord," she continued, turning away from him, "how could I have been so foolish! Jeremy, if ever I speak with authority on the usual viability of gossip, I give you my full permission to remind me of this moment. We've been blinded by gossip, by everyone telling us that the object of Nathan's murder was inheritance. Oh, good heavens!"

"Emily, would you please tell me what you're talking about!" Ransom demanded in the severest tone he'd ever taken with her.

She turned back to him and adopted the schoolmarmish attitude she exhibited whenever explaining something. "The object of the murders was not the inheritance, at least not directly. You're right, that was far too complicated. The object was safety. The safety of the murderer, that is." She stopped and her expression became more vacant as a new idea occurred to her. "Of course, the problem is we don't know how Nathan discovered what was going on. Although it doesn't really matter, I suppose."

"*Safety?*"

"Yes. And Sara's life was never in danger. At least, not before. I fear that it is now, because I think the murderer is getting desperate. Oh, Jeremy! We must do something about this immediately!"

"Emily," Ransom said firmly, "we're not going anywhere until you explain to me what you're talking about!"

Emily took a deep breath to order her thoughts, then calmly told Ransom what she was thinking. When she'd finished, Ransom drew back against his seat. He extracted a cigar from his coat pocket, lit it, and took a long drag at it. Though Emily was so lost in her thoughts she seemed largely unaware of what he was doing, she did take a moment from her preoccupations to roll down her window.

"That's fantastic," said Ransom at last.

"But it does fit."

"Yes, it does. Especially with what you said earlier, about children turning out so much like their parents." He sighed and wrinkled his nose. "If you're right, I don't think I'll ever get over that gargantuan woman holding the key to the mystery." There was another pause, after which he added, "Except...you do realize that he doesn't have to be David Bartlett's son."

Emily replied, "Perhaps not, but it would account for why Nathan was murdered."

Ransom stubbed the cigar into the ashtray, and suddenly realized what he was doing and turned to Emily. "Oh, I'm sorry! I didn't mean to smoke."

"That's quite all right," said Emily magnanimously, "you needed it."

"Now I think we'd better go and decide what to do about this business. It's not going to be easy," said Ransom as he turned the key in the ignition.

Emily laid a thin hand on his arm. "Jeremy, I think we should go to Jeff Fields."

Ransom sat back in his seat and looked at her. From his expression he was obviously displeased. "Why?"

"Because it's Christmas Eve," she replied with a mischievous smile, "and I think we should give our first Christmas present."

THIRTEEN

THE SNOWFALL continued to grow steadily heavier into the late evening. By nightfall the prospect had ceased to be picturesque and had instead become worrisome. Still, it wasn't bad enough for Ransom and Emily to abort their plans and stay home from the carol service.

They arrived at the First Presbyterian Church of LeFavre shortly before ten o'clock when the service was scheduled to begin. The narthex was once again full of people shaking the snow off their hats and coats, but generally the atmosphere was more quiet and subdued than it had been for the Nativity play. Though Emily knew that this was most likely due to worries about the snow and the more somber nature of the occasion, she couldn't help feeling that the church and all its members were holding their breath to see if her little plan would work.

The crowd was making its way into the nave to find seats, and Ransom and Emily were being swept along with it when Ransom heard someone call his name. He turned to find Johnnie Larkin just pushing his way through the couple nearest them. His trademark smile beamed in their direction.

"Hi, Mr. Ransom, Ms. Charters. Merry Christmas."

"Thank you," said Emily.

"I see Sara didn't make it again."

"Did you expect her to?" said Ransom, raising his right eyebrow.

Johnnie glanced at the floor sheepishly. "God, I guess not. 'Specially not with another murder." He glanced to the left and to the right. "You seen Amy?"

"No," Ransom replied after a beat.

"Well, I suppose I'll go look for her. I should say hi to her if she's here. It's only right."

"Um hm."

"Enjoy the show," said Johnnie as he started to make his way back through the crowd, "I mean, enjoy the service."

"Oh, dear," said Emily in her most disapproving tone, "are we now to suppose that he could turn to Miss Shelton again?"

"Now that Sara has made her position clear?" said Ransom with a curious smile in the direction in which Johnnie had disappeared. "Any port in a storm, I guess."

Emily held Ransom's arm as he ushered her halfway up the aisle and into a pew. She pulled a hymnal from the rack in front of her and placed it on her lap, then opened her program on top of it and proceeded to read.

While she was doing this Ransom scanned the crowd, looking for familiar faces. He didn't find any.

Emily looked up from the program, and said, "It looks like it will be an interesting evening."

Ransom sighed. "Yes, it does."

THE MURDERER stood obscured from view by the barn, taking an occasional stealthy peek around its corner to reassure himself that the coast was clear. He was filled with a sense of déjà vu, though this storm was not quite so bad as it had been the night he'd committed his first murder. The house was still visible, though the only light coming from it was the glow from the parlor window dimly lighting the driveway. Sara's car was there, but the guests' car was gone, just as he knew it would be. He started for the house.

Sara sat reading in the parlor, or at least trying to read. She found it impossible to concentrate. The words seemed to float off the pages and spin around her head like an alphabetic tornado. She shook her head and the words and letters would scatter as if caught in the eddies on a brook, then flow back onto the page, only to spring up around her again the moment she tried to focus on them. She sighed heavily and looked up at the tree, whose lights seemed curiously lifeless. She hoped once everything was settled she'd be able to find some joy again...somewhere.

She gazed at the tree for a moment, hoping that it might manage to lift her spirits, but in spite of the glistening glass ornaments and the small white lights, it looked to her to be little more than a lifeless monstrosity.

The silence was oppressive. Although the snow was falling heavily, this storm was not as violent as the one on the night that Nathan had been killed: there was no rushing, howling wind and no sound of snow pelting against the window as it was swept against the house, all of which made the silence so acute that Sara felt she could hear the snowflakes as they landed on one another.

It was because of this undue quiet that Sara could hear the creak of the back door as it opened, though it was obvious that whoever had entered was trying not to be heard. It required all of her restraint for Sara to keep herself from calling out to the intruder, or to keep from crying out. She knew it didn't matter. She was the one he had come for and she was sure he would have no trouble finding her. But that didn't stop her from being startled when he spoke her name.

"Sara."

She looked to the archway and there stood Johnnie Larkin. He was wet with snow and had a length of rope coiled into a loop and draped over his shoulder.

"Johnnie," she said in a surprised tone, "I didn't hear you drive up."

"I used the access road. Back by the vineyard."

"The access road..." Sara repeated weakly. She had to fight the urge to ask him to explain why he'd done that. She already knew. She swallowed, then said, "I thought you would be at the carol service."

"I am," he replied with a smile that Sara no longer found ingratiating. "I think what they say is 'I put in an appearance.'"

"What...what do you want?" she asked after a pause.

Johnnie's smile disappeared. "I can't have what I want. I just wanted you and that would've solved everything. Nobody would've gotten hurt. It's not like I don't care about you."

There was so much sadness in his tone that Sara, though she knew she had to keep to the subject, couldn't help but respond.

"I never did anything to lead you on."

A trace of Johnnie's smile returned, but it faded quickly. "It would've been easier if you had. But you couldn't give me a second look, you were too stuck on the cornfed moron, Jeff Fields, even after he thought you murdered your brother! Jesus!"

"But why did you have to murder Nathan?" Sara asked, tears welling up in her eyes. "Why, if you didn't want to hurt anybody? Why did you do it? You were the one who killed him, weren't you?"

"He found out who I was. By mistake. By a stupid mistake. My wallet...my wallet fell out of my pocket when I was helping Nathan out, just like it did the other day in the kitchen...and he saw inside."

"What?"

Johnnie reached into his back pocket and withdrew his wallet, then flipped it open and shoved a picture at her. It was slightly yellowed with age, but the image was still quite clear. It was of a man who looked to be in his midforties, his hair slicked back and just beginning to gray. There was something vaguely familiar about the face. Sara felt almost compelled to reach out and touch it, but when she did, Johnnie snatched it away and shoved it back into his pocket.

"Who is that?" Sara asked tentatively.

Johnnie's eyes narrowed, his expression becoming infused with contempt. "Our father, Sara."

"*Our* father..." Sara faltered, then as the full weight of his words began to hit her, her eyes glazed over as if they'd been covered by an invisible barrier to protect her from what she was seeing.

"Our father, who you've never cared about but who's lying in a goddamn, filthy nursing home, the best that public aid can buy. And would someone like you help him?"

"I didn't know...if I'd known how bad things were..."

"You would've helped him?" Johnnie snapped.

"I...don't...know..."

"He wrote to you and you didn't help him!"

Sara received this like a slap in the face. She couldn't deny it, and couldn't explain to the angry young man the confusion of her feelings at the time, and how time had slipped away from her.

"I didn't know," she said slowly. "I didn't know things were that bad. He didn't tell me in the letter."

Johnnie paused as if this had brought him up short. His jaw slackened and he looked down at the floor sadly. "He didn't know at the time. Neither did I. He started to develop Alzheimer's disease and by the time we realized what was wrong…it doesn't matter…but now there's nobody to take care of me."

Sara took a step toward him. "Johnnie, I…"

He looked up at her quickly, tears coursing down his cheeks. "I didn't want to hurt anybody. Especially you. I just wanted to marry you. That would have solved everything."

"*Marry me!*" Now knowing their relationship, the disgust she felt at this prospect broke through the barrier she'd erected.

Johnnie's face hardened. "But it's too late for that now."

"What are you going to do?"

"First you're going to show me where your will is."

"Then what? Are you going to kill me, too?"

The right side of his mouth slid upward. He tapped the rope. "No, you're going to kill yourself. 'Cause you're so despondent. Everybody knows how you've been since Nathan died. Nobody'll be surprised."

Sara hesitated a moment, wondering whether or not she should challenge him and ask him why she should bother giving him what he wanted if he was going to kill her anyway. But she decided against it. It wouldn't really serve any purpose.

She crossed the parlor and passed him. He followed her through the living room and up the stairs to the bedroom that had once belonged to her brother: her *real* brother, she thought with pride. Johnnie continued to follow close on her heels as she crossed the bedroom to Nathan's desk, where they'd always kept all of the business papers and their important personal papers. She opened the lower right-hand file drawer, rifled through it for a moment, and pulled out a single sheet. As she stood back up, Johnnie slipped the rope around her throat, twisted it behind her neck, and pulled it tight.

Sara's hands instinctively flew up to her neck and grappled with the rope as she choked and tried to gasp out a scream. Johnnie pulled backward on the rope, stepping back to elude her grasp, and causing her back to arch in a way that made it difficult if not impossible for her to reach her arms backward and hurt him, or to kick back at him without losing her balance and toppling over.

There was a sudden jerk backward, and for a flash Sara thought he was going to make very quick work of her, when suddenly the rope was released and Sara flew forward, sprawling out onto the floor. She wheeled around and saw what had caused the last pull of the rope. Jeff Fields had caught Johnnie by his long, dark hair and jerked him backward. Johnnie let out a low, guttural scream, like a cornered animal, as Jeff spun him around and plunged his massive fist into Johnnie's stomach. Johnnie doubled over and Jeff swiftly brought his knee up into contact with the young man's jaw. Johnnie's head snapped back, banging against the footboard of the bed. He crumpled to the ground, unconscious.

Jeff flipped Johnnie over, pulled his arms behind his back, and handcuffed him.

"Are you all right?" he demanded of Sara as he turned Johnnie over on his back.

Sara sat on the floor rubbing her neck, dazed both by the blood resuming its flow to her head and the suddenness of the attack and her rescue.

"Yes...yes...I think so." Tears were already welling in her eyes.

"You didn't think you left me behind, did you?" said Jeff as he helped her to her feet. "I followed right along with you, but I had to be careful coming up the stairs. Those damn things creak."

Sara's eyes were fixed on the limp form of the man she now knew to be her half brother. She slowly turned her eyes to Jeff, who looked down at her with a mixture of relief and love. Suddenly Sara could feel the door to the void in which she'd lived for the past years had been flung open, and the emptiness that had been there rushing away like a gust of wind.

"Oh, Jeff!" she cried, burying her face in his shoulder. "It's over! It's finally over!"

FOURTEEN

"YOU DON'T KNOW how much excitement this is going to cause,"
said Millie as she poured out tea, first for Emily, then for Ransom.
Millie had been just returning home from the carol service when
Ransom called her at Emily's insistence. Emily felt quite strongly
that Sara would be in need of a familiar female presence after
her ordeal, and Millie was, if anything, a completely comfortable
choice. As she fixed two more cups of tea on a tray she added,
"To think that after all this time, Jeff goes and nabs the killer!"

Ransom paused for barely a second in the process of lifting the
cup to his lips. Without a word he took a sip.

"And I can't tell you how glad people are gonna be that it was
an outsider!"

"Indeed," said Ransom flatly.

Oblivious to his tone, Millie lifted the tray and hurried out of
the kitchen. "Be right back!"

"Now, Jeremy," said Emily with such overt amusement that
Ransom had to fight to keep his cheeks from turning red, "you
said yourself that it doesn't matter who is responsible for catching
a murderer as long as the murderer is caught. And we all know
who's responsible for solving this case."

"Yes, we do," he replied, eyeing her significantly, "and I can't
take any of the credit. You were ahead of me all the way. You
were the one who put it together."

"Well," said Emily, blushing with Victorian modesty, "I can't
really take the credit, either. Most of that goes to Myrtle Girdler."

"What?" Ransom exclaimed, dropping his cup onto its saucer
with such a clatter that he was moved to quickly inspect it for
damage. "I hope you're joking. Just because she told us there
was another son? We could've found that out easily enough."

"Perhaps. But she was also the one who told us of David

Bartlett's propensity for marrying himself out of financial difficulties. It was like I said before, children have a tendency to turn out like their parents, for better or for worse. Nathan and Sara were raised by their mother, who was a practical woman most likely made even more practical by the experience of being married to their father, who was her polar opposite. I daresay that Gina Bartlett's anxiety over the fate of her and her children's money was not just for their benefit, but for their father's as well. I'm sure she believed that the only thing that would ever straighten him out was for him to have to make his own way. Johnnie Larkin, or Johnnie Bartlett as I presume we'll have to think of him from now on, was raised by their father, and so became like him. I suppose, in a way, Johnnie was even lazier than his father. Instead of relying on trial and error for finding a woman with money to marry, he went to a woman he knew to have some, ignoring the social implications involved in marrying his half sister.'' Emily gave a little shudder and took a sip of tea. ''I'm afraid Johnnie doesn't have much in the way of moral sense.''

Ransom had to smile at her gift for understatement. It was so like Emily to look at the lesser transgression as a true sign of a murderer's mettle, not that she would ever discount the seriousness of murder.

''Anyway,'' Emily continued, ''the knowledge of their father's character, coupled with the show Johnnie made of being devoted to Sara and the little scene I witnessed in the kitchen earlier is what put the idea into my head.''

Millie bustled back into the kitchen carrying the now-empty tray and smiling broadly. ''What a Christmas this is gonna be!'' she said as she ran some water over the tray. She gave it a light scrub with the dishrag, then grabbed up a towel and proceeded to dry it. ''I just wish I knew how anyone knew that Johnnie would try to kill Sara tonight!''

''We didn't, really,'' Emily explained, ''we were just taking a chance that he might. Sara made her feelings quite plain to Johnnie yesterday where he was concerned, so it must've been obvious to him that his plan had failed. And you must remember he'd put a great deal of time and energy into his little plan—probably more energy than he'd ever expended on anything before. And here was Sara telling him not only that she was not interested in him, but that she planned to return to Chicago with Jeremy and myself. That didn't leave him a lot of opportunity. He could, I suppose, have followed her to Chicago and either tried to pursue her there, or murder her, but that would have been far too risky a proposition. It's more than likely that following her there he would be noticed. Here was a last golden opportunity to finish what he'd started before she had a chance to get away, and we provided further opportunity by leaving her 'alone' in the house.''

"But she had a will and everything!" Millie protested. "What good would killing her have done?"

Emily replied, "I'm afraid that Johnnie Bartlett is a very, very foolish young man. I don't think he had any concrete plan in mind when he came here. He knew that Nathan and Sara had money, but not how it was entailed. He soon found that they had wills...I don't know how...." Emily turned her twinkling eyes on Millie.

Millie wasn't embarrassed enough to blush, but she did choose that moment to turn away to put the tray in a cupboard. "Well, people will talk," she said lightly.

"So Johnnie came up with what he thought was a better plan, to follow in his father's footsteps and simply marry someone who was financially stable. He saw only two obstacles to that. One was that Sara was already interested in Jeff Fields, and, if reports are to be believed, was on the road to marrying him. The other was more serious, and that was that Nathan, quite by accident, had discovered Johnnie's identity. He'd seen a picture of his own father in Johnnie's wallet. Unlike Sara, Nathan had a dim recollection of what his father looked like. So out of curiosity he went to visit Myrtle Girdler, who unfortunately told him not only about his father's subsequent marriages, but also of the existence of another son. Apparently Nathan confronted him about it, and Johnnie killed him. This turned out to be a fortunate move on Johnnie's part, because not only did it give Sara even more money, it all but destroyed the relationship between Sara and Jeff Fields, his rival for her affections.''

"But why did he kill Hansen Crane?" Millie asked.

"Well, of course this is only speculation," she said with a mischievous glance at Ransom, "but we think that Nathan was killed shortly after nine o'clock. Crane was adamant about having been asleep at eleven, when Sara came to his door, but he couldn't account for nine. We suspect that he either heard a sound from the barn below or perhaps heard Nathan cry out, and then looked out the window, where he would have seen Johnnie leaving the barn."

"Pure speculation," said Ransom.

Emily nodded. "The double meaning of the word. Crane was blackmailing Johnnie, but could only do so against his future prospects."

"So that's why he stayed around here!" Millie said with satisfaction, as if this had been the bigger mystery troubling her. "And that's why Hansen used to ride Johnnie so badly and Johnnie just took it."

"I assume so," said Emily.

"But why kill him now? So long after the fact?"

Emily turned to Ransom. "I think that was a testament more to your prepossessing demeanor than anything else. Like most basically foolish people, Johnnie had a rather inflated ego, fed in this case by the fact that he had, for all intents and purposes, gotten away with the first murder. That certainly made him feel superior to Jeff Fields. But you were an unknown quantity, and you were asking questions. After you questioned Crane, he went into town ostensibly to buy tobacco."

"He chose to buy tobacco that he didn't need," Ransom explained to Millie, "because the only place to get it nearby was the drugstore, and Johnnie lived above the drugstore, so Hansen could park there and see Johnnie without anyone being any the wiser."

"I suspect that he started pressuring Johnnie to get on with his plan, and Johnnie either didn't like the pressure or was afraid that Crane would somehow give him away. Or it could be that he simply didn't relish the idea of being blackmailed. Few people do, you know. Least of all people who have murdered.''

"But why do you call him foolish?" said Millie. "Seems to me Johnnie's been pretty clever."

Emily glanced at Ransom, who returned her smile.

He said, "Well, putting aside the fact that it was stupid of him to think he could get away with murder in the first place, the second murder was very badly planned. In his haste to make sure Crane was dead, he struck too hard, more than once, and didn't know that a trained eye would be able to see the difference between an attack and an accident. But his most foolish act was tonight.''

"Though we must remember that he was getting desperate as he saw his plan slipping away."

Ransom gave her a nod of concession as he proceeded, "He was foolish in thinking he could kill Sara and destroy her will. I don't know how he could possibly have thought there would only be one copy."

"He's young," said Emily as she took another sip of tea.

"Well," said Millie, grabbing her coat from the peg by the door, "I'm gonna go home and try to get some sleep, but I don't know how I'm gonna do it! I'm just too keyed up!"

"You're not going to stay here with Sara?" said Emily, raising her eyebrows.

Millie smiled broadly as she slipped her arms into the sleeves of her winter coat. "Oh, no! I think she's in good hands. You just go and see!" She headed out the back door as she added, "I just can't wait to tell people what's happened! They'll be so tickled to know it was an outsider!"

The door closed behind her and Ransom heaved a heavy sigh. "She seems to forget that Sara is an outsider, too."

"Oh, I don't think she will be any more."

"Really?" said Ransom, allowing his right eyebrow to arch.

She nodded. "Now that the truth is known, I think it most likely the locals will feel somewhat ashamed of the way they acted, and will now welcome her as one of their own."

"Trial by fire," said Ransom with disdain.

"Exactly," said Emily, "and now that Sara has the answers she's needed, perhaps she won't hold it against them. Sara is most likely a practical enough young woman to accept their suspicions as a matter of course."

"Hm," said Ransom doubtfully. He wasn't sure he thought that was a good thing.

"The one thing I don't understand..."

"There *is* something?" he interjected in a mildly sarcastic tone.

She smiled at him. "...is why Johnnie had his affair with Amy Shelton. Since his object was always Sara, I would think the last thing he would've done is risk that."

Ransom looked at her for a moment, unsure of whether or not she was simply tossing him a bone to assuage his pride, but the gaze she returned was so genuine that he proceeded. "Simply a matter of ensuring his safety. Amy was right when she said Johnnie needed to talk after Nathan's murder, but she assumed he could have talked to anyone. What he *really* needed was to talk to her and make sure that Nathan hadn't told her anything of his suspicions.

"Of course!" said Emily brightly. "Of course!"

They finished their tea in silence and then Ransom helped her up from her chair.

"It's after one in the morning," he said. "It's well past time you were getting to bed."

"Jeremy, I can honestly say I haven't felt this good for years. You were quite right, you know, this rest has done me a world of good."

Ransom narrowed his eyes at her. "Emily, I suspect you're having a joke at my expense."

As he led her to the staircase, they noticed a faint light coming from the parlor. Emily held Ransom's arm as they went to the archway, where they stopped and looked in.

Jeff Fields and Sara Bartlett were standing in front of the tree. Jeff had returned to the house after seeing Johnnie safely into a cell at the sheriff's station. They stood with their arms around each other, admiring the tree. To Sara, the lights that had so recently seemed to her little more than a reminder of death now seemed to dance with life on the branches. She rested her head on Jeff's shoulder and sighed as he tightened his arm around her waist.

"I thought you said a sad tale was best for winter," Ransom whispered to Emily.

"Ah, yes," she replied with a benignant smile, "but a happy ending is best for Christmas."

BENEATH THE SIGHS
Walter Satterthwait

WHEN I GOT TO VANESSIE'S on Monday night, around eight, the place was nearly empty. Not too many years ago, at that hour on any night of the week, you wouldn't have been able to find a seat at the broad rectangular bar.

But there was a new owner now, and there was a new piano player behind the big black Steinway, and there were new cocktail waitresses wearing the familiar black skirts and white tuxedo shirts. Gordon, the literary bartender, was off in Europe somewhere—writing a novel, I'd heard—and I didn't know the man who was pouring drinks these days. He was younger than Gordon had been, and he was certainly younger than I was. He looked about twelve.

And the few customers who were there, sitting around the piano, or huddling at the small tables near the two big fireplaces at opposite ends of the enormous room, were all younger than the people I remembered. It seemed that every day there were more and more of these young strangers in town, jostling and bustling, pushing the rest of us farther and farther away from the center of things, and closer and closer to the edge of the ledge. They probably thought that we belonged at the edge of the ledge. Or over it. And maybe they were right.

But Jim was at the bar, as Jim usually was, sitting in one corner, hunched over his snifter of Rémy Martin. He was wearing an opened shearling coat and a black Western shirt with mother-of-pearl buttons. On his head was a black Stetson. Jim was originally from New York, but he'd been here for twenty years and he took his Western wear seriously.

When I unzipped my leather jacket and sat down next to him, he smiled at me wearily and raised his glass. "Merry Christmas, Joshua."

"Merry Christmas," I said. It was the twenty-second of December. Two more shopping days until the Big Event. We hadn't had any snow for nearly a month, but the new piano player was softly singing "Winter Wonderland."

Jim took a drag from his cigarette and said to the bartender, "Give my father here whatever he wants."

The young man looked at me and I said, "Jack Daniel's on the rocks, a water on the side." I turned to Jim. "How's it going?"

"Same old same old." In his late fifties, overweight, Jim didn't look well, and he hadn't looked well for a long time. His loose jowls were gray, his cheekbones were flushed with the exploded capillaries of the heavy drinker. "My lungs are shot," he said, "my stomach's going, and I've got a pancreas the size of a football."

My drink arrived. I held it out and Jim clicked the snifter against it. "To good health," he said.

His hand was shaking slightly. It would shake less and less as the evening wore on, and by the end of the night, when he could barely walk, it would be rock steady.

"How about you?" he asked me.

It was a good drink, fire and silk, my first of the day and as welcome as a ticket home. "Hanging in there," I said.

"You heard from Rita?" Exhaling smoke, he stubbed his cigarette out in the ashtray.

"No," I said.

"She's on the Navajo reservation, right? Doing something with kids?"

"What I hear."

"You know where, exactly?"

"No."

"But you could find out, right? I mean, you're a detective. That's what you do."

"She asked me not to. She wants some space."

He nodded. "Plenty of space on the Navajo reservation."

"Yeah."

"Must be hard," he said, "losing a partner like that."

I didn't say anything. Rita had been more than a partner.

Jim took another sip from his Rémy. "You keeping up with the work?"

"What there is of it."

Jim frowned suddenly. "Hey. I got an idea."

"Got to be careful with those, Jim."

"No, I'm serious. You want a job?"

I looked at him. "Doing what?"

"Finding someone."

"Who?"

"You know Phillip? The homeless guy with the beard, hangs out at the library? Wears the monk's robe?"

"The one who makes those signs?"

"Yeah. It's poetry. You ever read any of it?"

"No."

"It's pretty good. I mean, some of it's a little loopy. UFOs and aliens. "X-Files" stuff. But some of it's about the sky and the trees, the arroyos. Nature. I like it." He took another sip of brandy. "At least it scans, which is more than you can say for most poetry these days."

"He's missing?"

"Yeah. I asked at the library today. They said they hadn't seen him for three or four days."

"It's winter," I said. "And it's cold." The temperature hadn't climbed above freezing for a week. "Maybe he left town."

"Yeah, right. He chartered a Learjet and he flew to the Caymans. He's homeless, Joshua. He hasn't got dime one. And he's been here for six or seven winters that I know of."

"Why the interest in him?"

"What? Oh. You remember that last wedding? Mine, I mean?"

"To Sophia?"

"Sophia was the one before. This was Evelyn, the cocktail waitress." He tapped a cigarette from a pack of Camel Lights, stuck it in the corner of his mouth.

"Right," I said. "Whatever happened to Evelyn?"

With a gold Dunhill lighter he lit the cigarette. He inhaled deeply, exhaled a cone of blue smoke. "Took the divorce settlement,'' he said, ''and went off to Phoenix. Opened a bar of her own. Doing pretty well, I hear. All of them are. All five of them. I'm like that MacArthur guy, with the Genius Grants. Except that none of my wives needs to be a genius. All she needs is a lawyer. And he doesn't need to be a genius, either.''

He sipped at the brandy. ''Anyway, I didn't really know Phillip. Saw him in the library for years, working away at those signs with his Magic Marker, but I never said a word to him. Or vice versa. And I don't know how he found out about the wedding— don't know how he knew who I was, even—but I'm over there one day, in the library, and he comes up to me and hands me one of the signs. A big sheet of white cardboard, about two feet by three. It was a poem. About the wedding. My wedding. And it was a pretty nice poem, too. I still have it somewhere.'' He frowned. ''Unless Evelyn walked with it.''

He drank some more brandy, inhaled some smoke, exhaled. ''I thought it was damn sweet of him. I offered him money, but he said he never took money for his work. He's not much of an entrepreneur, Phillip. So what I did, a few months later, when I saw him at Christmastime, I gave him a twenty. A Christmas gift, right? Had nothing to do with his work. And I've been dropping a twenty on him every Christmas, last couple of years. I don't know what he does with it. Doesn't use it to get that damned robe dry-cleaned, that's for sure. Maybe he spends it on Magic Markers.''

I smiled. ''You're a soft touch, Jim.''

''That's what Gonzales says. My divorce lawyer. Anyway, no one's seen Phillip for three or four days, and Christmas is coming up. Look.'' He reached back, tugged out his wallet, brought it around in front of him. He opened it, slipped out two fifties and laid them on the bar. ''How much of your time will that buy?''

''Put it back. I'll check around, see what I can find out.''

He lifted the fifties, folded them and slipped them into my shirt pocket. ''Don't be a jerk. Take the money. I'll only waste it on this poison, anyway.'' Lightly he waved his glass. He noticed that it was empty. He looked up at me. ''Speaking of which, you ready for another?"

"Sure. But this one's on me."

IT BECAME A LONG NIGHT. We talked about the people we knew who had left Santa Fe for other towns, or other worlds. There were a lot of people. By the time I got out into the parking lot, it was nearly one in the morning. Fat gray flakes of snow were slowly spinning down through the yellow lights of the street lamps. Maybe we'd be having a white Christmas after all.

By the time I woke up, the snow had stopped falling and the sun was shining. Outside the window, everything beneath the blinding blue of the sky was blinding white. I was feeling a little rocky, and I poured myself a beer. It tasted better than it should have tasted at eight o'clock in the morning. There was some left-over pizza in the refrigerator and I tore off a chunk and nuked it in the microwave.

While I ate, I turned on the weather channel. Lately I hadn't been using the television for much of anything else. A large part of my living room was taken up by a twenty-one-inch thermometer with stereo sound.

According to the experts, the local temperature was twenty degrees, and the high today would be twenty-eight. I felt a bit better after the beer and the pizza—a well-balanced meal will do that for you—but after seeing the forecast, I wanted to crawl back into bed.

I had promised Jim, though, so I showered, dressed, slipped on my sunglasses and stepped out into the cold.

IN TOWN, the four inches of snow had already turned to gray slush in the streets. Land Rovers and Ford Broncos and Chevy Blazers all took turns splashing it at each other as they whizzed by.

The main library is on Washington Street, in the same building that once held the police department, before the P.D. moved out toward Airport Road. It was in this building, years ago, that I'd first met Sergeant Hector Ramirez, who had introduced me to Rita. Normally when I went to the library I didn't think about that, but I did today. This would be my first Christmas in a long time without her.

Janice was working behind the desk. She was a trim, handsome woman in her fifties, wearing Levi's and, over a white blouse, a red crew-neck sweater with a white band at the chest, where reindeer pranced. Like a lot of women in Santa Fe, she had let her hair grow naturally gray, and she wore it wrapped atop her head, attractively careless in a thick loose bun.

"Merry Christmas, Joshua."

"Merry Christmas, Janice. How's the book business?"

"People still read, amazingly enough. How's Rita? Have you heard?"

"No. Listen, Janice, I'm trying to locate Phillip. The guy who hangs out here. With the robe?"

Her face went concerned. "Is he in trouble?"

"Why do you ask?"

"Well, if you're looking for him..." The sentence trailed off into a question.

"A friend of mine knows him," I said. "He wanted to give him something for Christmas, but he hasn't seen him around."

"No one has. Not since last week. I saw him—when was it? Thursday, when I gave him a sort of early Christmas present."

"What'd you give him?" I was curious what sort of gift you gave a homeless man who wore a monk's robe while he painted poetry on cardboard signs.

"Just an old watch. Like this one." She held up her wrist and showed me an electronic timepiece. "I just bought this for myself. I had an earlier version, and it seemed silly to throw it out, so I gave it to Phillip. It holds phone numbers."

"Phillip makes a lot of phone calls, does he?"

She smiled. "You don't have to use it for phone numbers. You can use it for whatever you like. Phillip put poetry in it. I showed him how to do it with the computer."

"The computer."

"The watch downloads from a computer monitor. You type in the information, then hold the watch up to the monitor."

"Black magic."

She smiled again. "More like a bar code reader."

"Like I said. Black magic."

"You really are a Luddite, aren't you, Joshua?"

"Want to see my membership card? It's hand-printed."

Another smile. "Anyway," she said, "I put the software onto one of our computers, and then I helped him to get started. He was very excited. It was fun to watch him. He likes the computer, likes using it for his poetry. And now, he said, he could carry it around with him wherever he went."

"And where would he go, Janice? Do you know where he lives? Where he stays?"

She shook her head. "Up in the hills, I think. I think he has a shack somewhere, up behind St. John's College. But I couldn't tell you where, exactly."

There were thousands of acres of forest land in the hills behind St. John's.

"Does he have any friends?" I asked her. "Does he hang out with anyone?"

She frowned, thinking for a moment, and then said, "I've seen him with Brent. Another homeless person, an older man. He's usually here—most of them come here in the winter, during the day, for the warmth. But he hasn't been in today. Thank goodness."

"Why thank goodness?"

She frowned. "Well, I don't like to say anything unkind about these people. The homeless. Some of them obviously don't have any choice. And some of them, like Phillip, are really very sweet. But Brent—there's something…unpleasant about him."

"Unpleasant how?"

"Furtive. Sneaky. We've had a couple of people lose things here—purses, book bags. No one could prove it was Brent, but I'm fairly certain it was."

I asked for a description and she gave me one—in his fifties, bearded, bald, thin, usually wore a long black overcoat.

"Anyone else?" I asked her.

"There's a Native American man named John. He's a panhandler. I always see him asking people for money, just outside the library. I've asked him to stop, but he only goes across the street, in front of the bank, and does it there.''

"Big guy, long black hair? Usually drunk?"

"Yes. Do you know him?"

"I've seen him over there. Okay, Janice. Thanks."

"Will you get back to me?" she said. "Will you let me know if Phillip's all right? I've been a little worried. He's usually here every day."

"Sure," I said.

JOHN, THE PANHANDLER, wasn't across the street. I went through town on foot, looking for him and Brent.

John I found on the Plaza, hitting up the tourists in their color-coordinated ski costumes.

He was a big, bulky man wearing an old red parka, greasy Levi's, battered cowboy boots. Leaning against one of the elm trees along San Francisco Street, I watched him for a while. His approach to panhandling walked that fine line between begging and extortion. He would come looming up to a tourist, all broad shoulders and long black hair and bleary red eyes, the stereotypical Drunken Indian, and he would say, in a gruff and whiskey-scarred voice, "Got some spare change, bro?" Almost all the tourists found some cash for him, happy to get away alive, and with their scalps intact.

After a few minutes of watching, I wandered over to him. "Hey, John," I said.

The red-rimmed eyes squinted at me. "I know you, bro?"

"Joshua Croft." I put out my hand and he took it. Neither of us was wearing gloves. He might have been drunk, but his hand was still strong. It was also damp.

I let go of his hand, and I was careful not to wipe mine against my pants. "John," I said, "I'm looking for Phillip."

He looked at me blankly. "Who?"

"Phillip. The guy who writes those signs in the library."

His big body was wavering slightly, forward and back, as he stood there. He was an inch or so taller than I, with a broad Indio face and slack, thick lips and that dull, blank expression. I didn't like him much, but not because of his face. I didn't like him because he was a drunk, and he reminded me of that beer I'd finished off at breakfast.

"Oh," he said. "Yeah. Phillip." He squinted again. "How come?"

"His family is trying to find him."

He shook his head. "Phillip don't have no family, bro."

"Not in Santa Fe. Back East. An uncle. There's some money involved."

The eyes narrowed again. "For Phillip?"

"Yeah. And for anyone who helps me. I hear he's got a place up in the hills. You know where it is?"

The eyes darted briefly to the right and then his glance found mine again. "What're you? Like a cop?"

"Private detective."

"Like Magnum P.I.? The guy on television?"

"Yeah." Apparently John hadn't been watching his television for a while, either.

He put his big head slightly back. "So what's it worth to you?"

I pulled out my wallet, opened it, slipped out a ten.

He reached for it and I jerked it back. "Hold on." I slid the wallet back into my pocket, tore the ten in half.

"Hey!" he said.

"Here." I handed him one half of the bill, put the other in my pocket.

"This is no good," he said, looking up from the torn banknote.

"You tell me how to find the place. When I find it, I'll come back and give you the other half."

He mulled that over. Then, squinting once more, he said, "How do I know you'll give it to me?"

"What am I going to do with half of a ten-dollar bill?"

"Yeah, but how you gonna find me?"

"I found you this time."

"Yeah, but maybe I'll be out of town."

On another chartered flight to the Caymans, maybe.

I took out a pen. "Here, give me that."

He pulled his hand away. The thing had been worthless until I reached for it.

"Don't worry," I said. "I'll give it back."

Reluctantly he handed over the note. I took out a pen, wrote my office address on it, handed it back. "If I don't find you, you come find me."

He looked down at what I'd written as though it were Sanskrit.

"Okay," I said. "How do I get to Phillip's place?"

He told me.

I PARKED THE CHEROKEE along the side of Camino Cabra, the road that led up to St. John's College. Through the narrow clearing on the east, its grasses bowed beneath the snow, a narrow white unmarked pathway led up toward the nearby hills, among the juniper and piñon. I got out of the car and I started walking.

I walked for over a mile, the snow crunching beneath my work boots, the path wandering higher and higher, above the scrub pines and up into the dark ponderosas. I was panting and my heart was thudding against my ribs. I was out of shape. Not enough swimming in the municipal pool lately, and too many Jack Daniel's in the local bars. Too many beers for breakfast.

I kept walking, and I missed a turnoff I was supposed to take, and I had to backtrack to find it, nearly sliding down the slippery slope, and then I kept walking again, through the dimness beneath the big solemn trees. In some places the branches overhead were so thick the snow hadn't reached the layer of pale brown pine needles covering the ground.

After almost an hour I found it, tucked at the rear of a small flat clearing, half-hidden beneath the slumping, snow-draped boughs of a ponderosa.

Shack was optimistic. It was about four feet high and about seven feet long. It had been hammered together with bits of plywood and scrap lumber. Its roof was a sagging sheet of rusted corrugated iron. There was a rough wooden door with a loop of rawhide for a handle. I pulled on it.

Tumbling out of the shack came the reek of unwashed human. I took off my sunglasses, stuck them into my jacket pocket. I was still panting from the climb, but I turned my head, took a breath, squatted down into a duck walk and went inside.

No Phillip, and not much of anything else. A cheap thin mattress on the hard-packed dirt floor. Carefully folded into a neat pile at its foot, three or four old woolen blankets. Beside the mattress, a Mickey Mouse coffee cup that held three Magic Markers. Beside that, a plastic designer-water bottle, its sides scratched and dented as though it had been refilled many times. It had been half-filled with water, but now the water was ice.

I was breathing in there, but not happily. I looked around some more. In one corner of the tiny room there was a small pile of ash and, next to it, an old aluminum saucepan. Stacked neatly against the wall there were three or four of Phillip's white cardboard signs. I lifted one, held it so I could read it by the light from the open door.

Two lines in thick block letters.

and beneath the sighs,
only the perfect Silence

I put back the sign and scuttled out the door. I stood up and sucked in a deep lungful of sweet fresh air, edged with the spiky scent of pine. I walked away from the shack, into the clearing, and I stopped to look out toward the west.

The sun was shining and the cloudless sky was that cobalt blue you sometimes find on old Chinese porcelain. The ground dropped off at the far end of the clearing, and I could see past the tops of the ponderosas, wrapped in snow like old men in shawls, down to the brown adobe clutter of Santa Fe, all the tiny roofs frosted over now, here and there a thin gray streamer of smoke curling upward from a tiny chimney. Farther out, beyond the thin brown line of trees that marked the Rio Grande, I could see the distant white slopes of the Jemez Mountains. Everything looked clearer and cleaner and sharper than it had any right to look.

Something happened then, and I'm not sure why. Maybe it

happened because I was seeing all this after being trapped inside the cramped, tidy misery of that little shack.

My heart was still thumping in my chest. I could hear it. I could hear my own breathing. Somewhere nearby, a raven cawed. Closer, somewhere, a small clump of snow slipped from a branch and made a faint puffing sound when it landed.

And then, suddenly, as I stood there below that sleek blue bowl of sky, in that dazzle of white, in the center of that fierce bright beauty, I could hear the sound that lay beneath all the others, the sound that Phillip had written about. The perfect Silence.

It didn't last for long, for a moment or two, maybe for only a second or two. But while it lasted, I was a part of it. Everything else fell away. Rita, the failures, the triumphs, the griefs, the joys, the sorrows, the hopes. Everything. If I had died just then, it would have been okay. It would have been perfectly acceptable.

And then two more things happened. They seemed to happen simultaneously, but one of them may have caused the other. I don't know.

Somehow, abruptly, the Silence changed its pitch, became higher; and I noticed a narrow mound of snow near the north side of the clearing.

The Silence disappeared as I walked toward the mound. I squatted down at one end of it, brushed away the snow. Phillip had blue eyes, clouded over now as they stared up at the cloudless blue sky.

"YOU SHOULD'VE STAYED there," Hector Ramirez said.

"How was I supposed to call you from up there?" I said. I was back at the library, using one of the pay phones outside the building.

"Why don't you break down and buy a cell phone?"

"Listen, Hector. It won't be hard for your people to find him. My footprints go right up to the body. But you're going to need a good-sized crew to get him down from there."

"You didn't fool around with the scene any?"

"I told you. I went inside the shack. I touched one of those signs. I touched the body. I cleared the snow away from his face and away from his wrist. That's it.''

"I want you in here, making a statement.''

"Soon. I've got to do a few things first.''

"It's always got to be *your* way, right?''

"If I hadn't found him, you wouldn't know he was there.''

"Two hours. And then I want you in here.''

"Right. See you later.''

He hung up.

I went into the library, to tell Janice.

THERE AREN'T A LOT of pawn shops in Santa Fe, and it didn't take me long to find the one that had what I wanted.

"That watch there,'' I said, and pointed.

The fat man opened the door at the back of the display case and took out the watch. He wiped it off with a gray cotton rag. I didn't bother trying to stop him. If it was the right watch, fingerprints wouldn't matter.

"This is very high-tech,'' he said. "Stores your phone numbers, your addresses, what have you. You download it all right from your computer. Right off the monitor.''

The air inside the shop was stale and stifling. Under my leather jacket I was sweating.

He wasn't wearing a jacket, only a black T-shirt, but he was sweating, too. He handed me the watch. "You need the right software,'' he said, "but the company, they've got a web site you can download it from. You're on the web, right?''

"No,'' I said. I pushed one of the buttons on the watch. The liquid crystal face lit up. Wrong button. I pushed another. Some letters went scrawling across the face and they became words. *and beneath the sighs.*

I put the watch down on the countertop. It made a small clicking sound as the metal met the glass.

"Who brought it in?'' I asked him.

"Sorry, buddy. I can't divulge my clients' names.''

I nodded. "Mind if I use your phone?''

"Local call?"

"Yeah," I said. "The cops."

I TALKED TO HECTOR, and then the fat man talked to Hector, and he told Hector who had brought in the watch, and then I talked to Hector again and told him I'd come by to make my statement as soon as I checked the mail at the office.

Fifteen minutes later I was about to unlock the office door when I heard a sound behind me.

The office was on the second floor of a three-story building. John had been sitting on the flight that led up to the third floor, waiting.

He lumbered toward me in his red parka, his bulk filling the narrow corridor. "You found it, right?" he said.

"I found it."

"So can I have my money now?"

"The guy at the pawn shop said he gave you a ten for the watch, John. That's the last ten dollars you'll be making for a while."

He was big but he was slow and he was drunk. Six months ago he wouldn't have been able to touch me. But I was out of shape and I was still exhausted from climbing through the mountains.

His big right fist came up from the floor, it seemed like, and I dropped my keys and almost managed to block the punch with my left arm. But the fist slammed into the side of my head and scraped back along my ear, and for a second I was stunned. He threw another punch, a left, and it caught me on the shoulder. My right arm went numb.

I needed some room. I smashed the toe of my boot against his shin and he grunted, and I straight-armed him in the chest, ramming him away from me. I backed up. My right was beginning to work again.

He didn't stay away for long. He was finished with the fancy stuff. No more punching. He moved toward me, hands out, fingers open, wanting to tear me apart. But his expression hadn't changed. It was still the same dull, blank expression it had been when I first met him. It probably hadn't changed when he clubbed

Phillip, or when he stripped the watch from his wrist. It probably changed only once in every day, when he had that first drink of the morning, the one that promised to wipe away all the pain.

He lunged for me, head and shoulders down. There wasn't room in the corridor for me to play bullfighter, so I braced myself and let him come, and when he hit me, shoving me back, I slammed both my hands, fingers locked, at his neck. He grunted again and I brought my knee up into his face, as hard as I could. His arms dropped and I smashed him with the other knee. He made a huge crashing sound when he met the floor, and then, immediately, as though he'd just rolled over in bed, he started to snore.

I found my keys. It took me a while to locate the right one, and then it took me a while to get it into the lock. The lock kept jumping around. But finally, I managed it, and I went inside and called Hector.

AFTERWARD, AFTER HECTOR and the others had left, taking John with them, I called Jim and told him.

"Ten dollars?" he said. "He killed Phillip for ten dollars?"

"Yeah."

For a few moments he was silent on the line. Then he let out his breath in a long slow sibilant sigh. "Sometimes," he said, "I don't think there's any hope for any of us."

"Yeah," I said. "I know the feeling."

When I hung up, I noticed that the mail was waiting in the brass box beneath the slot in the door. It had probably been there the entire time. I got up from the desk, went across the room, pulled out the envelopes. I carried them back to the desk, sat down and started to go through them. Three or four Christmas cards from friends, a brochure from some "security equipment consultants," a few bills.

And an envelope that had my name written on it in a neat, familiar script, and a postmark from Chinle, Arizona. Chinle was on the Navajo reservation.

It was a simple card with a simple, almost childish print of a

Christmas tree on the front. Inside, she had written, "Merry Christmas, Joshua. Soon, I think." And then her name.

Soon, I thought. And what then?

I opened the drawer of the desk and took out the bottle of Jack Daniel's and a water glass. I opened the bottle, poured myself a drink. I swiveled the chair around and sat back and put the heels of my boots up on the windowsill. I took a sip of the drink and I stared up at the white mountains shouldering into the clear blue sky.

I sat there for a long time, slowly drinking, in the silence.

But it wasn't a perfect Silence. I couldn't remember what that had sounded like.